Baghdad Burning

A Thriller

JOSEPH MAX LEWIS

ALSO BY JOSEPH MAX LEWIS

The Diaries of Pontius Pilate
Separation of Church and State
Baghdad Burning
Hell Rises
Final Warning
Aftermath

SHORT STORIES
Just Verdicts
John Hancock – July 4, 1776
John Hancock – The Final Chapter
Black Site

LEARN MORE AT:
www.josephmaxlewis.com

PART ONE – IRAQ – MARCH

1991
AS SALMAN AL NAJAF / AD DIWANIYA

CHAPTER I

———

MAYBE HIS LAWYER COULD PLEA bargain the "Treason" and "War Crimes" charges down to one count of "Murder." Maybe.

Murder was a charge Sergeant Ralph Jackson thought he could live with. Green Berets after all killed people. They did not, however, betray their country, though sometimes their country did betray them. Treason bothered him but War Crime, on the other hand, was preposterous. The *real* war crime would be following orders.

In any event, what he couldn't live with was walking away from the kids, about 70 Iraqi children who he knew practically worshiped him. It began as "winning the hearts and minds" of the villagers and it wasn't hard. Ralph came from a close-knit family with three younger brothers and some of the Iraqis weren't much younger than he was. So he played soccer with them, joked with them, and taught them English, using the lyrics to American pop songs. Well, kind of using the lyrics. Ralph remembered them all lined up, singing at the top of their lungs:

Fame! I want tooo live toooooo gather!

Um, "forever" guys.

"Tell me one thing that's funny, Ralph," Sergeant Ted Kehr said.

"It's either laugh or cry, Ted." He must have been smiling.

Ted Kehr was one of Ralph's teammates on Operational Detachment A716, or 716. In the same way the Jones family called themselves "The Jones," Green Berets referred to themselves as members of their detachment, so collectively Ralph, Ted Kehr, and the others were "716."

"Yeah," Ted said.

The last of the sandstorm blew itself out by eight o'clock in the morning. Ralph was the first one out of the bunker.

After all the months of cursing these storms, the one time you wanted one to last and it blew out early. Ralph used a set of binoculars to scan the horizon for movement. Outside of As Salman, the terrain in this part of Iraq consisted of shifting dunes of yellow sand, stretching wave after wave, as far as the eye could see. Fine sand still swirled up off the dunes as the final wind gusts blew themselves out. From this distance, in what turned out to be an omen, the sand looked like a yellow mist blowing toward land off of an unearthly sea. As Ralph began sweeping in closer to the village, its water supply and palm trees, the ground changed to a darker color of sand mixed with dirt and the occasional sprouts of grass.

Nothing.

Despite a tickling in his throat and a sudden desire for a drink, he didn't stop. You started close to the village and swept out in a grid pattern, and then you swept back in, whether you saw anything on the way out or not. He did it that way because that was the right way to do it and that was the way Ralph Jackson did things, the right way. That was why the United States Army put him on one of its fabled Green Beret "A teams" at an obscenely young age. Ralph not only always did things right, he had a real knack for combat, for killing. There was just no other way to put it.

He swept his gaze past the chest-high mud-brick wall surrounding the village and rested upon the first cinder block house on the outskirts. An old man with a red checked kafia walked outside. Ralph put the binoculars down. Captain Mel Harris, Ralph's team leader, stepped up behind him, his approach masked by the snapping sounds of men removing condoms from the barrels of their M-16 rifles or unwinding Saran wrap from the action receiver area. Particularly in a sandstorm, keeping the weapons clean and clear by any other means was near to impossible.

Ralph knew what he was going to do, but needed help. He had to figure out how to get the rest of the team on board. He un-slung his canteen and took a long pull.

"Sir, there's no way these people can escape now," Ralph said, "and if they stay here, they'll be slaughtered."

The rest of the team filed out of the bunker and drifted off.

"Hey Ralph, what can we do?"

"They've got weapons, Captain. We can set them up to fight."

"Most of the weapons they have, we gave them. They're all Korean War surplus."

Master Sergeant Dave Grayson, the Team Sergeant, joined them. As Team Sergeant Grayson was the senior enlisted man on the team, but he chose to remain silent.

"They kill people just fine, sir," Ralph said.

Ralph was the newest member of the team and young for the job. At first, that made the dangerous men he worked with nervous. In a twelve man A-Team, any weakness in one member threatens the survival of everyone else. He knew they watched him. Most of the time he was friendly and easy going and he acted his age. He joked around, usually took no offense and especially liked children. To his colleagues, these were not characteristics that inspired confidence. Then the killing started. After that they didn't get nervous about him being young, they got nervous about the red haze that seemed to surround him.

"Look, I know you've got a real soft spot for these kids and it's partly my fault," Captain Harris said. "I probably should've warned you to back off a little, but it helped us with villagers. You can't let it affect your judgment."

"Sir, think about all the help these people have given us over the last eight months. They've supplied us, hid us a couple times, given us shelter, intel . . . and if they'd been caught . . .“

”You don't think I know that?"

It was true, Ralph thought. Everyone was upset. Ten hours earlier they'd received word via a secure burst transmission from Kuwait that the United States and Iraq had agreed to end hostilities. "All material support for insurgent groups is to terminate." "A Teams," otherwise known as Operational Detachments, including Operational Detachment A716, were to wrap up their involvement with the indigenous people, blow all "externally originated" ordinance in place, and exfiltrate the area.

In other words, they were supposed to disarm the people who'd befriended them and then abandon them to their fate.

After receiving the message, Captain Harris called the Americans together and issued the orders: "Gather up all their weapons and ammunition. Clean up any evidence of our operations in the area. Get ready to exfiltrate."

Just as they'd begun directing their prior allies and former friends to stack their weapons in central locations, a second radio transmission came in. It was from Special Forces Headquarters and every bit as troubling as the first one.

"Just received at SF Headquarters - satellite intelligence indicates enemy troop elements moving in your direction. Large unit identified as a fragment of Republican Guard Mechanized Battalion. Approximately 6 BTR-60 armored personnel carriers and truck transport for 120 infantrymen. Estimated time of arrival, 10:00 hours."

By the time they received and decrypted the message, the sandstorm began in earnest. Since the storm was blowing east to west across As Salman, the Republican Guard unit approaching from the north was not impeded in until it got near town. The Iraqis who befriended 716, along with their wives and children, however, were snowed in. Then, just as the storm shifted to the north where it might slow down the enemy convoy, it blew out.

"I know you do sir, but-"

"We've got our orders, Sergeant Jackson."

Sergeant Jackson, huh? Two could play that game.

"Remember the police station at Al Khidr, Captain?"

"You little turd."

Ralph didn't move, he barely let himself breath. There was no forgetting what 716 found after capturing the Al Khidr police station during the invasion. Images of blood, gore, and horrible metal implements flash before their eyes. They found videotapes, confiscated them and watched enough of one to know what they contained. God only knew what Saddam Hussein's political party, the Baathists, would do to their friends given the chance, but 716 had a pretty good idea. Bringing it up was Ralph's strongest card and playing it might backfire. Harris never talked to anyone like that. After what seemed like forever, he spoke.

"Dave, what do you think," Harris asked his team sergeant.

"Well . . . it's not exactly unprecedented, sir."

Special Forces Detachments engaged in unconventional warfare and "unconventional" meant unconventional. There was a long Special Forces tradition of "improving upon" ambiguities in orders. Refusing to run from an enemy planning to butcher friends of America fell into this "improving upon" category. Morally, there was no reason not to disobey, but the entire team would have to agree. If they were caught, they'd be court-martialed.

"I'm inclined to go with Ralph on this, but first let's see if it's doable. We gotta think through the tactics, especially what we're gonna do with those armored personnel carriers. If it's doable, I say we lay out the legal consequences and then poll the team," Grayson said.

Success, Ralph thought.

"Agreed. We review the tactics and if it's feasible, we put it to a vote," Harris said. "But before we go that far, let's check the tactics."

"Yes!" Ralph blurted out, clenching a fist.

"Shut up, Ralph," Harris said under his breath. "Not a word out of you until we know it might work."

"Sorry, sir."

The rest of the team was fanning out into the village, yelling for the villagers. They were already assembling the ordinance, moving it from private homes and hiding places into the village streets.

"We've got about 120 infantrymen to deal with, but the old small arms don't bother me. We've got plenty of M-16 ammunition and the villagers will have the element of surprise," said Harris.

"Keep them moving, Sergeant Penn," Grayson shouted over Harris's head. "Stack em up, then stand by."

The rest of the twelve man detachment glanced over at the three men huddled together, then continued working with the villagers.

"What worries me are those APCs," Harris said, referring to the Armored Personnel Carriers.

"Me too," said Grayson. "Maybe we could use some of the C-4, Molotov cocktails . . ."

"Penn says there's a couple crates of old LAWS in the villagers' stockpile," Ralph said.

"When'd those come in?" Grayson said. He'd often been away from the village conducting patrols and didn't see all the ordinance as it was airdropped in.

"You've been working on this, haven't you?" Harris said to Ralph.

"I'm just saying, sir."

Ralph was referring to a rocket launcher that replaced the bazooka known as the M-72 Light Antitank Weapon (LAW). The LAW was developed in the 1960s. It was old and most soldiers had never seen one. In Special Forces, however, obsolete and foreign weapons were frequently supplied the allies or even to SF detachments. 716 knew more than a little bit about the LAW, including how to use it.

A donkey brayed from somewhere inside the village and Grayson raised an eyebrow.

"They should work on the APCs," he said.

"Ralph, get me an uplink," Harris said, leaving nothing to chance.

"Yes, sir." Ralph walked over to a line of rucksacks just inside the bunker, grabbed his and hauled it back to where the other two men waited. While Ralph set up the microwave dish and tranmitter-receiver set, Grayson stood up and scanned the northern horizon.

"It's still early, Dave," Harris said.

"If those time of arrival estimates are off, and it wouldn't be the first time, this is all academic anyhow," Grayson said. "We'll be lucky to get out of here in one piece ourselves, sir." A-716 didn't put a lot of faith in the intelligence reports they'd been receiving. Occasionally they were completely wrong and often they were flawed, but they were 100% accurate just often enough to keep you guessing.

They're worse than the local weather reports back home, Ted Kehr once said.

"Bingo," Ralph said, indicating he had a successful satellite uplink.

"All right," Harris said, "you know where I'm going with this. Tap into the DOD tactical mainframe."

Ralph did know what Harris wanted. Harris wanted to use the Department of Defense, or DOD, computer to find out if the LAW rockets were powerful enough to penetrate the armor plating on the armored personnel carriers.

The tactical mainframe was a computer database maintained by the Department of Defense. The database contained information on almost any conceivable military unit, tactic, firearm, aircraft, warship, vehicle, tank or other piece of equipment. Operational Detachments had the technology to tap into this information via satellite while thousands of miles away, on the battlefield.

The beauty of the database was that while the Pentagon would be alerted when 716 used it, no one would be able to determine what the informational queries were. If someone in an office somewhere could see what a team in the field was asking about, they might be able to figure out what the team was up to: which was one more unnecessary avenue for the leak of classified real-time operational data. Therefore the system was set up so the mainframe operators in Washington couldn't see what information detachments on the battlefield were looking at.

Of course the information was recorded and encoded onto a computer chip in Ralph's communications gear and . . . if the gear wasn't tampered with or, say, um, smashed or damaged, the chain of command would be able to check up on them once they were safely back at their base. None of the three Green Berets anticipated that particular function of the communications equipment was going to operate properly in the Iraqi desert. Thus, no one would be able to ask difficult questions.

Sorry General, it must've broke, Ralph thought, while mentally crushing it under his boot.

The liquid computer screen produced a white Department of Defense seal centered on a blue field. There was nothing else on the screen except for the initials "DOD–TDB" and a data entry box right below the seal. Ralph placed his cursor in the box and typed in 716's access code which appeared as stars on the screen. When he hit "enter" the screen changed, producing a banner at the top, "Department of Defense – Tactical Data Base." The system offered drop-down menus and options for complicated searches, but Ralph wasted no time choosing "ordinance."

"The LAWs first, sir?"

"Yep."

Ralph typed "LAW" for Light Antitank Weapon. The screen cleared once again and reassembled showing five diagrams at the top of the page. The diagrams depicted the weapon completely folded, extended and illustrated certain of its features. The technical description was below the photos.

"The M-72 series Light Antitank Weapon (LAW) is a lightweight, self-contained, anti-armor weapon consisting of a rocket . . ."

"Come on, Ralph."

Ralph punched his page down key.

". . . tubes, one inside the other, serves as a watertight packing container for the rocket and houses a percussion type firing mechanism that activates the rocket."

"Scroll, scroll, scroll," said Harris, inpatient.

Ralph scrolled down the screen. Sections of text with the occasional diagram flew past.

"Got it," Ralph said. The men leaned over and read together.

"The LAW is capable of penetrating a foot of armor, but its effective range is only 170 to 220 meters. Manufactured by Talley Industries in the U.S., early versions were frequently inaccurate, corrected by an improved sight and a more powerful rocket motor."

Talley was a good manufacturer, but the men were still a little cautious of a "Capable of" evaluation from a weapons manufacturer. Plus, these LAWS were old now. All three men calculated in their heads just how optimistic the manufacturer might have been and how old the explosive charges in the rockets were.

"All right, let's call it 3 to 6 inches," said Harris.

"What I thought," said Grayson.

"I want to be sure on this, Dave," Harris replied.

"Yes, sir."

"Okay, let's see about the APC's," said Harris.

Ralph "escaped" from the LAW section and returned to the main inquiry page. He chose "vehicles," and typed in "BTR–60." The screen showed five photos of an armored vehicle. Below was text.

"The BTR–60 armored personnel carrier, Soviet Union. Crew: 2 plus 4 passengers, eight-wheeled APCs. This vehicle protects its occupants from small arms fire but is vulnerable to anything heavier. Top speed: 60 kilometers. Armor: light. Armament: 1 x 14.5 mm KPVT heavy machine gun, 1x 7.62 mm PKT machine gun (coax)."

"Light armor could mean anything," Captain Harris said.

Ralph quickly scrolled past the text down to the physical description and characteristics of the vehicle itself.

"Got it!" he said.

"Right," said Harris, less enthusiastically. "Before you get too excited, check out the co-axle machine gun."

"Sir, we hit them before they ever get a chance to use the machine guns," Ralph said.

"Right," said Harris again.

All three men were looking at the screen, which indicated that the BTR–60 was equipped with 1 to 3 inches of armored plate, depending upon the version. The LAW rocket launchers would penetrate at least 3 inches of armor plating, and probably a lot more. They were in business.

"All right then," Harris said. "Sergeant Grayson, Sergeant Jackson, tell the rest of the team to stop what they're doing and send out a couple of villagers to the north. Put 'em on the first ridge line and make sure they take signaling mirrors. Then set up security and get the entire team back here, ASAP."

"Yes sir," the two men said in unison. Each left in a different direction at a trot.

While Grayson worked the other side, Ralph grabbed two of the villagers and asked them to put out sentries on the sand dunes.

"About half a mile out," Ralph said. "Tell them to each take a signal mirror and flash us if they see any military movement."

Cutting off questions, Ralph told the villagers he'd explain later.

He made it back to the team bunker just as the final members of 716 were arriving.

"Okay," said Harris, "here's the deal. Everyone knows we've received a direct order to blow all the weapons and return to Kuwait. You also know satellite imagery is showing a Republican Guard unit coming our way, and gentlemen, there ain't nothing out here but As Salman. It seems pretty clear what's going on. Saddam's coming for some payback, or to re-occupy, or whatever . . . it'll be the same thing for the villagers no matter what. We might have been able to get them all out if we'd started last night, but the sandstorm fixed that. If they go now, with the women and children, they'll get caught in the open desert. If they stay here . . . I don't think anyone's forgotten that police station at Al Khidr.

A couple guys flinched.

"Obviously, our orders are to blow everything in place and evacuate. Sergeant Grayson, me and Ralph are having a hard time with that. So, here's another option. We tell the Iraqis what's going on, leave em the weapons, get them set up for an ambush, and then leave."

Harris waited a minute and looked around. No one said anything, so he continued.

"We don't like that much either. They're brave men and we'll
probably feel better about ourselves, but they're villagers. The
chances of them taking on Republican Guardsmen backed up by
APC's and winning isn't very good. But, the thing is, even if we're
caught, absolutely red-handed, we can just say the Iraqis wouldn't
give up the weapons and we'll walk away. The last option is we stay,
ambushed the column and let the villagers kill everybody, and I
mean everybody, captured and wounded. Then we evacuate."

While Harris was talking, Ralph watched his teammates, especially Ted Kehr. Kehr was a Christian and real straight arrow.
Everyone stood poker-faced. Ralph couldn't read any of them.

"I don't think this is very complicated," Harris said, "but I'm not
taking any chances on someone not understanding it. If we leave
them the weapons and the Army can prove we did it intentionally,
we're all getting court-martialed. If we stay and fight, we're war
criminals and maybe traitors. We're going to execute, okay, we're
going to murder those Republican Guardsmen if we stay. If we
don't, why stay? Saddam will just send more men. We can't leave
any evidence of what happened. Let em think they got taken out
on the way here by air power, while they were still in the desert."

"I've been thinking about this and here's how we're going to do
it. Like I said, three of us want to stay and fight, but this is an all
or nothing proposition. If we stay and get caught, we're all going
to jail for a very long time, maybe for life. So, we don't stay unless
everyone agrees. I'll make up my mind about what to do with the
weapons myself and you can either back me up or not. Finally, no
one on this detachment ever mentions this vote again, no matter
what. No recriminations. That's it, everybody take a walk, have a
smoke – you've got five minutes, then we're voting."

"What's to think about?" It was the heavy weapons Sergeant,
Brian Penn. "We're wasting time."

Now, it wasn't just Ralph, every member of 716 looked at Sgt.
Kehr.

"If there wasn't any chance, that would be one thing," Kehr said
slowly, almost to himself. "But that's a small enough unit to take.
God forgive me, but . . . we can't leave these people in the hands
of the Republican Guards. I say we take them out, buy our friends

time to get into Saudi Arabia and we then evacuate."

Almost in unison, everyone on the detachment in one way or another said, "that's right, we can't just leave them without a chance."

After a moment they stopped talking and looked at their team-mates.

"Let's take the five minutes," Harris said.

"Come on sir, the heck with five minutes, let's go," Ed Dillon, the team medic said.

Ralph watched the eleven men who were his teammatesand, at least in his mind, like his brothers. Harris grinned. Kehr was sol-emn. Grayson shook his head with a sardonic smile. Ralph Jackson was young, but he understood the magnitude of the risk they were taking. He knew there was at least a −50-50 chance they would end up regretting this decision for the rest of their lives. But right then, looking at "his" team and over their heads at the waiting villagers who trusted them, he'd never felt better about himself in his life.

"Here's what we do then," Harris said.

CHAPTER 2

Isha Hami / AL NAJAF

THE WOMAN AWOKE TO THE smell of vomit, sex, and blood. She was laying spread out, face down, the rough concrete floor digging into her cheek. Her dress was in rags. Isha Hami opened her eye and began to stir, but then collapsed with a gasp. What she'd been taught as a girl to refer to as her "nether regions" burned. She lay motionless, waiting as waves of pain washed over her, blotting out the ability to do anything else but endure. She cried through the one eye that still worked and prayed the pain would at least ease.

"Lord Jesus." It came out as more of a sob than a prayer.

When the pain finally receded to the point where she could think, she preferred the thoughtlessness of the pain. Her last memories were of being raped by a room full of men while her husband and son were forced to watch. When the last man finished with her a Baathist security officer cut the throats of her men in front of her. Afterward, the men laughed, unwound garden hoses and washed down the concrete floor and the table where she had been tied. They kicked her family's bodies close to a floor drain, like garbage. Two other men grabbed her arms and drug her out the door and down a dim passageway as she sobbed.

"Don't cry. If you behave, I'll visit you again. Does that make you happy?"

The men laughed, unlocked a heavy iron door and threw her into a small, damp cell. They slammed the door shut with a clang, locked it and plunged her, literally and spiritually, into darkest night.

Now she curled up on the floor and prayed to merciful Jesus. She wasn't asking for strength, she wanted none. She wasn't asking why, she knew why. Educated abroad, she and her family were already suspect in the eyes of Saddam Hussein's regime. But beyond this, she was the daughter of a clan leader of a small but powerful Christian tribe with links to Tariq Aziz and the wife of another powerful Christian leader. After the American military buildup in Saudi Arabia and the Gulf states, she, her husband and her son began quietly encouraging not only their people but certain Shia tribal allies to prepare for resistance.

Soon after the war started, they, like all Iraqis, were astounded by the ease with which the Americans defeated Saddam's henchmen. So even while the fighting continued, Isha and her family took the Americans at their word and began to resist the Baathist government. Soon the Shias in the south burst into outright rebellion. The Baathists could barely defend themselves against the Americans so the Shias and their Christian allies ran wild. Those were heady times and Isha's husband, son, and father and father-in-law took leadership roles. Then the Americans ordered a cease-fire at the end of February. Stunned, the Shias waited to see what would happen. On March 3, 1991, Iraq formally accepted all of America's terms and signed an agreement to end hostilities. Isha felt like screaming.

"Don't you know what a liar Saddam is? What will happen to the uprising ?"

They soon found out. With their armored vehicles and attack helicopters freed up, the Baathists soon broke the back of organized resistance. Thousands of Shias and many Christians died fighting, trying to combat armor vehicles with rifles and home-made bombs. Even before the last of the organized resistance sputtered out, the mass roundups began. Iraq security forces eventually arrested a total of 15,105 people for participating in what they called "the disturbances."

The Hamis listened to the Voice of America and other international broadcasts with grim expectancy. The post-uprising roundups were particularly sweeping in the Shia holy cities of Karbala and al-Najaf, where Isha and her family lived. Those taken included hundreds of clerics. Between March 19 and 23, 1991, authorities in al-Najaf arrested the 95-year-old Shia spiritual leader Grand Ayatollah Sayyid abu al-Qassem al-Khoei, and 105 members of his family, his associates, and his associates' families. Those arrested included the Grand Ayatollah's son, the 89-year-old Ayatollah Murtaza Kazemi Khalkhali, and citizens of Lebanon, India, Pakistan, Afghanistan and Bahrain.

The roundups, arrests, and executions continued from March through April 1991, then died down in the south. The northern Kurds used mountainous terrain to their advantage and continued to defy Saddam and demand independence. Baathist attention and wrath thus fell upon the Kurds and the south enjoyed a period of peace. April became May, and drug on into June. The Hamis began to hope that in the pandemonium of the war and the uprising they had escaped the Baathists' notice. So many Baathists had been killed, so many facilities and security buildings were bombed into oblivion, their optimism didn't seem unrealistic. In late May, they moved out of their home, to Ad Diwaniya, far, but not too far, from Najaf.

Someone betrayed them. One July night they were awoken by kinsmen guarding their home. Almost immediately thereafter the front and back doors were simultaneously smashed in. Special Republican Guardsmen and security officers poured into the Hami home. Isha's son and his wife, Isha and her husband, were captured and bound. In a taste of things to come, rough men crowded around her, touching her and squeezing her where it was not decent. For some reason, Isha's pregnant daughter-in-law, Manal, was left unmolested.

The Hamis were forced into the back of a military truck and taken to the regional police headquarters in al-Najaf. They arrived late at night, nauseous and lightheaded from the diesel exhaust. The Baathists pushed and kicked them into the building. Once inside, Manal was pulled down one hallway, the others, screaming and crying out for her, down another. They would soon discover Manal was the lucky one. Isha, her son, and her husband were pushed and pulled down two flights of stairs, into the darkest police dungeon. Then the terror really began.

A set of keys rattled in the distance, the sound pulling her up from a twilight somewhere between unconscious and conscious. The jangling grew louder. Isha hardly dares breathe. Perhaps her cruel jailers would pass her by un-noticed and find their amusement in someone else's cell. She hated herself for hoping that, but then she prayed it. The footfalls stopped outside her door and a key sunk into the lock. Her heart jumped, but only for a moment.

Why, what's left?

The door swung open but Isha lay still. Eyes closed. Silence.

"Ahg."

Ice water. She contorted into a half sitting position and gasped, first in reaction to the bucket of icy water, then in pain as her damaged body rebelled against the abrupt movement. The jailers didn't wait. Each grabbed an arm and half walked, half dragged Isha out of her cell. A third man clad in a white doctor's coat stood behind a stainless steel wheelchair. The jailers dropped her into the chair. One of them threw a sheet over her body and tucked it around her neck and arms. The other yanked part of the sheet back and pinned her exposed left arm. Isha felt a sharp bite in her arm and then watched the hypodermic needle slide out back of her flesh. An immediate sense of relief washed over her. She leaned back to make eye contact with the white-coated man.

"Just enough so the pain won't distract you," said Mr. White Coat.

There was no mercy in those eyes, no mercy anywhere. She fought the tears but soon found herself sobbing. White Coat pushed her down a gloomy hallway toward a distant slice of light. The jailers plodded along beside her. The sweet relief from her pain continued, sweeping through Hami's body, out from the center of her chest, below her waist and out her limbs. She sunk back into the chair until the back of her head rested against Mr. White Coat, then jerked forward, horrified she had touched such a creature. No one seemed to notice.

The tunnel grade sloped upward toward a closed set of double doors leaking light. As they approached one of the jailers strode ahead and threw open the doors. Isha blinked her one good eye at the sudden sunlight and heat. White Coat pushed her through the doorway and into a large, walled-in courtyard dotted with a few trees. They rolled on, over hard packed dirt toward a group of soldiers standing beside three long tables. The walls were high and constructed of well-laid brick. Two of the men were carrying video cameras, just as they had when she was attacked. They rolled on, toward the center of the courtyard, closer to a young man on his knees with his hands tied behind his back and his ankles tied together. He was sobbing and shaking his head.

"No."

Over and over, softly, "No." One of the tables was covered with a dark green cloth. Bright, shiny instruments of metal glittered. She heard Manal scream.

"Mama, Mama."

The sight of her daughter-in-law, whose belly was just beginning to swell with her first grandchild, made Isha moan. It was a sound seemingly made by someone else. Even some of the guards turned away from her to look at the ground.

Isha recognized one of the men who held her gaze as the same Special Republican Guard Major who led the raid on her home. In the sunshine, she noticed that he also wore a badge of the "Mukhabarat," or Iraqi secret police, on his uniform. She shivered despite the heat.

"I cannot feel sorry for you. All this you have brought this upon yourself. It is only because of the mercy of our father, Saddam, that your daughter-in-law did not suffer your fate and then both of you the fate of your husband and son." Turning his head he said, "Bring her." Two of the soldiers grabbed Manal's arms and walked her toward the kneeling man. Hami was wheeled alongside Manal.

"You think you have been treated harshly?" the Major said, "I think your ingratitude and treason has been dealt with leniently. Soon you will agree and when you do, go from here and tell others not only of the justice of Saddam but also, as you have both tasted it, his mercy. Never forget, no matter how much justice you have suffered, you are not alone and there is always more." He turned from Isha to Manal, and back.

"Now," he said, "watch."

Another Baathist officer had been talking to the bound, kneeling prisoner. The officer looked up.

"Now, Major Allawis?"

Allawis nodded. The kneeling man was crying, but he finally nodded his head in resignation.

"Yes, yes."

The officer turned to the table and removed a small set of forceps and another shiny object which the women couldn't see. A second guard grabbed another set of forceps and the two men approached the kneeling man. Two other burly men restrained the kneeling man's arms.

"Open."

The man opened his mouth. Almost gently, the officer gripped his tongue with the forceps while the other guard held his mouth open with his forceps and slid a scalpel slowly and methodically across the man's tongue. He removed the tongue and held it up in front of women. Other policemen approached the kneeling man with towels and water buckets and tended to him. The Officer tossed the man's tongue onto Isha's lap with a flick of his wrist, staining her white sheet brilliant red. Isha gasped and squirmed, but White Coat and a jailer held her in place. Manal screamed until someone clamped a hand over her mouth. For a long moment, there was silence. Then, grinning, the officer clicked the blood covered forceps together and open, together and open, with a metallic, clack, clack. He looked at Isha, winked, and then stared at Manal Omar Hami and her belly.

"Who's next?"

Major Allawis spoke for the first time since the amputation began.

"Thank you, Captain Qazi. An unpleasant task, but a necessary service to our glorious leader and our triumphant republic. Clear the courtyard. Once this criminal is stabilized, take him to his home and release him. Let us hope others may learn from his tragic example."

It was now clear why Manal had been spared. Leverage. Isha was taken to a prison infirmary and cleaned up by female matrons. Her injuries were treated and five days later both she and Manal were released. They were taken home in the back of a government sedan. The neighborhood was different. While their house stood, many of the surrounding homes had been demolished. A once thriving neighborhood was pockmarked with empty lots. The normally busy streets were deserted. When the sedan opened its doors in front of Hami's home, the remnants of their friends and kinsmen peered out through windows or gates, but no one came to assist them. The two women managed to hobble into their house. Once inside, they both collapsed into chairs. Manal never spoke. She hardly ever spoke again.

Despite the young woman's silence, the Baathists eventually

killed her too. It just took them longer. When Manal died, Isha knew she could never give up her opposition to the Baathists. Some things decide our fate.

It began with the birth of her granddaughter. When Manal's pangs grew close, Isha and her cousin Khalima rushed her to the hospital. It was Manal's first child and her eyes shone with uncertainty and a little fear. The two older women helped Manal into the hospital. A small, innocuously dressed man slid into the waiting room behind them. Isha yelled at everyone in a white uniform.

"Please, let my mother-in-law go with me," Manal said as the hospital staff loaded her onto a gurney.

The head nurse glanced over Isha's shoulder, toward the corner of the room.

"I am sorry. We can't allow anyone into the delivery room."

"Wait," Isha began, "when I had my son . . ."

"I said no, I am sorry," the nurse said. She turned away and helped hustle a wide eyed Manal through the swinging double doors that led to the delivery room.

So Isha sat with her cousin in the waiting area, wringing her hands and praying for her daughter-in-law and soon-to-be grandchild. While squirming on the wooden bench in an attempt to get comfortable she glanced at the swinging double doors and then into a corner of the waiting room.

She pretended to ignore the small man seated by himself, hiding his face behind a newspaper. Occasionally she caught him peeking.

Baathist, she thought.

An old plastic clock numbered in Arabic numerals hung above the delivery room doors. It's minute and hour hands mocked her.

"Surely it's been longer than ten hours."

"Isha, I'm sorry," Khalima said. "I must leave."

Isha reached out to squeeze her shoulder.

"I know cousin," she whispered. "Have you had any word on Tariq?"

"The rumor is he's held at As Shawn prison. I just can't..."

Khalima cried.

"I'm sorry," she said after a moment, "it's just that there are so few of us left. I worry, but . . ." Khalima wiped her eyes and looked at Isha. "What about your husband's family?"

"Much the same as ours. I know for certain that Ahmed, Aziz, and Hafez are dead. Their families have been moved north. Kaliq and Ramzi were in Nakal prison the last we know. I spoke with Shaala last week," Isha said referring to Ramzi's wife.

Khalima stood up, now composed. She cast a quick glance at the corner and lowered her voice.

"If I can return, I will, but the ride is long. At least we can do this," she said. She slid around, blocking the Baathist's view with her body and took Isha's hand, wrapping it around a small package.

"What," Isha began.

"This is something from our families to you. As badly as we've been harmed, many of us are better off than you. Even now we're not without resources. It's not as much as we would like, but with Manal's health and a new baby and you will need . . ."

Isha squeezed her cousin's hand. "It's a gift from God and so are you. The Baathists left us with little."

Khalima squeezed Isha back. "We'll do all we can, but I don't know how you'll care for your family."

"The Princess is not helpless."

"A British Law Degree will not-"

"I'm working on a garden . . ." Isha had always been rich, beautiful, intelligent and married well. If Khalima thought that had made her soft . . . she tried a smile. "I can cook, sew, . . ." Her voice broke. She waited, tensed her face into a hard look and slipped the money into a fold of her dress. "My family needs me and I will care for them."

The women embraced one last time and Khalima left Isha alone with grim thoughts. Eventually, a weary looking nurse pushed through the doors. They swung in her wake, back and forth, back and forth, as she crossed the room.

"Mrs. Hami?"

"Yes," Isha said rising, "is my daughter-in-law well? Has my grandchild been born? Is the child healthy?"

The nurse held up both of her hands, palms out.

"You have a healthy granddaughter whom you will soon be able to see and even hold. Your daughter-in-law has had some complications."

"What comp...."

"She lost a great deal of blood but is now almost stable. The doctor will speak to you as soon as he can."

"Why did she lose so much blood, does she need..."

"Mrs. Hami the doctor is the one to answer your questions, not me."

"Of course."

The nurse smiled, patted her on the shoulder and left to push her way back through the doors.

Isha watched the clock until a second nurse appeared and motioned for Isha to follow her.

"This way, Mrs. Hami. You have a beautiful young granddaughter waiting to see you."

Isha bolted up, smiling despite her concern for Manal. The nurse gave her a professional smile and led her down a long, tiled hallway. At the end of the hall, they made a left-hand turn and entered a room filled with wooden cribs. Matrons in white uniforms buzzed around the cribs like bees around flowers.

"Hami," the nurse said in a loud voice.

A matron walked up with a small bundle in her arms. The nurse placed a hand on Isha's back and spoke gently.

"Only a short visit, for now, Mrs. Hami. By the time it's over the Doctor should be able to see you."

Isha nodded but had eyes only for the baby. She held out her arms to the matron and took the infant. Isha smiled down, holding her close and rocking her in her arms, back and forth, just like she'd rocked her son. After a moment, hot tears rolled down her face.

"Your daughter-in-law said her name is Naba."

"Yes. Naba. Grandmother loves you Naba. Grandmother will make you a better life than she had."

After what seemed like only moments, the matron re-joined Isha and Naba.

"I'm sorry Mrs. Hami, it's been 15 minutes and we're very strict on the day of birth. Tomorrow the child will be stronger and probably with her mother." The woman smiled a warm, human smile that surprised and touched Isha. "In not so long a time, you'll long for a day when someone like me offers to give you some rest, a break from this little bundle."

Isha smiled back and took her time handing Naba over. She left the nursery and walked down the long hallway, the child's face still clear in her mind's eye. She pushed through the heavy doors and returned to her seat. Before she could sit, a man's voice called to her.

"Mrs. Hami? I am Doctor Tublai."

Doctor Tublai was a handsome man in his late 40's wearing a green surgical gown with a white mask hanging from his neck. He glanced down at a chart. Isha thought he looked weary.

"Manal lost a great deal of blood. She's stable but very anemic. I'm sorry to say the blood loss aggravated some of her other health problems. She's out of immediate danger but will need to be careful with her health. Do you have someone to help you at home?"

"We live alone, Doctor."

"Talk to your family and friends. I'm sure someone can stay with you for a few weeks to help out."

"I'll try. But, whatever Naba and my daughter-in-law need, I'll provide it for them. May I see Manal?"

The doctor sighed, pinched the top of his nose and rubbed his fingers back and forth. Finally, he looked up.

"I want to look in on her again myself, so you can come with me. Just let me warn you, she's pale and very weak, so . . . Come along."

The doctor led her through a series of hallways, up a short flight of steps, and into a white tiled room that Manal shared with another woman. Isha expected her daughter-in-law's pale appearance, but not the empty look in her eyes. What Isha saw frightened her. She walked to the side of the bed and took Manal's hand.

"I've seen our beautiful, beautiful girl. I'm so proud of her and of you."

"Now I will sleep."

The doctor was on the other side of the bed, removing a blood pressure cuff.

"Leave her sleep, Mrs. Hami. Come back tomorrow"

"Thank you, Doctor. For your good care."

Isha left the hospital and decided to walk home to save money. It was late afternoon, the weather was pleasant, and it was easy to stroll along lost in thought. When she turned the corner into her neighborhood she had no clear recollection of how she got there.

A handful of men were striding along streets, scrutinizing telephone and power poles, the sides of buildings and even the trash receptacles. In spite of her weariness, Isha was curious. One of the men reached up and pulled off some sort of poster tacked up at eye level.

"What are they doing?"

She slowed and watched the men, trying to decide what they were up to when two neighborhood men spotted her. They jogged toward her.

"Mrs. Hami, Mrs. Hami!"

One of the enlarged posters that so intrigued the men was visible on a nearby pole, but before she could get close the men moved to one side, blocking her view. With a quizzical smile, Hami turned toward another pole and got the same reaction. This time, one of the men actually reached out and grabbed her shirt sleeve, something very unusual in polite Arab culture. He was just a second too slow. Isha caught a glimpse. She was so surprised it took a moment for the poster image to register. It was her, her clothes ripped, her body exposed, while two Baathists were in the midst of their assault on her. The fact registered only as she turned to face Abdul who wore a smile that was really a leer.

CHAPTER 3

———

R ALPH SPENT ABOUT 15 MINUTES with Captain Harris and the rest of 716, working out the strategy and tactics they'd use against the enemy Armored Cars and infantry. Although Harris was in charge, as usual, he wanted input from everyone: especially the heavy and light weapons Sergeants, Team Sniper Ted Kehr and Team Sergeant Dave Grayson. 716 had been in As Salman for over a year, so they knew the terrain and the men they'd be leading. They came to a quick consensus on strategy: hide, draw the Republican Guard unit into the village square, then attack.

The tactics were a bit more contentious. "Strategy" meant what they were going to do, "tactics" meant how they were going to do it. Several members disagreed about the proper placement of the LAWs, the villagers and where Ted Kehr, the team sniper would best be positioned. After hearing everyone out, Captain Harris broke the tie. He'd take Kehr with him and set up an observation post inside the village. They'd disburse the Iraqis around the village in select locations alongside the Green Berets who'd been assigned to them ever since they'd arrived.

The plan was to use a handful of villagers to draw the fire of the Republican Guard Unit. The hope was the guards would then chase the villagers into the large open village square. Except for a concrete fountain, the square was clear of buildings, statues or trees for 40 yards in any direction. A perfect ambush site. However, if any of the Republican Guard saw additional armed men lurking about, it would probably ruin the whole plan.

Finally, Ralph Jackson would be the point man, the one who'd work with the lookouts and act as the lone American sentry on the north side of the village. He along with a handful of the townsmen would be the one baiting the Republican Guards, drawing them into the town square. He'd be the one on the wrong side of town holding the bag if anything went bad.

"You okay with that Ralph," Captain Harris asked.

Ralph was okay with it. He knew what 716 thought of him and wondered if they weren't right. Today people were going to be killed and he was going to contribute more than his fair share to the killing. In the last eighteen months, he'd personally killed twenty-seven men, all of them armed and all of them expecting him, or someone just like him. His teammates wondered if he was out of control, but that didn't stop them from winding him up, pointing him in the right direction and letting him go. Like he was some kind of doomsday machine or something.

"I'm okay with it, make's sense to me, sir."

That's what he does, that's all he does, Ralph thought, recalling a line from the movie "Terminator." He smiled from under his four hundred dollar sunglasses and then stopped, hating how his thoughts always wandered while he was waiting.

"Ralph? I'm taking the pills for this one," Harris said.

"Me too, sir," Ralph said. Harris was worried. Of course, he was going to take the pills, everyone always took the pills, even Kehr.

Captain Harris, of course, was referring to a fast-acting cyanide-based poison pill SF members used to commit suicide if it looked like they might get captured. The practice originated as a result of SF's involvement in covert operations. At times, the teams operated almost as surrogates for the Central Intelligence Agency spies, so in Special Forces, covert, unacknowledged or black operations were common. These operations, at least as conducted by Special Forces, were small military actions in a foreign country, without that country's permission. The reason the operation was often called unacknowledged was because the United States would deny that the men killed or captured were US soldiers. On unacknowledged operations, the detachment was inserted into the area of operations "sterile." Sterile, in SF speak, meant when you are inserted, there was nothing to identify you as an American or an American soldier. The Green Berets were dressed in old surplus East European combat fatigues without any identifying insignia or patches. They carried firearms manufactured in South America, canteens and web gear from Thailand and combat boots from

Canadian military surplus. In the event they were killed, there would be no way to identify the nationality or affiliation of the dead soldier. This is one of the reasons why a tattoo, anywhere on one's body, disqualified a soldier from even applying for Special Forces Qualification.

The nature of the operations meant that if captured, one would certainly be tortured. Since the operation was going to be denied by the United States, no one was going to negotiate for your release or complain about how you were treated. Rescue was unlikely. Death eventually followed prolonged torture. Unprotected by the Geneva Convention and denied by your own government, you could expect an extended stay in hell. Early in Special Forces history, captured team members were subjected to unimaginable treatment. From then on, Special Forces Detachments favored poison rather than facing torture and risk betraying teammates or the United States.

The process was short and straightforward. The team medic kept the capsules in his medical kit and passed them out, three to a man. Ralph stuck one of the caps in an easy to reach cargo pocket, then ripped off a couple strips of industrial grade duct tape and taped the other two just above the ball of his right and left shoulder. If both your arms were blown off or trapped, you could still reach the poison and bite down on the cap. It actually happened once, an SF guy got shot down, lost one arm and found the other pinned below some of the debris. The enemy captured him. About two months later, someone dropped off a can of 8 mm film at the US Embassy in Karachi. It revealed the gruesome last weeks of the soldier's life.

The tape was still played as part of the class on escape and eva-sion in the final phase of the Special Forces Qualification course. No one was required to use poison. No one in Special Forces ever refused it.

After they finished, Harris and Kehr left to set up the observa-tion post. The rest of 716 split up, each guy heading to a different part of the village to assemble their men. Ralph worked his way toward the northern wall. Months ago, 716 formed the villagers into squads based upon where they lived and assigned one Green Beret to each 12 man squad. Ralph and the others called out to their men in the Arabic they knew and waited. What had been a sleepy village came alive. In moments, each team member had about 12 adult males forming an inner circle around them, with another, a larger circle of women, children, and old folks lining the periphery. Slowly, the murmurs grew into a hum. The hum covered the entire village and then burst into a chorus of voices, jabbering in Arabic. The circle of Iraqi men broke up and ran to their weapons. Within moments the villagers were armed and lined up.

Ralph and the other Green Berets explained their plan and how the villagers fit into it. After answering a few questions, the groups of men followed the Green Berets to their assigned battle positions. The three most senior leaders were asked to join Harris so he could explain how 716 thought the enemy would approach and why they placed the men where they had. The village leaders, satisfied, returned to their men, moving from group to group, encouraging them and answering questions in their turn.

When they were done, everyone else trotted off to their assigned positions. Ralph Jackson led his small group of villagers toward the north wall of As Salman.

———

Three hours later, Captain Harris and Ted Kehr were waiting on a nearby rooftop. They had chosen a building for their observation post that was set back fifty yards from the perimeter where the townsmen and American soldiers lay in wait. The location and elevation of the building gave them a wide, unobstructed view of the battlefield. Both men were hunkered down, hiding behind the roof's three-foot high parapet and thus concealed from any oncoming enemy who crested the dunes outside the town. They sat together and leaned back against the parapet, watching the heat reflect up off the roof's surface in shimmering waves. Both were chugging water from their canteens, wiping the sweat out of their eyes and waiting to be notified that the enemy had arrived. The microwave communications system was set up and sitting beside Harris.

"The intelligence reports said they were supposed to be here an hour ago," Harris said. Normally, Harris would have only shared his reservations with the team Sergeant, but he and Kehr were both Evangelical Christians and their shared faith led to a closer than usual friendship.

"You surprised sir?"

"Par for the course. I'm expecting the same with the evacuation."

Promises of support from headquarters were no more reliable than the intelligence reports. Special Forces command advised Harris to expect a fifteen-minute delay between calling for the evacuation choppers and their arrival. The Captain was expecting a least a half an hour wait for the helicopters and half an hour was forever in combat. He set up the communications gear so they could call in the team's evacuation on a moment's notice.

"Maybe I should have put one of the individual radios out on the dunes. I'd like to know what we are really up against as soon as possible."

Once again the Captain questioned whether he should have sent one of 716s' personal radios out to the dunes with the Iraqi observation team. On the one hand, such a move might have enabled him to receive an advanced report on the size and composition of the enemy force. On the other hand, 716 only had twelve of the sophisticated devices, one for each team member. Equipping the Iraqis would've meant taking one of his men out of direct contact with the rest of the team. Out in the open desert, with the sand and uncertain ability of the Iraqis to use them . . . it seemed best to maintain inner team communications. Coordinating the movements of his outnumbered men would be crucial in achieving victory or surviving to escape. Still, he would've liked immediate confirmation of the size and composition of the enemy force.

You'll know soon enough, Harris thought.

"Come on sir, our Iraqi friends are big on character, but they're not exactly technical whizzes. Besides, with all the sand blowing out there it would probably be ruined by now. I wonder if it wasn't a mistake stationing Ralph near the kids. He got way too close to them, the soccer . . . he's not that much older than some of them."

"Ralph? Yeah, he's young and too close to the kids, but he's a wrecking ball once the shooting starts, like he was born for it. We put him right where he belongs— the point of impact."

Harris almost laughed at Kehr for worrying about Ralph. They say some people, prodigies, sense things other people can't detect. In music, they compose melodies no one else can hear until they're played. In art they find shadow, light, and color no one else can see until they reduce it to canvas. They're the Albert Einsteins of their calling. Ralph Jackson was like that. During battle he could see angles and cover, he knew how men would react and which way they would move. He could sense where it was safe and where death lay waiting. He was a dead shot with bullet train reflexes and an emotional thermostat set a few degrees below zero. Harris liked Ralph, but he was one spooky kid.

"At least the team's hooked together," Harris said after a minute. "Once this starts I'll need to coordinate everybody and there's going to be no room for error."

"Sir, you always get like this. Pregame jitters. You're the best small unit guy I've ever seen."

Kehr was still sitting beside Harris, cradling a scoped sniper rifle he knew how to use with devastating effect. Once they got the call, Harris planned on peeking through a hole in the parapet and coordinating the attack with his personal radio. Kehr would use his sniper rifle to provide long range support, lending unseen fire-power to any area that was threatened.

Ralph Jackson's voice rolled in on top of a sudden burst of static, piercing the silence.

"Boss, we've got movement. Wait one."

"Roger," Harris said after triggering his mike. He turned back toward Kehr.

The Captain looked at Kehr and nodded. Harris bowed his head momentarily and Kehr crossed himself before removing the lens cover caps from the sniper rifle's scope.

Showtime.

CHAPTER 4

———◆———

ABDUL CHATTERED ON AND ON about Manal until Isha's head cleared. The man wasn't leering, after all, he was smiling. His tone was friendly and his look concerned as he tried to distract her.

"What happened, where have you been, are congratulations in order?"

It was too late. The Baathists had posted photographs of Isha's rape throughout her neighborhood. Her friends and neighbors spread out, working to take them down before she saw them. Isha turned from Abdul for a second look at the offending poster. Another man already had it is his hand. He smiled at her, crumpled the poster into a ball and stuck it in his pocket.

"What do you have," she asked in a high-pitched voice.

The man looked at the ground and actually scuffed his toe in the dirt.

"Nothing Mrs. Hami," he said. His eye remained locked on the ground.

"What do you have in your pocket?"

"Nothing, Ma'am," he said. He turned around and walked off. Before Isha could decide if she should chase him Abdul was in front of her, blocking the way. His eyes were kind.

"Mrs. Hami, what's the news? Some things, they're like bad dreams and disappear. Other things, they last. Tell me of the things that last. Tell me about your grandchild."

Isha was shamed so many had seen her so exposed, but shame was an emotion she couldn't afford. A family relied upon her.

"I am glad to tell you that besides being blessed by Godly neighbors, I have been blessed by a beautiful, healthy granddaughter."

When Abdul smiled, Isha felt her own smile, a real one, spread across her face.

"As you say, some things last."

But across the street, unfriendly eyes watched and bided their time.

———————

"Grandmother, grandmother, knocking door, knocking door," Naba yelled as she came running into the kitchen.

"Very well child," Isha said to the three-year-old. If only she could bottle Naba's energy and use it herself. She picked up a nearby dish rag and walked toward the front door, wiping flour off her hands.

"Khalima? What a . . ."

"Won't you ask me in?"

"Yes, yes."

The two women laughed and embraced. Khalima bent over and hugged Naba.

"How she's grown."

"I am three years old now."

Isha closed the door and walked arm in arm with Khalima to the kitchen.

"The door, window, and its box are so fine. When I left last year I thought I'd see the box lying on the ground when I returned."

"The neighbor boys replaced it," said Isha, "right around the time Manal died."

"I'm sorry I missed her funeral, we all are, but with Tariq being released and his health ..."

"I know. Naba says she can barely remember her mother. She cries and holds onto her doll. Manal's last gift. I don't know what to tell her."

The women sat at the kitchen table in silence.

"How is Tariq," Isha finally asked, referring to Khalima's son.

"The leg prosthesis still causes him problems. He struggles with skin infections." Khalima shrugged. "We'll never get a better fitting leg. We were lucky to get one at all."

"They took his leg," Isha whispered too low for Naba to hear, "they could at least let him have a prosthesis that fits."

"At least he's alive. Most of our men are dead. Some in the 'disturbances,' some after. I thank God they let him live."

"Let me show you my doll, Aunt Khalima," Naba said. She dashed out of the kitchen and sprinted down the hallway toward her room. The two women smiled at each other.

"The joy of my life," Isha said.

Khalima, who was actually Naba's sixth cousin, grew solemn.

"Then what are these rumors I hear? That you are involved with the mullahs and their followers in resistance? We're Christians, Isha, haven't you suffered enough? What about Naba?"

"I am not involved with the mullahs," Isha said in a low voice. "On occasion, when I'm in the market chatting with someone, I might mention they would enjoy the friendship or companionship of another person I know."

"Tah. You're helping establish connections between resistance groups. You know you're watched. You and I have seen them. What about receiving and passing messages?"

"That's only happened on two occasions. Who told you this? If it's someone in our family, I hope they keep a tight rein on their tongues."

"Our tongues are kept in our mouths, except around family. Did you expect us to say nothing? Before the war we were not close, but we are family. We are all we have left. Haven't you learned? You of all people? You are a woman, know a woman's place!"

"First, I'm not watched all the time. Do you think me a fool? As for a woman's place, my neighbors don't seem to share your ideas."

"Ah! As long as you take the risks, they smile at you on the streets, address you with respect and even fix your house. But ask them to risk for you!"

"I do not want Naba to grow up in a country where what happened to me can happen to her."

"I do not want black house flies in my cupboard when . . ."

Khalima had raised her voice. Now she took a breath and removed a small airmail envelope from her bag.

"What does it matter what we want?" Khalima said. "I must catch my bus, it's a difficult ride home. This is not a lot of money, it's not as much as we would like to send. Still, if you want support from our family you should care about what we think. We think you are being reckless. If the money is to continue..."

"Aunt Khalima, Aunt Khalima! Do you see my doll? Grandmother made me a new dress for her."

The child came to a dead stop in the doorway, the smiled dying on her face.

"Aunt Khalima? Must you go Aunt Khalima? It's been so long since you visited."

Khalima looked at Naba and let a smile play across her face.

"I'm afraid so child. It is a long bus ride for your old aunt. Sometimes I think maybe you should come and visit us." Khalima looked at Isha and the smiled disappeared. "Perhaps a long visit would be good."

"Yes! A long visit with you, me and grandmother. Grandmother, grandmother can we go?"

Khalima and Isha stood with their eyes locked, knowing that if Naba went for a long visit, Isha would not be invited and Naba might not come back. Khalima broke off the gaze first and walked to Naba, knelt on the one knee and embraced the child.

"Perhaps, Naba, perhaps."

The three of them walked to the front door where the women embraced.

"Thank you for your visits and your help."

"Isha, I am your blood." Khalima softened her tone. "Think of what I said."

"May God give you a safe trip. Send our love to our families."

Despite Khalima's concerns, it was easy for Isha to continue assisting Saddam's opponents. She didn't think she was likely to be found out. In her opinion, the Baathists weren't trying to spy on her, they were trying to intimidate her and those around her. The Mukhabarat's actions seemed to support her conclusion. Isha and her associates were vigilant, yet often weeks passed with no evidence of secret police surveillance. When she was under surveillance, the men who followed and watched her didn't try to hide who they were or what they were doing. They seemed to want her and those around her to know she was being watched. Whenever she had the slightest concern she might be watched, she suspended her work. When she sensed the threat was lifted, she started helping again. Despite the displeasure of both sides of her family, she continued to receive their circumspect financial support. She was, after all, a Hami.

"I'm as safe as a Hami in Iraq can be," she thought on a day when she was free of the Baathist shadowers. The weather was beautiful and the oppressive police surveillance was nowhere to be seen. Her spirits soaring, she walked with Naba to the market and planned to pass along a coded verbal message to a resistance sympathizer. It was low risk activity, otherwise, she would have never involved Naba. The shopkeeper was one of her normal suppliers of produce. He was also a resistance sympathizer.

"Say hello to your friend Abdullah for me," she said quietly. She paid in brightly colored Iraqi dinars. The man smiled, nodded and handed over her change along with a bag of vegetables.

Isha thanked the merchant in her normal voice and turned to Naba.

"Come, child, let's go home."

They walked back from the market, chatting about Naba's friends, until they were across the street from their home. At that point, Isha stopped to survey her domain. She had a fine house which she loved, and although it reminded her of her husband and son, she had made it a home for Naba. On the outside, she worked to water and care for the small trees, shrubs, and plants that grew near the front patio. She hung potted plants from the wooden latticework above the patio and grew fragrant herbs and colorful flowers. When a strong breeze blew in off the desert, the plants swung back and forth, soothingly. As always she took pleasure and pride in how the green vegetation contrasted with the red tile sides of her house as well as the darker walls and plant wells that surrounded the patio.

After they stored the groceries Isha and Naba went outside, finding shade under the latticework. The lattice was interwoven with desert Ivy which blocked the sun's strongest rays and provided a cool, fragrant haven. At first, Naba played while Isha did her work, chattering away to her beloved doll. Later, Naba began to "help" with the gardening work. As always, they continued to heal, a little at a time, in the shade filled refuge she and Naba created for themselves.

A burst of raucous laughter made Isha look up from her gardening and gave her a chill. A group of rough looking young men were walking along the side of the street in their direction. One boy pushed another and two of the boys raised their voices, pointing fingers at each other and laughing loudly along with their friends. Isha shivered and Naba grew still, her eyes flickering back and forth from the boys to Isha. When Isha held out her arm, Naba scooted under it and leaned against her grandmother. One of the young men in the group lowered his voice and tugged on the sleeve of another. The boys went silent, then looked up and over in Isha's direction. They lowered their voices and mumbled amongst themselves until they drew near to Isha's sidewalk.

"Good afternoon, Mrs. Hami," the largest of the boys sang out in a respectful voice. The other youngsters added their greeting and waved at Naba. Isha smiled and waved to the boys.

"Good afternoon."

She returned to her gardening and felt her granddaughter relax. The boys returned to their roughhousing, their voices fading as they walked away. Isha's arms were covered with goosebumps. Even now, men's rough laughter took her back to the night her family was killed, but now the spell was broken. Isha took Naba inside and began to prepare dinner.

After they ate Isha sent Naba into the front room while she cleaned up. She'd just finished and was heading toward the toilet or "water closet," when someone knocked on the front door.

Amah, from next door, wanting to borrow something. It never fails, Isha thought. She really had to go. Let her wait.

"Grandmother, grandmother, knocking door, knocking door."

"RRRR, WAIT CHILD !"

Something crashed and the door splintered as it gave way.

"Yeeee ..Yeee .. Grandmother!"

Naba sounded hysterical. Isha sprinted down the hall and grabbed her just as a uniformed Republican Guardsman was preparing to strike the child. She huddled over her granddaughter, shielding her and tensing to receive the blow. It never came.

"Enough, clean the place out," ordered a familiar voice.

Major Nadim Allawis stepped through the door wearing a pressed green uniform. Gleaming black boots. Shining Mukhabarat badge. Butcher of families, cheerleader of rapists. Isha straightened and released Naba.

"Grandmother! Why are they here! I'm scared."

Naba moved closer, clutching Isha's leg. She could feel the child's small body trembling. Isha prayed.

"Stand there and do not move," Allawis said.

He turned and walked down the hallway while his men spread throughout the house. In minutes they were removing the Hamis' possessions and loading them onto two trucks parked in front of the house. Isha knew better than to say anything. Two men emerged from Naba's room with her bed and slammed the headboard into the door frame, gouging out a large chunk of wood.

"That's my bed, that's my..."

Isha clapped her hand over her granddaughter's mouth. Naba sobbed, her tears rolled down her cheeks and over her grandmother's hand. The guardsmen around them stopped and glared at Naba. Isha went down to one knee, holding the child close and whispering in her ear.

"Quiet child, quiet child, please Naba, quiet."

Every man in the house had stopped to glare at the Hamis. Isha was disoriented by the sudden, roaring silence and started shaking. Far away, a dog barked at the sun. No one moved. After several long minutes, Allawis returned to the living room and glanced around.

"Carry on with your work."

As though a spell were broken, the men resumed ransacking her home.

"May we use the water closet?"

"Stand right where you are and don't move."

Allawis stood over them and looked down, his face neither cruel nor compassionate.

"You and the child will not be coming back."

Naba subsided, so Isha took a chance and released her. She stood with her arm around Naba's shoulders and looked at Allawis.

"Why? Where are we going, why?"

She hated herself for the subservient tone she heard in her voice. Still, she waited with her eyes cast slightly down.

"This is none of your concern. Your fate is sealed, but that of the child is still undecided."

He smiled, leaned down and brushed the back of his hand gently across Naba's cheek. Naba cringed against her grandmother.

"Several of my men have commented on what a beautiful child she is."

For the next half an hour, Isha and Naba stood in the corner of their home where Allawis placed them. The guardsmen came and went, loading individual pieces of furniture and some clothing. They didn't bother with most of the household items, except to kick them aside or send them crashing off of tabletops or countertops. Naba shook every time it happened, but she'd stopped crying. Finally, it occurred to her.

They're going to kill me or . . . send me to prison. The only reason they don't just come out and say it is to keep me quiet. That's why they're plundering my home, its booty, like a conquering army. Lord Jesus, what will happen to Naba?

Rough men's voices cursed and laughed while Isha stood stiff, tears streaming down her face. The air was filled with the crashing sounds of breaking items and smashed furniture. Naba turned away, burying her face into her grandmother's thigh. Occasionally Isha could feel her tremble. All the while, despite the terror, Isha was distracted by the growing discomfort, bordering on pain, in her bladder.

Nadim Allawis returned.

"Take your granddaughter and follow this man."

"May I go to the water closet first," Naba asked.

Allawis smiled. "Of course. Private," he yelled, motioning to a second man, "take the child to the toilet. Take your time, we're in no hurry." Allawis picked up an overturned chair and sat in it with a sinister smile.

An ill kept, leering man approached and saluted Allawis, but his eyes kept darting to the little girl.

"Thank you, sir. Come, child," he said, reaching for Naba.

CHAPTER 5

———

THEY'D BEEN IN AMBUSH POSITIONS for three hours and there was still no signal or movement from the ridgeline look-outs. Every minute crawled. The morning sun continued rising and so did the intensity of the heat and glare it generated. Metal and glass burned the flesh of anyone careless enough to touch it.

The men squinting into the desert couldn't concentrate for longer than a few minutes before turning away, blinking and grateful they weren't the ones posted out in the desert. An occasional wind stirred up the bright sand, creating a yellow, almost mist-like cloud off in the distance. As the wisps of sand swirled, the town streets were deserted and silent. Everyone in As Salman fought against the drowsiness that whispered in their ears.

Ralph Jackson stood in the shadow of a house on the northeast boundary of town and was the first man to see the flashes of light from the ridgeline. After signaling once, the sentries jumped on their bicycles and raced full speed, down from the dunes toward the outskirts of the town, flashing the stainless steel mirrors as they pedaled. Ralph triggered his radio mike.

"Boss, we've got movement. Wait one."

"Roger," Harris said into his ear.

"Move the kids into the stone house, Akhmed," Ralph said. He still couldn't see anyone except for the two Iraqis on their bicycles.

The town fathers decided that a house constructed of flat stones near the center of town was the safest place for the children. They'd considered an old Baathist bunker the Americans had used as a team house, but parts of the bunker were in disrepair and the kids might wander off and get hurt. Since the stone construction of the house was resistant even to heavy caliber machine gun fire, it was safer for the kids.

When the kids lined up to enter the house, several turned and waved at Ralph. He waved back, waiting until the door closed behind the last of the little figures before squeezing the transmit button on his radio.

"I don't see anything yet, but I told the Iraqis to put the kids inside. The observation post team is signaling like crazy and coming back now, best possible speed, over."

Ralph tightened his grip on the rifle and leaned back in the shadow. They'd be coming soon. Well over one hundred Guardsmen against their twelve, plus the Iraqis. Harris and Kehr were religious men and they would be praying, no doubt. Not him. He was ready. Everything was in its place.

"Let me know, over," Harris said through his earpiece.

Ralph ordered his men into their concealed positions just about the time he heard raised voices in Arabic over the wind. The two observers might have been 100 yards away, peddling their way closer to town and yelling. Ralph turned to his interpreter.

"What are they saying?"

"I'm not sure. It might be . . . No, no."

The bikes were rapidly closing the distance and Ralph could hear the lookouts, screaming in English and Arabic.

"There are tanks, they have tanks!"

Bull, Ralph thought. He knew how fear could distort a man's perception. Then he remembered how often their intelligence reports were distorted or incorrect. What if, he thought, there really were Tanks instead of the personnel carriers? For one thing, the tank's main gun would knock that stone building down; right on top of the children inside.

"Get the kids out of the house and into our bunker, next to the square," Ralph said. "Now!" The interpreter yelled at the villagers, who scrambled to relocate the children. Ralph keyed his mike.

"Sir, this is Jackson, I think we might have a problem."

"What, Ralph?" Harris immediately replied.

"They're not back yet, but we can hear the lookouts screaming that the Republican Guard brought Tanks, sir."

"Find out what's going on."

"Roger."

Ralph grabbed a LAW from a nearby Iraqi position and ran

toward the two bicycling lookouts, closing the distance, yelling at the top of his lungs.

"How many and where?"

Most of the villagers spoke at least a little English, so he hoped for a quick reply since time was . . . a large shriek interrupted his thoughts just about the time the lookouts disappeared in bright light. A roaring wave of sound and heat rushed toward Ralph, picked him up and threw him about 8 feet. He landed with the back of his head, shoulders, and upper back making contact with the ground, stunning him. Three tanks crested the ridge and opened fire with cannon and machine guns.

Ralph regained consciousness, his ears ringing. The right side of his face was warm or wet or something. Furious, he shook his head trying to clear it. It took a moment, but he found the LAW lying off to his left. Ralph crab crawled to it on his hands and knees. The first tank crashed through a small mud wall that surrounded the village. It and its enormous cannon was less than 25 feet away.

Murderers, Ralph thought.

He reached the LAW, pulled out a safety clip, popped off the covers and pulled the ends apart, expanding it like a telescope. The tank's front machine gunner spotted him and sent a stream of bullets flying his way. Ralph dove behind a brick building, rolled to his feet and completed the extension of the LAW, locking it into place. He found an open window, climbed through it and sprinted down the narrow hallway. When he reached the end of the building he stuck his head out another open window. There it was, the tail end of the first tank.

Ralph smiled.

He straddled the windowsill, one leg in, one leg out and wedged his boot into a crack in the outside wall. Before he could shoulder the LAW, the tank's top hatch popped open and a soldier grabbed a mounted machine gun. Ralph tried to dive back inside, but his wedged foot was stuck. The enemy swung the machine gun around.

I'm dead, Ralph thought, at the same time a sniper rifle shot killed the soldier and threw him back against the rim of the tank hatch.

"Get out of there Ralph," Kehr said through his radio earpiece. "I can't help you against armor."

Ralph sucked in air, wiggled his foot free and took aim at the first tank when a second one crashed through a mud brick building about 45 feet away. Ralph shifted his aim, lined up the second tank's thick metal track in the red "V" of the sight and fired. The rocket whooshed off. Seconds later it exploded, cutting the left track in half. It spun around and spilled out onto the ground. With only one track operating, the tank was thrown into a hard right turn. Before the driver could cut the engine, the tank slammed into the remnants of a building and became wedged, unable to move. While the driver spun the remaining track backward and forward, three or four Iraqi villagers swarmed the tank and fired into its observation slots.

With the second tank disabled, Ralph jumped over the windowsill and hit the ground running. He pulled out his pistol with one hand and a hand grenade with the other.

The fifteen feet between the window and the first tank seemed to expand. Time slowed. Although Ralph kept his eye trained on the top tank hatch, the tank's front machine gun was in his peripheral vision. Time seemed to work just fine for the gun barrel—it swung toward him with unearthly speed. Ralph could hear himself pant. His legs seemed mired in quicksand and the gun barrel neared his left shoulder.

I'm never going to make it, he thought.

Then real-time reasserted itself and he sped past the arc of the machine gun barrel, climbed onto the tank track and onto the body of the tank itself. Ralph kept one eye on the top hatch, then grabbed a hand grenade and pulled the pin. The top part of the grenade flew off while he used his forearm to push the dead tanker backward. The corpse dropped down into the tank. Someone squealed in Arabic. Ralph counted "one" and then snapped his arm and wrist over the top of the open tank hatch, whipping the grenade into the interior of the tank. He pushed up on the open hatch to close it, but the grenade detonated first, hurling the hatch back over with a metallic slam. Metal vibrated even after the explosion. Ralph was confident the crew was dead.

"Ralph," Kehr said into his earpiece, "third tank, your one o'clock, third tank, your one o'clock." Ralph keyed his mike.

"Got it."

He was thinking, two down, a thousand to go, when he spotted the third tank, almost dead ahead. The next LAW rocket launcher was hidden about twenty feet away but before he could get started a high pitched howl rushed over his head.

It was a cannon round, heading toward some small arms fire aimed at the third tank. The shell slammed into the ground just to the right of the underground bunker sheltering the kids. It was a deep bunker, so Ralph didn't worry about it until he heard a secondary explosion. By the time he turned around a small plume of yellow mist oozed out of the ground. Ralph's eyes went all white.

"Oh God, please no."

The yellow mist thickened into a yellow fog, spreading out and then covering the bunker. Access to the bunker was through a metal door, flush with the ground. It flew open with a clang and the first child staggered out. He was small, perhaps five or six years old.

His name was Hussien. Ralph taught him the lyrics to a Beach Boys song, "I Get Around," one night while they were playing soccer.

It looked like someone smeared him, head to toe, with greasy yellow Vaseline. When he walked through the bunker's entrance, he pulled away from the door. A large strip of his flesh stuck to the door handle. Ralph couldn't move, but he knew what was coming next. The screams.

It was one thing to know they were coming, another to hear them. Frozen, Ralph watched the cloud continue to thicken as more kids staggered through it, their faces and bodies blistering, oozing, like special effects from a horror movie.

A second set of screams sprung from another direction. The parents. Their children were literally falling apart in front of them. The men were closer, and they abandoned their weapons along with all thought for their own safety. As they rushed toward the bunker entrance and they made easy targets. The remaining Republican Guard tanks opened fire with their machine guns just as the first group of men reached their kids. They were cut down. Still, the men continue to run toward their children and they continued to die. By this time their wives, mothers, and sisters had arrived from deeper in the village, drawn toward the screams. They stopped short. The town was littered with the bodies of their men and the dissolving scraps of what was left of their children. For one long moment, no one moved or made a sound.

Ralph Jackson was standing with the women. Moments earlier, it occurred to him that the Republican Guards didn't fire a mustard gas round at the bunker. In fact, the cannon round ignited concealed chemical munitions buried off to one side of it. That was the secondary explosion he'd heard. Upon detonation, the explosion blew the plasma and gas off to the path of least resistance, into the bunker itself. The bunker where he'd order the town's parents to stash their children, "so they'd be safe." As he was thinking, the same bullets killing the villagers were whipping over his head and whizzing by his shoulders. They seemed incapable of touching him.

I put them there. The thought paralyzed him.

———◆———

Elder Abdul Hahcar stood stoic beside Mel Harris, gazing over the parapet in the direction of the town square. Kids burned and melted like yellow candles. Parents died in groups of two or three. Hahcar began to speak, then stopped to compose himself. With great effort, he started again.

"You and your men must leave Captain. It is now inescapable that we will die. That is enough evil for one day."

In the distance, four armored personnel carriers appeared and began to dislodge troops.

"Quickly," Hahcar said, "withdraw your men and we will provide such delay as we can manage."

Dave Grayson was standing at the edge of the roof, watching as the disaster continued. He lowered his rifle and walked toward Hahcar, not stopping until they were no more than eight inches apart. Grayson studied the Arab's face, as though memorizing it. Then he lowered his proud eyes and bent forward, in a sort of a bow. Straightening, he turned without looking back and packed his gear. Harris began to speak but Hahcar cut him off.

"There is no time and no words. Between true friends, none are needed. Go with Allah."

After Hahcar dropped through the roof hatch, Grayson and Harris took a long look at each other across the shimmering asphalt.

"Sir, better call for exfiltration. Those tanks will be coming any minute."

Harris leaned over the satellite dish and hit "send." The microwave transmitter simultaneously triggered an encryption program built into the radio unit.

"This is Detachment A-716 requesting immediate exfiltration from As Salman. Time critical. Zero Ten Hundred intelligence incorrect. Iraqi vehicles tanks, not APC's. Request gunship escort for exfiltration."

Harris released the encryption button and toggled it the other way to decrypt the response. The headquarters' powerful transmitter blasted back at them within seconds.

"716 this is Group. Exfiltration site Southeast of town. Exfiltration time ten minutes. Two transports and one Cobra gunship already on station, diverted to your location, and currently en route. Out."

Harris turned from the radio and yelled into his walky-talky, "Rally one, rally one, rally one," not because he was rattled, but so that his distracted men would hear him over the sound of explosions and gunfire. Except for Ralph Jackson, everyone on 716 responded to the evacuation code and disengaged from combat. The team had already lost control of the townsmen. When the bunker exploded, the defense crumbled, so now all that was left was to either escape or die. Harris could see them trotting off in the direction of the preselected exfiltration site.

Harris and Grayson scrambled down the ladder, slid out the door and double-timed it along a narrow dirt alley toward the exfiltration site. Additional team members linked up with them as they twisted between the buildings and jogged down streets and alleys, web gear rattling as they went. Finally, the first group of Green Berets led by Harris reached the Southeast end of the town. While certain team members turned back toward the town and went down on one knee, scanning for the enemy, the final stragglers joined them. Grayson conducted a headcount while Harris and Penn found a gap in the mud brick wall and set up the machine gun.

"Sir, Jackson's missing," Grayson said.

"*What?*"

Grayson and a couple of the other men watched him. The kid knows better, Harris thought. Maybe he got hit, but knowing Ralph, he might have decided to stay. How was he supposed to order other men to risk their lives because ...

Damn kid, he thought, expecting to see an APC or tank come flying down the street at any minute. Then for some reason, he began grinning. Grayson looked over and addressed him in a "what the heck's so funny" tone of voice.

"Something I'm missing here, sir?"

Harris looked up. Grayson and three other guys were looking at him.

"Sorry. I was just thinking about Ralph's pie choir for some reason."

Despite the tension, everybody else smiled too. Ralph Jackson's "pie choir" was a group of Iraqi kids Ralph taught to sing American pop songs. The group got their name because Ed Dillon had a real taste for chocolate pie. When the Team inserted into Iraq, one of the few personal items Ed brought along was a "Baker's" brand chocolate pie, one of the old kind you often find on a convenience store shelf, covered in dust. For some reason this struck Ralph as incredibly funny.

"Those things might taste like crap Ed, but I gotta give you credit, they got the same half-life as Uranium."

Finally Dillon's birthday rolled around. After dinner that evening the Americans sat outside the team bunker and Ed produced his precious chocolate pie. After ceremoniously unwrapping it, he began eating it with exaggerated relish. Halfway through his desert a large group of Iraqi children appeared and lined up in three rows, like Christmas carolers, shortest to tallest, right in front of Ed.

Without any prompting from Jackson, who looked on innocently, they began to sing in English. Jackson had taught them a complete set of lyrics, all to the tune of "American Pie" by Don McClean, but Harris could only remember the refrain.

"Say good byyyy byyyyy, to Ed's American pie."

"That kid sure does have a weird sense of humor," Grayson said laughing along with the rest of the men. After a short moment, the laughter died out and the men grew solemn.

"Ed, take Brian and go get him. You can shoot him in the leg and drag him back here if that's what it takes but . . . make it fast. We've got ten minutes and I don't know if I can hold the choppers so . . ."

"Yes sir," Dillon said. "Brian, on me."

Harris turned to Frank Hendrix, the junior weapons man. "Take over on the SAW, Frank," Harris said referring to the machine gun.

Dillon and Penn jogged off, a small cloud of dust in their wake.

Ralph's absence was the kind of complication that often got men killed. The thing was already going sideways and timing on the evacuation was going to be tight. Harris chewed the inside of his lip.

"Sir, maybe it wouldn't hurt for me to tag along behind the other two guys in case they need to carry him," said Rich Synder.

"If it's all right I'll go along with him," Hoffman said.

"Go," Harris replied. "Everyone else, let's secure the LZ."

The rest of the detachment fanned out to create a large circle. Each man faced out, separated by about twenty-five yards. Altogether, the team formed a wide circle, with a diameter of about fifty yards for the landing zone. This made enough space for the helicopters to land in the center, while the team was still in position to respond with suppressing fire to an attack from any direction.

Dillon and Penn jogged toward a yellow cloud still hovering over the old bunker until they heard screaming and machine gun fire. Dillon hesitated, then pointed. The two men ran to the rusting hulk of an old, dilapidated truck, then crouched behind it, panting.

"Smell that?" Dillon said.

"Yeah. Some kind of chemical, something else too, something I don't want to think about."

"I'll circle the left side and you circle around the right," Dillon said, point at a two-story concrete building.

The open town square lay on the other side of the building. The bunker was on the far side of the open square. Penn nodded and the men checked their watches.

"Ninety seconds and we pop out," Dillon said. "Go!"

They sprinted toward and then around opposite sides of the building, hugging the wall and slowing as they neared their respective corners. Both men went to their knees, then their stomachs, pulling their weapons close to their bodies and crawling inch by inch toward the corner. The air grew increasingly caustic. When they peeped around the side, they weren't observed. All eyes were on the smoking bunker, staggering children, and fathers struggling to reach them through a relentless hail of machine gun fire. Standing in the center of the carnage was Ralph Jackson, one side of his head blood encrusted, screaming at the top of his lungs. He'd found an ancient bolt action rifle somewhere and was working the bolt back as and forth as he fired. Dead men lay scattered around him, their limbs jutting off in every direction.

Ralph's target was one of the Republican Guard tanks some hundred yards away. Sparks jumped off of the tank turret without effect, but he kept plinking away. Inexplicably, none of the machine gun or cannon fire had yet touched him. He was out in the open, legs planted wide, swaying and screaming.

Ralph's teammates lay still, evaluating the scene. Dillon was no doubt trying to decide the best course of action. Penn was wondering what Dillon was planning. It was obvious Ralph wasn't rational and unless they moved him, his time on earth was limited. Penn' initial reaction was to dash out, grab Ralph, and get the heck out of Dodge. The problem was the BTRs had offloaded infantry. Until they located the enemy soldiers, they weren't going to move.

"Go now," someone hissed.

Penn already had his pistol out and was rolling onto his back before the sentence ended.

"Jeeze," he gasped, barely restraining his trigger finger. The townsman knelt alongside him.

"For now we have the Baathists pinned down, about two blocks away. There are not many of us left. Take Sergeant Jackson and leave, before it's too late."

The Arab reached out, squeezed Penn' forearm and left.

There wasn't time to think, so Penn reacted. He jumped to his feet and raced into the town square, running right at Ralph Jackson. He yelled over his shoulder as he ran.

"Dillon, on me."

Dillon was up and running in less than a second, scanning for enemy infantry as he ran and probably hoping Penn knew what he was doing. Penn began shouting.

"Ralph! Let's go, evac, evac."

Ralph Jackson lowered the rifle stock from his cheek. He took a half turn toward Penn as he barreled closer, but then froze in place. Penn reached him, grabbed his rifle and stripped it out of his hands. Dillon joined him and they grabbed Ralph and began dragging him toward the exfiltration site.

For some reason the Republican Guard machine gunners were still not targeting them, but there were plenty of "to whom it may concern" bullets flying all around. Ralph tried to shake loose.

"No way I'm letting these s.o.b.'s get away with it," he said.

His pupils were dilated. Blood oozed from his ear. He looked savage, even primitive. Penn made his decision without a second thought. He released Ralph's arm, put both hands on his rifle and pivoted at the waist, slamming the flat side of the rifle butt into Ralph's solar plexus. The kid's knees buckled, but Dillon got an arm around his waist and held him up. While Ralph gasped, his teammates each grabbed an armpit and drug him away from the battle. When they rounded the corner of the concrete building they were out of the direct line of fire. Dillon stopped and clicked his voice mike.

"We've got Ralph, but we could use some help, over," he panted.

"Help's on the way, keep moving," Harris' answered back.

Ralph was no longer resisting them, but he was dead weight. Both men were already tiring and they were barely out of the town square.

"Wait a minute," Penn said.

He slung his rifle, letting the weapon hang and freeing up both hands. When he bent down, Dillon helped him, grabbing Ralph by the front of his shirt and one pant leg. Penn did the same and between the two of them they hoisted Ralph onto his back. He straightened, grunting, but managed to stand. Penn got the load as well positioned as possible, then shuffled into a trot with Ralph bouncing on his shoulder. The street was a composite of light brown dirt and sand that seemed to stretch on forever. Penn grunted. Dillon moved along beside him, facing to the rear, shuffling backwards and sideways, keeping his weapon pointed to cover their retreat. They kept up a slow but steady trot until Sergeants Hoffman and Synder jogged up to them from the other direction.

"Let's move," Synder said.

"Yeah, right," Penn replied. He stopped, bent at the waist and dumped Ralph. You could hear the air rush out of his lungs when he hit the ground.

"Serves you right," Penn said gasping for air.

Ralph groaned.

"You otta spend a little more time in the weight room," Synder said. He grabbed Ralph and swung him onto his shoulders with relative ease. Most SF guys were quick and ripcord strong, big on calisthenics and obstacle courses. Synder was the team muscle man and a disciple of free weights.

"Kiss my rear."

Synder grinned and jogged off toward the exfiltration site without bothering to reply. Hoffman dashed ahead of him, clearing the way. Penn and Dillon pulled rear security. The men arrived at the exfiltration site just before the first chopper landed.

Captain Harris stood to one side, waving them on. The bird set down with a splash of rotor wind and threw sand in every direction. Synder ran through the LZ security perimeter, straight to the helicopter. Once the crew chief helped get Ralph on board, Dillon climbed in behind him. Ralph was coming out of his stupor and mumbling things that didn't sound very helpful, so Dillon ripped open his medical bag.

"Let's use the choppers against the tanks, let's . . ."

Ralph tried to get up. Synder pushed him back and the medic measured out a syringe of morphine, stuck Ralph in the rump and emptied it. The last thing they needed was Ralph raising Cain in the helicopter. He went limp.

The remaining Green Berets ran the exfiltration like a half-time show. Every second team member in the circle got up and sprinted to the first helicopter, reducing the circle's manpower by half. While the Cobra helicopter gunship patrolled overhead, the first "slick," or troop carrier, took off and the second landed. One by one, the remaining Americans loaded onto the second transport which took off with a jolt as soon as the last man was aboard. Seconds later they were 300 feet in the air, gaining altitude and moving swiftly toward the Kuwaiti border. Penn looked out the open helicopter door. The Cobra veered off to join them. Wistfully he thought about what his team could have done to the Baathists with the help of the gunship. His last glimpse of As Salman was a snapshot of a putrid yellow plume rising from the ground, surrounded by the small black dots of the bodies of townspeople, fathers, victims, and friends of the United States.

Penn turned in response to a hand on his shoulder. It was

Grayson, leaning over him and gesturing with his head toward the center of the helicopter. While the chopper bobbed and swayed, Penn pushed off with his feet and slid his rear across the metal flooring. The six men gathered into a tight circle, their heads close together. Wind rushed through the open doors and swirled around them, so Grayson shouted just loud enough to be heard over the roar of the rotor and howling wind.

"Okay, this is the only briefing we get. First, we got the message to evacuate, but the storm hit before we could get the weapons. Once the sand cleared out we tried to get everyone lined up the square, but the Baathists showed up. The Iraqis grabbed their weapons and fought. Nothing we could do about it, so we called for evacuation. That's it. No deviations from the story, no freelancing. Any questions?"

Captain Mel Harris was conducting the same briefing on the other helicopter with the rest of the team. Ralph Jackson was stretched out on the helicopter floor beside them, mumbling.

"What about Ralph?" Hoffman shouted.

"Ralph will play that story back to them better than we will."

Everyone looked at each other and nodded. Ralph Jackson was an odd kid, but he didn't choke. They just had to make sure he knew they were running the cover story and no one got to him before the morphine wore off. Harris continued.

"Sergeant Ralph Jackson suffered a concussion secondary to a near miss from cannon fire during the evacuation. He's a little confused and disoriented."

More nods. Harris leaned over and put his lips inches from Jackson's ear.

"Ralph remember the cover story. The town was attacked before we could collect the weapons. When the Baathists attacked, the Iraqi's wouldn't give them up, so we called for evacuation."

Ralph mumbled.

"Ralph, look at me." Harris grabbed Ralph's hair and used it to twist him around so their eyes were inches apart and locked on each other.

"Ralph, what happened?"

The young man's eyes cleared briefly. His brow furrowed as he concentrated.

"I know what to say, but not now." Ralph managed to nod his

head once and then his eyes focused behind Harris on some morphine induced daydream.

Harris straightened and glanced at his men, shouting to be heard.

"We - are - all - together!"

After that the team spread out, each man sliding along the floor until his back ran into something to lean against. They drifted into their own thoughts, lulled by the vibrating rotors.

Their landing in Kuwait was anticlimatic. The Generals and politicians were interested in victory laps, not debriefings, so Operational Detachment A-716 was checked in and released, debriefing to follow in the next few days. A couple of hours later the team sat by themselves at a big circular table in an NCO club. The bar was dark, air-conditioned cold, and loud with the jukebox sounds of Guns and Roses. The other occupants of the club kept a respectful, or maybe prudent, distance from the table. A Special Forces Detachment just in from the field was considered unpredictable by everyone, even members of other Special Forces Detachments. They were best left to themselves. The men of A-716 had been drinking steadily and eating jalapeno peppers from a quart jar in the middle of the table. Harris and Grayson sat on either side of a cleaned up Ralph Jackson. Most of the morphine had worn off and Ralph seemed to be himself again.

"Ralph, I would have put those kids in the same place. The only difference in any of this is who got stuck giving the order, because all of us would've done the same thing. We're all responsible, not you, A-716. If you take the hit for what happened to those kids, you're done."

"It's easy to say that, Dave," Ralph said. "I gave the order."

"Yep," Harris said, "but you would've never got the chance if I hadn't given the order to stay."

"Yeah, I hear you sir, but . . ."

Dillon and Penn were on the other side of the table and while they couldn't hear Ralph's "counseling session," they had a pretty good idea of what was going on.

"He's got a very nasty concussion and should be in the hospital," Dillon said. "He sure as heck shouldn't be drinking."

"He's a tough kid and all they'd do is observe him anyway, right?" Penn said. Dillon didn't say anything. "Besides it's probably good for him, for all of us, to stick together." Penn gestured with his hand, vaguely, "It was a hell of a thing to watch, to go through, but Ralph will get through it, we all will. It's just going to take a little time."

"What worries me is the morphine injection I gave him on the helicopter," Dillon said.

"What does that have to do with anything?"

"Some of the literature indicates . . ."

"Literature?"

"Medical books, smart aleck. Maybe intense memories can be reinforced, kind of burned into the brain, if the memories, graphic experiences, are combined with the effects of powerful drugs."

Dillon, like all Special Forces Medics, was as well or better trained than medical doctors in many third world countries and often more competent in trauma medicine than most American general practitioners. They took the medical side of their profession seriously.

"The North Koreans and Soviets were famous for experimenting with the use of intense experience, combined with powerful drugs and repetition. They called it brainwashing."

"Wait a minute," Penn said, "you're telling me it's your fault Ralph got hung up on all of this because you stuck him with some morphine? Come on. What's with everybody's sudden martyr complex?"

"You get pretty annoying after a couple beers, you know?"

"Okay, okay, sorry. What are you thinking?"

"I'm thinking I did the right thing. Ralph was out of control and had to be put down. But yeah, it's possible . . . seeing all those kids . . . friends of his . . . the intensity of it . . . the concussion, the effects of the morphine . . . together, that might have burned that town into his brain . . . burned it there in a different way than normal memories . . . he might end up reliving it, over and over, like a loop of film or a tape recording."

"I hope you're wrong," Penn said. "I like that kid. That would be one hell of a thing to have to relive all the time."

"Yeah," Dillon said.

CHAPTER 6

———◆———

"NO! NABA YOU DO NOT have to go to the water closet!"
"But Grandmother ..."
"NO!"

Allawis chuckled. "I'm sorry child. Your grandmother says no."
His voice turned cold. "Hold yourself."

"But I really have to ..."

"Naba, SHUT UP!"

Naba eyes darted from Allawis to her grandmother, her eyes
wide and confused. She clutched herself and bit into her lip. When
a tear leaked out of one corner of her eye and rolled down her
cheek Allawis seemed satisfied. He stood up and walked out the
door.

Isha grabbed Naba's hand and followed a uniformed Republican
Guardsman out the door and into the back of a government sedan.
When she looked back, the guardsmen were streaming out of the
house. The lights were still on and the doors and windows were
wide open. The soldiers jumped into the trucks as they roared to
life and pulled out.

After fifteen minutes of driving, Isha knew they were leaving
the city.

"Sir, we're leaving the city? My granddaughter and I are too..."

"Shut up, witch. You'll discover your future sooner than you'll
like."

Isha and Naba rode in silence through the late afternoon and
into the early evening. Naba cried.

"Grandmother, I am sorry but I could not hold myself."
She sobbed.

"Oh child, child," Isha said. She left her own bladder release and felt a rush of relief and shame as the smell of urine filled the car. She and Naba put their arms around each other, sobbing in unison. The driver looked back at Isha through the rearview mirror with a satisfied smile, catching her eye and holding it as he spoke.

"Pig ... and piglet."

As they approached Baghdad, Isha's mind raced. Where were they planning to kill her? Would they make Naba watch? Who would tell her family? Who would have the courage to come and get Naba after she was executed? Where would Naba go to school? Isha dug deep and steeled herself. Whatever happened, she'd be strong for her granddaughter.

Isha was lost in these thoughts when the caravan turned off the highway and twisted through the side streets of a small village on the outskirts of Baghdad. The vehicles stopped in front of an industrial looking apartment building.

"Stay," the driver said.

As soon as the trucks rolled to a stop, the Guardsmen began unloading them. Isha watched them disappear into the apartment house's main entrance with her housewares. Curious faces appeared in the windows of nearby homes and from behind half-opened doors. A few courageous souls stopped on the street to watch. Isha was struck by the care with which her belongings were now handled, especially after the obvious disrespect shown to them at her home. When the trucks were emptied, Major Allawis and two other uniformed Baathist officers approached the sedan. The driver jumped out and circled to the back door. He bowed toward Isha through the car window, jerked her car door open, and stood stiffly at attention, one hand on the door handle.

"Out, witch," he said under his breath.

Isha and Naba climbed out of the sedan. Allawis and two other waiting officers saluted, then bowed. Major Allawis removed a wad of money from his pocket and wrapped Isha's hands around it. Isha stood dazed, holding the money in her hands with half a smile on her face. Allawis saluted again, then dropped his salute. His face was a mask of sudden fury and he spoke in a harsh whisper.

"If it were up to me, your whole treacherous family would be wiped out, beginning with your quote-unquote, granddaughter. You think she's your son's daughter?" Allawis laughed. "We had Manal under surveillance, of course, and you're just as big a fool as your son. But," he said, mastering himself, "Saddam will not turn you into a martyr. Your apartment is on the third floor, 3B. I think you'll find your standing in this community is a bit different than it was in al-Najaf."

Allawis smiled, spun on his heel and marched off to a waiting car. His men followed his example with military precision. Truck doors slammed, engines cranked and vehicles roared off. Before Isha had a chance to react, her driver slammed the car door behind her, climbed into the sedan, and drove off.

They were left standing in the middle of the street, the woman and the little girl, holding hands, the seats of their dresses still damp, stained dark and fragrant. For one moment Isha tottered on the brink of despair. The most unlikely thing brought her back.

It was one of the ever-present murals featuring Saddam Hussein. This one stood twenty feet high and depicted a bereted Saddam sternly watching over a crowd of Iraqis: a soldier, a scientist, and a doctor with a stethoscope, just to name a few. In the background, a satellite dish, oil refinery and other symbols of Iraqi industry loomed almost as large as Saddam.

Where Isha wondered, are the rapists with their pants around their ankles? Guess that wasn't considered sufficiently "revolution-ary."

"What's funny, grandmother?"

"Nothing, child, let's see our new home."

The apartment building the Baathists had chosen for them was modern enough. It was a seven-story, gray concrete box of a thing that towered over everything around it. Each story of the building was overhung by a fifteen-foot-deep concrete ledge, which the contractor had then framed into six small boxes per story, three to a side. They thoughtfully added a set of shabbily made sliding glass doors that opened onto the ledge, then generously labeled each tomb-like box a "balcony." Off to the left, one solitary palm tree's branches rustled in the breeze. Unfriendly faces peered down at them from many of the balconies.

Wonderful, Isha thought. She prayed in silence.

"Grandmother, why are all those people staring at us?"

Their new neighbors stared down, with contempt, no doubt, at a woman so honored by the hated Baathists. Steeling herself, she took Naba's hand and under the paternal gaze of the Saddam Hussein portrait, led her granddaughter toward the apartment building and their new apartment.

"We're their new neighbors, Naba. They're curious. Let's see what our new home is like."

The interior of the apartment was the same as its exterior, modern by Iraqi standards: cold and functional. They had two bedrooms, a living room, and a kitchen. The kitchen counter was fading yellow Formica, the cabinets were constructed of metal painted white. Their possessions were scattered throughout the four rooms in a haphazard fashion.

"Why is my dresser in the living room, grandmother?"

"I don't know, but it will make it easier for us to arrange things as we wish."

Allawis predicted that her standing in this new community would be different than in Najaf and Isha knew that was the truth. Without her family and support structure, the only impression the village citizens had of her was the one left by her abrupt arrival and the exaggerated deference of the Baathists.

That night she tucked Naba into bed. After they'd finished her prayers, Naba had questions.

"Grandmother, when can we go home?"

"This is our new home Naba."

"I don't like it here. My friends are all back in al-Najaf."

"I know, but we can't leave right now. Someday, but not now."

"But . . ."

"If we went home, the men who brought us here tonight would find us and bring us back. It won't be so bad, it will be like a vacation, you'll see. And it *is* very modern, isn't it? We'll make new friends."

"Yes, grandmother."

Isha kissed her goodnight and climbed into bed. Sleep eluded her. She laid awake praying and worrying, long into the night, wondering what she would do. When Naba woke her it was almost 7:00 a.m.

"Grandmother, I'm hungry. Is there breakfast, please?"

"Of course child," Isha slipped out of bed and rubbed grit from the corners of her eyes. Normally she awoke at 5 a.m. The late wake up left her off balance and touchy, something she'd need to be careful not to take out on her granddaughter

"Go set the table, please."

Naba left and Isha soon heard the clatter of cups and dishes. She padded through the main living area of the apartment in her bare feet, still disoriented and half asleep. Naba was in the small kitchenette.

"Let's see what we have," Isha said, joining her. She opened cabinet doors and the small ice box, hoping to at least find bread. Nothing but dust.

"Since grandmother was such a sleepy head, we'll have to go hungry until we can dress and go to the market. I'm sorry."

Naba looked up. Perhaps sensing Isha was upset, she smiled.

"That is fine grandmother. We'll see the people who live here before we go home. It will be fun."

Isha rummaged around for fresh clothes and decided not to bother correcting Naba about going home. Eventually, she found toiletries and clothes for both herself and Naba.

"Let's make ourselves presentable."

Half an hour later, Isha had both of them cleaned up and in fresh clothes.

They left the apartment hand in hand. Two of their new neighbors were in the hallway huddled in hushed conversation until Isha and Naba approached. Both women cross their arms over their chests and fell silent.

"Good morning," Isha said. "My granddaughter and I were moved against our will because the government is displeased with us. I know how it must have looked..."

"Yes, exactly how it looks."

The women turned their backs on Isha and walked toward an open apartment door. Isha followed them, reached out and touched one of the women's elbow.

"Excuse me, but you don't..."

The women turned on her, one knocked Isha's hand away and literally spit at her feet. The woman's friend grabbed her arm, pulled her into the apartment and slammed the door in Isha's face.

"Grandmother?"

Naba looked confused. No one ever treated Isha in such a manner, except for soldiers and police. But normal people were always very nice. The child's eyes glistened, but she remained silent.

"They're just angry we have such a fine apartment, Naba.

They've probably been waiting for a better place a long time and we just moved in. We're very lucky."

Isha took Naba's hand and led her down the staircase, the handrail cold against her hand. She did wonder why the neighbors were so hostile. Yes, their arrival looked bad, like she was a sympathizer, but everywhere she had been, a person was always given a chance to at least explain herself. Perhaps the Baathists were particularly brutal here. When they reached the bottom step, Isha pushed the door open.

They stepped from the gloom of the stairway into bright sunshine and onto a bustling street. Midmorning, Isha knew, was a busy time but people seemed to be delayed in going about their business. In both directions down the sidewalk, busy pedestrians would suddenly look up and slow their pace before quickly turning their head and putting on a burst of speed. Perhaps it was...

"Oh Lord."

"What's wrong, grandmother?"

"Stay here."

"But ..."

"Right here," Isha said, pointing.

"Yes, grandmother."

Isha scurried to a nearby metal trash container. It boasted a portrait of Saddam on one side and the Iraqi flag on the other. Someone taped a flyer to the top of the can. She ripped it off and read.

"We've run this harlot out of our town. Know that you live with the devil's helper. The Islamic Army of Free Iraq."

Of course, there was a photo. It had been taken during the sexual assaults she suffered at the hands of Saddam's men. Her breasts were visible and so were men. She glanced up. Naba waited were she'd been left, clutching her doll. Isha returned to the photo. She knew she'd been grimacing in pain, but the camera angle made it appear she was smiling. Her face was visible and recognizable.

Her cheeks grew warm as she flushed. It felt like everyone on the street was staring at her. She risked a quick look around, then crumpled the photo into a ball and tossed it in the can.

How many more copies are posted around the city?

It was hard not to cry. She was ruined. Everything was ruined. For the second time in less than twenty-four hours, she teetered on the edge of surrender.

"Grandmother?"

From the edge of the abyss, she looked back at Naba. She saw love. And need. A sudden sensation seized her. It was as though her backbone was transformed into a steel rod. She straightened and her face hardened. The price was almost unbearably high, but she'd discovered things about herself few ever learned. Although there would be other bad days, she would never give up, never let them break her, never let Naba suffer her fate. Blessed with beauty and intelligence, a rich, powerful family and a good marriage, she never thought of herself as tough or strong. Now she knew. As difficult as things would soon be, it was at that moment that Isha fought her most challenging battle. She knew at that instant what she would face, what she would endure and who she would endure it for. She strode back to Naba and smiled.

"Come with me child. Let's find the market."

So they began the process of learning to survive in the new town. Isha was, of course, a pariah. The women in particular were vicious. They insulted her to her face and in front of her grand-daughter. Initially she fought, driving the gossips and slanderers back on their heels. But one day, as Isha confronted them, they found her weak spot.

"How dare you say such things in front of a child, my grand-child?"

One woman, chuckling, responded.

"How do you even know this is your grandchild? Don't you think that your son's wife could have had the same morals as you? Child, do you know what kind of woman your grandmother is? Do you know she may not even be your..."

"Shut up, you ..."

Isha balled her fists but stopped when the woman pulled out one of the Baathist flyers. She waved it at them but kept the photo hidden.

"How dare I? How dare you be indignant, hypocrite!" Sensing Isha's desperation, she puffed out, emboldened. "Be glad I don't remove all doubt from the girl's mind," she said, shaking the paper.

Naba tried to get a better look at the flyer but Isha's opponent, aware of the power it gave her, held it so the rape photo was con-cealed. Isha grabbed Naba and left with their laughter ringing in her ears.

Now the vultures knew her soft spot. From then on whenever they went to the market, the women, whom Isha had taken to calling the 50 thieves, had great fun stalking her. Rather than confront the women and risk an eruption of venom that might harm Naba, Isha ignored and avoided them. In exchange, they tormented her, but with enough discretion that Naba remained confused. When the thieves taunted her, she'd grasp Naba's hand and walked by them with her head held high. When Naba ask questions, Isha only reply was, "Ignore them."

One day she made Naba go outside, hoping the neighborhood would be content to ostracize her, but leave her young granddaughter in peace.

"It is too nice a day for you to stay in. Go downstairs and say hello to those children," she said pointing over the edge of the balcony. "I'll be right here, working our new garden and mending this sock."

"It's not a real garden, not like our garden at home."

"Just remember, do not go anyplace where you can't see me. If I look up, I want to be able to see you. Yes?"

"Yes, grandmother."

Isha worked at mending the sock from a chair near their balcony's railing where she could keep watch. After a few moments she saw Naba's small figure appear from beneath the building, pause, look up and wave. Isha waved back, then motioned toward the group of girls playing across the street. Naba waved again, then crossed the street. The girls stopped playing and formed themselves into a small group. Isha held her breath when Naba approached them. Then, the girls broke apart to form a circle around her granddaughter. She could hear their taunts and laughter, even from the balcony.

"Naba, come up here!"

The shout easily carried across the street and the girls broke apart, looking over the street and up toward the balcony.

"Now, please."

Isha was surprised at Naba's posture. Even in the distance she could sense a kind of anger radiating out from the little figure. She didn't run away from the other girls, she walked purposefully, her back straight and her chin thrust up in the air. Soon she crossed the street and disappeared below the apartment building.

Isha went into the hall and waited for her. When she emerged from the stairwell the young girl's face was defiant but stained with tear tracks.

"What did they say Naba?"

"Nothing grandmother, they just laughed and were mean." Isha could tell she was lying because she stared at the floor when she said it. She was going to let it go, but Naba looked up at her, tearless.

"You are wrong though. The people are not mad because we got this apartment, they are mad because I have the best grandmother and they don't!"

After that day, whenever possible, Isha stayed close to home in an effort to shield Naba and herself from as much of the abuse as possible. The approach of Naba's school year was a worry Isha wouldn't permit herself. One worry at a time was her new motto. They often went to the park across the street and it was there she did her sewing. Naba played alone. Despite the contempt the apartment people expressed toward her, they were quick to take advantage of the low prices she charged to take in sewing, some wash, and some cooking.

I'm paying the pariah tax, she thought to herself.

She raised vegetables on her balcony, made and repaired their clothing and otherwise provided for as much of her and Naba's needs as she could. Nevertheless, at least once a week they had to go to the market for necessities. There were kind merchants who quickly and courteously filled her orders and there were the weak and cruel, who took the opportunity to torment her. One particular male flour merchant always watched for her. In her own mind, Isha referred to him as "Saladin," after the handsome, romantic Arab prince of old.

It was the same experience every time she went to the market. The flour merchant booth was strategically located at the entrance to the market, just on the outskirts. Once he saw her, he rushed from behind his stall and began chattering. "Saladin" was in his 60's, about 5'6" tall, thin, with perpetual beard stubble and acidy body odor. One of his eyes was brown, the other's cornea a creamy blue. What passed for the bad eye's pupil always pointed upward and to the left, no matter where Saladin looked. He never removed the cigarette from the corner of his mouth and his good left eye squinted against the smoke.

"Ah, my Baathist beauty, will you not celebrate with me as you have other comrades? Your eyes my love, brown, but with the red of a desert sunset ..."

Some days were worse than others. One day the merchant drew near and as Isha shielded Naba, he reached out and grabbed her breast. Isha yelped and kicked out at him, but he danced away before she could strike him.

Naba cried.

"Leave the child," Saladin laughed. "She can watch the stall while we go in the back."

Naba clutched at Isha's sleeve, her eyes wide. She tilted her head up and whispered.

"Don't go with that man grandmother. I don't want to watch the stall by myself."

At times Isha couldn't imagine life would ever improve. The struggle seemed futile. She called these her "despair days." Outside her apartment she walked with her head held high, avoiding the tormentors when possible and when not, ignoring their barbs. She always fought Saladin and sometimes even sarcastically referred to herself as a "crusader" because she was about as successful against her Saladin as they were against theirs. But, once inside her apartment, she couldn't always stay strong. On those "despair" days, Naba shadowed her everywhere, resting her head on Isha's lap whenever she sat down. Isha didn't know and never asked if Naba was acting out of fear or trying to lend her comfort. She did know she drew strength from it.

In addition to the social difficulties Isha faced, she was also under financial pressure. Support from her family had to travel all the way from Najaf to Baghdad under the watchful eyes of the Mukhabarat. It was always difficult and often too dangerous to deliver her money. No employer in the village would hire her, so Isha paid her pariah tax by taking on odd jobs in the neighborhood for low wages.

One day she entered the market after dodging Saladin only to see her husband's fifth cousin, Halli, in the market. They made eye contact but before Isha could point him out to Naba, he shook his head, "No." Perplexed, she nevertheless complied with his wishes and ignored him. She conducted her business and chatted with Naba, but of course snuck glances at Halli speaking to a group of male merchants. As she was loading her market bags she felt eyes upon her. Several of the men were nodding their heads, watching her, as Halli spoke. Isha felt a familiar ache of worry deep in the pit of her stomach, but fought it back. No matter what mischief this meant, she'd done nothing wrong. Naba needed her and she would not quit. Jesus knew this. It was enough. Still, she was relieved to finish her business and return home without incident.

The next week, Isha and Naba left the apartment for their weekly market trip, as always. As always, they were forced to walk by the flour merchant's stall. Isha stiffened, but kept walking. Naba's hand tightened on her's and she looked up with a bright smile. Isha did her best to smile back, sad that one so young had learned to give comfort to those who should be giving comfort to her. Saladin appeared as always and rounded the corner of his stall to enter the street. Isha tensed. Something was different, wrong. She could see that, even while he was still in the shadow of his stall. Something was different, but . . . the merchant moved stiffly. As he left the shadow of his stall Isha could see his left eye was swollen shut. His face was scratched and bruised.

"Please, wait one moment, Mrs. Hami."

Mrs. Hami? What's this, Isha wondered.

So she waited, steeling herself. Saladin stopped a respectful distance away and bowed at the waist, his beating now apparent.

"Ma'am, I have shamed myself. Forgive me. You will never again be treated by me with anything but respect. May I leave and allow you to go your way?"

"Yes," a stunned Isha replied.

Naba opened her mouth, but Isha led her away before she could speak.

"Now is a time to be silent, child."

Naba walked alongside her grandmother, her little feet moving rapidly, trying to keep up with Isha's quick, somewhat nervous pace. Ahead of them loomed the market, the gauntlet. The entire market consisted of twenty-seven structures, with a beaten dirt path encircling it. There were wood and tent-like merchant stalls, outdoor braisers, livestock corrals, and butcher's blocks. Even at this time of day, midafternoon, it buzzed with bleating, clucking, mooing, people, and activity.

Often bored, the three ringleaders of the "fifty thieves" con-gregated alongside a market stall on the outermost ring of shops. When they saw Isha approach they laughed and chattered, pred-ators who delight in toying with helpless game. Isha's stomach churned and she fought back her anger. When she drew near to the thieves' stall she noticed a different group of merchant women and wives were leaving their own stalls and marching toward her.

Now what, Isha thought. No more enemies, Lord, please. For a moment she thought she might cry.

Since the three ringleaders were distracted by Isha's approach, the second group of merchant women was almost on top of the thieves before they were noticed. She and Naba weren't that far away when they heard the confrontation erupt.

"Don't you women work?" one of the merchant women ask.

"Such laziness," a second woman said. "No wonder some people have so much energy to run their tongues."

Many of the thieves drifted off, obviously intimidated, but not the ringleaders. They were tough women and prepared to fight back . . . until they saw the numbers arrayed against them. Literally half the market emptied with the express purpose of confront-ing the thieves in what was clearly a fight between women. Not a single man approached the thieves, only their wives. The hus-bands stayed at their stalls, observing. The buzz was so loud Isha couldn't hear what any individual said, but everyone seemed to have an opinion. The voices were loud, the words hostile, and they were all directed at Isha's tormenters. The three "ex-tormentors" decided to beat a quick retreat, but their way was blocked as fresh reinforcements of merchant women converged on them. These women surged around their targets and formed a circle around the three persecutors of Isha. Perplexed, Isha altered her course so as to veer around the large circle.

Instead, she took Naba down the middle of the market's path-way, dazed by the unexpected turn of events. Try as she might, she could not remember all the items she came to purchase. Someone spoke in a voice that cut through her stupor.

"Mrs. Hami, Mrs. Hami. Over here, I have some of the lamb that I know you prefer."

Isha turned toward the butcher, hesitating. She didn't want to offend the man, but her funds were limited. Her income was unreliable and some time had passed since she'd received financial aid from her family. Lamb, especially of the quality sold by this merchant, was something she could only afford right after receiving a gift from family.

"Come, come," the man said, smiling. "This is the last on the bone and if you don't take it off my hands, I'll be delayed butchering for the rush. Two dinars may sound expensive, but not for this quality of lamb."

Isha and Naba walked over to the butcher.

Two dinars, she wondered.

Any slice of lamb the size he was holding would easily cost twelve dinars. But before she could object, the lamb was in her hand, securely wrapped in waxed paper, and she'd paid her two dinars. The butcher wished her a good day, asked her to come again, and turned to the next customer. And so it went for her that day, from merchant to merchant. She seemed to get the quickest service, the best quality, and the best price. She wandered from merchant to merchant, smiling, almost staggering with disbelief.

"Thank this kind man . . . thank this kind lady," Isha told Naba.

As always, Naba listened to her grandmother. She smiled brilliantly and thanked every merchant in a soft, shy voice. Finally, loaded with a bounty of supplies, the Hamis prepared to go home.

"If you would, please, my dear lady."

Isha looked up, recognizing the voice. It belonged to Ahmed Khalilzad, the leader of the Merchant Association in the market and thus a leader in the community. To the extent she wasn't exposed to cold silence while conducting her business the last three months, she'd heard good things about this man. Although tough, he was fair, courageous, and no friend of Saddam's. Lowering her head, Isha turned and walked toward him.

"My name is Ahmed Khalilzad."

Isha smiled, bowing slightly at the waist and said, "This I know."

"Today I have received news from a reliable source. Your name has been wrongly sullied by agents of Saddam and others. None of them are worthy of the breath it takes to mention them. By this statement, I place my life in your hands."

He bent to look into her eyes.

"I hear it is well-placed. You come from two noble families with whom I have no connection, but for whom I have respect. Christian, yes, but good friends to the true followers of the Prophet, and people of the book." Khalilzad smiled. "Fear not, I'm a Muslim, not a Wahabe."

Isha smiled back. Wahabism was a brand or deviation of Islam that believed in the abrogation doctrine, a theory that claims some parts of the Magnificent Koran was deleted or abrogated by other parts. One of the things "abrogated" was a special status to Christians and Jews as People of the Book. People of the Book were not Muslims but were respected by and entitled to protection by Muslims. Khalilzad was telling her she was as safe as a non-Baathist could make someone.

"Your family's reach no longer extends as it did before the Americans came," said Khalilzad, "but their reputation does. Here no one is safe from Saddam, but you will be as safe as one can be. I understand you are trained in the law. Can you apply this law equally between Sunni, Christian, Jew and Shia?"

"Yes. I reject the Baathist law as immoral. As you know, with the Baathists, I have placed my life in your hands."

"It is well-placed." Ahmed Khalilzad smiled. "It is not always possible to submit our disputes to the mullahs. Sometimes it is possible, but the amounts or the controversy is too small. For disputes between merchants, it is not good for a merchant such as me to decide. Of course, the Baathist's courts decide in favor of whoever has the largest bribe. No one trusts them. So, if this is something you are trained for, you can make a living. Money will be hard to come by, but payment in food, clothing and other items is worthwhile. Is this something you will do?"

"It is."

"I will see to it."

"Thank you."

This time, she bowed low. At her side, Naba followed her grandmother's example, bowing also. Ahmed Khalilzad smiled at the child, turned and left them. Isha took Naba's hand and led her away. And so it began. First merchants, at the direction of Khalilzad, began to approach Isha to resolve commercial disputes. She poured her heart into this work. After all she'd been through, the displeasure of the merchants was something she was prepared to face. She preferred to risk losing what favor she'd gained by being honest, rather than to keep it by being dishonest. She showed no favoritism and searched out the truth. Often she investigated disputes herself, questioning the merchants and village people, asking questions and watching. Her judgments were so fair, eventually her integrity so unquestioned, that soon village people came to her with small neighborhood disputes as well. Then, one day, she was asked to appear in an Iraqi courtroom. Despite her fear, she took the case. For some reason, perhaps the Kurd agitation in the North, she seemed no longer important to the Baathists. She practiced law without interference, but kept as low a profile as possible. She prospered, after a fashion. But always, she looked over her shoulder.

After some years, a new American President was elected. Then, the horrific events of September 11th occurred.

PART TWO

Baghdad, IRAQ – 2003 / 2004

CHAPTER 7

———

IT WAS A SCENE OF obvious serenity and therefore couldn't have been more misleading. In other words, the situation epitomized the reality of Baghdad in the year 2003.

Three men of the four men were in their mid-sixties, wearing traditional Arab headdress and out of fashion, mismatched western dress pants, dress shirts, and suit jackets. After the American occupation began they agreed to meet every few weeks to resolve points of disagreement arising amongst themselves and their vassals. Open conflict was bad for business. So they reclined around a large brass "Houka" filled with strong Turkish tobacco and waited. From time to time, one of the men would draw on a hose for a lung full of tobacco smoke. Others sipped green tinted tea from what an American would call a water glass.

Two of the older men were respected elders of Shia tribes, the third was a Kurd from Northern Iraq. War and peace hung in the balance.

"We still need one more Judge," said Mahmoud Bahr al-Uloum, one of the Shias. "No one is better suited than Al Asar."

"I must say this is not accurate, my brother," said Ayad al-Jaberi, the other Shia. "Even the Americans respect my candidate."

A fourth man, younger than the others, sat somewhat apart, erect and watching with what for him was uncertainty. His Western-style clothing was new and fashionable. Bareheaded, he'd abandoned the kafia years earlier. Though uncertain he remained mentally coiled and after waiting for the others to make the first moves, he decided it was time to speak.

"Both of these Judges are unacceptable to me and my people. It was bad enough when we did business under the Judges of

Saddam. They were corrupt, but at least they believed as we did. Both of your Judges, from your families and with beliefs not our own, will not treat us fairly."

Both Shia leaders and Ibrahim Othman, the Kurd, suppressed looks of distaste. The young man, Sameer al-Hakim, was no family leader, no religious leader and certainly not a man one could trust. Sameer was what the Americans would probably call a crime boss. His family wasn't a blood family, but instead an army of vicious and efficient criminals. Sameer was a Sunni, but not of the tribe of Saddam Hussein's from Tikric or of their closely allied tribes, which formed the heart of the Bath party. Sameer al-Hakim was a criminal. Sameer al-Hakim was a criminal under Saddam, Sameer al-Hakim was a criminal under the Americans and Sameer al-Hakim would continue to be a criminal under any government that existed in Iraq. The support of Sameer, however, was crucial. His opposition to any political decisions in Baghdad would mean street fighting. His manpower, ruthlessness and organizational skills were only matched by his boldness. It was Sameer, for example, who organized the plundering of the Iraqi National Museum. He had to be reckoned with.

"My concern, my interest," Sameer continued, "is in appointing an honest, fair Judge to cover this section of Baghdad. A Judge my allies and I can rely upon to enforce the law without favoring the government, the Americans, or the government's allies."

"All of our Judges will enforce the law and treat all the same," said Mahmoud with just a touch of anger in his voice.

Sameer proceeded carefully.

"True, my friend. As always you speak the truth with wisdom. But," he added delicately, "the four of us, whose opinions matter, haven't been able to decide between these two fine candidates. This is our third meeting in three months and the Americans are growing impatient. They're badgering our friends and representatives in government for the names of these Judges. They point out, with some justification, that resolving differences and maintaining order in Baghdad affects the entire country. And I agree. Both Ibrahim Othman and I have deferred to your judgments in areas that affect the Shias, but this issue concerns me, perhaps more than any of you. If the Americans decide to appoint a Judge without further consultation, this could prove very difficult. Therefore, I think it is time that I, as an outsider, propose a candidate for this final sensitive position."

The men watched each other with hooded eyes. Their relationships were still in a state of flux because the quick victory of the Americans and their strange way of doing things scrambled Iraqi power relationships. Before the second Gulf War, Shias always had to conduct their affairs with one eye on the Baathist enemy. Their own tribal relations were always governed by their mutual hatred and fear of the Sunni tribes of Tikric, Saddam Hussein's city. At that time, the goal of the leaders of these numerous and powerful Shia tribes was to survive and thrive as best as possible under the dictatorship.

Now, for the first time in their lifetime, each man there had the ability to wield real power. At the same time, the other men in the room had the same ability, and all were loyal to their tribe and their family. Men who for decades schemed against an unbeatable power suddenly found themselves facing the real opportunity of grabbing that power for themselves.

Both Mahmoud and Ayad started to speak at once. They were certain that Sameer, as a criminal, only wanted a weak Judge who could be bribed or intimidated. Sameer held up his hand.

"Please wait. I think I understand your concerns but listen. What I look for is an honest Judge with integrity. All I ask for is a Judge who will follow the law impartially. If there is such a Judge, I can conduct my business taking into account the business risk the law represents. I do not ask you to agree to a Judge who can be bought or intimidated. For your part, you can't expect me to support a Judge who will show favoritism or overlook unlawful police activity. If I have an honest Judge, I can conduct my business, as can those who look to me for leadership. I propose Isha Hami as Judge for Southern Baghdad District 17."

Sameer waited out a long silence. The other three men sat stone-faced.

Finally, the Kurd squinted. "A woman, for Judge?"

"She's a Christian, but suffered under the Baathists for aiding many of my kinsmen," Mahmoud said. "She lives with integrity and dignity. I do not reject this suggestion out of hand."

Ayad sneered. "Of course, a Christian woman. Those Americans will love it. They'll probably give us money and new things just for suggesting it."

All four men began to laugh despite the tension.

"We're learning under your wise tutelage," said Ayad and they burst out again. When the laughter finally died down, Othman was still smiling, but his tone was grave.

"Of course, this will eventually become a problem."

Mahmoud nodded.

"Many things will change once the Americans leave including, no doubt, the identity of one or two Judges. Until then, I think our wise friend has proposed a solution that will work. Hami is a woman, but for a woman, she has remarkable integrity. Sameer can be confident she'll ensure the government follows the Americans' rules and not prosecute his interests too efficiently. For the rest of us, Hami's Christian tribes are too weak to effectively support her or prevent her removal when the time comes."

"While I've heard that she has integrity," Ayad said, "I've also heard she has a strange sense of humor and Western tastes. She has a Western law degree. What kind of message will this send to our people, if not only awoman but a Westernized Christian woman holds such a position of power? I agree there are advantages to this appointment, but there are many dangers as well."

"The four of us live at a time in the history of our country where every decision we make is dangerous. But if this is unacceptable to you, I'm still prepared to support Aziz," Mahmoud said, smiling and referring to his candidate.

Ayad smiled back. "Very well, Hami is acceptable . . . at this time. When the Americans leave, or if she becomes more of a problem than we anticipate, I reserve the right to revisit this decision."

Sameer al-Hakim and Mahmoud Bahr al-Uloum both nodded.

"This decision will be re-examined."

The three Arabs looked to the Kurd who nodded his assent.

———◆———

Across Baghdad, Hank Jenkins was back at his desk after a week in northern Iraq. A large stack of written material awaited him and he plowed through it as best he could. Among the more interesting items was a transcript from a recent Baathist cell phone intercept.

"Interesting," he thought.

The Baathists were beginning to worry the Shias, Kurds, and

disaffected Sunni's might grow bold enough to oppose them. Before he could reach the end of the transcript someone knocked on his door.

"Come," Hank said. The transcript was classified, so he covered it with yesterday's International Herald Star.

Hank's military liaison, General Michael Fitzgerald, walked in and dropped onto a battered metal chair.

"Morning, Hank."

"What's up, General?"

"We've got a situation here. Three days ago that butt head Akmed Amani blew off an IED and got a couple of our guys. He also got some poor little girl. Her family found out about it, went to his house, drug him into the street and killed him."

"Outstanding," Hank said. "I've been after that turd myself for three and half months and was always a day too late."

"You can take him off your list, but, we've got another problem. The new Iraqis have arrested the father, uncle and two cousins."

"What? Are they nuts?"

"The problem's not the government, it's the police and the prosecutor. Instead of looking the other way the cops interviewed the witnesses, including our guys, and took it to the prosecutor. All these guys were trained by our Military Police, Criminal Investigative Division and Judge Advocate General people and they weren't screwing around. Charges are filed, the Western media just found out about it and it's too late to stop it. The case is heading toward an evidence hearing. We've transferred Alpha company, the guys who were there, up North to Mosul. The Iraqi government's winking at us on that, but they can't get the charges dropped, not now. I'm thinking about sending Colonel Board over to talk to the new Judge who drew the case assignment. Let her know our soldiers won't be available to testify."

"Her?"

"A U.S. Navy signals section picked up a transmission between a couple of Shia militia groups and we got an intercept. Looks like the big tribes couldn't agree on the third Judge, so they settled on a neutral as a compromise. This female, her name is Isha Hami, is the only one they could all trust. They're going to propose her as a dramatic surprise at the next Provisional Authority coordinating meeting. The Shias don't know it yet, but Hami's Judicial District drew the lot to hear this case. Anyhow, the government's behind us, but the new Judge is a bit of a stickler, with a lot of prestige."

"Does the P.A. know," Hank asked, referring to the U.S. Provisional Authority.

Fitzgerald smiled. "Andrea Dell represents State at those meetings." That meant, "No." No one trusted Dell and they sure weren't going to go out of their way to help her.

"Just great. Any other good news?"

"I'm afraid so."

"What?"

"All newly appointed Judges, including the one in this case, it seems, are assigned a US lawyer through the Star Foundation to advise them in matters of judicial independence, etc."

"Great, great, great. You want me to go with Board and counsel the lad?"

"It might be a bit more complicated than that, Hank."

"Yeah?"

"When the Star guy applied for his visa to enter Iraq he got flagged. The State Department Intelligence Division pulled his file and cleared him, but they didn't see everything. Take a look at this."

The General took out a thick file folder emblazoned with a bright red banner and slid it across the desk toward Hank. Fitzgerald slumped in his chair while Hank opened the file. The first, outer folder, was a large manila filing folder called a "jacket" that was only graded "Classified." It contained information on one Ralph Jackson, US Army: pay grade, enlistment, discharge and promotion dates, as well as some of his awards and qualifications.

"This is the Star adviser?"

Fitzgerald just nodded, so Hank returned to the file. The second folder fit inside the "jacket" and was called a "vest." The records of certain military personnel were segregated, depending upon the security classification of what they contained. These folders within folders were designed to be easily removable and easily reassembled in the event of an official inquiry. A freedom of information request, for example, would typically generate a redacted or "whited out" copy of the outside folder or "jacket." The "vests" were removed before anything was copied and their contents would never see the light of day. The first of Jackson's vests was graded "secret" and listed additional training, qualifications, decorations, and details of classified operations Jackson had participated in. Hank took his time reviewing the first two sections before looking up at Fitzgerald.

Most often men with advanced combat skills who took early retirement from the military became an "operator," usually with the CIA or State Department. A few became employees, but most signed and worked out a contract with the CIA. They were paid a certain amount of money per week, plus certain benefits and were expected to perform dangerous task overseas, installation security, rescue and bodyguard type work, usually. They were gunslingers and since they worked in the open, acknowledged by the government, there was little secret about them. The second type of contractor was rare, they were intelligence contractors who worked as spies and according to some, even assassins.

Hank knew and worked with both types of men. In fact, a number of the gunslinger types worked for him now, in Iraq. The intel contractors were a different breed, secretive, dangerous and sometimes difficult to control. Loners usually. Every now and then one went rogue, killed a bunch of bad guys without permission and disappeared with their money. The Agency didn't approve, but they didn't go looking for them either. A disproportionate number of them came from Army Special Forces, the Green Berets. Because they worked undercover, their civilian identifies were kept secret and most of them created various cover stories. Sometimes they claimed they were leaving to study abroad, sometimes they managed to lose a job or discovered health problems or even fake mental problems. Hank knew one guy who created a string of heartbreaking relationships. A smart, handsome guy, he only dated beautiful, rich young women. They always dumped him. Heartbroken, he disappeared from sight, "to heal," he said, laughing. Hank asked him if he ever felt guilty about manipulating the women. The guy laughed.

"No, Hank I don't. Understand something, these are not nice people. They're the ones that end up betraying me . . ."

"You set it up."

"By introducing them to one of my 'friends,' really? No kidding, I've learned as much about betrayal from a couple of these girls as I have from the French."

The French Intelligence Services were usually effective and notoriously treacherous.

Hank thought about it. The most important thing for an intelligence contractor was to create a believable cover so if he was ever jailed abroad no one would suspect he was a spy, but instead conclude he was just a nosy tourist. He held up a photo of Ralph Jackson. Good looking kid, young, but there was something else, it kind of made you uneasy. He found a second photo, a team picture of the men of Operational Detachment A-716. They stood in front of a burned out T-52 battle-tank, holding their weapons and bunched together. A very nasty looking group of meat eaters. Even so, everyone stood back a step from Jackson. It was like he radiated something, something you could catch.

Ralph Jackson had intelligence contractor written all over him.

"Is he working off the books?"

Since there was a discharge date listed in the file, Hank' question meant, 'did Jackson officially get discharged from the Army, only to return secretly, unofficially or as a contract operative with a government agency?' That sort of career path was not common, but by no means was it rare. Legitimate retirement by someone with Jackson's training and experience, on the other hand, was very rare. Obviuosly, Hank didn't believe the discharge date.

"Read on," Fitzgerald said.

Hank opened the last separate, detachable portion of the file, the second or inner "vest," marked "top secret" and began flipping pages.

"This just keeps getting better and better," he said. "I've been working for eighteen months to get the Iraqis to help us fight the Baathists. Just when it looks like I'm making progress, this happens, this crap. Cops who don't know when to look the other way, a prosecutor with no common sense and case assignment to the only honest, politically connected Judge in Iraq. Now she's backed up by this Jackson guy." Hank flipped pages as he spoke. "Ex-green beret," flip, flip, flip, "limited circulation Silver Star with oak leaf cluster," flip, flip, "voluntary separation from the Army and now a lawyer."

Hank stopped to think about it. A Limited Circulation award was a military decoration awarded for action on a classified or "secret" mission. Recipients weren't allowed to wear the decoration on their uniform and the award wasn't entered in the "jacket" portion their official record. Since the mission was classified, the award was granted in secret and few people would ever know it had been bestowed upon the recipient. "Circulation" of that information was "limited." The Silver Star was the Army's third highest award for heroism. An oak leaf cluster meant the decoration had been earned and awarded twice, once each for two separate combat incidents. It was a pretty big deal. Hank looked up at Fitzgerald.

"A real *infant terrible* in the late 80's, early 90's. I didn't even know we were doing some of this stuff."

Fitzgerald remained silent, so Hank flipped a few more pages, then stopped.

"Wow."

A long pause and a slow page flip.

"Poor s.o.b."

"Yeah," Fitzgerald said. "I wondered when you'd get to that."

"As Salman. That's that town in the south-west Iraqi desert. I read the technical reports on this stuff right after it happened. Some kind of souped-up mustard gas we didn't know about. Instead of blistering in fifteen or twenty minutes, the stuff took off skin like paint remover."

The men sat together in silence for a few minutes.

"What the hell is he doing here," Hank finally asked.

"We are looking into that right now," Fitzgerald said. "It'll probably take a couple days to get the records and field reports back. I'll let you know as soon as I do."

"Shssss. We've got a problem."

"Maybe, maybe not," Fitzgerald said. "But I want you to go along with Board, try to get a feel for Jackson. Maybe he'll be on our side."

"Yeah, right," Hank said. "If President Bush hadn't ordered an evacuation of U.S. military personnel from the Kurd and Shia areas, this," he said, taping the folder with his finger, "would never have happened. This guy is no doubt p.o.ed at the U.S. government in particular and the world in general. He'll be difficult just on general principles. Does Board know about this?"

"No, Hank. With Board's security clearance he'd need a lot more than a Court Order to see the inside of that. Besides, you speak Jackson's language. Why don't you push him a little, see how he reacts."

"General, I recommend going very slow and being very careful. You know these Special Forces guys as well as I do. They've got a very different culture from most Special Operations people. They're as much spies as they are soldiers. Sneaky little s.o.b.s. When we were hunting Noriega in Panama City one of them took a . . . Anyway, if we push Jackson, he'll probably agree to whatever we say and try to look harmless, maybe even scared. But as soon as we turn our back he'll come up with a way to rip out someone's spine. I don't want it to be mine."

"So, what do you want to do? That's why I'm here, to get your opinion."

"Why don't we wait and see what happens? First, let's see if Hami actually gets the appointment. I'm scheduled to attend that meeting anyway because of Sameer, al-Uloum, and al-Jaberi. I don't think we should tell Hami our soldiers aren't going to be there either. Why warn her? If the Prosecution doesn't have witnesses, how is the case going to go to trial?"

"What are you, a lawyer now?"

"No way, I work for a living. Give them nothing, Fitz. Sometimes problems fix themselves. If they don't, then Board and I can pay them a visit. If we don't push Jackson he may not even care about any of this. Besides, by then we should know more about him, plus we can see what happens at the evidentiary hearing."

"All right Hank, I'll tell Board wait to call Hami."

"Wait a minute, Isha Hami?"

"Yeah."

"It is coming back to me now. Isn't she the one whose family was wiped out in one of those rape torture rooms? Then, when she got out, she still snuck around, helping the resistance? Isn't she a Christian?"

"The same lady," Fitzgerald said. "Neither al-Uloum, al-Jaberi, or the Kurd factions are particularly thrilled with her, but their people think a lot of her. And yeah, she is a Christian. Her husband and son were both considered heroes by the Shias. Hami, however, never learned how to play ball, Iraqi style. She was educated in London, Law Degree, a lot of Western cultural tastes."

"We'd better keep an eye out for her then."

"Maybe, maybe not," Fitzgerald said. "It's a little too early in

Iraq's development for someone like Hami."

Hank didn't say anything.

"I know we disagree about that. You know we'd never do any-thing, but this could be big problem for us."

"Fitz, if it's a big problem for us, it's a big problem for the new Iraqis too. We can't let anything happen to Hami, just as long as we don't do it ourselves. I'll color outside the lines to get bad guys, you know that, but we're not the same as they are. Some things I won't do. If we won't protect someone like Hami, even if she is a problem, then what are we doing this for?"

"Are you saying the new Iraqis might assassinate Hami?"

"General, I've worked in Asia and the Middle East for a long time. If it comes down to it? The new Iraqis won't kill her, they'll set it up so the Baathists kill her for them."

"Maybe you're a little too cynical about our allies."

"This is a part of the world where cynics are rarely surprised. If this soon to be Judge is as clean as she seems, I will not let anything happen to her," Hank said, pushing Fitzgerald.

Fitzgerald stood up and took the file from Hank.

"Neither will the United States military, Mr. Jenkins."

"Of course not, General."

Fitzgerald left, obviously annoyed, but he and Hank went back far enough that both would get over it. Fitz is a little too calculat-ing sometimes, Hank thought. After twenty years in the darkest, deepest areas of covert operations, Hank Jenkins had learned a few things. One of the things he learned was that with all the intrigue, the secret agendas and all the lies, doing the right thing without regard to your interests often worked out as well, or better, than intricate planning. In a world of liars, consistently telling the truth was the most deceptive technique of all. So Hank Jenkins told the truth as often as he could, and always tried to do the right thing. He'd survived in a very tough business, for a very long time, because people trusted him. And because he'd become, when nec-essary, a very capable, very heartless killer.

Hank leaned back and considered the current situation and the potential Shia murder trial. He agreed with Fitzgerald that pre-venting the prosecution of the citizens, in this case, was the right thing to do. Post Saddam Iraq was fragile, so actual justice was the most important thing to protect. The proper procedural and legal safeguards for its citizens were something that would have to evolve over time. However, the country's judicial system itself along with its law enforcement had to be protected. Hank decided he and the Special Operations people he controlled would just have to work around them. His job was to protect and nurture a legitimate, Democratic government that was still in its infancy. While he was not going to defy Iraq's institutions, neither was he going to allow the Iraqis to tear themselves to pieces in the name of procedural safeguards.

Before Fitzgerald's visit, Hank' main concern was tracking down and killing Baathists and encouraging the Iraqi population to help him. Now, he had to balance killing Baathists against ensuring the physical safety of the judicial system. In addition, he had to play all three major Iraqi factions against each other and against the terrorists. Finally, he had to account for a wild card, Sergeant Ralph Jackson, retired.

CHAPTER 8

———◆———

HANK JENKINS FOUGHT AN ALMOST irresistible urge to stick his hand between the buttons on his shirt, claw underneath his T-shirt and polyurethane "fat man" belt and scratch like crazy. He'd been wearing the belt for six hours, first outside in the heat, and now inside. He'd been itching for the last fifteen minutes. The belt of course, was not designed to be comfortable. It was designed to make him look twenty pounds heavier and it was good at what it did. It made his stomach itch.

The Provisional Authority, or temporary governing body for Iraq, was meeting in the old Iraqi Constituent Assembly building. After entering the building, two floor-to-ceiling iron wood doors opened into a large auditorium-like room with blond wood seats bolted to the floor. The seats were arranged outdoor stadium style, one seat after the other, forming a half moon shape. Three red carpeted walkways ran between the rows of seats, one leading from the doors directly to a raised podium in the front of the hall and the other two walkways running from the left and right, angling toward the center of the hall. What had once been a ten foot by ten foot portrait of Saddam Hussein was now ten foot by ten foot of empty space, punctuated by holes that had once accommodated support bolts.

The Provisional Authority set up its conference table in the open floor space between the seats and the podium. There were plush cushioned chairs for the principals and metal folding chairs a few feet away for staff and assistants. Hank occupied one of the folding chairs near the wall and sometimes wondered if the ghost of Saddam didn't hover where his old portrait had hung, looking down and laughing at the proceedings.

Hank's job wasn't to take notes for diplomates but to observe the interaction between Mahmoud Bahr al-Uloum, Ayad al-Jaberi, Sameer al-Hakim and Ibrahim Othman for intelligence purposes. Besides looking for clues about the relationship between the men, he wanted to see if Isha Hami was really going to get her Judgeship. For the last three months these individual leaders had been jockeying to influence police, state prosecutor and most importantly, Judgeship selections in Baghdad. The alliances and subtle warfare amongst the four men were of crucial importance to Iraq and its future. Since these issues were important to Iraq's future, the United States of America was concerned. Whenever the United States of America was concerned Hank Jenkins or someone like him, was usually present.

Yeah, Hank thought, someone like me, wearing one of these belts.

His most intimate friends and colleagues might not have recognized him from even a few feet away. He'd died his sandy hair red, rounded and softened his waist with the fat man belt and tolerated small polyurethane cheek inserts to keep his facial features consistent with his belly. Finally, he sported his trademark nerd suit and nerd glasses. Certainly fellow computer and publication employees, his cover job with the Provisional Authority, wouldn't recognize him. Neither would Harvey Henderson of United Wire Service and Hank certainly hoped operatives and sympathizers of the Baathists and foreign terrorists wouldn't either. Ironically, his suit and glasses were the only reason even his colleagues would have the slightest chance of recognizing him. Otherwise, the transformation was remarkable.

Hank made himself as small and unnoticeable as possible while concentrating on the words, facial expressions, tones of voice and posture of the four men on the Iraqi side of the table. Three open Judgeships were on the day's agenda. The first positions went to the men he'd expected. They were creatures of Mahmoud Bahr al-Uloum and Ayad al-Jaberi respectively and since each Judgeships' geographic jurisdiction roughly coincided to their areas of influence, the selections made sense. Othman, the Kurd, and Sameer al-Hakim had no tribal or geographic interest in these Judgeships, but possessed sufficient political power to make their approval necessary. In exchange for their approval, they expected similar concessions when their interests were impacted.

The last Judgeship, District 17, was the interesting one. It covered a geographic area straddling both Shia and Sunni neighborhoods. Its jurisdiction included a section of South Baghdad along the Tigris River and the lucrative Tigris River boat docks. Further complicating matters, District 17's Shia area contained nearly equal elements of both Mahmoud's and Ayad's tribal allies. As if all this were not enough, Sameer al-Hakim and his allies diversified criminal enterprise engaged in activities ranging from hijacking cargos to collecting protection money from the American contractors to stealing or destroying the equipment of Americans who didn't see fit to employ his services. Coincidentally, Sameer was just beginning to speak.

"The open Judgeship for District 17 is a demanding position and requires a special type of person. Therefore, special considerations apply in choosing that person. As you know, Districts 12 and 14 are mainly populated by families and friends of Mahmoud Bahr al-Uloum and Ayad al-Jaberi. So, it is only proper that their concerns and advice be given weight in selecting those Judges. But District 17, I believe, is emblematic of the future of Iraq."

Oh boy, Hank thought. Sameer was dressed like an investment banker and now he was talking like one.

"It is Shia and Sunni, business and neighborhoods, new and old. It symbolizes the hope all of us have for the new Iraq. In this spirit, I, Sameer al-Hakim, at the risk of offending my friends and my colleagues, Mahmoud Bahr al-Uloum and Ayad al-Jaberi, as well as Ibrahim Othman, propose a Judge for the future, not the past. I propose Isha Hami for Judge of the 17th District."

The two Arabs and the Kurd were theatrically impressed, their faces the very definition of surprised shock. Hank, who knew from the intercepts this had all been prearranged smiled to himself. Even the issue of who would propose Hami's selection to the Americans would have been negotiated.

On the American side of the table, State Department official Andrea Dell gasped with joy. Even General Abott and Thomas Hopper, the provisional authority representative, seemed pleased.

Dell, without giving the Arabs or Kurd a chance to object, almost burst into song.

"I know Isha very well. I also know that she'll be honored

to accept this position. Of course, this sort of diversity and for-ward-looking thinking is what many of us have hoped for in the new Iraq. I, personally, am prepared to recommend that our new State Department facility be constructed in this area of South Baghdad. Mr. al-Hakim, we would, of course, consult with you regarding the site selection, appropriate local contractors, and other issues. I know now is not the time for these discussions, but may I contact you later in the week for your advice and insight?"

"Ms. Dell, I would be honored," said Sameer with a bow the waist.

"Gentleman," General Abott asked, "do you object to this appointment?"

Sameer leaned back, poker-faced. The other two Arabs no doubt struggled to keep the avarice off their faces as they contemplated the new State Department building. All of them were going to grow even richer. Still, they were hardened, experienced men, so they managed to appear hesitant and glanced at each other, saying nothing for several seconds. Dell decided to speak for them.

"Surely, since you men have been unable to give us a recommen-dation for this position . . . you don't object to the appointment, do you?" With dangerous gentleness, Dell added, "It's not because Hami is a woman, is it?"

Despite the fact that everything was going exactly as the Iraqi leaders planned, the four men were now furious. Dell's attempt at intimidation was about as effective as Baghdad Bob's optimis-tic propaganda. Hank wondered what was wrong with her. These were four men who survived Saddam Hussein. And she thought she could intimidate them? Three of them concealed their anger so quickly it might have been imagined. Ayad, however, stared at Dell. Dell blinked and looked away. Hami's Judgeship suddenly hung by a thread. Hank held his breath, shrinking into himself so as to be as unobtrusive as possible.

Talk about winning the battle and losing the war, he thought. Sameer recognized the look on Ayad's face and tried to salvage the appointment.

"Ms. Dell you really must . . ."

"A moment, please," Ayad said, holding up his hand. Sameer waited and Ayad turned back to Dell. "This recommendation is a surprise to us. The fact that she's a woman, while not common, is not unprecedented. Surprise should not necessarily be mistaken for resistance or objection." Ayad's voice was well modulated and under control. His eyes were not and they blazed.

"Then we should take this to the Ambassador for final approval," said Dell, now returning his gaze and looking pleased with herself. Before Ayad could respond, Mahmoud spoke up.

"Of course all three Judges are presented as a slate, Ms. Dell."

Hank fought back a smile.

Without a thought, Dell bought the farm with a nod. The four Iraqis stood, bowed perfunctorily toward the Americans and filed out of the room with everything they wanted.

I'm going to have to be very careful with these guys, Hank thought.

Once the door closed, Dell, oblivious, glanced around the room, beaming.

"This is a breakthrough, gentleman," she said. "The Hami appointment is something the press should be aware of as well as the U.N. organizations. It will go far with the world community and the Europeans in establishing that Iraq is a worthwhile recipient of aid dollars." She paused. "Is there anything else for today," she asked. She couldn't wait to call and spread the good news to friends and allies.

"Nothing for today, Ms. Dell," said the Provisional Authority representative. "I'll memo this meeting via email to everyone, pending final approval. We can discuss when and how to present these proposals with the Civil Administrator next week. Tuesday, the 17th at 10:45 a.m.?" he said, looking at a hand-held device.

Dell pulled out a similar gadget and after some fidgeting said, "Good for me, I've got it marked."

"General?"

The General and his staff officer referred to a paper pocket calendar before nodding.

"Good enough, Sir," said the General.

"Thanks, everyone. Good work, we're adjourned."

Yeah, congratulations, Hank thought. You've just agreed to make a multi-million dollar contribution to the Baghdad Mafia.

———◆———

Isha Hami hung up her phone, stunned. She'd just accepted a

judicial appointment for the 17th District of Baghdad. The phone connection with Andrea Dell was fuzzy and at first, she thought she'd misunderstood. She asked Dell to repeat herself.

"That's right," Dell said, "the Provisional Authority wants to appoint you Judge for the 17th District of Baghdad."

Hami hesitated. She'd come into contact with Andrea Dell through the U.S. Army. Earlier in the year, so-called civil affairs units roamed Baghdad as part of the American effort to win the hearts and minds of the Iraqi people. Congress and State Department staffers arrived on a fact-finding mission to investigate the effectiveness of these efforts. Civic affairs chauffeured a group of five congressional staffers and five State Department officials, including Ms. Dell, all around Baghdad.

Hami learned from her friend, Ahmed Khalilzad, how the meeting came about after the fact. During the tour, the civic affairs team escorted their charges from meeting to meeting with an assortment of community leaders. They met with bankers, merchants, and family and tribal leaders. In the middle of the afternoon, Andrea Dell spoke up in a loud voice.

"I must tell you that I find it very troubling that after an entire day of meetings with community leaders, I haven't seen a single woman. I find it hard to believe that in a country this size, with a capital city this size, there are no women of substance. I certainly hope this isn't another example of the institutional sexism in the military."

Major Jill Lamp, the Civil Affairs Unit Commanding Officer, groaned to herself.

"Ma'am," Lamp replied, "I'm not aware of any institutional sexism in this unit or in the United States Army. You'll also see the U.S. Army has reached out to include female leaders in our efforts."

"That is exactly the kind of sensitive, forward-thinking approach that I would expect from female military leadership," Dell said smiling.

Lamp smiled back and nodded. With that, one of her men herded the big wigs and Iraqi interpreters toward their air-conditioned bus. Lamp motioned her soldiers to move ahead and walked behind them, joined by her First Sergeant, Al Collins.

"That's the kind of forward-thinking leadership I would expect...," Collins said, snickering. Lamp managed a smile and rolled her eyes.

"I'm forward thinking enough to know that if I don't come up with a female by tomorrow, my sensitive rear end will end up a sling."

Lamp had been bluffing Dell. Civic Affairs didn't have female leaders on the agenda for the next day.

"Well ma'am, I could get myself one of those 'moo moo' things, those tent dresses, and a veil, dress up and represent the new trend in female leadership in Iraq."

"Al, Dell's a pain, so if I don't get her a female, she's going to create a mud storm and mud rolls downhill, right into the foxhole."

Collins grinned. She thought and talked like an NCO.

"I need a female leader," she said," and a couple of doctors babbling about their concern for women and children's health won't cut it."

First Sergeant Al Collins had been in the Army for eighteen years and during that time suffered under two female officers, both inept. A past political administration valued political correctness over national security. As a result, female officers were promoted at a rapid pace, regardless of qualifications. It always made Collins smile when someone said a woman had to be twice as good as a man in the Army.

Not in this Army, he thought.

Lamp, however, was a different story. She came to command with no ideological agenda and from a military family with a long history of service. Part of that history taught her to value and rely upon her NCOs and to support and back up her men. She wanted to be a good officer and lead the best civic affairs unit in the United States Army. Lamp was young, but turning out to be a fine officer. One of a First Sergeant's jobs was to make sure nothing bad happened to good officers and if he failed, there'd be hell to pay in the NCO Club.

"Ma'am, request permission to fallout and see if I can find us a female leader or two."

"Take the supply Humvee. I'll radio for another one to join us in route. Good Luck."

Collins drove off, looking to run down some of the insiders he knew in Iraq and around Baghdad. For the last six months, he'd been developing relationships with various merchants, community and tribal leaders by passing out surplus American goods and other booty. It was time to call in some favors, so he drove around town, dropping in on his contacts. Eventually, he ran into Ahmed Khalilzad who supplied the translators for Collins' Civic Affairs Unit. After explaining the situation to Khalilzad, he made it clear that anyone who helped him would enjoy the favor of the Provisional Authority. Khalilzad told Collins about Isha Hami.

"This sounds too good to be true."

Khalilzad introduced Collins to Isha and like almost everyone else who met her, he was impressed. Hami spoke fluent English. She'd been trained in the Law in the City of London. Not only did she act as a Judge with regard to neighborhood and commercial disputes, she had actually appeared in Baathist courtrooms.

"Jackpot," Collins said to Khalilzad.

The next day, the entourage met Isha Hami. In an authoritative, well-modulated voice, Isha explained her involvement with her community, her impressions of the challenges facing Iraqis in the future and the concerns and problems of the average person in the street. Lamp and Collins thought Dell would wet herself. Collins looked at Khalilzad and winked.

"Al, the beer is on me," Lamp whispered.

Thus, Isha Hami met Andrea Dell and she didn't think much of her. According to Dell, everything Hami did was monumental. Isha's actions were symbolic of the irrepressible aspirations of women everywhere. Isha thought, "It's a disagreement about who gets the side of beef and who gets the rump. It was about one merchant honoring his commitment to a second merchant." Hami was educated in one of the finest Inns of Court in London. She knew what a big case was and she knew what a small case was. Little cases and small disputes, the kind she handled, were the stuff of life. To try and transform her work into something grandiose, a strange political statement, seemed to insult the average person who worked hard and to whom these disputes were very important. Hami's opinion of Dell was that she was a big faker or worse, a zealot. Whether Wahabi, Baathist, or something else, Isha disliked zealots. Dell called her every few weeks and asked for her advice and input. Hami unease only grew, but she thought it was her responsibility to remain on good terms with the powers that be, so she cooperated with Dell despite her personal reservations.

When Dell called about the Judgeship, she was hesitant. Despite the American occupation and apparent decimation of the Baathists, Isha couldn't ignore her fear they would someday return to power. She defied them once before and they almost broke her. They killed her family and inflicted a personal kind of pain few people would ever understand. They almost stole her life. Now she was being asked to become a prominent symbol of opposition to the Baathists and the request came from the hands of someone she instinctively distrusted.

"Miss Dell, I'm very flattered by this offer. However, I have a granddaughter to raise and..."

That was how they got her. Dell cut her off in mid-sentence.

"The Judgeship salary is 200 Iraqi dinars a week. Since the P.A. recognizes the risk involved, it pays an additional 250 dollars a month subsidy to those who work with us, in U.S. dollars. Finally, judicial personnel have access to the United States and Provisional Authority canteens and commissaries. Like you said, you have a granddaughter to raise."

Three weeks later Isha stood alongside two other appointees on a recently assembled, modular steel platform draped with bunting. A substantial sized audience watched from brown steel folding chairs arranged in a semicircle in front of the rostrum. An Arab official administered an oath of office to Isha and her colleagues and they all swore to carry out their duties with honesty and fidelity to the newly constituted Iraqi government. The P.A. provided a translator for the international news media. As flashbulbs popped and cameras whirled, each new Judge gave remarks. The first two men droned on, praising the noble Iraqi people, praising their patrons, Mahmoud Bahr al-Uloum and Ayad al-Jaberi, praising the glorious future of Iraq and finally, praising themselves, their background and their qualifications.

Judge Isha Hami stood last.

"These are days I prayed for and thought I would never see. These are days when Iraq holds its freedom in its hands. All through my life, during the times of greatest joy, during the times of greatest sadness, during every time, always, in the background, was the knowledge that my life was not my own. It belonged to the Baathists, to Saddam. Many of you know that I lost my family, a part of myself and my dignity to Saddam. At that time, I knew my life was not my own. I swore to God that if it were in my power, my granddaughter would not live as I had lived, but too often fear kept me from doing what I should or from doing all that I should. For that failure, I asked for forgiveness. I doubted God, but God did not doubt himself. He brought about the destruction of evil in his own time, as He always does. I will doubt no more. I will never again allow fear to keep me from doing what is right, from doing all that is right. This I swear to you before God."

CHAPTER 9

A HOLLOW "BUMP" JOLTED RALPH JACKSON out of a deep sleep, leaving him with that peculiar sense of unease left after unexpectedly waking from an equally unexpected nap. He'd been dreaming an already familiar, but relatively new dream. Before, they'd always been the exclusive province of hopeless battles and burning flesh. Once he decided to return to Iraq, his sub-conscience or God or the Devil, something, decided to reward him with a bit of variety - self-destruction. The new twist featured Ralph holding a pistol and raising it to his head. For the hundredth time he struggled, the muscles in his arm as taut as steel cables, but to no avail. Slowly, inexorably, the pistol made its way to the side of his skull, grinding into his temple. Usually his thumb pulled back the trigger, but this time the bump woke him first. He remembered an airplane flight. The plane decelerated and the reverse thrusters roared. An overhead speaker vibrated with the Captain's voice.

"Welcome to Baghdad. Today is November 23, 2003. The current temperature at nine hundred hours local time is 89 degrees Fahrenheit with a slight wind from the Northeast. Please remember to have your passports, military ID cards, or press credentials ready for presentation as soon as we disembark. I'm required to notify you your baggage and person are subject to search without warning at any time in the airport or anywhere else in the country. If you resist the lawful authority conducting the searches, United Airlines, the Provisional Authority, the airport authority, and the government of Iraq are not responsible for any injuries you may sustain. Finally, you may be subject to arrest. Enjoy your stay in the Republic of Iraq."

Yeah, just like last time, Ralph thought.

He stood up, stretched and patted his chest to locate a leather document pouch strung around his neck. It held his passport, traveler's checks, packets of United States currency in various denominations and some Iraqi Dinars. He pulled back his shirt collar and shoved the pouch underneath his undershirt. The Star Foundation paperwork was stowed in his carry on.

Ralph got his bags out of the overhead compartment and shuffled down the aisle. When the crew threw open the door, the feel, smell and even taste of the Iraqi desert blew in from the East. After a twelve year hiatus, its distinctive aroma was like the face of an old enemy. Memories associated with the desert surfaced and left him feeling like a criminal forced to return to the scene of his crime.

That's not that far off the mark, Ralph thought.

Unlike now, he hadn't bothered with an airport the last time. He'd jumped out of an airplane in the middle of the night. Today, he disembarked on metal flight steps secured to the side of the plane. The handrail was already hot to the touch, even this early in the morning. A dry wind blew. Ralph reached the tarmac and peered through waves of heat rippling upward off the blacktop. The terminal building was a modern structure of poured concrete topped by a bank of darkened glass windows. The windows were covered with a Venetian blind-like grill that ran unbroken the length of the building. The second story consisted of the same poured concrete floor, wall and window arrangement. Large blue letters in English and calligraphy were bolted between the two banks of windows.

"Baghdad International Airport."

So this is how the other half lives, Ralph thought.

The last time he was in Iraq he possessed, though of course he didn't carry, a "Green Slash" military ID card. "Green Slash" was Army slang, referring to a military ID card with a green diagonal line that ran from the upper right-hand corner of the card down to the lower left-hand corner. The green line ran through text, part of the ID picture, although not the face and the rest of the card before it ended. The line's purpose was to prevent easy counterfeiting and to be easily recognizable. The real beauty of the green line, though, was that it let you crash borders. Your bags weren't searched and you didn't wait in line. All you did was flash the card long enough for a Customs, Immigration or Security official to ensure your face was the face on the card. Then you "crashed" right through the barriers.

Now a peon, Ralph followed his fellow passengers across the shimmering tarmac. When the group reached the terminal and opened one of the glass doors, a delicious wave of cool air washed out. Everyone jostled to get through. Ralph was lost in thought, so when a big, red-haired guy slammed into him, he was unaware.

"Where's the fire, jerk," asked the carrot top.

Ralph was still tired and cranky after his nap. For the briefest moment he made eye contact, ready to drop the man where he stood. The same thing that got him in trouble with the cops back in the states, he thought. Instead of striking, he looked down at his belt buckle.

"Look, ..."

The man was about three inches taller than Ralph and muscular. His forearms were thick and covered with fine red hair and freckles. Sensing easy prey, he flexed and took a step closer.

"Not looking is your problem, so don't tell me 'look'."

Ralph didn't say anything.

"What do you have to say for yourself?"

Ralph looked at him and thought about telling him his muscles were of limited use in real combat. He wondered if "Red" knew it only took fifteen pounds of pressure to break a human bone. So, strength was really not an issue. While Red's muscle mass helped protect the length of his bone, it did nothing to protect his joints, the bridge of his nose, his eyes or the base of his throat. Still, being strong has a lot of advantages. He picked up his bags and moved away.

"I'll just go to Customs, sorry."

Once inside the terminal, Ralph spotted a large overhead sign, "Passports," in both English and Arabic directing the new arrivals to Customs. Six agents waited for them in elevated booths enclosed with bulletproof glass. Each booth was split by stainless-steel railings. The passport lines resembled livestock shoots where lowing visitors were lined up and inspected like cattle. Customs tables waited on the other side. There, certain unlucky souls were selected to open their luggage for inspection.

Ralph heard the redhead calling him names or something, but

was so busy with his memories the taunts were little more than background noise. He lined up behind the last man waiting for the furthest booth from the one the redhead chose. Fortunately, the lines moved at a brisk, but uneven pace. The redhead was through his line, outside and into a cab long before Ralph was called up. His agent cleared the man in front of him and motioned for him to approach the booth.

"Passport, please."

Ralph handed over his paperwork, which the neat little man examined with bureaucratic care. He thought the Agent was satisfied until he leaned over a chrome microphone and said something in Arabic. It was broadcast over the loudspeaker and several uniformed agents at the Custom's tables looked him over. The little man slid Ralph's passport under the slot pointed to the tables.

"You, go there, NEXT!"

Ralph mumbled a low growl under his breath, picked up his luggage and carried everything over to the Customs table. Four uniformed Iraqis were waiting and gestured for him to put his things on the table. He hoisted two small bags of personal items and a medium-size cardboard box full of books onto the table. The inspectors didn't even bother with his carry-ons, but they were interested in the box of books. First, they ran it through an x-ray machine. Then they questioned him about its contents.

"What are these things?"

"I'm an American lawyer from the Star Foundation. I came to help and brought law books, Iraq's old legal code translated into English, the Provisional Authority Rules and Regulations and a soft-back, 2 volume, Arab to English dictionary ..."

"Papers, papers," the oldest looking of the men shouted, holding out his hand and shaking it.

Ralph dug into his carry on and pulled out the Star Foundation papers. The inspectors shuffled through them a second time, still chattering. Eventually they slashed through the shipping tape with a set of now infamous box cutters and rifled through his books. Evidently satisfied, three of the four men suddenly lost interest, turned on their heels and left for another table and whose victim awaited them. The final inspector looked somewhat embarrassed and produced a large roll of packing tape. He wound two quick, complete loops of the tape around the long end of the box, flipped it over and repeated the procedure on the short end. Satisfied, he cut the continuous tape with a flourish, smiled at Ralph and left.

Ralph shook his head, picked up his stuff and left the Customs area for the expansive main terminal. He took a minute to admire it. Recently refurbished by U.S. AID, the interior was striking. The ceiling, two stories above them, was exposed and supported by a set of illuminated metal arches. The arches stretched some fifty feet from the ceiling toward the ground in a graceful curve, then came to rest on steel support beams running the width of the airport. The floor was thickly carpeted and a spacious lobby was encircled by small shops lining the outside walls of the terminal. He found the front of the building, pushed through a swinging glass door and stepped out into the heat.

A long line of cabs waited outside the terminal, so Ralph mentally drew a straw and approached a dilapidated, rust red, four-door sedan. It was a Ford, manufactured around 1963, with no air conditioning and no back window, but a world-class sound system. The speakers blared the "Ying, Yang, Ching, Chang" sounds only Middle East and Asian music can produce. Gritting his teeth, Ralph threw his books into the back seat, climbed in with his carry-ons and showed the driver a slip of paper with his address.

"Would you turn off that noise, I mean music."

He was a little tired.

The driver ignored him, pulled the shift into drive and waited for an opening in oncoming traffic. The music screeched on, rattling Ralph's fillings. He clawed under his shirt, pulled out his pouch and found some of his precious U.S. currency.

"Look man, I know you speak English," he shouted over the blare of the 'music.' "Five bucks, U.S., just for turning that crap off."

Without bothering to look, the driver reached back, snatched the bill out of Ralph's fingers and turned off the radio, all in the same motion. Ralph held up another five and locked eyes with the driver in the rear view mirror.

"Don't take me to that address. Take me to a market where I can find things, anything. Then drop off my books and stuff at this address. I'll find you and make it worth your while."

"No," the Driver said. "Ten dollars now and make it worth my while when I show up tomorrow."

Ralph sighed.

"Five dollars now and five dollars tomorrow, plus your fare."

"Not good."

"Fine. I'm sure with all the soldiers around here there's no shortage of U.S. dollars."

"Give me the five."

Ralph handed him a sawbuck and thought, the old greenback may not be what it used to be, but it still comes in handy.

The driver made a sharp left turn, cut across traffic and was rewarded with blaring car horns and middle fingers.

"I'm looking for an American handgun. A revolver. One that works and hasn't been used to kill anyone. Recently."

The driver slowed and looked at him in the mirror.

"I will take you to a market where you can buy a handgun and almost anything else you want. Beyond that, you take your chances. Not only do I refuse to guarantee you a clean firearm; I won't guarantee your safety. I do hope you live, though, because I want the rest of my money."

They smiled at each other.

"Take me to the market."

They rode together in silence for about two miles, dodging traffic and occasionally changing directions. The area thickened with small, handmade booths along the road, selling everything from livestock to pots and pans. The driver stopped the taxi at the opening of a wide alley, perpendicular to the road. People, bicycles, and livestock milled around. Colorful booths crowded both sides of the alley and sported canvas awnings extending a few feet into the alleyway. Ralph climbed out of the cab, removed a small vinyl case from inside one of his bags and left the rest of his luggage with the driver.

"If I end up dead, this stuff is yours. Otherwise, if I don't have my things by 10 a.m. tomorrow, I'll begin to look for you."

Ralph smiled. The driver smiled back.

"Of course."

"You know, you stand to make a lot of money off of me in the next year and a half. If you have any advice, I would listen and it would be a good investment for you."

The driver stopped for a moment and considered what he said. Ralph waited. For the first time since he'd gotten in the cab, the driver looked at him as though he were a human being.

"Advice. First, you will have no trouble finding someone willing to sell you a handgun. However, those merchants will be deeper in the market than the outer booths and shops. You must wind through all the alleyways until you get close to the center of the market. You will be able to tell when you get there, the alleys are narrower, with higher walls. It is dark and crowded. Take nothing you don't want stolen. Items will be ripped from your hands and people will stand in your way if you try to pursue the thief. You'll be in the most danger, probably attacked, after you buy the gun. This isn't political danger—these are criminals. In the market, carrying firearms is discouraged, so your assailants will probably be armed with knives. They'll probably be young and will follow you for some time before attacking. They may have partners or assistants amongst the merchants.

I don't know you so I won't send you to a specific merchant. Later, if I get to know you better, perhaps. Once you are in the inner Shouk, ask the most prosperous looking merchant you see where you can buy a firearm. This is all I have to say. Except, give me five dollars."

Ralph reached under his shirt and removed his cash from the passport pouch, figuring he'd stick about a hundred bucks in his pocket and keep the rest in the pouch. He didn't want to flash around any more cash than was necessary and figured one hundred dollars should buy a serviceable pistol. If anyone, including his driver, knew or suspected how much cash he was carrying, he'd be attacked long before he got a chance to buy anything. He leaned into the cab with one foot on the ground and one knee on the front seat, dropped his bags between him and the driver. After a moment, he handed the driver a twenty instead of a five.

"What's this?" the driver asked.

"An investment."

Shielding his hands behind the bags, he counted out two twenties and six tens for the shouk and shoved the bills into his pants pocket. He put the rest in the passport case and looked at the driver.

"I'll see you tomorrow," Ralph said.

"In sha Allah," the driver replied.

CHAPTER 10

———◆———

RALPH SLAMMED THE CAB DOOR and plunged into the market. The alley was lined on both sides with booths, carts, and a few panel vans. Older Arab men, cigarettes dangling from their lips, wandered the alleyways draped with sandwich boards advertising the quality of some good or service in squiggly lined Arabic. Off to one side, live poultry squawked and beat the air with their wings in a hopeless attempt to escape from wooden crates sealed with chicken wire.

Ralph kept moving and did his best to memorize the market's layout. It appeared alleyways branched out from the center of the market like spokes on a wagon wheel. Each spoke or alleyway led into the heart of the market. If this market was like others Ralph had explored, it was no doubt originally the center of that section of the city itself. As the city grew, the streets and alleys expanded outward, until the market sat like a spider in the center of a web. Ralph dodged a group of market patrons and continued down a broad cobblestone alley in the direction of the dark center of the market.

Chickens, goats, dogs, and children mixed with cripples rolling around on small carts pushing themselves along. Old men and women mingled together, creating a gigantic assault on the senses. The street was covered with feces, gum wrappers, animal guts and other sorts of graphic debris. Ralph walked by a shopkeeper spraying the street in front of his store with a green garden hose. When the water hit the sludge, a cloud of foul, exotic odors blossomed up from the bricks.

Ralph was careful to maintain his pace, but he didn't hurry. Those who hurried in a place like this looked like prey. Prey attracted predators. Instead, he glanced to the right and left, as though shopping, while really scanning the crowd. At times he slowed or even stopped to look over the wide assortment of merchandise for sale.

He struggled not to smile once he entered an area of the market specializing in "knock off" sports apparel and designer clothing. The various names and slogans got all twisted around in translation and the results could be hilarious. "Barf Loren" one shirt proclaimed in small stitched letters underneath an equally sized stitched donkey. The donkey was carrying a helmeted rider who was swinging what appeared to be garden hoe at the ground. As soon as he looked away, he caught the gaze of a predator. Or maybe not. Maybe he could still get his gun and leave the market without incident. Ralph realized he was nervous, which made him angry, and . . . more nervous. He moved on.

As he walked by, merchants called to him in the half friendly, half mocking tone reserved for foreigners. Gesturing at their wares, they managed to look amazed when Ralph didn't stop, paralyzed with delight. The alley narrowed. Above him wooden balconies dark with age protruded from the walls, looming over the street below. Residents leaned over the balconies yelling across the expanse to the other side, laughing, chattering or cursing. Sensing a blur from above, Ralph managed to dodge a meteor shower of garbage, water and excrement hurled from above. To the delight of the Iraqis, a bit splashed up on his legs. He smiled good-naturedly and moved on, looking for the Arab he'd noticed before.

He emerged from the alley into the center of the market, greeted by a new combination of the same sounds and smells as before, but somehow combined in a way that felt like something from another country. The center of the market was a medieval maze, a hodgepodge of small, permanent storefronts, semi-permanent wood booths, and shabbily constructed temporary structures. Ralph dodged three young men coming in the opposite direction and squeezed by a large canvas sack full of red, aromatic, finely ground spice.

He spotted the predator. Somehow the young man had gotten ahead of him and picked up a couple of friends. Ralph ignored them but he knew he'd found his assailants and they their victim. The clock was ticking. The men would only wait so long before they attacked, so Ralph wanted to find his pistol merchant now. He didn't see anyone who fit the profile his driver had given him. He changed direction so he could approach one of the glass-fronted shops at an angle and use it as a mirror. He walked by, with a nonchalant glance at the window as he passed. His assailants' reflections were shortening the distance, no doubt waiting for him to near the mouth of one of the unoccupied alleys that occasionally branched off the main thoroughfare.

Just when Ralph thought things might get complicated, he found a likely gun dealer. His shop front was twenty feet wide, all in glass. Inside, bright merchandise of red, brass, and vivid green grabbed the eye.

This guy's doing pretty good for himself, so I don't see him letting people molest legitimate customers, Ralph thought. Then again, I'bad m hardly a legitimate customer. He went straight for the door, noticing his new friend accepted MasterCard, Visa, American Express, and Discover. The reflection above these logos showed his thug escort peeling off and hovering over the produce of a nearby fruit stand. When Ralph opened the door a bell over the top of the frame jangled loudly.

"Hello my friend, welcome, welcome, welcome, to my humble shop. I am Akmed and this is my son, Hussein."

Akmed looked like he was a little over 60. His huge, basketball like stomach stretched a brown t-shirt to the ripping point. It was lettered "Sad Boy Club," with a silkscreen of a silhouetted young man with spiked hair, holding an electric guitar. Hussein looked to be about thirty and was as thin as a rail. He was shod in plastic bathroom togs and wore generic jeans and a collared shirt. The shirt fit better than his father's and said "Los Angeles Steelers." Someone emblazoned a hockey stick on the front. Feeling somewhat underdressed in his khaki pants and a short-sleeved cotton shirt, Ralph decided to start slow.

"I was looking at the brass dagger and the candle snuffer in your window."

He made a show of looking around, wide-eyed, at Akmed's admittedly impressive display of merchandise, while really looking for cameras or security windows. He found two cameras, one on the door and one over the jewelry counter.

Manageable, he thought to himself.

"Certainly, certainly, my American friend," Akmed said. "We

have a fine selection of brass articles and make our own fragrances. Perhaps a special scent for your mother, wife or another special lady? Hussein, some tea for our guest." Hussein turned to leave and Ralph slipped the brass dagger into a side pocket of his backpack. Akmed came close and took Ralph's left hand in his right and gently led him to a wall display opposite the door.

The entire wall was floor-to-ceiling mirrors behind glass and chrome shelving. The shelves were lined with row upon row of small, medium and large sized cut glass fragrance bottles. Each held a liquid of varying shades of color. Everything was backlit from the top, bottom, and side, giving each bottle's heart a fiery glow. Everything seemed to sparkle.

The merchant regaled Ralph with charming descriptions of secret ingredients in the perfumes and fragrances. The special ones, ones he thought would be appropriate for a woman belonging to a man of Ralph's status had to be sampled. Akmed picked up each bottle, held the small stopper in place with his index finger and twisted his wrist to splash some of the fragrance onto the bottom of the stopper. Then he dabbed it on the inside of Ralph's wrist. Ralph raised his wrist to his nose.

"Enjoy, my friend. Can you not detect the rose petals whose essence is a part of this fragrance?"

Akmed continued the ritual with three or four other samples, explaining the processes as he went. Hussein brought in a tea service with three cups and a tray.

"Come, my friend, enough business for now. Please be my guest for tea and some fine biscuits in a relaxing atmosphere. You must be tired, having experienced our market for the first time."

He took Ralph's hand once again and led him into a spacious side room, windowless and upholstered with red velvet and brass wall decorations. A large eight hose houka dominated the center of the room. A deeply cushioned couch and several chairs were arranged around the houka. Ralph swept the room. No cameras.

"Sit, sit," Hussein said, smiling. "Please, let me be of assistance."

Hussein sat the tea service and a silver serving tray with biscuits on a side table.

"Cream with your tea, my friend?"

"No, my friend," Ralph replied.

"Do any of our poor, local fragrances please you? We here in

Iraq cannot compare with the sophisticated fragrances available in your country, but at least we provide fine quality and a unique aroma found nowhere else."

"You're too modest. These are perfumes that will please my mother and my sister and what else is more important than one's family," Ralph asked nodding toward Hussein.

"Yes," Akmed said smiling and nodding his head, "I see that you're a bit different than many Westerners who come here. Perhaps you have more of a Middle East perspective on life. You must let me give you the rose fragrance as my gift to your mother."

"This I cannot allow my new friend. Do you not also have a family to care for? My company has been generous with Iraqi Dinars to assist me as I settle in. I would be insulted if I wasn't allowed to the give you fair value for not only the rose but for the sage fragrance which I so enjoyed."

"Ah, the sage is one of my favorites," the merchant said approvingly. His face quickly registered and then concealed his disappointment over the fact that Ralph would pay with Dinars instead of U.S. dollars.

In his Star Foundation orientation materials, Ralph discovered that the new Iraqi government and the Provisional Authority were very conscientious about restricting the use of U.S. dollars and encouraging the use of the new Dinar. Like everywhere Ralph had been in the world, however, merchants were equally conscientious about obtaining so-called hard currency. "Hard currency" meant money that could be used to buy foreign goods because it was accepted by foreign merchants. Local currencies could be inflated to the point where they were valueless. Foreign hard currencies could not be debased by desperate dictators or a struggling new democracy. Of all foreign hard currencies, the U.S. dollar was still the most universally accepted and therefore desirable.

The men bantered back and forth over the price of the perfume while sipping tea. Akmed refused to accept any payment. Ralph offered an outrageously high price. Akmed agreed to accept some ridiculously small payment. Then Ralph offered a high price. Finally, Ralph offered and Akmed accepted a moderately ridiculous high price for his two bottles of perfume. Ralph set his teacup on the side table and removed a folded pack of red and lime green Iraqi Dinar bills from his pocket. As they say, it looked like play money. While shuffling through the bills he expressed his concern for his personal safety.

"I mean no disrespect when I say that your fine country is still dangerous for a westerner such as myself. It concerns me. In my own country, of course I would have a handgun and the ability to protect myself but here, possession of firearms is prohibited."

Ralph timed his pilgrimage through the currency wad so that just as he reached the middle of the wad, the part containing the U.S. currency, he reached his lament over his lack of a handgun.

When he looked up he caught Akmed staring at the U.S. dollars. United States currency, of course, looks like nothing else in the world. It's even illegal to privately own the type of paper and ink used to create it. Americans don't depict birds or ballerinas, famous artists or puppies on their money. In America, unless you were a Founder, there are only two criteria for being represented on the real money, the folding money. You must have been elected President of the United States, and you must be dead. President and Dead. Americans are serious about money. Therefore, American money is serious. This is known and respected around the world. Whether at home or abroad, U.S. Dollars make people, like Akmed for example, dance.

"These are dangerous times, said the merchant. "For you, already a customer and I feel a friend, to be without the ability to protect himself in a country he knows so little of concerns me."

"Thank you, my friend," Ralph said, handing him the Iraqi Dinar with one hand while still holding the wad open to the U.S. bills with the other. Akmed took the Dinars and handed him a small bag with his perfume.

"Of course, there are many different kinds of pistols."

"For me" Ralph replied, "there is only the .38 Special Revolver."

"We are indeed brothers," said the merchant.

"In many ways, but how do you mean," Ralph asked with as much innocence as he could muster.

"It may not surprise you to learn that an honest man, such as myself, even though Iraqi, must also be concerned with my safety and that of my store. So, and this is only between friends that I say this, I have a firearm here on the premises."

"Who can blame you," Ralph said. "You're a wise man and I envy you."

"What is surprising, my friend is that you and I have the same opinion of firearms. I own a .38 caliber pistol. It is a Ruger revolver."

Ralph merely smiled and slowly nodded his head, folding the money and placing it back in his pocket.

"You are much more at risk than I am, though. You must allow me to give you this weapon as a gift so that Allah will not hold me accountable should something happen to you."

He nodded to Hussein who left the tea room and returned after a few minutes holding a white towel folded over upon itself. Approaching his father, he bowed slightly and held out the towel in both hands for his father to accept.

"Leave us now, my son. It is better for you not to be here."

Hussein bowed once again, looked meaningfully at his father, nodded and left. He never took a second look at Ralph. A quick flash of anger passed Akmed's face, replaced with contrived disappointment. Shaking his head he said, "I'm afraid my son's feelings are hurt, but he does not understand the danger. I am embarrassed he did not even look at you, let alone properly excuse himself. He has much to learn."

Yeah, Ralph thought to himself. In this part of the world, being able to look a man in the eye and shake his hand before leaving to arrange his murder is mere competence.

Akmed and Ralph now repeated the same ritual that had preceded the sale of the perfume.

"My son does not realize how dangerous it is for me to give you this weapon. He thinks I insult him by dismissing him before I make you this gift. Instead, of course, I protect him. My friend, let me keep my conscience clear by giving you this weapon."

He laid the towel on a small table off to his side and unfolded it. Lying on the towel, now exposed, was a Ruger "Security Six" in .38 Special caliber. Beside the pistol lay six rounds of ammunition with the tips of the bullets "scooped" or hollowed out. Jackson was somewhat concerned about the lack of ammunition. Increasingly, governments everywhere were adopting the use of 9 mm pistols and other weapons. The advantage to this policy was the ammunition for all the weapons was interchangeable. All an Army, police force or terrorist organization had to do was purchase and ship one type of ammunition, 9 mm. It made no difference whether any particular unit needed the ammunition for rifles, machine guns, or handguns because, increasingly, they were all chambered to use the same 9 mm ammunition.

What this meant for Ralph, as an old timer who preferred older weapons, was that ammunition other than 9 mm was difficult to obtain outside of regular channels. Still, he needed this particular type of weapon and the hollow point ammunition because of where he was and the rules that locale imposed upon his freedom of action.

Ralph was operating, and not for the first time, in a friendly or neutral governmental environment. Moreover, that environment had a functioning police force and judicial system. After all, he had come to Iraq to help strengthen it. A legitimate police force imposed certain restrictions on Ralph's freedom of action. While SF people had no qualms about breaking the laws of allied or neutral countries to get bad guys, the use of deadly force against their internal security forces, usually the police, was strictly off limits. It was like shooting your own guys. They were one edge of the sword, the military was the other edge. Since employing deadly force against such individuals was an SF taboo, evasion was the only recourse. If the Cops caught you, you didn't fight back. You were caught.

So if he did have to shoot someone, he couldn't afford to get caught with the gun. The way you got caught was keeping the gun and leaving behind intact bullets or spent casings. The bullets or casings would identify the gun. The gun would identify the shooter. It was dangerous keeping a used gun. But it was also dangerous throwing away guns because it was dangerous getting new ones.

Therefore, he was taught to use bullets that fragmented upon impact and to never leave the ejected casings, or "brass" lying around. On the bullet, a pistol left rifling marks from the barrel which the police could use to match up against the pistol barrel. On the brass cartridges, the casings were marked by the firing pin in a certain location and were scored when leaving the ejection port. The weapon could be identified not just by the bullet itself, but also by an expended casing. If Ralph left the brass at the scene, it could be used to identify the pistol just as easily as a recovered slug or bullet could. Picking up or "policing" the brass before you left was only an option in badly written novels. Who was going to risk hanging around after a gunfight to pick up all the expended cartridges? Even if you had a lot of time, those little buggers had a way of rolling into the hardest to find places.

Someone armed with an automatic faced bad choices. They could hang around until they found all the brass casings. They could forget the casings, leave, keep the gun and face the risk of being caught. Finally, they could discard the gun and take a chance on obtaining a new one. Because of this, anyone who knew what they were doing armed themselves with a mid-caliber revolver because it didn't eject the cartridges. The brass stayed in the pistol and you could get rid of it later. They loaded the revolver with hollow point bullets because the rounds almost always fragmented, especially in the mid caliber range because of the round's velocity. Since the bullets almost always fragmented, ballistics identification was difficult and usually impossible.

While not full proof, the likelihood of leaving enough ballistic evidence to get caught was low. Local police departments investigating any shooting might catch you with a gun, but they couldn't prove you used it to kill anyone. Often all you faced was deportation for an unregistered or illegal gun. Even if you faced criminal prosecution, it was a lot better to be prosecuted for possessing a firearm than for murder.

Thus, Ralph wanted more bullets.

"Only six rounds of ammunition? This doesn't seem like you. Your son must have overlooked the extra boxes of ammunition you keep nearby." Akmed's eyes narrowed. He and Ralph were now done pretending this was a favor. He leaned back in his chair and smiled.

"My son is more of a disappointment than I thought. Yes, I have three boxes of the ammunition."

"I would have expected no less of a man like you," Ralph said while leaning forward in his chair, gathering himself. "But my friend, before you give these items to me as well, since they are now worthless to you, you must let me show my appreciation. While you bring the rest of the gift, I must consider this."

Frowning, the merchant started to stand up. One hand remained on his lap.

Ralph raised his left hand in a 'Stop' gesture and pulled out the dagger he'd lifted from the display case with the other. He drew the dagger from its scabbard and made a show of admiring its blade. Then he picked up the revolver and using only his left hand released the cylinder, which swung out of the weapon. The brass bullet casings gleamed duly in the shop light. While twisting the dagger's blade in the light with one hand, he pulled back the pistol hammer and pulled the trigger with the other while the cylinder was still hanging out of the weapon. The hammer clanked metallically on the recoil plate. Ralph looked away from the brass dagger for the first time and locked eyes with the merchant.

"Let me assist you in correcting this oversight," he said, gesturing toward the towel with the dagger.

Akmed's frown turned into a glare as he handed Ralph the firing pin and firing pin recoil spring. Ralph's look had gone cold.

"Sit down."

The fat merchant sat down.

Ralph sat the blade down within easy reach, spilled the shells onto his lap and snapped the cylinder back into the pistol. Turning the weapon around to the front, he cocked the hammer back. With one hand he held the pistol and with the other he pressed the end of the post on his belt buckle into the recoil plate pin. He released the pin and plate, inserted the firing pin and its spring, and then reassembled the pistol. Although it had been a while since he'd had any practice, he still managed to re-insert the firing pin and reassemble the weapon in under a minute. Akmed looked on dumbfounded.

Ralph eased the hammer back, pointed at the floor and pulled the trigger. The pistol now emitted a springy click. His eyes still on the merchant, Ralph picked up the bullets and thumbed all six rounds into the cylinder, slapped the cylinder shut and pulled the hammer back. This rotated a bullet into the barrel of the pistol. All that was required now was that he pull the trigger. Ralph aimed at the wall about six inches to the left of Akmed's face. Pointing it directly at the fat merchant would have been in an insult that couldn't be overlooked. Ralph would have either had to kill him or be looking over his shoulder the rest of his time in Iraq. Like the cab driver, Jackson thought he and Akmed could do business. Akmed looked grim.

"The pistol seems in fine condition, my friend. Would you be so kind as to bring the other items we discussed."

Ralph brought out the money wad, removed a sufficient number of Dinars to pay for a cab and dinner and placed the rest on the
side table. He left the U.S. dollars facing up. Akmed looked from
him to the currency and waited.

"I'm not like most Americans you've met," Ralph said. "I think
you and I can be of great help to each other over the next two or
three years. I have many needs that are difficult to satisfy and I find
you resourceful."

The fat man stared hard at him.

"You are not like most Americans. I will return in a moment."

Ralph nodded. When Akmed left, he stood up and switched
chairs. Now, he was facing the doorway with a view out of the tea
room, able to see the front door and the side door Hussein and
Akmed used. Ralph pulled the hammer back, placed the butt or
handle toward him and covered the pistol with the towel. It was
within easy reach, as was the dagger.

Akmed reemerged from the curtained doorway carrying a second towel encased package, both hands visible outside the towel.
If they hadn't been, Ralph would have shot him. Or stabbed him.
Or both. In any event his hands were visible and he reentered the
tea room and sat across from Ralph, their positions now reversed.
The merchant laid his package on the table and pulled back the
towel, revealing three boxes of 50 rounds each, 38 caliber hollow
point ammunition. Ralph nodded and gestured with his free left
hand to another side table. Akmed grabbed two ends of the towel
with the towel still unfolded and placed it on the table.

"The money is yours," Ralph said.

He opened a small pack around his waist, a so-called belly pack
and placed the .38 inside with its hammer down. He stuffed the
ammunition into a small carry bag that only held a sweatshirt
when he came. The sweatshirt stayed out.

"Now what," Akmed asked.

"Now nothing. I leave. Until next time."

"This we will see."

Ralph stopped and turned around to look at him.

"As a sign of respect, I will say no one can control today's youth.
For this, they are not responsible. The children themselves, should
they be where they should not be, must expect to be held respon-

sible."

Ralph didn't want to kill or injure the merchant's son and he suspected Hussein would try to get in on the action unless his father stopped him. Akmed nodded.

"I will address this when you leave. As a sign of respect to you, I will say this. There will be three who will come for you. They will use knives. I doubt you will be able to avoid them, but if you can, do so. If you can't, try not to shoot them. Gunfire draws attention to us that no one wants."

Gee, that's awfully important to me, Ralph thought, as he fantasized about shooting the three thugs in their kneecaps. He nodded.

"Of course, you will be observed," Akmed went on, "and if there is no choice, this will not be held against you. Go."

Ralph's carry-on bag had shoulder straps and he used them. He released the straps and stuck both arms through the straps. He'd brought a long-sleeved, cotton, sweatshirt which he now folded in half and draped through the right shoulder strap and allowed it to slide down near his waist. The material was really too heavy to wear except on the chilliest of evenings, but he hadn't brought it to wear. Ralph left the shop, its bell jingled and he stepped into the street, his eyes sweeping left and right. No sign of the three young thugs. Yet. The bell jingled again and Akmed stuck his head out, looking undecided.

"You were respectful enough with my son . . . and not to point the pistol at me."

He hesitated, trying to decide something.

"I would not trust the first six rounds of ammunition if I were you."

He slammed the door, locked it and dropped the drapes.

"Closed," the sign now read.

CHAPTER 11

———◆———

WARNING OR BLUFF? RALPH CONSIDERED reloading
with some of the ammunition stored in his backpack. Way
too many people, he thought. Someone would call the police, or
worse, U.S, M.P.s. Besides, maybe that was what Akmed is counting on. Maybe the first 6 rounds are good and the 3 boxes are bad.
Some of the passers-by were looking at him, quizzically.

I've been standing here too long.

Ralph moved down the street, dodging other market goers
who it now seemed watched him with hostile faces. He retraced
his steps out of the market, glancing right, left, and behind while
checking for hostile reflections in shop windows. His stomach
danced to a tune called by nerves, an active imagination, and an
unreliable pistol. He'd been counting on the pistol to scare off
the thugs. Now he might have to rely on his hands. It had been
some time since Ralph faced such a situation and he could barely
remember what it felt like.

Still, what does an ex-green beret tough guy like me have to
worry about from 3 skinny kids, he thought, mocking himself.

He was walking back his original route and considered changing direction. The physical layout of the market was confusing,
dark and filled with dead-end streets and hidden dangers, but
Ralph was blessed with a good sense of direction and experience.
Experience had taught him that unpredictability and surprise are
powerful allies. His assailants and their friends would expect Ralph
to follow the same route out of the market.

The surprise was worth the risk. He veered to the left, cutting
across other market-goers' pathways, crossed the street and trotted
down a narrow, dark alley. The cobblestoned surface was shadowed

by high, dark brick walls and before he'd gone ten feet he was swallowed by the gloom, unobservable from the street. The architecture lent an ominous air to the route. The doors and windows dotting the alleyway walls were arched, veering upward to a point, a distinctly Middle Eastern feature. The alley was deserted.

He turned to see if he'd been followed, then broke into a dead run, his rubber soles soundless on the cobblestones. After perhaps forty yards he came upon another, even smaller, side street cutting across his route. Mentally tossing a coin, Ralph zigged to the left, running down an alley that paralleled the street he had taken out. He was now heading in the opposite direction from the one he had been traveling a few moments ago.

That should throw them off, he thought.

He slowed from a run to a rapid stride, hoping to use another cross alley intersection and change direction yet again. He found what he was looking for a short distance ahead, just as the engine of a large diesel truck roared into life, then subsided to a growl. Ralph rushed toward the intersection, but a large panel truck beat him, crossing it and stopping when only the white metal side panels were visible. The length of the vehicle completely blocked the alleyway with no room to get around it. The truck was heavily loaded, its frame sunk down only inches off the ground. He was blocked. The only way out was to retrace his steps or try a small archway leading into a common area between two buildings. It was dark and filled with bicycles, wash tubs and shadows.

One of the residence doors fronting on the alley opened and then slammed behind the three men who'd been stalking him. Another door opened above him. A cold faced, middle-aged man leaned over the dark balcony, staring down. Ralph looked away, grabbed the .38 and pulled the hammer back. He aimed at the first thug's knee and pulled the trigger.

"Click."

He moved toward the arch using the half run, half walk shuffle of someone afraid not to run and afraid not to walk. In other words, as he shoved the pistol back into the pack, he moved like the cornered prey he was.

The Arabs trotted toward him, grinning and flashing their knives. Ralph shuffled through the shadows toward the archway and looked over his shoulder. Then he dashed to the left and under the entrance. As soon as he was out of sight he slowed to a walk and pulled his sweatshirt off the backpack strap. All the butterflies were gone. That old, cold rush enveloped him. Time slowed down, giving him all the time in the world to evaluate the terrain and see in his mind's eye exactly how it was going to go down. It was a gift. Or something. He grinned.

He grabbed one sleeve cuff in his left hand and swung the shirt around his arm like a whip until it covered his left forearm from the wrist to the elbow. Finally, he pulled it tight and gripped both sleeve cuffs in his left hand. Ralph held his sweat-shirted arm across his chest to keep it hidden from the view of the assailants when they burst around the corner. He didn't have long to wait. As he had hoped, the first man was a few steps ahead of the others. Ralph looked over his shoulder and shuffled forward. The assailant ran to catch him, so Ralph ran too . . . for about two strides, then he stopped dead. The man had difficulty stopping because he was wearing a pair of those stupid flip-flops. He half slid, half stumbled toward Ralph and slashed at him when he got near. Ralph spun to his left, snapping his forearm up so it was straight up and down, elbow toward the ground, fist in the air. Spinning on his left foot, he whipped his forearm around and his sweat-shirted forearm and the knife blade collided. Ralph twisted his protected forearm down, deflecting the knife. Reversing his earlier movement, he planted the other foot while thrusting out his arm. His right hand, fingers bent down, knuckles exposed, shot straight out from his body, directly into the throat of the young man charging toward him. The Arab's head snapped back, as though impaled, but the rest of him continued moving forward, stretching him out as far as possible until his feet left the ground and he slammed down on the cobblestones, back first, gaging. Ralph picked up the assailant's knife with his right hand and kept his eyes on the archway.

The other two men entered. They were surprised and hesitated just long enough to save the first one's life. Instead of the man's own momentum impaling him on the knife as Ralph had planned, he stopped. Ralph was forced to change tactics. He switched his grip on the knife, grabbed the blade and he hurled it at the throat of the third assailant. Now Special Forces members amuse them-selves in many strange ways and knife throwing was one of them. Ralph, therefore, was unthinkingly confident. But it had been years since he'd consistently thrown knives at plywood targets in his team house. Like most things in life, practice makes perfect. So, instead of sticking the knife into the third guy's chest or throat like in the movies, he inadvertently bounced its handle off the man's upper lip.

"Ouch," the third Arab said.

"Crap," Ralph replied, already moving toward the closest thug.

By the time Ralph reached him, his opponent was still trying to recover his balance after slamming on the brakes in the flip-flops. In no time his peril dawned on him. He stabbed straight out at Ralph's stomach. It wasn't a very quick or graceful thrust and Ralph easily deflected it. He continued his shuffling advance toward the man, bunched his right hand into a fist and brought it up behind his ear in a windmill motion. Once it was over his head he whipped it down with as much force as he could muster, right toward the end of the Arab's nose. The man's eyes grew wide, but it was too late. Ralph felt a satisfying crack of cartilage as Arab number two's nose gushed blood. Ralph was already moving toward the third man and his fat lip.

The third guy had dropped his knife and was holding his face. He wanted to put up a fight, he really did, but things were happening too fast. As Ralph approached, the Arab moved his hands up in a defensive posture. Instead of throwing a punch, Ralph was already sliding in at an angle toward the other man's left leg. Ralph picked up his foot and extended it out as hard as he could in what is known as a sidekick. It connected with the other man's knee with enough force to jolt back up Ralph's leg. Then the assailant's knee cartilage and tendons gave out and Arab three collapsed to the ground, howling.

Ralph spun around and returned to the assailant with the broken nose. He was bent over so Ralph bludgeoned him. The Arab stopped moving. The first assailant was still on the ground, gagging and grasping his throat. With everyone on the ground in various stages of disrepair, Ralph considered his options. His first thought was to kill the men, but he decided against it. They might want revenge, but that danger would be nothing compared to the danger Ralph would face from the men's families if he killed their relatives while they lay in the street. He left.

Ralph returned to the alley, looking for the cold-faced man. As

soon as they made eye contact, Ralph pointed back to the courtyard.

"They're still alive. A gesture of respect."

Cold Face nodded toward the blocked intersection and left the
balcony. The panel truck was already moving, clearing his path.
Ralph wasted no time reaching the now unblocked intersection.
He was half expecting someone to jump out at him as he rounded
the corner, but was pleasantly disappointed. The alleyways were
deserted in both directions. Ralph made a right hand turn and
kept moving. The balconies above him were clear. The only thing
he could think was that he had been targeted by the three youths
and they owned first shot at him. Since no one had expected them
to fail, there was no backup. Ralph was hoping to just walk out.

Hoping, not counting on.

In little time he reached the next intersection and was paralleling
the main thoroughfare of the market. He ran across isolated shoppers strolling lazily around canvas sacks rolled down like a shirt
sleeve. Squatting merchants measured out grain by what appeared
to be ceramic pitchers. Other men rolled down accordion-like
steel garage doors that served as the storefront for their small
enterprises, padlocking them to the ground during their extended
lunch break. It was hard to believe that only a block away, less than
fifteen minutes earlier, Ralph was fighting for his life.

He popped onto the main thoroughfare of the market and
blended in with a flowing stream of humanity. Now even isolated
Western faces could be seen amongst the crowd. Ralph stayed
with the flow of shoppers leaving of the market.

Coasting alone, bobbing along with the flow of humanity, he
thought, I'm going to make it out of here.

Long dormant habits re-asserted themselves and he remained
alert. Colors were vivid. Detail seemed to jump out at him. The
excitement of trial work in the States suddenly seemed a poor
substitute for what he'd just experience. He moved faster, bypass-
ing the slower shoppers because he knew it was only a matter of
time until he'd run out of adrenaline. Then his vigilance would
flag. Then he would want nothing more than a relatively safe place
to rest, to have a few beers and relax. He was out of shape, out of
practice. Of course, he would see visions from As Salman.

Ralph was already on automatic pilot and could feel his focus fade. He got out of the market and got lucky. There were a number of cabs passing by and the first one he hailed stopped for him. He slid into the back seat, glad it was over. When he decided to return to Iraq, he knew he was going to have to face this sort of situation again. There was no way he could live in Baghdad without a gun and without re-activating long dormant skills and reactions. During the flight over, he concluded the best thing to do was kill two birds with one stone. Entering the market as he had marked him as a target. At the same time, the market was the best place to buy a pistol. He needed a pistol and needed to go through what he had just experienced. Now, thankfully, it was over and all things considered, he was pleased with how he'd performed.

Ralph handed his driver a slip of paper with his new address written in Arabic. The driver nodded, threw the transmission column lever into drive and jerked out into traffic. Ralph felt the after effects of fear, anger and excitement surge through his body. While everyone's external reaction to combat related stress was different, the physiological effects were the same for everyone. In the end, sooner or later, everyone crashed. Some people crashed by sleeping, some by drinking, others by running or talking. One way or another, you had to learn how to deal with the rocket fuel that your body dumped into your bloodstream during combat situations. Ralph tried to remain vigilant on the off chance the driver was unreliable or he was being followed. Evidently, he was not quite up to it, a troubling sign. In what seemed like five seconds, the driver surprised him in unknown Arabic.

"What, what," Ralph asked in English, flinching in his seat.

The driver began in Arabic and pointed to the side of the building. "371" printed in white paint on the cinder block. "There, there," said the driver.

Ralph got out, paid the driver with his remaining Dinars and walked up into the depressing lobby of his new apartment building. He spotted the reception desk on his right hand side. As he approached, an Arab man stood up.

"Name, please."

He checked Ralph's name off his list and gestured for Ralph to follow him up the staircase. They climbed to the third floor and walked down an ill-lit hallway. The man stopped outside Room 301, removed a key, opened the door and pointed.

"Your apartment."

Ralph pressed a Dinar note into the man's hand and asked him to close the door when he left.

"Wait. Recommend a Western restaurant with Western beverages and food."

The apartment building was provided by the Star Foundation, so this Iraqi was likely familiar with Western tastes. He should know Ralph wanted an establishment that served alcohol.

"I understand from other guests that the Riverside View café has fine food and a menu suited to Western tastes. It's in a heavily patrolled section of Baghdad behind the Green Zone and is favored by Westerners. If you wish, I can arrange transportation."

The man had a lot to lose by offending the Star Foundation and therefore could probably be trusted. In Baghdad, "probably" was the best he would get.

"Please do that. Also, my luggage will be delivered tomorrow. The cab driver has been of some service to me, so I will have an envelope for him. If I leave this with you, can you ensure he gets it when he delivers my things?" Before the Iraqi could answer, Ralph handed him two more Dinar bills.

"This is very important to me. Please, close the door behind you."

CHAPTER 12

———◆———

RALPH'S FIRST CONSCIOUS IMPRESSION WAS of a bright yellow needle piercing through his eyelid. Groaning, he opened his eyes to a face full of sunlight streaming in through the bedroom window. When he sat upright he knew he'd made some good choices.

The restaurant Jackson's apartment manager sent him to did serve alcohol. Since his drink of choice was beer, he gravitated toward kindred souls and spent an hour and a half drinking beer with a table full of Australians. Somewhere between all the beers, Ralph managed to eat two cheeseburgers and an order of oven cooked french fries. Evidently, they didn't use deep fryers in Baghdad. Despite the Australians, the availability of beer, the street fight in the Shouk and the post-traumatic stress over the quality of Iraqi french fries, Ralph managed to limit his intake to five bottles. By ten p.m. he bade farewell to his new friends and caught a cab back to the apartment. He was sound asleep by 11:00 p.m. It was one of the few nights in the last decade he had slept the night through. A good sign.

Ralph went to the sink, shaved and washed up for an 11:30 a.m. appointment with his Star representative. He dressed in khaki pants, rubber soled leather half boots, and a light cotton, button–up shirt. His pistol was stashed underneath the mattress so he pulled that out, gathered the boxes of extra ammunition from their hiding places and stacked everything between his feet. He unlocked the cylinder of the .38, dumped the old cartridges on the bed, selected two bullets from each box and re-loaded the pistol. He was just nestling the .38 and some spare rounds into a hand towel when there was a sharp knock on the door. Ralph stuck the towel into his belly pack, zipped it closed and used his feet to slide the ammunition back under the bed. The apartment manager and the cab driver from the airport were waiting when he opened the door.

"This man says he knows you. Also, he fits the description you gave me and these," the manager said gesturing, "appear to be your bags."

"You did well."

The cabbie took the luggage into the room. Ralph dismissed the manager.

"How did you find the Shouk?"

"About what I expected. I need a place to test the reliability of one of my purchases. Some of the items I bought didn't perform as I expected."

The driver smiled ruefully.

"I heard about what happened. The boxes of ammunition are good. The first six rounds you might as well throw away . . . or take back to the shopkeeper. They're designed to look real but they're duds."

Ralph took a twenty out of his passport pouch.

"How safe are my possessions in this hotel?"

The cab driver shrugged and took the twenty.

"The staff is reliable. Nothing, however, is safe."

"Indeed. Can you drive me to the Baghdad Hilton?"

"Of course. It will run about 10 Dinars on the meter."

"You drive a hard bargain."

Smiling back the driver said, "What time is your appointment?"

"Eleven."

"It will only take 15 minutes to get to the hotel, why not call another driver?"

"Because," Ralph replied, "I want you to take me somewhere I can fire this pistol. It is not that I don't trust you, but I don't trust what others told you."

"Very well. In that case, it will run you 30 Dinar."

Shaking his head Ralph said, "Let's go."

They left the building and climbed into the cab.

"Most of the places where you can fire your pistol are not places where you want to get out of the cab. From what I hear, I'm not so much worried about you as I am for the safety of our younger

. . . businessmen. Besides, why waste the time?"

"I want to make sure the weapon and ammunition are reliable. Drive where you want and tell me what to do."

The driver pulled out, twisted and turned along the city's major thoroughfares, its narrower streets and finally down a dirt alley. The cabbie slowed to a stop and pointed out the right-hand window toward a large garbage dump. It was in an open field, the nearest structures two shabby, ten story buildings. Most of the windows were broken and no one was in sight.

"Shoot out the car window into the center of the garbage mound. Be quick, this is the closest place, not the best. You said you wanted to test the ammunition. No aiming. I don't think you're a man who needs practice but if you do, tell me and I'll take you to safer place."

Ralph unzipped the belly pack, removed the pistol and pulled back the hammer. He sighted on what appeared to be a coffee can and began firing. He tracked the can, banging bullets off it as it jumped around on the garbage mound. As the driver suspected, he wasn't a man who needed practice. When the sound of the last round echoed down the alley, Ralph leaned forward.

"Drive."

The cab rolled off, slow, then picking up speed, and then easing off once it was moving. In the meantime, Ralph had replaced the six empty casings with fresh bullets. He held the six expended shells in his hand.

The driver watched him in the rearview mirror.

"I can dispose of those if you wish."

Jackson rubbed each casing on the hand towel and spilled the casings from the towel directly into the driver's hand. No fingerprints.

The driver shook his head, as though dismayed the world had grown so cynical.

Fifteen minutes later they approached the Baghdad Hilton Hotel, only to be stopped some one hundred thirty feet from the main entrance. The Hotel ran a privately maintained checkpoint, staffed by paid contractors from Eastern Europe. They maintained a buffer around the hotel, estimating that one hundred thirty feet was a sufficient distance to diffuse the most powerful initial surge of a car bomb blast. Of course a large car bomb would still be devastating at one hundred thirty feet, but this was Baghdad in 2004. One did what one could. The contractors, who sounded Polish, swarmed Ralph's cab. One of the men, armed with only a pistol and a clipboard approached the vehicle. Ignoring the driver, he looked at Ralph.

"Do you have a room here?"

Remembering the pistol in his belly-pack, Jackson said, "I'm a lawyer meeting the director of the Star Foundation for lunch in the hotel. Inside the belly-pack is a .38 caliber revolver I have for personal protection."

Raising an eyebrow, the Pole held out his hand without a word. Ralph handed him his passport, his Star Foundation letter of introduction, and a Provisional Authority travel pass. The man scrutinized the documents while his crew searched under the hood, the trunk and the wheel wells. Last, they rolled a dolly with a large mirror underneath the cab. The leader looked up from the papers and waited. After a few minutes moving the dolly around, another Pole looked up and nodded at his boss.

"Open the belly-pack."

Ralph unzipped it and slid to the window. The man leaned in, pulled back the zippered flap and rummaged around.

"Very well, Mr. Jackson. Leave the pack with me. I will return it when you leave."

Ralph unclipped the pack and handed it out the window. Pole took it and gestured to his men. The assault weapons and check-point gate swung away from the cab.

"Enjoy your lunch at the Hilton, sir."

"Man, that must cost a Fortune," Ralph said.

Shaking his head the Driver said, "Nope. East Europeans are good and they work cheap."

Since the whole procedure had taken less than five minutes and was obviously thorough, Ralph could hardly argue. They pulled up to the front of the building.

"You can let yourself out."

"Right. Want to stay?"

Smiling, the driver shook his head and pulled out as Ralph was closing the door. Ralph walked past the bellman, who held the door for him, through the lobby and over to the main desk. He noticed another European seated in the lobby, looking him over from behind a newspaper. The reception desk directed him to the dining room. Entering, he swept the room with his eyes as he had been taught many years before. Seated by the far window, alone and aloof, sat Harold Ford, III a man who's first impression screamed snob, know it all, nice taste in clothes.

Ford had Ralph's file open on the table in front of him. He immediately recognized him, obviously from his photo, and waved Ralph toward a chair. Ralph walked over and introduced himself, holding out his hand.

"Ralph Jackson, Mr. Ford."

"Of course," Ford said, sounding bored. He gently took Ralph's hand without rising and quickly released it.

"Please sit. I would offer you lunch," he said, "but I must tell you it's barely worth eating." He looked exasperated. "As you may know, I'm the Star Foundation Director for the entire Middle East. Because of the situation here, I, personally, have to come to this country and perform tasks not normally undertaken at my level. I've other pressing duties, so I'm sure you'll forgive me if I am brief."

Since Ralph was already certain he didn't like Mr. Ford, this sounded fine to him.

"Please proceed."

"Well," he said flipping through Ralph's folder, "you're not what we typically look for in a candidate, but given the conditions, you may fit in. That is, if you're accepted."

"Accepted? There was nothing in the materials about accepted. I thought I was already accepted."

"Accepted by the sponsor, the Judge you'll be working with. It's not in the literature because it's almost always a formality."

Ralph leaned back in his chair, gestured toward the waiter and said nothing. He looked up.

"Please continue Mr. Ford. I'm going to eat."

"Of course, of course. Your proposed advisee is one Isha Hami. She's recently been appointed Judge in South Baghdad District 17. This is a very significant matter for a woman to be appointed to such a position in a Muslim country, he said condescendingly.

"Really," Ralph said.

"Yes, quite. In fact, I must say I am of the opinion that she was a compromise between warring factions. Because she's a woman and a Christian, no doubt they think they'll be able to push her around. You know from your orientation in the States that the Star Foundation is here to reinforce newly emerging traditions of judicial independence."

What a pompous ass, Ralph said to himself.

"With this Judge in particular, you'll need to be supportive. Also, we would like you to watch her to ensure that her treatment of the Sunnis is fair. Her family suffered greatly under Saddam Hussein. Many members of her immediate and extended family were killed. In fact, her husband, son, and parents were all murdered by the Baathists. Finally, there are ugly rumors that she herself was physically mistreated in the worst possible ways."

Ralph sat there, wondering why he was being told this and wondering if the Star Foundation expected him to spy on his advisee. He decided to keep his concerns to himself.

"You see, there have been some problems with Judge Hami."

"What do you mean?"

"You're the, ah ... fourth candidate for the Judge. I'm afraid she has already rejected three prior advisors."

"What if she rejects me?"

"Of course, there are a number of other countries under the Star Program that could benefit ..."

"Wait! What do you mean other countries! I signed up for Iraq for a reason."

"Please lower your voice, Mr. Jackson."

Ford glanced around the bar and looked uncomfortable. Several tables of bar patrons had indeed interrupted their meals and were watching them. When a waiter started over he held up his hand, shrugged with a smile and then waved. The waiter broke off and conversation resumed in the bar. Ralph continued in a lower voice.

"Mr. Ford, I left a successful law practice, specifically to serve in Iraq. I was promised Iraq, I have no interest in serving anywhere else in your organization ..."

"I understand Mr. Jackson, although why you would want to serve in such a God forsaken area is beyond me. However, the other positions in Iraq have been filled by the other candidates, so ..."

"Move them, find me another Judge."

"There are no other positions available in the country and the other advisors have been working with their Sponsor or advisee for months now. It's impossible. Judge Hami hasn't rejected you yet and you'll be better prepared than the other candidates. Fore-warned is forearmed after all."

Ralph almost reached across the table and grabbed him. Instead, he took a sip of water and then the menu from the waiter.

"A bottle of Becks and a club sandwich. Thank you. Why did she reject the others?"

"She thought they didn't bring anything to the program."

"What do you mean?"

"Judge Hami sees herself as a formidable person. She comes from a very prestigious Christian tribe and family. After being educated in London at Cambridge as an undergraduate, she read for law at one the finest Inns of Court in London and then returned to Iraq. She married into another powerful Christian family, one with links to Tariq Aziz, and participated in the uprisings during the first gulf war.

"What do you mean, she participated in the uprisings?"

"Are you angry with me? You asked me . . ."

"Sorry. Please go on."

"As I started to say, she, her husband, son, and her extended fam-ily led armed citizens in battle against the Baathist army during the war. Once the American's signed the armistice, the uprising collapsed and the Special Republican Guards initiated a series of massive roundups. As I mentioned her family was decimated, she was jailed for some time before being released, and then she was forcibly relocated. Virtually abandoned, she somehow raised an orphaned grand-daughter and worked her way back into a position of prominence and respect in her own right. Much of this is based upon rumor and some very ugly rumors, but she is impressive. Although not as impressive as she seems to think," Ford sniffed.

"What does that have to do with the Star candidates?"

"She thinks they're all dilettantes."

"How so?"

"She said they were all, 'Successful lawyers who decided to move to Iraq and advise the same way they might take time off to climb Mount Everest,' or sail down the Danube, something like that."

"She said that?"

"In so many words, yes, and I don't see what's so funny. Are you really going to eat here," he asked.

"Of course I am. The Star Foundation is paying."

While Ford was busy looking aghast, Ralph was trying to decide how to dump him before meeting Judge Hami. He had no idea just how much damage the cretin had already done to his chances, but he did know he wasn't going him the opportunity to make it worse. Ralph had to convince the woman he was the right man to work with her for the next 18 to 36 months and the thought that her first impression of the Star Foundation was Harold Ford was sobering. It also might explain why the other candidates had failed to pass Hami's interview. Getting rid of Ford was the only shot he had. He decided to try to establish some rapport with Ford.

"For heaven's sake, I'm joking. If I'm going to live here, I'd better get used to the food."

"Ah," Ford said, "I see. I will not eat here unless it is unavoidable. Which brings me to my next issue."

"Please move right along," Ralph said, wanting out of the man's presence as soon as possible.

"Yes, well, I would like to leave tonight. I've already been here longer than planned . . . because of this one Judgeship. Don't get me wrong, I admire you for volunteering to serve in this place, but I find it horrid. Normally, as the Star Foundation representative, I would introduce you to the Judge at your three o'clock appointment tomorrow and assist you in the interview. If I do so, though, I'll have to spend another day in this dreadful hotel. I'll almost certainly have to eat more of this dreadful food. As I told you, I met Judge Hami last night, in fact, over dinner. She took me to one of the best restaurants in Baghdad, in her opinion, and it was horrid. The thought of repeating such an experience is not appealing. Is it at all possible that you can introduce yourself to the Judge and manage the interview process? I know after the problems with the other candidates that's not really fair, but it may actually help. On the one hand, you will miss out on my experience and relationship with the Judge, but on the other hand, you might appeal to her if you showed up by yourself. If you would be willing to do this, I would be eternally grateful and I could leave tonight instead of tomorrow. Regardless of how the interview goes, the Foundation remains committed to your room and board until we decide what to do next."

"Mr. Ford, a man of your taste and responsibilities would best serve the Star Foundation elsewhere, I am sure. Though I'll certainly miss the benefit of your guidance, as you said, that may work in my favor. I'll introduce myself to the Judge. For my part, you may leave tonight."

"You are a delightful man. So many of you require such hand holding. This is not something that I will forget, let me assure you. These," Ford said, "are packets of your reporting forms. You will see that for the most part, they ask open-ended questions. In the past, our counselors submitted essay type reports, which often did not address the areas of most concern to us. Rather than relying upon serendipitous reporting . . ."

What an ass, Ralph thought.

". . . we now prefer paragraph answers to these open-ended questions."

Ralph scanned the forms, noting questions such as: "Discuss your advisee's attitude and response toward being contacted by government officials regarding a pending case. How does your advisee deal with situations where he may have a conflict of interest because of past association, business or family ties? How have you addressed this issue with your advisee? How did your advisee respond to your advice?"

"As you can see, there are twelve of the three-page forms. In addition, there are twelve prepaid international overnight mailing envelopes addressed to my office. My staff will review your reports and advise you in writing as to any concerns we have or actions we would like you to take. At the end of your first year, either I or another representative will return for a more in-depth interview."

Just then the waiter arrived with Ralph's sandwich and bottle of beer.

"Of course," said Ford. "That strong beer will quickly erase the aftertaste of this horrid food. After all your courtesy to me, Mr. Jackson, I hope you'll forgive me if I take my leave now. I have to call for transportation and reserve a seat on tonight's plane. After that, I'll need to pack and get to the airport. Sitting here, contemplating my escape, I can't tell you how devastating it would be if I missed my chance because I was late."

Ralph stood up.

"Mr. Ford, leave me to my sandwich and I'll leave you to your plane."

Ford stood and shook his hand.

"I will not forget."

Ford scurried out of the dining room and out of sight. Ralph sat down, pleasantly surprised by his luck with Ford and with what was a delicious looking sandwich.

CHAPTER 13

———

THE TRAFFIC AT 2:00 P.M. was as light as it ever got in post-war Baghdad. Ralph sat in the back of an air-conditioned cab bobbing and weaving its way between the other vehicles. He'd tossed and turned most of the night, worrying about how he'd handle the interview with Hami and what he'd do if he didn't get the position. When he finally drifted off, just before dawn, he suffered through one of the most disturbing variants of his As Salman nightmare. His new friend Kalib the driver had been nowhere to be found, so Ralph had the apartment manager call for a cab. In addition to the fare, it cost another $5.00, U.S., for the taxicab driver to turn off his "ying yang, ching chang," music.

Money well spent, Ralph thought.

As the road bent closer to the river, he gazed out to the far bank. Construction cranes sprouted everywhere and new buildings seemed like forest trees, struggling for room to grow. The view was quite different from the intelligence and satellite photos he had seen in the '90s or from the pre-war video feeds on Fox.

Another example of the American imperialists exploiting the Iraqis for oil, he thought.

His cab rolled to a stop in front of a barricade manned by the US Army. An up-armored Humvee was parked nearby, its machine gun covering the cab as two American paratroopers strolled up to the vehicle.

"Names, IDs and your purpose," said a no-nonsense sergeant.

Ralph handed over his U.S. passport, his driver's license, and a letter of introduction to Judge Hami on Star Foundation letterhead. He'd known better than to bring the gun.

"What's your business here, sir?"

"I'm meeting with Judge Isha Hami. I'm an adviser appointed to give her a western perspective on the judicial system."

"Have you ever met this driver before?"

"No, why?"

"Did you tell someone where you were going before they called your cab?"

"I might have told the hotel manager at the Star Foundation boarding house," Ralph said. "I'm not sure."

"Okay, sir. We can do this one of two ways. If you don't mind, you can get out and walk across to the Ministry on your own. If we let your cab any closer, we will have to roust it first."

"I'll just walk."

After he got out and paid the driver, one of the other paratroopers searched his backpack and flipped through the legal supplies and Star Foundation info and released him. Ralph crossed the barricade and walked into an area of the street where traffic was blocked off by concrete Jersey barriers.

The Ministry was housed in a three-story building constructed of cut and dressed stones whitewashed so brightly they almost hurt the eye to look at. Four deep concrete steps were stacked on top of each other in a half moon shape, arcing from one side of the building to the other. A four-pillared porch supported a porch roof and the roof supported a brass lamp at the end of a chain. The building was topped with a medieval parapet. Calligraphy was etched into the wall just below the roof line and ran all the way around the building. The lamp was a little worn, but otherwise the building was tiredly majestic.

Ralph mounted the steps under the gaze of the two Iraqi guards who nodded and warned him in English, "Security check inside, sir."

Ralph swung his backpack off his shoulder and stepped inside, waiting for his eyes readjust to the gloom.

"Over here sir," a third Iraqi policeman called out in passable English. His bags were competently checked at a nearby security station while a fourth guard ran an electronic wand over him.

"Where can I find Judge Isha Hami's courtroom," Ralph asked.

Both men scrutinized him a second time.

"Second floor," the first officer said, pointing to a wide marble staircase. "At the top of the stairs, make a left. The third door down on the left opens into the Judge's secretary's office. Do you have an appointment?"

"Yes, I'm her Star Foundation adviser."

Without waiting for a response, Ralph turned for the staircase. The policeman picked up a telephone and spoke into it in rapid Arabic.

"No doubt my introduction," Ralph thought.

Ralph wound up the staircase, impressed by the architecture and construction. This wasn't one of Saddam or his cronies' personal buildings, so it was less extravagant than the many palaces dotting the country. Since Hussein had crappy taste the building, meant to be functional, was actually classic. Ralph liked it and liked the idea of working in it.

"Decent security too," he thought, reaching the third floor. He found Hami's office right where they said it would be and knocked. A female voice said something in Arabic that Ralph decided meant, "Come on in." So he did.

He was caught in the crossfire of two stares. The Arab women were smiling, glancing at each other sideways and Ralph thought maybe winked. The woman seated at the desk was obviously Hami's secretary. Ralph just knew the second woman, standing, was Judge Isha Hami. He waved to the secretary, but his gaze was drawn toward Hami. She was remarkable. At about 5 ft. 7 inches, she stood tall for an Arab woman. Her short Star Foundation biography said she was 66 years of age, but Ralph decided she couldn't have been a day over 50. The Judge was still a very attractive woman. Ralph and Hami stared at each other for a moment, both suddenly solemn.

When Ralph broke the spell and approached, Hami held out her hand, Western-style. She looked him in the eye as they shook.

"You're rather young, are you not?"

"Everyone says that your Honor, but I'm older than . . ."

"I hope not, because we're not running a nursery here."

Without giving him a chance to reply, she turned on heel and marched into her office, forcing him to follow. Hami's Secretary snickered behind his back. As Ralph followed her they passed a glass-panned inner door that projected a reflection of the Judge. She had a small, good-natured smile on her face. In spite of himself, Ralph grinned.

"Sit, sit," she said, moving behind her desk. The smile was gone and the side chair was on the decrepit side. "Mr. Jackson . . ."

"Ralph, please."

"We'll see about that. As I was saying, Mr. Jackson, I'm not enthusiastic about the idea of someone who's never been to my country, especially one so young . . . looking . . . advising me how to run my Courtroom and how to apply the law."

"Your Honor, I don't see my role as telling you . . ."

"I do wish you would stop interrupting me, Mr. Jackson. I agreed with my government to give this program a chance and I hope I am a woman of my word. I also thought the staff grants from Starr to my secretary and some others would improve their lives, but it's just not to be."

Hami stood up and extended her hand toward him. Ralph could almost hear the screams from future nightmares and knew this was his only chance. He panicked.

"Judge, please. I have to have this position and I have been here before. I do know your country and I'm not here on a vacation or on a whim, its, it's a matter of survival."

He was shocked how the words tumbled out of his mouth, how his voice quivered, that he was so desperate. He knew he'd lost his chance. No Judge wanted a basket case around. He sagged in his chair and waited to be dismissed again. Instead, Hami sat down and appraised him for what seemed like a long time.

"All right, Ralph. If it's a matter of survival, I'll at least hear you out. Tell me why it's matter of survival and why you want to be here."

"I was a soldier in the first gulf war and I served here, in Iraq, working and fighting with Iraqis. Shias. I can't tell you a lot of the details, they're still classified Judge, and . . . I hope I'm a man of my word, too, but bad things happened."

"Bad things happened to a lot of us in that war, Ralph."

"I know your Honor, but I caused some of the bad things."

"Go on," Hami said. She was now sitting up and leaning over her desk.

"I tried to protect, to help some of your people, Judge, and it all went horribly wrong. Maybe I wasn't thinking right, maybe I was too eager to fight the Bath. I'd seen some of what they'd done to people and I wanted to fight them. Maybe too much."

Ralph pointed over to a water pitcher.

"Can I, I mean I don't normally do this."

Hami nodded, so he got up, went to a nearby table and poured himself a glass of water. His hand was shaking as he poured and a little water ran off the side of the glass onto the table top. Ralph glanced back, but Hami made no sign. He took a quick slurp of the cool water and walked back to his chair, wiping his chin where some of it had run down.

"In the twelve years since I was last here, I haven't had an uninterrupted night's sleep. The nightmares started the night after . . . the mistakes I made. At first, I could handle it. I got out of the Army and went to school, so the fact I couldn't sleep right was something I could work around. I scheduled my classes so I could sleep for two or three hours, then wake-up, sweating and shaking. Since I was wide awake, I'd study or eat, go to a class and then fall back asleep, exhausted. The next day, I did it all again, three years of college and then three years of law school."

"How have you been managing for the last, what seven years? Since you left school?   Did your dreaming, your nightmares improve?"

"No. I had to start working for myself as a lawyer and for a while it was tough, but I got used to it. I overcompensated and pretty soon I was doing good. Lack of sleep will make you mean Judge, and I was so afraid of not being prepared, I just used coffee and willpower, maybe fear more than willpower. I did car accident cases, big ones, and I won two or three large verdicts."

"What about the rest of your life, friends, family, did you get married?"

"I guess I really only had part of a life. Except for my family, I'm not close to anyone. My only real social activity was coaching my nephew's soccer team."

"An American coaching soccer? What about American football?"

For the first time, Ralph smiled and spoke with obvious pride.

"You should have seen these guys. They were small and young but they played hard and earned a 7-0-1 record against older, bigger kids."

No one said anything for a few seconds, so Ralph took another drink of water and waited. Hami waited him out, so he went on.

"My closest friend was a 12-year-old collie-dog that I had to put down right before I decided to come back. I really don't have any other friends, except my brothers. My girlfriends last an average of a month and a half. My greatest joy in life, next to peewee soccer, is making people look like fools on a witness stand."

Hami smiled at him and asked, "What about professional help?"

"Psychiatrists?"

Hami raised her eyebrows.

"I will not soak my brain in drugs and I will not blabber like a fool to another fool while I'm stretched out on a couch. I'm a WASP, your Honor . . ."

Ralph hesitated, but Hami was already smiling at him.

"That means White Anglo . . ."

"I went to school in London, Ralph, and I know what 'WASP' stands for. And . . . I'm flattered that you don't think I'm a fool."

"WASPs don't believe in drugs and psychiatrists, we believe in alcohol and bartenders. I'm blabbering now because it's the truth and because . . . I need to stay here because trying to make amends for the last time . . . it's the only thing left I know to do and, well, you're the last ticket in town, Judge."

"Hmm, I'm the last ticket. I don't mean to be critical, but you should think about working on your interviewing skills."

"A lot of people say that."

"What was the final straw, what made you decide to apply to this program and come back here?"

"I started to think I could go on like I had been forever. But one night I really crashed and it scared the hell out of me."

"What?"

"I won a big case, the largest jury verdict in my career, so I stopped off to celebrate with some of my staff. I was drinking pretty hard, but around midnight, when the party broke up, I went home when everyone else did. That night I was really afraid to go to sleep, sick of the nightmares, so I got dressed and went back out, 'for a nightcap'. The nightcap expanded into ten nightcaps and I went from bar to bar for the next four or five days, I can never remember, drinking, passing out at tables, waking up, ordering bar food and drinking again. Eventually, I ended up in a big brawl, injured several of the patrons and . . . a police officer . . . and got myself thrown in jail."

"I suppose that would do it."

Ralph was thinking about the first nightmare, where he woke up with his pistol in his hand. For years he had nightmares where he couldn't keep from putting a gun to his head, but he never actually had a gun in his hand before. It scared the crap out of him. He had no recollection of grabbing the gun and couldn't account for his blistering headache. Until the next time. The next time, he woke up, again with the pistol in his hand, but he was grinding the barrel into his temple. His head ached and he realized it wasn't the first time it had happened. He thought about getting rid of his guns, but disarming himself was against his nature. He wasn't sure what to do. He'd heard of sleepwalking, but sleep suicide?

"It wasn't just that, Judge, it was also the fact that I couldn't remember any of it. I was trained to . . . anyway, I know how to hurt people and if I started doing stuff like that . . . someone was going to get hurt, bad. One way or another, I knew I had to deal with As Salman. But how? This is the thing I could think of."

"As Salman? That small town in the southwest desert? Can you prove any of this?"

"Why in God's name would I make up something like this?"

"Mr. Jackson, can you prove any of this?"

"Yes, your Honor. I can show you my Starr packet, including the applications and the recommendation from the District Attorney who handled the criminal charges. He gave me a recommendation anyway. His phone number is in there."

"In where?"

Ralph pointed to the floor where his backpack lay. Isha and Ralph stared at each other for a few seconds.

"Anything else?"

Ralph decided not to mention the part about the pistol magically rising to his head.

"No, ma'am."

"Let me see the papers."

He handed over photocopies of the entire application packet he'd submitted to Starr. Hami took her time reviewing it and paused more than once to take notes.

"The District Attorney says he reviewed your military record."

"I read that too," Ralph said with a smile. "I told you my Iraq service is classified and it is. Unless the DA got elected to Congress and put on an intelligence committee, he didn't review my military record. Maybe he saw part of it."

"Perhaps you may actually be of use here," Hami said. "You seem to have seen your share of pain and loss. Assuming this checks out, I . . . Come, don't be angry with me, I actually do believe you. Some say I am a good Judge of character. You and I might grow to be friends."

"Your Honor, I'm not here to make friends" Ralph replied, still stinging from the insult. "Besides, I've found friendship to be overrated."

"Well then, why don't you instead begin to instruct me in the wisdom of Western jurisprudence so that all may be milk and honey here in my battle-scarred land? We have an interesting case here already."

"We?"

"Assuming you're not lying, in which case I will throw you into jail on charges of making an Iraqi Judge look like one of those fools you're so afraid of associating with. Anyway, on Tariq Street, last month a "former" Baathist political officer, Akmed Amani, a Sunni, was allegedly murdered by four Shia men after he allegedly installed and later detonated an IED."

The improvised explosive device, Ralph knew, was hated by the Iraqis almost as much as by the American soldiers.

"So they caught him in the act?

"No, of course nothing that simple or I wouldn't need your Western insight."

"Come on, Judge," Ralph said interrupting her.

She smiled, nodded, and continued.

"The device was located and exploded right near where Amani was seen loitering earlier in the day. Remember, Tariq is a Shia section of Baghdad. In addition to killing one of the soldiers and wounding two others, it blew off the leg and arm of a small girl returning home from the market. She survived, but will be disfigured and crippled for the rest of her life." Isha sighed. "Her father, an uncle, and two cousins went to this man's apartment, pulled him into the street and beat him to death. Most or all of this was witnessed by an American patrol from the same unit that suffered the casualties from the IED. They arrived sometime during or right after the attack. There's some question as to how aggressively they intervened. The Army is conducting a parallel investigation."

"How did this case end up assigned to you, your Honor?"

"The cases are assigned according to a lottery system in the Clerk of Court's office. Your American soldiers are involved in it. They use a large wire basket with slips of paper. They spin the basket and pull out numbers. The numbers correspond with certain cases. Why do you ask?"

"Trying to get my bearings, Judge."

"In that case, why don't we review some of the other cases currently on my assignment list. I have an idea from Mr. Ford what the Star Foundation expects from our relationship, but I would be interested to know what you expect."

Isha pulled out a clipboard from her desk drawer and ran down her case list. Case-by-case, she went down the list in chronological order, describing the type of case, her initial impressions, how long she thought the trial would last, how many witnesses would testify and whether or not there were any novel legal questions. She had thirty three active cases and Ralph was impressed, not only with the Judge's diligence but with what appeared to be her acute legal insight. Maybe she was bluffing, but until he had a chance to find out more about the cases, he wouldn't know.

Isha returned to her earlier question about what Ralph's expectations were of their relationship.

"Also, I am still curious why you wanted to know how I ended up with the terrorist case. Let me be frank. I suspect that you've heard I have reason to hate the Baathists. You know enough to know that these are Sunnis. You wonder if I arranged to have the case assigned to my docket and wonder if I can be fair and impartial in a trial that features Shias killing a Sunni Baathists who murdered a little girl."

"You're half right, your Honor. I didn't mean to imply you arranged to have the case assigned to your court. I am, of course, curious to know if there is manipulation or potential manipulation of case assignments. But suspect you of doing the manipulation yourself? No. I do wonder if you can be impartial under this set of facts. I also wonder whether or not you would recuse yourself if you weren't sure."

For the next hour and a half, Isha and Ralph discussed the law, Iraq, the future of Iraq and the future of their relationship. Ralph discovered Isha agreed she had prejudices and biases, especially as they applied to the Sunni Bath, but was determined to compensate for them. In her opinion, without fairness toward the Bath and self-restraint on the part of the Shias in power, there was no hope for the country. She wanted to set an example for other Judges and law enforcement officials.

"Just let me be clear, without being rude, Mr. Jackson. I am willing to accept your presence in my Court in exchange for Star Foundation grants, but you are not my boss."

"I understand that Ma'am. You know how badly I need this position, but I will report what I find, and not you, the Iraqi police, the Provisional Authority or the terrorists will dissuade me from my job."

That was as testy as it got. Afterward, they were swapping amusing antidotes and laughing aloud. As they parted company with a handshake, Ralph found himself very impressed with Isha. For her part, the Judge decided she liked this Ralph Jackson fellow.

"Tomorrow," both thought, "will be the first day of work."

Unbeknownst to Hami, she was followed home that evening by determined men.

CHAPTER 14

———◆———

RALPH JACKSON WITNESSED THE DAY Judge Isha Hami's life took a turn for the worse. Neither of them knew it at the time, but it began in the old Baathist Court Room Isha had taken to hear cases. The room was impressive but unfortunately situated in a section of the Ministry Building that received direct sunlight during the hottest part of the day. The Provisional Authority installed powerful window unit air conditioners, but the large room remained hot and uncomfortable.

People entered Isha's Court by what would appear to Americans to be an old-style schoolroom door, the kind made of light-colored wood with a small window. If anyone should happen to peer in, they would see rows of seats for the spectators, ending in a three foot high railing or "bar" dividing the public seats from the rest of the room. In the center of the railing, two small gates were hung to allow easy entry. The lawyers, witnesses, and court personnel entered the back of the courtroom along with the rest of the public, but then passed through the gates, past the bar and into seats in front of the Judge's dais. A large round clock was mounted over top of the public entrance door for the Judge's convenience.

Ralph, lawyer though he was, sat in the public seating area, back against the wall. To his right, the air conditioners struggled mightily and he felt his eyes growing heavy. During the last case, he'd fought against the heat, the monotonous hum from the a/c units and the monotonous lies from the witness stand with limited success. That case involved a contract dispute between merchants in the Baghdad market. He'd forced himself to lean forward and pay attention.

There'd be no trouble staying awake for this one, though. In front of the bar, three Arab men in western style suits sat at a large table alongside four other Iraqis in prison garb and shackles. Two prosecutors and a uniformed Iraqi policeman were seated at a second table to their right. Everyone rose as Isha entered her Courtroom, sat on a tall leather chair and looked over the parties.

"Be seated. The case currently before us is the Republic of Iraq vs. Abdul, Habib, Aziz, and Abdul. Mr. Prosecutor?"

Ralph and his interpreter had already agreed the interpreter would spare the American the long, sometimes confusing Arab names. The interpreter shortened things for Ralph, who could see the names of the parties and witnesses if he wanted by using an abstract of Court information transcribed into English ahead of time.

"Thank you, your honor. The people call police officer."

"Very well, have him sworn."

The police officer walked to an elevated witness box beside Isha's raised dais or "bench." Off to the side, an Iraqi flag hung limp from a wooden pole. The Officer stood long enough to take an oath before God, to tell the truth that violated several U.S. Supreme Court decisions, then sat ramrod straight in a spartanly constructed wooden chair.

"Please state your name, occupation, and location on October 26, 2003."

"My name is police officer . . . and I'm a law-enforcement officer with the Provisional Authority of the Republic of Iraq. I was so employed on October 26, 2003. On that day, I received radio instructions to report to the scene of a riot in a Shia section of Baghdad. Upon my arrival, I saw that a U.S. Army patrol had already arrived and that other police vehicles were arriving. A large crowd had gathered."

"What happened next?"

"I got out of my vehicle and ran to an American Army Captain who was gesturing to me. He was trying to placate the crowd while keeping them away from something. His men were in a circle, surrounded by the crowd. Their weapons were slung and they used their hands to hold back the crowd. Everyone began shouting at me, 'Don't let them protect a killer, that man's a killer.' I couldn't see it at first, but they were pointing to a body in the middle of the Americans. And that's when I saw an Iraqi civilian lying in the middle of the circle of US soldiers."

"What was his condition?"

"I'm not sure if he was still alive. If he was he didn't live for long. His clothes were in shreds, both of his arms and legs were bent back in the opposite direction and he was covered with blood. He wasn't making any noise, and with those injuries ... if you were still alive you would have been making noise. The crowd wasn't sure though. Everyone was screaming, there must of been a hundred people, and it was like being in the middle of a sandstorm. Captain Jones said a hurricane and had to explain to me. I agreed with him." The policeman smiled.

"Objection your honor, does the policeman think this is funny," asked the youngest looking of the defense attorneys.

"Overruled, continue."

"Go on, officer."

"Overruled? Overruled?" A second Attorney, also named Habib, had bolted to his feet and was almost screaming at the Judge.

Isha turned from the witness to defense counsel, gazing at them over top of her reading glasses.

"I will say this one-time counsel. I treat everyone in my court-room with respect and civility. Everyone in my courtroom will treat me with respect and civility. Sit down. Proceed, Mr. Prosecutor."

The look Isha flashed the attorney froze him where he stood. The third lawyer, a grim-faced older man, reached up and grabbed the back of the other's suit jacket and pulled. The lawyer collapsed into his seat.

"Officer, continue."

"I was just trying to tell the Court it was like being in a storm. I had to shout at the American officer to be heard above the crowd. I asked what happened and he said he arrived..."

"Objection your honor," rang out once again in Isha's court-room. This time, however, it was the third, older defense lawyer who'd spoken. He'd stood, buttoned his jacket and respectfully waited until Hami addressed him.

"What's the basis of your objection counselor?"

"Your Honor, I object to what will certainly be hearsay testimony from this police officer. Based upon documents we've received from the government, this witness will say the Americans saw my four clients kill this Baathist terrorist. The Iraqi government has had plenty of notice when this hearing would take place. Nevertheless, not even one of the American soldiers is here to testify, first-hand, as to what he saw. I cannot cross-examine a man who is not here. My clients are on trial for murder. This policeman should not be allowed to testify for someone who is not here. Thank you, your honor."

"Mr. Prosecutor I must tell you I'm also concerned about the absence of any soldiers from," Isha looked at her notes. "The Alpha company patrol." She switched to English. "I see a representative of the American military here. JAG corps, I believe?"

"Your honor, I must respectfully object," the old defense lawyer said. "It is the government's duty to make their case, not your Honor."

"You are correct, within certain parameters, counsel." She switched to English again.

"Major?"

"Your honor," the American officer said, standing. "I was ordered to attend this hearing with my interpreter and report the outcome to my superiors. I don't have any information on the whereabouts of the U.S. military personnel."

"I understand Major. Nevertheless, the Court suggests you report to your superiors that if they have any interest, in this case, proceeding they might wish to confer with the Iraqi government regarding the location of these individuals."

"Your Honor, I must ....."

"Overruled, Counsel. I understand your position, but I will not allow a murder case to be dismissed unless all other avenues have been exhausted. Both sides are entitled to justice."

"Your Honor," the prosecutor spoke, "this proceeding before the Court is only to determine if there is reasonable evidence to proceed against these men. We understand our duty to produce the soldiers if they are available at the time of trial. We request the Court issue subpoenas for the personnel identified in the reports we submitted to the Court. In the meantime, your Honor certainly has the power to consider this officer's testimony as to what he was told and make a preliminary determination as to its factual sufficiency."

"Your Honor, I renew my objection. If you listened to closely to the prosecutor, as I know you did, he said he had a duty to produce these men at trial quote if they are available closed quote. Your Honor, the government is not even pretending to know if these men will be available for trial. Therefore it's improper to entertain this Officer's testimony under these circumstances."

"Nevertheless, counsel, again, your clients are charged with murder. Therefore, the Court is obligated to give the government a chance to prove its case, given this unique time in our country's history. But, Mr. Prosecutor, the defense makes a powerful argument. I'll issue subpoenas to each and every member of the Alpha company patrol you listed in your reports. But it is your obligation, Mr. Prosecutor, not only to have the subpoenas prepared for my signature but to serve them upon the appropriate American unit commander. Do we understand each other, counsel?"

"Yes, ma'am."

"Very well. Proceed with your witness."

The old defense lawyer sat down thinking, "Your Honor, you have just signed your death warrant."

"Officer, please tell the Court what happened next."

"Captain Jones told me that as they arrived on the scene, they saw the four defendants in the center of a circle of other Iraqis. These four were kicking the terrorist, one was standing on his arm while another one pulled it up, and the others were stomping on his legs. The Americans were eventually able to surround the man and keep the crowd away until we arrived."

"Did you establish the identity of the man who died as a result of this attack?'

"Yes. His name was Akmed Amani."

"Do you see the men Captain Jones identified as the murders in the courtroom?"

"The four men are the Defendants sitting at the defense table with their lawyers."

"No further questions your honor."

Isha looked at the defense table. "Counsel?"

"Subject to my objection your honor, I have a few questions. The dead man's name was Akmed Amani, correct?"

"Yes."

"Amani was a Baathist security officer, wasn't he?"

"Objection!"

"Overruled, answer officer."

"Yes."

"In your duties as a police officer, have you ever known of Baathists, especially security officers to be attacked or killed by other Iraqi's, especially Shias?"

"Yes."

"This incident occurred in a Shia section of Baghdad, correct?"

"Yes."

"And you testified that at least one hundred people, Shia's, surrounded Amani's body when you arrived."

"Well, the Americans ... yes."

"You didn't see any of the attack on the terrorist, did you officer."

"No."

"Did anyone except for the Americans tell you what happened?"

"No."

"Isn't it a fact that for all you know the Americans may have been told what happened by someone in the mob who didn't like my clients and the Americans just wanted to impress you?"

"Objection!"

"Overruled."

"That's not what happened."

"How do you know, you weren't there? Did you ask the Americans if they were told what had happened by Arabs in the mob?"

"No. I didn't have to because . . ."

"So you don't know."

"They said they were there and . . ."

"But I can't ask them, can I Officer, because they're not here?"

"Objection."

"Sustained."

"No further questions your honor. However, I do renew my motion to exclude this testimony and move to dismiss the charges."

"Very well," Isha said. "I find sufficient evidence, in this case, to hold the matter for trial. I know that does not please the defense and your motion is denied at this time Counselor. Let me remind the Prosecutor that the defense makes a strong argument and it is in the government's interest to produce the Americans at the time of trial."

Isha effortlessly switched to English.

"Finally, Major, advise your superiors that my Court will be issuing subpoenas for American soldiers and we would be grateful and expect that our subpoenas are honored by the provisional authority. This proceeding is closed." She banged her gavel and stood to leave.

Glancing down at his yellow legal pad, Ralph flipped back the pages to a four-page Star Foundation evaluation questionnaire he'd hidden underneath. Part of his job, after all, was to evaluate Hami's performance on the bench. He checked off "outstanding," or "exceeds expectations" on every evaluation question. The short-answer questions could wait. When he looked up the younger defense lawyer was speaking again. Isha stopped at the side of her chair.

"Is there anything else you would like to add, Mr. Habib?"

Habib was still talking and his voice rose as he stood. He gestured once toward the Judge. When he continued his rant, the Judge raised an eyebrow. The older defense lawyer stood again and cut off his colleague in mid-sentence.

"Your Honor, excuse my co-counsel. He is young. We have nothing further to say."

Perhaps sensing his peril, Habib closed his mouth and stared at the floor. It was too late. Three bailiffs were on their way to the defense table. As the first bailiff approached, Habib sat.

Isha surveyed her Court Room, considering the situation. The bailiffs hovered above the motionless Habib, waiting. The room was dead silent. Isha let the lawyer twist in the wind for a long sixty seconds before she spoke.

"Very well. We are adjourned for the day."

Still stone-faced, she winked at Ralph, turned and left. Ralph stood until she was gone, thanked his interpreter and walked back to her chambers.

The three defense lawyers left the Court Room, heading in separate directions. They all had their cell phones out. The oldest defense attorney placed a call to Ayad al-Jaberi, letting him know the murder case would proceed. He listened for a few moments and then spoke again.

"No, I am afraid it is even worse than that. Even if the Americans are willing to ignore her subpoenas, I'm not sure if the case will be dismissed. She may decide that if the Americans refuse to honor the subpoenas, she's justified allowing the hearsay evidence. I cannot predict what this Judge will do. She's very skilled and will find a legal justification to do whatever she wants. Yes, sir." He hung up.

Not even a block away, the younger, fiery lawyer Habib called his cousin, who, in turn, for a fee, provided a satellite phone hookup to another "sat" phone far north in the Kurdish autonomous zone. The young lawyer didn't have the same uncertainty as to how Isha would proceed as did his older colleague. The men on the other end said nothing while Habib talked except, "I understand, go on." When Habib had finished, the connection was abruptly cut at the Kurdish end without a word.

Thus, the fuse was lit.

Meanwhile, Ralph entered Isha's outer chambers, smiled at her Secretary and followed the Judge into her office. She was just hanging up her black robe when Ralph came in and took one of the side chairs.

"Ralph, were we boring you in there with the merchants," she asked. Isha was referring to the first case of the day and ignoring the murder case.

"Listening to that case is like slow death, Isha. The merchant's such a poor liar I don't know how you put up with it. He agreed to rent the stall when he thought he would gain advantages from the Americans. As soon as it became clear he wouldn't, he broke his deal."

"A slow death is better than a fast one my friend, just ask the dead," she smiled. "You're a natural born advocate, Ralph. Someday, when you are much older, you might even become a good Judge. Because I agree with you, I had to be even more careful than normal. Remember this Ralph, even people who know they're in the wrong and broke the law must feel they had a fair chance. If they did feel they had a fair chance, that their side was heard, their pride will not be as damaged as it would if we immediately branded them a "liar." Some people, when they've obviously done wrong, are impressed when they're still given a chance to defend themselves. The system of justice itself, even when it works against someone, can help enforce the law in the future. It can do so by showing wrongdoers what fairness is. It can show them an example of how to act."

"I'll think about that, but you made up for the first hearing with the second one. Are you really going to stop the government from trying its case if they can't produce the witnesses?"

Isha ignored the question. "How did I do today?"

Ralph took the questionnaire from underneath his legal pad and slid it across her desk. She glanced down and slid it back.

"Why don't you join Naba and I for dinner?"

Ralph was taken aback.

"I would like that very much, your Honor."

"It's the same everywhere. Promise a man a meal and suddenly I'm 'your Honor' again." She smiled. "I'll have my driver take you home afterward."

Ralph and Isha continued to argue about the law as they walked to the rear parking garage. Judge Hami's Provisional Authority supplied Ford Explorer pulled up and they climbed in the back, still talking.

"Hussein, my Star Foundation friend will be joining Naba and me for dinner. Would you or another driver be available to take him home?"

"Of course, Judge. Good evening, Mr. Jackson."

"Hello, Hussein. Thank you for the inconvenience in advance."

Hussein looked at Ralph in the rearview mirror, nodded and smiled. The driver was a member of Judge Hami's extended family, provided to her by her family. Although Isha and her husband's family were both ambivalent about women Judges, it was an honor a family member was appointed and a family obligation to protect her. Hussein was one of thirty clan members who came north, along with their families, in order to serve as courthouse staff under Judge Hami. All these extended family members were paid from Provisional Authority coffers. Nevertheless, it was American money well spent. Nowhere else would a judicial official receive such service, security, and loyalty in 2004 Baghdad.

They resumed their conversation as they drove out of the immediate ministry area. Around them, the quality of the houses and surrounding structures in the neighborhoods deteriorated. At first, all the buildings were a uniformly muddy cocoa color. Most appeared to have been built in the early 1920s with questionable construction materials. But the scenery changed while they talked and the Explorer drove out of the more densely populated areas of the city. The buildings were not so densely packed and idled construction cranes were visible, dotting the skyline throughout the city.

By the time they left Baghdad proper, urban sprawl gave way to fields under cultivation. Palm trees were everywhere. Ralph noticed the line of cultivation was limited to an area bordering the river. The vegetation ended abruptly, as though God had laid down a ruler and then used a gigantic razor to neatly trim the Tigris' green beard. The visual effect was striking, bright blue water, then lush green vegetation, followed by light yellow sand and dirt. The terrain lay like a huge multi-colored ribbon of cloth and ran off into the distance.

Soon after they passed through the last of the vegetation, they entered a medium-sized village on the outskirts of Baghdad. Here even the most humble homes were vastly superior in quality to those surrounding the Justice Ministry. More walled courtyards were seen. There were even trees and other vegetation visible from the road. While Isha talked, Ralph listened and watched the buildings become increasingly more attractive and well-constructed. Eventually, they entered a residential area that was clearly upscale. Instead of cinder block, brick and mud brick, these buildings were made with fire-brick tile exteriors. Likewise, the roofs were made of the corrugated red tile that reflected the sun in shimmers. Soon, bright white stone buildings and homes dotted the streets. Hussein guided the Explorer down one of the side streets onto a hard packed dirt driveway. At the end of the twenty-foot drive was a carport. Kind of. That's how Ralph thought of it, anyway. Hussein drove into the carport and turned off the engine.

Across the street, they were observed through binoculars by vigilant eyes. Their time of arrival and the number of vehicle occupants was dutifully noted.

"Welcome to my home," Isha said.

As Ralph approached the door he noticed a large ceramic tile actually bricked into the wall and covered with flowing calligraphy.

"Verses from the Bible," said Isha. "Be still and know that I am God."

Ralph nodded, he hoped respectfully. As he glanced around the kitchen, he saw a plate on the counter braced in an upright position by a small wooden easel. It too was covered with calligraphy, again Ralph assumed, from the Bible.

"Normally Iraqis entertain in formal living rooms, but since you are American I thought we would eat out on the patio."

The home was a clean, pleasing mixture of the old and the new. Although the kitchen was equipped with appliances, they'd been manufactured in Iraq or imported from other Middle Eastern countries. The design and function of the stove and refrigerator reminded Ralph of the 1950s. On the other hand, the Judge had several smaller appliances on her kitchen counter. Ralph saw a modern blender, a coffee pot, a microwave oven, and what appeared to be a mixing bowl with an electric mixer hanging over it. All these appliances could have been taken directly out of a kitchen in New York or Pittsburgh.

"I hoped that you would accept my invitation, so, I took the liberty of providing Kibi, Shish Kabob with some vegetables, and pita bread for dinner. The Kibi and Shish Kabob I've prepared. The bread, I'm afraid, I purchased at market. Do you know Kibi?"

"Actually, I do Judge. And I must say it is a favorite."

"I'm glad I chose correctly. I know how much you hate Chickpeas's so only Naba and I will have peas. I made the Kibi from lamb slaughtered this morning while I waited in the market. The same is true of the meat on the shish kabobs. The vegetables are fresh as well. Finally, at the risk of my reputation, I spoke to an American soldier on our security detail. He kind enough to purchase a number of bottles of beer on my behalf."

Isha walked over to her Ozzie and Harriet refrigerator and pulled open the door. Inside were a least six bottles of European beer, obviously cold.

"Have one. I will have a chilled tea."

Ralph reached over and took the beer Isha handed him. Twisting off the bottle cap, he lifted the bottle to his lips and took a long drink. Finishing, he looked at Isha with a broad smile.

"Just one more example of your judicious nature and keen intellect. I would have expected no less than . . ."

———◆———

Ralph stopped in mid-sentence and Isha followed his gaze to the other side of the kitchen. Naba, Isha's eleven-year-old granddaughter, stood at the entryway in a pale yellow cotton dress, clutching a bundle of rags to her chest. At one time, Ralph decided, the bundle of rags was almost certainly a doll. He shifted his glance from the rags back to the child's face. She had huge, almond shaped eyes and long black hair. She looked at him, unblinkingly, with the most solemn gaze he had ever seen from someone her age.

"Naba, this is my friend Ralph."

"I told her that I thought you'd be coming for dinner this evening. She speaks a little English, but struggles. From time to time I'll break off in Arabic and explain parts of our conversation to her. Please don't be offended. The doll was a gift to Naba from her mother, purchased before she was born. She values it, though it's not much more than rags."

"Welcome, Ralph. My name is Naba. I am very pleased to meet you."

Though she'd spoken haltingly, Naba's gaze had never wandered from Ralph's face. She no longer looked quite so solemn, but instead intrigued.

"Thank you, Naba. My name is Ralph as you know. I hope we can be friends."

"You're eyes are blue like the sky. It is like there is only air in your head behind them."

Both Isha and Ralph burst out laughing. Naba went from intrigued to injured in a microsecond. She was on the verge of tears, certain that Isha and Ralph were laughing at her. Before Isha could stop him or even say anything, Ralph closed the distance to Naba and dropped to one knee in front of her. Isha was astounded by how quickly he moved. Before she could say, "Wait Ralph," he put his hand on Naba's shoulder. To Isha's surprise, Naba didn't scream, cry or run away. She didn't even flinch. She'd always been very shy with strangers, especially men. Isha held her breath.

"Naba, I am sorry. My laughing was not to make fun of you or because you said anything wrong. In my language, the way you described my eyes is a very funny joke on me. Except that we upset you, I am very glad that you said what you said. I like to laugh and the best jokes are always the ones on yourself. That way, you know no one's feelings were hurt."

"Really?"

Naba stopped sobbing and looked at her grandmother. She asked two or three questions in Arabic and finally began to smile.

She looked at Ralph.

"Now I understand. If only sky is behind your eyes, it could mean you are empty-headed. Grandmother says Americans call such people 'airheads.' Are sky heads the same as airheads? Please know that I did not mean to insult you."

Naba's English was a little hard to follow, but he got it.

"Naba, I am not insulted. I thank you for the joke."

"Why don't you take Ralph to the patio," Isha said. "Ralph, take your beer and follow Naba. I'll prepare the food and bring it outside. We have a small. . . barbecue you might call it. We can cook there."

Naba reached up, took Ralph's hand and lead him out of the kitchen, chattering in broken English. Ralph followed her out with a big smile on his face. Isha began preparing the meal and re-running the last five minutes through her mind. She had never seen Naba interact with someone new so openly. Humming, she brought out the food and began to cook while they all talked. When the food was ready, Isha said grace and they ate.

The rest of the evening was gone before anyone realized it. Isha's meal was a huge success, even by her standards. Ralph avoided all beans and vegetables, but the meat and beer didn't stand a chance. He did eat some of the onions and pita bread, but the main course was meat. Between mouthfuls, and Ralph raving about the food, they talked nonstop. They talked about the law, about Naba's school, about the American invasion and different personalities at the courthouse. They told Naba and each other about different places they'd visited. Naba didn't always understand every word or sentence, so Isha occasionally updated her in Arabic.

Naba was simply fascinated by Ralph. She was fascinated by how much he ate. She was fascinated by the fact that he drank beer. Isha suspected that Naba was simply fascinated by the fact that Ralph was a man and would have sworn that Naba's English improved during the course of the evening. By 9:30, everyone agreed it was time to say good night. After they put Naba to bed, Isha called for Ralph's transportation.

While they waited for his ride, Isha was surprised to find herself telling Ralph some of her family history. She worried that Naba was closed in and self-contained and wanted Ralph to understand how vulnerable the child was. Somehow, she found she could talk to this strange young man about what she and Naba had suffered, though she had never discussed her ordeal with family or anyone else. Still, she was not explicit. She mentioned the death of her and Naba's family and the attack she'd survived, but focused on what happened to Naba. She told Ralph about the dirty looks, the insults and how people went across the street to avoid her and her granddaughter. Ralph listened intently, silently. Only when she mentioned the First Gulf War did he seem ready to speak. Before she could ask him, he encouraged her to finish.

"What about your family that did survive, like Hussein for example?"

"Most of our immediate family, on both sides were killed or are missing. The ones that are left, like my cousin Kahmila and others, are fifth or sixth cousins. They are dear to me, but we are somewhat estranged. They are more conservative than I am and have never entirely approved of me."

"How so? Do you mean politically, religiously? From what I can see and know it is obvious you take your faith very seriously."

"I do and I hope someday you will consider the sacrifice Jesus made on your behalf, but I don't condition our friendship on that. I'm willing to allow you to drink beer in my home, as long as it is in moderate amounts."

"Beer?"

"We don't drink Ralph. Someone like Kahmila thinks it is a sin for me to even extend this courtesy to you. In fact, even though you are young enough to be my son, many would be scandalized that you and I are here alone in my home. But even more than those issues of faith are the families attitude toward my education, my profession, really how a modern woman can act and still be faithful. Then there is their interest in Naba."

"Their interest . . ."

"Before the second invasion, I thought they might try to take her from me."

"What?"

"I did not ever want Naba to live as I had, all my life, without at least trying to change things. Though I was watched by the Mukhabarat from time to time, I still helped resistance groups. This is the type of activity that generates rumors. Kahmila actually told me Naba should stay with her and that 'I did not know a woman's place in the world.' I have always acknowledged my husband as the head of our home but the idea that Naba could not have a future and that she might . . . Enough."

They sat in silence, waiting for Ralph's ride. When the vehicle pulled into the driveway, he got up to leave but stopped at the door. When he turned around he looked embarrassed.

"I had a great time. I hope we can do it again. I'm not inviting myself to your home but we could go ...."

"What about the same time next week," Isha asked.

From that day on, dinner at the Hami's became a weekly institution for the three new friends. Every Wednesday after work, Ralph and Isha rode home together, ate dinner with Naba, and spent the evening together.

CHAPTER 15

———◆———

HANK JENKINS WAS BARELY MIDDLE aged, but he'd already developed snow white hair. His eyes were a shade of blue seldom seen in human beings. The result was a memorable physical appearance that he'd learned over the years to conceal. Today he showed up for work in what he called "his undercover clothes." He wore a brown suit three sizes too large for his physique, which gave him a soft, rumpled look. Perched on his nose were large, brown framed glasses with clear lenses. They helped hide the shade of his eyes. Finally, there was his inconspicuous attitude. Hank couldn't explain how, but it was a fact you could learn to conduct yourself in such a manner that people overlooked you. It wasn't the power of invisibility, but it was the next best thing.

Before he could sit down, his telephone rang.

"Hank Jenkins, Provisional Authority Publication Office."

"Mr. Jenkins, this is Colonel Henry Board."

"Good morning, Colonel."

"Mr. Jenkins, I will be by the Provisional Authority Administration Building at 12:15 to pick you up, if that's acceptable."

"I'll see you then."

Isha Hami and the cursed Akmed Amani murder trial. When they'd first met on the case, Hank had talked General Fitzgerald out of taking any action. The Judge was Christian and knew she would enrage the Shias if she bound the case for trial. Surely, Hank had thought, the Christian Judge will dismiss the charges against the Shia for killing the Sunni terrorist and the situation would fix itself. It hadn't. Hami held the thing over for trial. Hank considered the situation for probably the hundredth time. He smiled and, to himself, paid Isha his highest compliment.

Crazy witch, he thought.

Recent reports, news releases and transcripts from hard wire and cell phone intercepts regarding the military and political situation in Iraq were not encouraging. Two days earlier, a large explosion killed fifteen police recruits traveling from their barracks to a firing range. The IED completely decimated the bus, maiming those it didn't kill. One of the dead was the favorite nephew of a powerful Shia cleric. The cleric was placing increasing pressure upon the Shia leadership to take reprisals against the Sunnis for Baathist atrocities.

When he was reading through the reports, Hank thought, This country can easily explode into Civil War. It's just missing the right spark.

He considered the situation with the four Shia family members awaiting trial for Akmed Amani's murder. One way or another, Hank knew those four men weren't going to be convicted. The Shias wouldn't tolerate it and their leaders were particularly sensitive to the passions of their countrymen in the current environment. Shaking his head, he thought, we'd better be able to resolve this situation with the Judge or else the new Iraqis will.

Hank decided to read up on Hami after the meeting with Fitzgerald. He obtained her education and bar records from the British and was briefed on her family and their role in the post gulf war uprising. He interviewed her neighbors, learned about the rape room and the birth of Hami's grand-daughter. The deeper he dug, the more he respected her. Hank decided the Judge was someone who was going to survive post Saddam Iraq and help lead Iraq into its future. When the time for the Amani hearing approached, he assigned security personnel to covertly guard her home and escort her vehicle to and from the heavily guarded Ministry complex.

He kept that security in place after the initial hearing when Hami held the Shias for trial. The noise from his informants and operatives was the new Iraqi's were almost hysterical about the case. The Shia street was furious and fearful. Rumors were flying that the case was an example of Baathist power, that they could still manipulate the government.

"None one," the rumors said, "can attack Baathist operatives safely." Some were whispering that the Baathists would return to power and wreak vengeance on all who cooperated with the occupiers. The seriousness of the threat became clear three days ago. Hank took a call from one of his colleagues in the CIA's Special Activities Division, stationed up north in the Kurdish area of Iraq.

"Hank, the Kurds are fretting about this Amani case. They're worried it may end up cowing the Shia's and if that happens, they think the same damn thing that happened in 1991 could happen all over again. We pull out, the Baathists get back in power and the Kurds get gassed. My people tell me there's going to be a high-level meeting of the top family leaders, just on this."

"Do you have someone inside?"

"No. Too small and high level a group, but I can tell you this. There's no way the Kurds won't react to this. They see it as life and death."

"If you hear anything, let me know."

"Right."

It was awfully difficult to argue with Fitzgerald now, Hank thought. Judge Hami was unlikely to dismiss the case on her own, so a little push might be worth a shot. Besides, Hank was worried about the Judge and wondered if Ralph Jackson, with his American Lawyer sensibilities, hadn't had a role in Hami decision. So, an hour later, Hank was riding in the back of an air-conditioned sedan with the Assistant Provost Marshall, Colonel Henry Board to meet with Hami.

"Mr. Jenkins, Fitz told me that I was to defer to you on how to approach this situation."

"What I think, Colonel Board, is that you should take exactly the tact that you propose to me."

"What about this Jefferson ..... no Jackson, the civilian lawyer?"

"Well Colonel, it seems to me that he's here at our sufferance. He's an observer and an adviser, so that's what he should do. I think he should be handled that way."

"Very good Sir, that's what I'll do."

Hank stared out the window and reviewed a mental checklist. He knew how Board would handle Ralph Jackson. Board was a bit of a bully, used to hiding behind a badge and using his authority to push people around. Although he was convinced that was the wrong way to deal with Jackson, he wanted to watch the ex-Green Beret's reaction to Board's bullying. He planned on staying in the background, observing. If things really went south, he could always step in. That made him think.

"You know Colonel, I do think we should handle the Judge as respectfully as possible. Rather than directly challenging her, I think we should be differential, cooperative, and then just keep delaying her."

"That's my feeling too, Mr. Jenkins. This civilian though, I still think should be kept in his place."

"You've done a lot of interviews and interrogations Colonel. If that's what you think, then I'll go with your recommendation."

"Thanks, Mr. Jenkins."

Hank nodded, smiled to himself and thought about Jackson's background. Wait until Board gets a load of Jackson he thought.

"Something funny, Sir?"

"I was just thinking about that civilian trying to butt in. We're sure not in Kansas anymore, are we Colonel Board?"

Board smiled like a shark and said, "Not by a long shot, Mr. Jenkins."

The sedan stopped at the Ministry of Justice barricade and Board's driver rolled down his window. An American paratrooper wearing desert camouflage stuck his head inside the car.

"Good afternoon, Sirs," the Sergeant said. "Please flash me your IDs."

Both Board and Hank removed their picture IDs and held them alongside their faces. The Sergeant took his time, comparing each picture to each face. Then he leaned back and checked out the driver.

"What is your business here Colonel?"

"Interview with Judge Isha Hami and her adviser regarding the citizen execution of the terrorist last month."

"Good. Good luck, Sir. Please pass," he said and motioned toward his men.

The other soldiers pulled back the barricade, allowing the sedan to drive to the front steps. Board and Hank wore game faces when they got out of the car and climbed up the steps. After clearing security they climbed the staircase and entered the chambers of Judge Hami. Hami's Secretary stopped them in the outer office and checked their credentials.

Inside chambers, Ralph and Isha were waiting for them. As soon as the two men entered, Ralph scrutinized them. The first man was in uniform, the second was dressed in a frumpy brown suit, with short white hair and ice blue eyes. They introduced themselves as Lieutenant Colonel Board, U.S. Army, and Mr. Jenkins, on behalf of the U.S. government. Ralph swept his eyes across Board's chest, quickly taking in the ribbons. If you know how to translate, military ribbons are the equivalent of wearing your heart on your sleeve. Ralph knew the language. In seconds he pigeonholed Board with his chest full of non-combat awards and his Military Police branch insignia as an efficient bureaucrat and a bit of a bully. On the other hand, Mr. Jenkins was at first glance opaque. But things began to sink in. Besides the suit, Jenkins was hiding those creepy peepers of his behind a pair of non-prescription, vanity glasses. Jenkins didn't strike Ralph as a vain kind of guy. The frames, like the clothes, seemed intentionally nerdy looking. Ralph decided to watch him.

In the meantime, Judge Hami invited everyone to sit and introduced Ralph as her civilian adviser and observer.

"So, how can we help you, gentlemen?"

"Obviously, this situation with Amani has placed you in a very delicate position," said Colonel Board.

"Really? How so."

"Well, this is a case that will be almost impossible to try."

"I don't agree," said Judge Hami. "The incident occurred here, the witnesses are here, and the defendants are here. What's difficult about this case?"

"What witnesses do you have? Didn't this occur in a Shia neighborhood to a Sunni Baathist?"

"You should know," said Judge Hami. "The government's witnesses are members of the United States Army."

"Our internal investigation indicates that none of our men actually witnessed this incident."

"Wait a minute," Isha said, "the prosecutor has statements taken by Baghdad police from identified members of the Alpha Company patrol who witnessed the entire incident."

"Your Honor, there must be some mistake, perhaps in transla-tion. Our men did not witness the terrorist's death, they only saw the crowd, stopped and then repeated to the police what they were told by bystanders."

"First, Amani is an alleged terrorist and second, this contra-dicts the statements from the police reports." Hami paused for a moment, then continued. "But, I suppose the jury will be able to determine whether the police got it right or not. I still don't see what's so difficult."

The pace of the conversation picked up. Board and Isha were still civil in tone, but their sentences came out crisply.

"I'm afraid a jury's not going to hear the testimony of those men because Alpha Company has been transferred north to Mosul."

"Transferred or not, the witnesses will appear in my Court and they will testify."

"No ma'am they won't. Alpha is now participating in a crucial 'sweep' operation."

"Wait a minute," Ralph spoke up, "what do you mean they won't testify? Under Iraqi law and the Provisional Authority regulations, the Judge's subpoena power covers the entire country."

Ralph had done his homework and like any other teacher's pet, he wanted people to know it.

Board turned a laser beam gaze upon the other man, obviously unhappy. Ralph retaliated by putting on his most innocent, 'Hey I don't know what's going on here' look. Of course, he knew well what was going on. They were trying to stiff Hami. Still, the Judge didn't look pleased with him either.

"My understanding," Board said, "is you're an observer here. It might be appropriate for you to observe instead of interjecting yourself into a situation you don't understand and don't belong in."

"Ah... ah... I didn't mean to interfere. It's just that I was talking to that Henderson guy from the Associated Press. He told me that the Army was very cooperative with the Iraqi judicial system."

Ralph was looking at Board's shoes while trying to look sheep-ish and sound apologetic at the same time. Of course, Henderson had said no such thing since Ralph had never spoken to him. Still, Ralph thought raising the issue of media coverage might prove helpful.

"I think you're absolutely correct about that Mr. Jackson." It was Jenkins, speaking for the first time. "I suspect these logistical concerns we came to iron out can and will be resolved successfully. All we wanted to do at this point was give Judge Hami a 'heads up' on the transfer and let her know that there might be some slight delay in providing the witnesses from the Alpha Company patrol. We've accomplished that. Now that we know she needs those individuals, Colonel Board and I can look into it for her. Right, Colonel Board?"

Board broke off the death stare he'd directed at Ralph and turned to Judge Hami.

"Certainly your, Honor."

Ralph felt a flush of self-directed anger. Despite his promise to himself, he'd forgotten Jenkins.

How the heck did that happen? Ralph wondered.

"Actually, we must be going," Hank said.

They all stood.

"Thank you, gentlemen, Isha said. "This certainly turned out better than I first thought it would."

"Yes, ma'am," both men said as they walked toward the door.

Stopping at the door, Hank turned.

"Go on ahead Colonel. Mr. Jackson, could you spare me a moment?"

Ralph looked at Isha as he followed Jenkins out the door, but before she could speak, the phone rang. Her secretary answered and said something in Arabic which sent Isha back through her inner door and into chambers. Outside in the hall, Hank stopped at the head of the staircase. Board gave Ralph a final glare and headed down the stairs. Hank waited, then glanced around to make sure they wouldn't be overheard.

"What the heck do you think you're doing," Hank said.

Looking at Jenkins, Ralph opened his mouth and stammered, " I..., I...."

"Knock it off," Hank said. "I'm not Board, so don't give me any of that SF 'there's no one here but us church mice' crap, OK."

Uh oh, Ralph thought.

"We've been waiting for over a year for the Iraqi population to take an active role in helping us clean out the Baathists and now that they have, we're going to prosecute some of them for murder?

I don't think so."

"Look, Jenkins, or whatever your name is, I don't make the rules," Ralph said. If we want to encourage and legalize vigilante action, then let's have the rules say so. I'm a lawyer. I follow rules. I'm here to encourage the Iraqis to do the same, even when it's not popular. So, your problem's not with me, it's with the Provisional Authority and the U.S. government."

"Right now, my problem is not the PA, it's you. Left to her own devices, Judge Hami will reluctantly understand her jurisdiction doesn't extend north to Mosul . . . in this particular case. You do her no favor by convincing her otherwise. Like it or not, American and Iraqi lives are at stake here. How many fewer IEDs might be installed if the Baathists have to worry about their own people killing them or turning them in? How many Americans and Iraqis will die, over your half cheek principles, because citizens are afraid of being prosecuted by their own government and its allies if they help us? Think about it," Hank said, "because these men will not be prosecuted and that is a fact."

With that, Hank turned and was halfway down the staircase before stopping and looking back up at Ralph.

"Don't forget about Hami either. If this case continues, she's going to be in real, Iraqi style danger. Who's going to protect her? You? This isn't a Courtroom, this is Baghdad. Good day, Mr. Jackson."

"Love the glasses," Ralph shouted after him.

Burning at the insult, he fought off the urge to follow Hank down the steps and find out who was going to protect him from Jackson. Instead, he walked back to the Judge's office.

Calm down, he told himself.

Hami hung up her phone as he entered.

"What a coincidence. Our Prime Minister just called regarding this case. It seems there's not much desire to prosecute these four defendants. What did Mr. Jenkins say to you?"

"Something about the rodent population and some church," Ralph mumbled under his breath. He was staring down into a corner of the room with his brow furrowed.

"What?"

"Nothing your Honor." Ralph looked up. "Basically, Jenkins told me to mind my own business."

"And this case and your assignment to me is none of your business, correct."

"Yes ma'am."

"How do you feel about that?"

"I determine what advice to give, subject to the guidelines from Star I agreed to."

"Good for you," Isha said. "Still, they can make your life rather difficult."

"They can make yours difficult too, your Honor."

The Judge laughed at that.

"The last military government here, our friends the Baathists, used forceps and razor blades to remove the tongues of those who disagreed with them. Perhaps you have seen this on that video they were selling in the States. I have seen this in person. So, the possibility that some American boy might make me stand on a box with my underwear over my head is not particularly intimidating."

Ralph burst out laughing.

She smiled. "I am concerned, however, with how the inability of my Court to compel the attendance of the US Army witnesses will affect the proceedings before me and the ability of those men to obtain a fair trial. Conversely, I am concerned that the prosecution be able to move forward with a valid case."

"Tell Jenkins-"

"Jenkins? Why not Board?"

"Forget Board, Isha. Tell Hank Jenkins that you'll allow the police to testify as to what the Alpha Company witnesses told them."

"What? Allow a murder trial to go forward on the basis of 'eyewitness' testimony not subject to cross-examination? Here in Iraq we call that inadmissible hearsay."

"I'm not-"

"What's your argument? What's the hearsay exception? We know the defense is going to claim that the statements the police took from the soldiers were really the interviewees repeating to the police what the actual eyewitnesses related to them. Ralph, the actual eyewitnesses are here in Baghdad and still available."

"The actual eyewitnesses are Shias and the Shias will clam up," Ralph said. "Since Iraq has a common law tradition from the British mandate days that-"

"Oh yes, we'll use the old common law 'the Americans are covering up' exception to the hearsay rule," Isha said.

"I'm not saying let the police testimony in your Honor. I'm saying threaten to let the testimony in. Hank Jenkins wants these civilians acquitted, so it will be better for him to have the soldiers themselves here and able to testify rather than to have the police testify as to what the soldiers told them. We all know the police testimony will be damming to the accused."

"If the Army thinks those soldiers will perjure themselves if ordered to do so, yes. I wonder if they're sure. In any event, an idea worth considering my friend, but for now, there is the matter of rental fees at the market Whalid Shouk and Mr. Abdula's failure to pay his fee. The lawyers wait in the Courtroom."

"Your Honor, forgive me. I'm off to the water closet. I'll sneak into the Court Room through the public entrance and sit at the back."

"Very well." Hami headed off toward a private door which led directly to her elevated seat in the Courtroom.

Ralph reached down, grabbed his travel bag and headed down the hall toward the public restroom. There was only one occupant, so he went to a stall to wait and closed the door behind him. The stall was nothing more than a concrete slab with the metal sewer pipe exposed and a facet suspended over it to wash away the debris. Not only was there no toilet lid or seat, there was no toilet. Just the squat hole.

Bombs away, Ralph thought.

He stood hunched down, waiting for the other guy to finish his business and leave. Finally the water ran, then the outer door closed. Ralph stood up, walked over to the door and kicked the rubber door stop firmly under the door. Then, he withdrew a flip phone and dialed the number of a professional acquaintance.

Who was going to take care of Hami? Jenkins wanted to know.

If Jenkins wanted a fight, Jenkins was going to get a fight.

CHAPTER 16

IT WAS A DEFT, BUT unequivocal demand for an assassination. Ibrahim Othman had requested the meeting three days earlier, over a secure satellite phone from his village north of Mosul. Even over an encrypted satellite phone, he'd been cautious with his choice of words. All he'd said was he wanted to be sure his old friends were still gathering at their favorite shop on Thursday at 12 o'clock for coffee and to reminiscence about old times.

When Othman and a second Kurd entered the South Baghdad Coffee Shop, Mahmoud Bahr al-Uloum, Ayad al-Jaberi, and Sameer al-Hakim were waiting. The Shop fronted the street with three 10 by 10 foot glass window panes painted red with the week's specials. Inside were an old style, glass-encased deli cooler and a black and white square linoleum floor. When the Kurds opened the door, three young Arab men stood aside, allowing them to enter.

Othman walked to an art deco metal table where the three Arabs sat drinking strong coffee from miniature cups. The other tables were empty. Even the shop owners were nowhere in sight. Othman smiled a friendly smile.

"This is Aziz Yacoub," he said, "my dear friend and kinsman. He knows the same old friends that we know and hopes to share in a story or two."

Ayad al-Jaberi nodded and said lightly, "Please friends, try this excellent coffee. You know it's why we choose this shop year after year."

As the Kurds sat at the table and were served coffee, six more young men entered the shop, in groups of two, and sat at three different tables. Outside, three more men, similar in facial features and dress to the Kurds, joined a group of Arab men. A similar number of aggressive young men, in the same relative numbers, stood outside of the only other entrance to the shop.

Despite the tension in the air and at the table, the five men sipped thick, sweet Turkish coffee in silence. Given the strength of the coffee, the cups were tiny and each man was careful to only sip his portion, savoring its flavor and aroma, but swallowing very little. There was more than enough tension in the room without adding highly concentrated caffeine into the bloodstreams of the participants. Although time seemed frozen, the men discussed each other's health and then droned on about family, friends, weather, and even soccer, for over twenty minutes. Finally, Ibrahim Othman obliquely approached the reason he had requested the meeting.

"Despite the fact that I can find no coffee as fine as this outside of Baghdad, I'm still grateful to live in the North. It must be very difficult to live with so many of our former enemies amongst you. I thought it noteworthy that even in the face of this difficulty, the police managed to apprehend citizens who expressed their opposition to the Baathists with violence. In my part of the country, citizens are becoming increasingly bold. They no longer tolerate Baathists among us, particularly if these Baathists are trying to bring back the bad old days. Such lawless behavior is regrettable, but it does speed up the process with which democracy and freedom become established."

Othman spoke without irony in his voice because that would not only have been disrespectful, it would have most likely have proven fatal.

"I'm sure such citizen involvement is not practical in Baghdad," he continued. "We wonder whether recent incidents may not make our people see the error of their ways."

The three Arabs were uncomfortable. Othman was obviously referring to the execution of the murderer Amani and the arrest of the patriots who'd killed him. The Kurds were concerned any persecution or prosecution of Iraqis who opposed the Baathists would discourage others from doing so. This, to them, was unacceptable. The Baathists were to be crushed, now, once and forever. In Iraq, there was a deep-seated, multi-generational fear of the Baathists and Saddam Hussein that often paralyzed resistance. The leadership of the Kurds, Shias, and non-aligned Sunnis struggled

mightily to overcome this fear. Thus, anything that detracted from
the effort to destroy the Baathists threatened the Kurds. They did
not send representatives to South Baghdad to drink coffee. They
were here to express their displeasure over the Armani prosecution and they had to be taken seriously. Not only were the
Kurds twenty percent of the country's population, they were fierce
fighters. Their tribal support systems spanned eastern Turkey, all of
Northern Iraq, and Northwestern Iran, and frankly, the Arabs all
shared the Kurds' fears.

The likelihood of the Bath regime returning to power seemed
so unlikely as to be ridiculous to those in the West. Western eyes,
however, hadn't been subjected to the same horrors as the Iraqi
people. Western eyes hadn't seen their sisters, mothers, and daugh-
ters raped before their eyes. They hadn't awoken to the knock in
the middle of the night and the image of their son or husband
being drug out the door, never to be seen again. Westerners didn't
understand the almost primordial, hereditary fear of Baathist sup-
pression the average Iraqi inherited. The Iraqi population worried
the Baathists were not through. They were convinced the Syrian
Baathists, in much the same situation as the Iraqi Baathists, were
harboring Iraqi Baathists, money, weapons and chemical munitions. Although a minority, the Baathists with chemical weapons,
organization, money, and desperation could return to power. Even
the new Iraqi leadership was not immune from this fear.

To a degree, none of the new leaders would admit to each other,
or even to themselves, their motivation in leading their people to
complete the destruction of the Baathists was fear for their own
safety. At night, in the dark, all of them, even Sameer al-Hakim,
struggled to blot out the images of Baathists' revenge conjured
up by the imagination. All three Arabs knew if the Baathists ever
returned to power, no place on earth would be a safe haven. They
wouldn't even be safe if they fled the country. Saddam's treacherous son-in-law, who had escaped abroad, was captured. He was
only briefly tortured, but he was a son-in-law. The Baathists would
keep the new Iraqi leaders alive for months, perhaps years, before
finally killing them. This fear was alive to them in a way that is
embedded in the soul. Iraqis, even the new Iraqi leaders, fear the
Baathists in the way a lamb fears the wolf.

So, all of the men in the coffee shop were aware that when

American trained Iraqis arrested the executioners of a Baathist murderer, they threatened the future of Iraq itself. The Iraqi population wouldn't believe the four men who killed the terrorist were arrested and prosecuted by new Iraq officials acting in compliance with the law. They would believe this was an exercise of Baathist power.

"Even in the new Iraq, with the Americans still in charge, no one can touch the Baathists," the people would say.

The men sitting around the coffee table were not immune from this doubt. If the people were suddenly frozen in terror, just when their leaders began to assert themselves, who could say what would happen. Perhaps the Baathists could force the Americans to leave. If the Americans left, who could say the Baathists wouldn't return to power. If the Baathists returned to power, the men in the coffee shop, sooner or later, would experience a little taste of hell. This one incident, therefore, now threatened to affect not only Baghdad and the triangle but Southern and even Northern Iraq. That was why the Kurds were in Baghdad. With all this in mind, Ayad al-Jaberi replied casually.

"It is difficult not to feel sympathy when people take vengeance on the Baathists. We must, though, as you say, also establish our own democracy and law. I wonder, given the fact that we are still at war, whether there will be enough witnesses, time and will-power to prosecute these innocent people. If the justice system dismisses the charges against these individuals for lack of evidence, rather than discouraging the people, this incident may encourage them. It may show them Iraqi justice covers even the righteous expression of their rage and is wise enough to make allowances for self-defense. We believe the Americans are concerned that Iraqi justice be vigilant, but they are also aware of all that concerns our country. We think that some effort will be exerted so that justice will be done in this case."

Ibrahim Othman nodded his head thoughtfully.

"Well said, my friend. This is all that an Iraqi Patriot could hope for. Even as bad as the Baathists are, this is not the only danger. We must always be concerned that our government and judicial officials are respected and protected. We must ensure that Kurd respects Sunni and Shia and that Mosul respects Baghdad."

Seconds ticked by and no one spoke. The silence lengthened

while everyone stared at their coffee. This silence was not a natural break in the conversation but a vacuum where the men struggled to catch their breath. Ibrahim Othman, very artfully, had just said that if the Baghdad judicial system persisted in this case, the Kurds would intervene to stop it. Thus his concern for the safety of government and judicial personnel. Of course, if the Kurds sent people down from the North to assassinate Sunni policemen and a Christian Judge in order to stop the trial, the Southerners would be forced to retaliate. Civil war would result. Ibrahim Othman knew this. That is why his threat had been well crafted, veiled. Probably it had been written and rehearsed over several days. Its final delivery had been practiced for hours. No doubt the statement itself was first approved by numerous Kurdish leaders. As delivered, the Kurd threat left open a crack for southern Iraqis to escape through without ever needing to acknowledge they'd been threatened.

Essentially the statement said, "We are afraid that this prosecution will start a chain reaction. The chain reaction will be that the average citizen will be afraid to help the Americans and the Iraq government. This will increase the chance that the Baathists will prevail. We Kurdish leaders are so afraid of this happening that we will risk Civil War before we will allow it to happen. We are telling you this in advance because we do not want to do it. We want you to do it and then peace will continue."

Mahmoud Bahr al-Uloum picked up his coffee, peered at each of the others at the table and then sat his cup back down. The others followed. Mahmoud said, "I wonder if my two friends agree with me. My opinion is that Baghdad must show its respect to Mosul and Sunnis and Shias must show their respect to Kurds. My belief is the Shias, Sunnis, and Kurds all have the same interests now." The pause was brief.

Ayad al-Jaberi said, "I think my friend is right."

All eyes turned on Sameer al-Hakim because he was now in the most difficult position of any man at the table. He'd suggested Hami as Judge. Sameer's eyes looked off in the distance as he thought. After a brief moment his eyes refocused, he looked at the two Kurds in turn and spoke softly.

"To me, this is not an issue. Baghdad will always respect Mosul, at least in South Baghdad."

The Baghdad Arabs had just assured the Kurds that the case against the killers of the terrorist would not go to trial.

"Sometimes," Sameer could not resist adding, "signs of respect come in unexpected ways."

Their business concluded, the Arabs and Kurds prepared to share a meal. For the next hour, the five men talked of their families, mutual friends, and acquaintances and engaged in other small talk between mouthfuls of food, served by the shop owners who returned for the occasion. Periodically steaming bowls of various dishes would be passed from man to man. Most of the food, however, was self-serve from a large pot of rice, mixed with chunks of seasoned lamb. Each man had a plate of steaming pita sitting in front of him on a cloth napkin. Between mouthfuls and snatches of conversation, the men would rip off a hunk of pita and thrust it into the bowl of rice and meat. Using the pita almost like a glove, they took turns grabbing handfuls of rice and meat. Often the bread was dipped into another large bowl of tachina, a paste made from crushed sesame seeds and lemon oil. Less common than humus – the Chickpea paste -- it had a strong cult following among the Southern Shias. Eventually they finished the repast, the conversation died down, and Ibrahim Othman and Aziz Yacoub nodded respectfully and stood.

"My friends, as always, it has been a pleasure to meet with you and share the news. Thank you for this meal," Aziz gestured toward the table, "the coffee and mostly the fine friendship built upon mutual values, interests, and concerns for the future. Ibrahim and I have a long journey ahead of us and we must be off. I know that our friends and family up North will be pleased to hear we were able to meet and comforted to know that we have such wise and generous friends as you." The Arabs answered politely and the Kurds left.

When the door closed behind them, Mahmoud Bahr al-Uloum gestured with his hand toward his son. The young man separated from the others and walked over to his father. Bending at the waist, he leaned so his ear was inches from his father's lips.

"Ensure that the restaurant is empty and then ask our friends to leave it and the keys with us for an hour. We're not to be disturbed for that hour."

The young man straightened. "I'm having my son clear and

secure the restaurant if that is acceptable."

Ayad and Sameer both nodded and raised a hand in the air at their respective security detail. So, confident that everyone understood each other, the three men sat with their thoughts, sipping coffee until Mahmoud Bahr al-Uloum's son returned.

"All is clear, father."

"Very well, son. Leave us and wait outside."

CHAPTER 17

———◆———

THEY JUST FINISHED DINNER AND Isha was clearing the table while Ralph relaxed in a nearby chair, sipping a bottle of beer. He watched Naba chattering away as she brushed her doll's hair with a smile playing on his lips.

In the West, little girls grow up too fast, he thought. They would have already abandoned dolls.

"It's a shame she doesn't have brothers or sisters," he said out loud to Isha. "She loves taking care of . . . Hey, why doesn't she have a dog?"

"What?"

"I said why doesn't Naba have a dog?"

Isha moaned. "What is it about you Americans and dogs? When I was in London I was friends with an American exchange student. The one thing I remember, whenever she would show me pictures with her family, there was her dog. Every other story she told her dog did something. We are Arabs, we don't like dogs the way Americans do."

Naba had looked up from her doll, watching her grandmother and Ralph with comprehension. In the new public school, the Americans had helped establish, English was a popular subject. Naba had English class three days a week, Monday, Wednesday and Friday and it showed. At first, the child had struggled, constantly complaining that "English does not make sense." Since Isha and Ralph had become friends, things changed. Even Naba's English teacher called Isha to comment on how much Naba had improved. Now she understood most of the conversation between Isha and Ralph. So it surprised neither when Naba spoke in English.

"Grandmother, might I speak?"

"Of course child, what do you think?"

"Grandmother, even though I am an Arab, it is as you have taught me many times. We are all different and in our way special. Even though you can never be wrong and most Arabs don't like dogs, I am like Ralph. I see them in the street, with their little tails that swing back and forth and their wet noses. Sometimes, grandmother, when they're happy, they bark and they prance around their friends in a little circle. Maybe I am not like most Arabs."

Ralph was trying to hide his smile behind his hand. Failing, he grabbed his beer bottle and put it to his lips.

Isha looked first at Naba, and then at Ralph. She placed her hands on her hips and put on her sternest look. Ralph had seen the same look used during twenty or thirty courtroom scenes in the last few months. It froze lawyers, shut the lips of even the most talkative witness, and brought order to a disorderly courtroom in seconds. Still swinging her eyes back and forth, she burst out.

"Woof, Woof."

Ralph choked, sending fizzing beer through his nose and down his chin. Naba began to laugh, clapping her hands and giggling. Still laughing and choking, Ralph grabbed a napkin and wiped his face and cleaned the beer dribble off his neck, shirt and chin.

"This serves you right. Now my granddaughter wants to bring a flea infested, eating machine into my home." The Judge was smiling.

"Yes. But it serves you right for exposing your granddaughter to my decadent Western ways."

"Grandmother. What does 'Decadent' mean in Arabic?"

"Well. You started this Ralph, you explain," Isha said.

"For the way we are talking now, Naba, in this context, as we say, it means 'dog lover.'"

Isha kept her hands on her hips, looked at Ralph and rolled her eyes at him. The girl said nothing. She looked thoughtful.

"This is good," Naba finally said. "Tomorrow, I have English class. I can tell Mrs. Osman that I am 'Decadent' just like my American friend, Ralph."

After two days of non-stop pestering, Ralph and Naba battered Isha into agreeing that Naba could have a dog. Triumphant, the two conspirators made plans to leave the Hami house at 6:00 p.m. the next Wednesday. At that time of year in Iraq, they could still count on two hours of daylight for the search without subjecting Naba to the worst of the day's heat. Isha refused to participate. In exchange for her consent to Naba adopting a dog, Ralph had to obtain the dog, delouse the dog, potty train the dog and ensure the dog's discipline.

"This is not America," Isha said. "No Bill of Rights, no speedy trial, none of that nonsense. If this dog is anything less than the best behaved creature on the planet, I will have you thrown into the deepest, darkest, dungeon Saddam Hussein ever built in this country."

Ralph was not entirely sure she was joking. Isha was obsessed with fleas and dogs were known to have … Ralph decided it might be prudent to call his brother in the States. Scott had Ralph's power of attorney and access to all his bank accounts. So, when Scott answered the phone that Friday, Ralph told him to spare no expense in obtaining and shipping dog supplies to Iraq by the next week. It was a close call, but Ralph had received an over-night delivery on Wednesday morning. The box contained a two year supply of not only flea collars but also flea shampoo and flea dip. Ralph didn't want to take any chances. Just to show that he wasn't really afraid of Judge Hami, he also had Scott send chew toys, a couple of leashes, collars, and chains. Finally, he ordered a new Raggedy Ann doll. It had never occurred to him that a red haired Scottish girl doll was not the best choice for a dark haired, Arab girl.

After he opened the box, he called home to thank his brother. Scott was out, but his sister-in-law answered. As they were talking, Ralph mentioned he hoped Naba would like her doll. Marsha broke out laughing.

"Ralph, you knucklehead," she said affectionately, "you should get a girl a doll she can identify with. Do you think one with bright red hair was the best choice?"

Ralph was horrified. It never occurred to him that the kind of doll he got was important, as long as it was cute. Now that Marsha had brought it up, he panicked. Clueless about the mystery of little girls, he worried about giving the child a complex. Would she think Ralph was insinuating something was wrong with her because she wasn't white and red haired? Would she withdraw from Ralph? Would she cry?

"Look Marsha, thanks again and I don't want to be rude, but I have to go."

Ralph smacked himself on the forehead, stood motionless, then decided. He grabbed his belly-pack and headed out the door. On the way out he stopped at the reception desk.

"You know where I can buy black dye?"

The clerk was of no help. So for the next three hours Ralph hunted for black dye. Eventually, he found a three-year-old packet in one of the markets. He wasn't even sure it would work, but he bought it anyway and returned to his apartment. Looking up at the clock, he discovered it was 4:30. He was scheduled to be at the Hamis at 6:00 and it took half an hour to get there from his apartment.

"Crap."

For the first time, Ralph read the instructions. "I have to dilute this in water?" He sat the doll on his clothes hamper and began to rip open the dye. The cellophane packing was brittle, resisted his efforts and then gave way all at once. The dye went over his hands and ran down the white ceramic sink bowl.

"Crap, Crap, Crap."

He reached up and pulled the drain plug on the sink to prevent the remainder of the dye from slipping down the drain. He went to the tub, turned on a small stream of hot water and tried to scrub off the dye of his hands. Nothing. While he was trying to decide what to do next, he reached up to scratch his cheek and stopped himself just in time.

"Oh geeze."

Ralph turned off the faucet and re-grouped. Finally, after half an hour, he managed to ruin four bath towels and two tooth-brushes, but, Raggedy Ann now had black hair. Ralph took a step back, hands on his hips, surveying the doll from a distance. He was pleased with his efforts.

It wasn't a half bad job, but he'd still managed to get the dye everywhere except on Raggedy Ann. Importantly though, the doll's hair was black but the the doll herself had no dye marks. Ralph stood up after stroking the last of the dye on to a light spot on the doll's hair with a big smile. He took bath towel number five, held Raggedy Ann by her foot and attached her foot to the shower head over his bathtub. Her hair hung down and began to air dry. Taking a step back, Ralph surveyed his work yet again.

"Not bad. Not bad at all."

Then he looked in the mirror. His shirt was covered with black specks of dye. His hands were covered too. In keeping with the spirit of the day, he saw that it was 5:25 p.m. Hussein had agreed to pick him up at 5:30 p.m. so they could get to Hami's house on time.

"Great."

He spent four minutes trying to scrub the die off of his hands with no effect whatsoever. The next 45 seconds were devoted to changing his pants, grabbing a shirt and his belly pack. Then he rushed out the door, pounded down the stairs and threw on his shirt and pack as he ran. It was 5:35 p.m. when he jumped into the front passenger's side seat and slammed the door closed. Hussein drove off, addressing Ralph in an accusatory tone.

"Will be late for dog hunt."

"I know."

"This important to Naba."

"I know."

A pause and a curious look.

"Why your hands black?"

"Mind your own business."

The doll was still in his apartment, its new black dyed hair drying as she hung in Ralph's bathtub.

It's a blessing in disguise, Ralph thought to himself. If I had the doll right now, it would be two gifts the same day. Better to split them up and double the excitement.

It seemed as though fate had relented because traffic was unusually light. Ralph was only a few minutes late, but Naba and Isha were still waiting for him by the door. Ralph let Naba rifle through the contents of his belly pack while he checked his watch.

"Okay, 6:00 p.m. Do we have everything, Naba?"

Naba was grinning and bouncing up on her tip-toes and then down again, over and over.

"Yes, Ralph. We have a collar, a flea collar, a leash, and -- what do you call these? Treats?"

"Treats, Naba. Now we go."

"Do you think we will find my dog tonight?"

Ralph's plan was to take Naba out into the streets with some snacks for the dogs that roamed free. He knew that in the Middle East one had to be careful of stray dogs, who tended to run in packs and had learned to distrust humans. In postwar Iraq though, many animals had become strays as a result of the war. Ralph saw them wandering the streets ever since he arrived. Often you would see a stray, many times with a collar, approach a stranger wagging his tail, hoping for food. More often than not, the dog was rebuffed with a kick or by being cuffed behind the ear. The way Ralph figured it, there was a pretty good pool of dogs out there.

"Can't tell for sure Naba. The best way to choose a dog is to let him choose you. So better we take a few days and get the right dog, than just get a dog for the sake of having one."

"I hope it's tonight, I hope its tonight," she said, bouncing up-and-down.

Ralph smiled. Isha had her "Judge" look on and was standing with her hands on her hips in the doorway.

"Okay Naba, let's go. Isha?"

"There is no way I'm going to search the streets for a dog."

She looked at him and frowned.

"Why in heaven's name are your hands black? Are you dying your hair?"

Scowling, Ralph turned and led Naba out the door. They began walking down the street and headed toward the center of the small residential area the Hamis lived in.

As they walked their attention was drawn toward a small group of men sitting bent over a table. Ralph had just about decided to ask for some advice when a loud "bap, bap, bap, bap" sound broke out and then stopped. A second of silence was followed by a burst of laughter. Four old men sat around a short, homemade wooden table someone had pieced together with discarded lumber. A battered backgammon sat on it, the center of attention. The men were now shouting at each other with obvious good nature. Since no one had a dog and everyone seemed enthralled, Ralph decided to keep moving.

He already had a particular area in mind. A certain block of Isha's village contained an abandoned building, sitting in the middle of a large field. Reasonably close to the river, the fields were overgrown with vegetation. In the evenings, when the sun was low in the sky, a menagerie of dogs appeared. From what Ralph could see while driving by, many of them appeared to be strong boned and clean-limbed. All things considered, they also appeared to be well mannered. Ralph suspected that many of them were strays who'd been displaced during the air war and subsequent ground attack. It seemed to him a good hunting ground.

They walked the two blocks toward what Ralph had been referring to as "the dog pound," holding hands and swinging their arms. Naba kept up a nonstop chatter about what kind of dog, what color of dog and how big a dog she would get. Ralph tried to keep her calm, reminding her that they might not find her dog that evening. He didn't want her to be disappointed, but words went in one of Naba's ears and rushed out the other. The closer they got to the dog pound, the more animated she became. Ralph found her excitement contagious.

"Okay, there they are."

"Where Ralph, I don't see them."

"In the shadow, on the left side of the building," Ralph said pointing.

"Oh. I see."

Leading Naba, Ralph moved across the field toward the dogs. Three or four came out of the shadows sniffing, wagging their tails, but keeping them low. Ralph stopped, dropped Naba's hand and opened his belly pack. This was where he'd stored the "treats" for the dogs, little cut up pieces of lamb wrapped in wax paper. When he pulled out the package, the wax paper rattled and the four dogs pranced backward a few steps, watching. He opened the first piece and the aroma wafted toward the abandoned house. More dogs appeared. Ralph took handfuls of the meat and threw it over the dogs' heads, in between them and the house. All the dogs bolted toward the meat, growling, snarling and maneuvering for position. In the meantime, Ralph kept half the meat, twisted the wax paper shut and pushed it into the pack. He held two pieces of lamb in his right hand. Naba watched him, fascinated. He went down on one knee, holding the meat out.

The smallest of the four dogs came back toward them, unnoticed by the rest of the pack. As he came closer, Ralph could tell he was a youngster with a slight limp to his right rear leg. The nail on his paw scratched as it dragged against the dirt when he walked.

"Okay Naba, just do as I say, all right?"

"Yes, Ralph."

Ralph handed one of the pieces of meat to Naba. The dog, a small black boy with white markings around one eye, inched closer. His tail was still held low, but it was swishing back and forth with regularity. Glancing at Naba, Ralph saw a huge smile on her face.

"Naba?"

No answer.

"Naba," a little more insistently.

"Yes, Ralph. I'm sorry."

"Hold your hand out, with the meat flat on your hand. Don't hold the meat or curl your fingers. Let the dog take the meat off your hand, like your hand is a plate."

A giggle.

"Okay, Ralph."

He stepped away from Naba, far enough away that the dog had to choose, but close enough should the dog turn aggressive. Naba was on his left, holding out the meat. Ralph kneeled back down and held his piece of meat in his right hand, out toward his side. The dog stopped in front of them, sniffed them both, and immediately headed for Naba. His tail picked up a little bit and continued to switch back and forth.

Another giggle.

As the dog closed the distance toward Naba, Ralph took a good look at him. His flews, nose, and eyes all appeared clean. Looking for pus or discharge, Ralph didn't find any. The dog gently took the meat off of Naba's open hand, wagging a little harder. Ralph stood up slowly and the dog glanced at him. He approached and held out the pieces of meat.

"Take this, Naba."

Naba took the meat and placed it on her open palm. The dog waited until she held her hand out and didn't try to snatch it from her fingers.

"Go-ahead Naba, pet him."

Naba petted the dog's head and side. The dog began to lick Naba's hands and knees, circled around her, then stopped. Ralph pulled up his rear paw and saw the cause of the limp. There was a small cut in one of his pads, but it appeared to be healing nicely. By this time, the other dogs had finished the meat and were beginning to wander over, curious. Ralph opened his belly pack back up and gave Naba another piece of meat.

"Hold this piece away from the dog for a moment Naba."

"Okay, Ralph. Why?"

"I want to see something."

With that, Ralph opened his belly pack and took out another handful of meat pieces. Drawing back, he threw them, baseball style, over the dogs' heads. Immediately, they broke off their meandering and bolted toward the meat. The black and white jerked and took half a step. Then he stopped, turned around and looked at Naba.

"Naba, do you want him or do you want to look for another?"

"Oh, Ralph, I want this dog. I want him so bad, he's going to be my best friend. It's just like you said, your dog comes to you. Even when you took all that meat, he didn't run away. I was so afraid he would run away. Can I have him, Ralph? Can I have this dog?"

"This is your dog, Naba."

Ralph removed a collar from the belly pack and reached around the dog's neck. He twisted for a moment but stopped when Ralph linked his arm around him. For a moment he whined, but by then Ralph had his collar on. He held the collar with one hand, snapped on a leash and then released the dog. Instantly, he stopped whining and licked Naba's knee.

"Hold this for a moment, Naba."

Ralph handed Naba the leash and reached into his belly pack. He pulled out the remainder of the meat and threw it toward the rest of the dogs. Then he took the leash from Naba with one hand and her hand with the other. The three of them walked home.

CHAPTER 18

———◆———

AFTER EASING HIS APARTMENT DOOR closed, Hank Jenkins threw his gear on the floor and slumped into an easy chair. His current abode was a newly constructed, government supplied apartment building located in a secure compound behind the so-called green line in Baghdad. It was one of fifty identical, white drywall, one bed, one bath units constructed for provisional authority civilians. Hank snapped on a dim table lamp and discovered it was 5:30 a.m. He was glad to be home, be it ever so humble.

Officially, he was employed as an Internet and computer technologist working on a contract with the Provisional Authority in its communications department. Although the job provided good cover, it limited his ability to interact with the locals and travel the country. Often he was forced to sneak around. Despite the job's limitations, he was satisfied. He chose it as cover because it was an unlikely choice, not because it was convenient.

"Besides, sneaking around is what I do," Hank said out loud.

He'd just returned from an unsuccessful foray into one of the many Sunni suburbs of Baghdad.

Hank brooded while massaging his temples and worrying the night's failure would lead to real tragedy, real soon. He'd received a tip that a meeting was being set up between rival terrorists Major Nadim Allawis of the Baathists and Abu Musab Al-Zarqawi of Al-Queda. A meeting between two hunted men like Allawis and Al-Zarqawi was unusual because it carried extraordinary risk and required extraordinary planning and security. The CIA learned two of the terrorists' retainers were meeting in a North Baghdad suburb to arrange the logistics and security details for the summit between their bosses. Hank and his men were waiting, hoping to capture the men and squeeze the location of Allawis and Al-Zarqawi out of them. Just a few blocks away from the rendez-vous site, both parties turned off. At the last minute the terrorists must have sensed, or been warned of, a trap. Hank's guys chased them, but after a brief gun battle, both groups of men managed to break contact with Hanks operatives and slipped out of the neighborhood.

Hank was willing to devote substantial resources to discover the purpose of the meeting and disrupt it if possible. Men like Zarqawi and Allawis didn't risk a face-to-face meeting unless it was neces-sary to avoid conflict between their groups or to coordinate their efforts on some "project."

What though, he wondered, squeezing around the breakfast bar. He opened the fridge door and grabbed a beer, wondering if get-ting his team to Gundar earlier would have made a difference. If the terrorists noticed a mistake in his hastily laid ambush, that was one thing, but Hank's gut told him they were tipped off at the last minute . . . by someone associated with the P.A.

He found himself wishing for half the intelligence network the Baathists had. While he and the CIA obtained good results from technological intelligence, such as "bugging" phones and other spy gadget stuff, they struggled to develop reliable human resources, spies, among the various Iraqi groups. Last week his buddy from the Mosul Area Special Activities Division or SAD called from a sat-phone with an update on the Kurd meeting. As they had suspected, security for the meeting was tight and no was saying anything to anyone, not even the Americans. The only thing he could find out was the Kurd tribes were sending some sort of delegation to Baghdad to meet with Arab tribal leaders. Both Hank and the other SAD members suspected it had something to do with the Amani trial. He called in every favor, tapped every phone and shook down every informant he had but couldn't find out anything. Something was going on, the pace of chatter and activity was picking up. He suspected the Baghdad meeting had already taken place and something big was in the works. Other-wise, he was in the dark, despite the light reflecting off of his white government issue appliances. The whole thing was frustrating and ominous.

Hank tossed the bottle cap in the trash, took a long pull on the brew and leaned against the stove, thinking in the earlier morning gloom. The Baathists already had wide-ranging contacts in pre-existing Baathist cells, undercover political officers and members of the military. These operatives, in turn, had their own network of operatives and informants. Hank put in long, frustrating hours trying to identify and eliminate these individuals, but knew it could have been worse. If he and his allies hadn't been successful in disbanding the pre-war Iraqi Army, the power of the insurgency would have been crippling. Of course, this reality was not widely acknowledged. After the stunning victory of American forces over Iraq in the Gulf War, the country had erupted in a spasm of crime and Baathist terror. Later, Al Queda began infiltrating foreign fighters into the select provinces. In the aftermath, the United States government and military received a great deal of criticism for disbanding the Iraqi Army. These critics, mostly academics claiming to be scholars in "security studies," along with journalists, and even a few retired generals, argued the United States had made a serious strategic error by not preserving the Iraq Regular Army. The Republican Guards and all the variations thereof, they agreed, had to be disbanded. The Army itself, they claimed, could have been preserved and used as a basis for the future Iraqi Army. Yes, perhaps certain individuals were beyond rehabilitation, but much of the crime and terrorism could have been restrained had the Army remained intact.

What frustrated Hank was how much credence this theory had been given. In his job he often had to tolerate unfair criticism because he possessed classified information unavailable to his critics. If the critics knew what he knew, they would likely support the government's position. In those situations, Hank had a fatalistic attitude and considered the criticism part of the job. This was different.

Widely available, so-called open source materials showed Saddam Hussein had been a student and admirer of Josef Stalin. Indeed, much of Saddam's political and security apparatus was structured along the same lines as the Stalinist Soviet Union. One of the features of his political system, like that of Stalin's, was complete infiltration of the military with political officers. The pre-liberation Iraqi Army was riddled with undercover political officers embedded down to the squad level. In Saddam's Iraq, no one knew for sure who was a Baathist informer and who was not. Therefore, to have preserved the pre-invasion Iraq military and convert it into the new Iraqi military would have been to install, in place, an up and running system of informants and terrorists within the Iraq military. This was obvious. The only two reasons that Hank could think of for this criticism was ignorance, stupidity, or a political agenda hostile to the United States.

His musings were interrupted by what he called the "cover" ringtone of his cell. His phone had the capacity to respond to two different phone numbers, each with a distinctive ringtone. Hank' contract operatives or superiors in Langley could call his secure cell phone and the number rang through to the phone in his hand. Alternatively, individuals he met when he was in his role as the bearded Steve Porto, make-believe internet computer guy, could call him on the same cell phone, using a different phone number. This number, when it rang through, had a different ringtone than the first number. By the ring, Hank knew it was one of his "under-cover" contacts. It was 6:07 a.m., but he decided to answer.

"Hello."

"Steve, you'll never guess what I'm hearing these guys are doing now," said the voice.

Speak of the devil, Hank thought.

The caller was Harvey Henderson, a newspaper reporter from WWP, World Wide Press. Henderson was one of the least informed and most critical commentators on U.S. policy in Iraq. Known as a real news hound in the business, his strident questions at news conferences impressed his colleagues more than the fact that his articles were usually proven wrong. Of course, it often took six to twelve months before Harvey's mistakes became obvious, so few in the news business noticed.

"Steve" and Henderson were "good friends." Like Henderson, Steve had deep misgivings about American policy and motives in Iraq. Steve was here just trying to make a living.

"But Harvey, my conscience bothers me. I'm complicit in steal-ing the Iraqis' oil," Hank Jenkins, a.k.a. Steve Porto, had confided to Henderson. Hank, whose tolerance for alcohol was legendary, allowed himself to be "loosened up" by five or six high balls of American whiskey before he admitted this deep, dark secret to the reporter. After that, Hank/Steve and Henderson become close friends, with Henderson often picking up the tab for Steve's meals and drinks. Henderson thought Steve's opinions about American policy in Iraq, Provisional Authority computer policy—"Those guys just don't understand technology, Harvey"—or the state of race relations in America, were fascinating.

Henderson hardly said a word when Hank/Steve was talking, although he would skillfully direct the topics of conversation. Hank/Steve, for his part, played a tricky balancing act by baiting Henderson with harmless, but newsworthy information regarding the Provisional Authority. Occasionally, he provided tidbits of somewhat damaging or (usually) embarrassing information on Provisional Authority personalities. Mostly, he ranted about the shortcomings of American society and the policy of the current administration. Of course, Hank had Henderson's phone tapped and it amused him to hear what Harvey really thought of Hank as Steve.

"A nerdy guy but with a real social conscience," was Henderson's evaluation.

Hank responded to Henderson with excitement. "No, what, come on, Harvey, dish, I've got to get to work pretty soon."

"All right," Henderson said "just remember I shouldn't be talking to you like this. I'm a reporter after all, but even reporters have to have friends, right?"

"Harvey," Hank said, making his voice sound pleased, "you know I wouldn't let you down. Your work is crucial to our democracy and keeping these zealots honest. Heck, you're like my only friend here."

"Thanks, Steve. Look, I got a call from a pretty good source that claims that our Provisional Authority, here to support Iraqi democracy, is actually ignoring the Iraqi justice system and its citizens' civil rights."

"No way," Hank gasped as he returned to his recliner.

"Yeah, two months ago some Iraqis drug a poor guy out of his house and killed him because he was some kind of spy or something. No proof. The worst sort of vigilante justice imaginable. Well, anyhow, it seems some of our soldiers witnessed this attack and were interviewed by the Iraqi police. Since the Bush administration wants everyone who disagrees with them in Iraq afraid, they're actually glad this attack happened."

"No way, not even I think they're that bad."

"Don't be naive Steve, the Bushes are playing for high stakes here. Oil. Anyhow, they moved those soldiers up North and hid them so they couldn't testify. That's what my source tells me."

Crap, Hank was thought, this is the last thing we need right now. With his mind spinning at a thousand revolutions a minute, Hank tried to decide whether or not to spend some of his capital with the reporter.

"Steve?"

There was no way around it. The Akmed Armani trial had the potential to plunge the country into civil war. He had to squelch the story. He fumed over the leak and suspected Ralph Jackson. Hank decided it was time to have a little conversation with Mr. Jackson, dangerous though that might be.

"I'd go slow on that one, Harvey," said Hank/Steve. "I know I shouldn't tell you this, but . . . turnabout's fair play. I know . . . I mean, you'd never get me in trouble, right?"

"Steve, even with sources that I don't like, my primary, my first obligation is to protect them. No newsman can operate if everyone's afraid to talk to him. But we're friends. I wouldn't do anything to hurt you. If I can't report this and know you'll still be safe, I just won't report it."

"Okay, Harvey, here goes. I don't know about this Iraqi murder or anything else. But, you might get embarrassed if you say the Provisional Authority moved those guys to keep them from testifying. Keep this under your hat, but I got an order at the tech shop. We had to format email and hard copy orders for some kind of operation up North with zero prep time. Drove us crazy. Anyway, they moved a lot of army guys on very short notice because . . .," Hank said nothing for several seconds, and then sighed.

"This is between us, right?"

"Come on Steve," Henderson said, sounding a little hurt and angry.

"Okay, they actually thought they had Al-Zarqawi cornered in northern Iraq. Everyone was freaking out, moving guys North as fast as they could. So I don't think it has anything to do with this innocent guy getting killed."

"Geez, Steve, I owe you dinner."

"That's okay Harvey, that's what friends are for. Just keep it under . . . ," Hank wrapped his knuckles on his end table. "Got to go, Harvey, that's my ride to work at the door. Don't forget, keep it quiet."

"I'll call you," Henderson said. Hank hit the end button on his cell phone.

At the click of the phone both men, at different ends of Baghdad, threw themselves back into their chairs and sighed. Whew, both thought, did I just dodge a bullet or what?

———◆———

At his end of Baghdad, Harvey Henderson was thinking, 'This is a perfect example of 'a story too good to check.' Thank God I did check it. That this Ralph Jackson guy was trying to use him and his paper in some kind of personal vendetta was obvious. A couple of months ago, Jackson walked up to him on the street and introduced himself as a recently arrived lawyer with the Star Foundation.

"I recognize you and I admire your work," said Jackson. "I thought it might be good for both of us and this country to know each other."

Flattered, and also sensing an opportunity, Henderson offered Jackson a seat and bought him an espresso. He should have known to be careful when Jackson approached him like that.

Ralph Jackson was right, Harvey Henderson was a good person to know, but what Jackson didn't know was that Harvey Henderson was also a bad person to know. Jackson had taken advantage of him and he wasn't going to forget it. It never occurred to Henderson that Steve, a/k/a Hank Jenkins, might have been the one with an agenda. After all, Steve had been solicited and seduced over many months. Although you had to sort through an awful lot of dribble, there was often useful information, proven, accurate, useful information, amongst all of Steve's philosophical ramblings.

———◆———

At his end of Baghdad, Hank's relief rapidly changed to anger. "That s.o.b. Jackson."

Hank took a quick shower, put on his normal work clothes and laced up a pair of sturdy leather half boots. After concealing an ever-present pistol and grabbing his cell phone, he left the apartment and took a roundabout path to the Provisional Authority motor pool. The only thing available was a battered, nondescript Toyota Land Cruiser, so he took it. By 7:24 a.m. he parked underneath Ralph Jackson's apartment window, stopped and used a small set of binoculars to see what he could see. His prey revealed an arm and about a third of his head around the edge of the window frame. Ralph was scanning the street and seconds later locked on to the binoculars. Hank pulled back from the windshield, but not quickly enough. Ralph spotted him.

Tough, Hank thought. If he doesn't know I'm here now, he will in a minute.

He knew Ralph was armed but was willing to bet the Ex-Green Beret wouldn't panic and start shooting. Jackson had been around. Besides, Hank was armed as well and unlike Ralph, he hadn't been retired for twelve years. He'd tried to avoid Ralph, then to reason with him, now he was just going to tell him. Recognizing he was angry, Hank waited to gather his thoughts and cool down.

Remember, Ralph's a good guy who's lost his way. Treat him like that if you can.

He climbed out of the Toyota, swept the streets and then the rooftops for threats as he moved. In seconds he was at the front door of Jackson's apartment building. Inside, Hank found himself in a large, dingy lobby with cinder block walls and a dark green and black linoleum tile floor. A lone bulb suspended high from the ceiling provided the only illumination, giving the place a dark, gloomy, 1930's mental hospital look. Off to the right an old Iraqi man sat behind the reception counter. As soon as he saw Hank was a Westerner he spit tobacco juice and returned to his newspaper. Hank stopped near the bottom of the staircase to wait.

It wasn't long until he heard Jackson's sure-footed stride pounding down the stairs. Hank removed his sunglasses and stood close to one of the building's support pillars. In the next second, he and Ralph were watching each other as the lawyer descended the stairs. Ralph didn't seem surprised to see an athletic looking Hank Jenkins, minus the nerd suit and glasses, waiting for him.

———◆———

Ralph knew it was Hank Jenkins with the binoculars and, of

course, he was standing at the bottom of the steps. Minus the baggy suit, anyone could see Hank for what he was, a whip strong, athletic looking guy.

"What? No Mr. McGoo outfit?"

"I told you when we first met to stay out of this," Hank said.

"What are you talking about," Ralph said. He was thinking, There's no way he can prove I called that reporter.

"Someone's been calling the news media down on the authority and the coalition military command, spreading rumors the U.S. is running roughshod over Iraqi sovereignty and its citizens' civil rights."

"Church mice can be such pests," Ralph said, grinning. The bell with Jenkins.

To his credit, Hank didn't flinch, try to kick Ralph in the testicles or even call him a smart sass.

"I pulled your jacket," Hank said, referring to Ralph's military records. "You saw some hard times in Desert Storm, especially that chemical bunker explosion with those kids. That's enough to set anyone back, but just because you dropped out doesn't mean the rest of us can. Everyone stops bailing, the boat sinks. You know that."

Unwelcome images flashed before Ralph's eyes. If Jenkins thought watching children being burned alive was nothing more than "hard times," he was tougher than Ralph was. He wished Jenkins had kept his mouth shut and just kicked him instead.

"What are you talking about," Ralph said

"Have it your way, James Bond. I'm so impressed with your tight-lipped style I'll spell it out for you. If you don't stay out of this, it's going to get very dangerous— not only for you but also for Judge Hami."

James Bond? What a smart sass, Ralph thought. In a parallel dimension somewhere, this guy and I are probably friends. Not in this one though.

"Are you threatening me, Mr. Jenkins?"

"Threatening you?" Hank came a bit closer. "I'm merely pointing out it's a lot more dangerous in Baghdad without a weapon than it is with one. That .38 of yours is illegal and I might decide to take it."

Ralph thought it through. The handgun, of course, was illegal, and if Colonel Board had demanded it , he would've probably turned it over and picked up another one. Jenkins was different. No doubt part of it was pride, but there was also the potential for miscalculation. If Colonel Henry Board, for example, thought he was a pushover and went too far, Ralph could deal with him with relative ease. Addressing miscalculation on the part of Jenkins, however, would be very dangerous, and not just for Jenkins and Jackson. Others were likely to get hurt in the crossfire. Much better to deal with this, right now, Ralph decided.

Ralph answered slowly. "You . . . take my pistol? I haven't been out that long."

He stared Hank, who was about 4 feet away, right in the eye. Hank held his gaze and inched forward until he was just out of arms reach, then ever so slightly shifted his weight so it was equally distributed between both feet.

Hank lowered his voice to a sinister whisper.

"Been out? Out of what, James?"

Both of them bent their knees and went up on the balls of their feet. Otherwise, they were careful not to move. They were standing really close to each other. As the seconds ticked by, Ralph began to think one of them was going to die and he wasn't sure who it would be. Actually, it had been a long time and Jenkins obviously knew what he was doing. Finally, Hank broke the silence.

"You're not dealing with street thugs this time. That pistol won't keep you safe. It definitely won't keep Judge Hami safe and it's not me you have to worry about. It's the new Iraqis. You might've been hot spit in your twenties, but you're just a washed up civilian now."

He kept his eyes on Ralph but took a step back.

———◆———

Ralph, who for a moment looked relieved, now narrowed his eyes. He shifted his weight, clearly angry and almost ready to step forward. Hank took another step back.

"This isn't just about what's best for Iraq. The Amani trial is putting Hami in danger. Did you think that ass Henderson wouldn't talk to anyone else about what you told him? People are furious and even worse, scared. I'm picking up all kinds of weird communications traffic that seems to be about the Amani trial and I can't get a grip on it. You can't keep Judge Hami safe – we can't keep Hami safe. I'm telling you, it's not us you have to worry about. It's the new Iraqis."

That stopped Ralph, so Hank turned around and left. Jackson's temper surprised the older man. As he walked out of the building, he thought, Jackson's going to get himself killed if he isn't careful.

Much of Special Operations work, he reflected, was similar to playing a sport or a musical instrument. You may have been a championship weightlifter, hockey player or concert pianist, but if you put it down and didn't play for 10 years, you deteriorated. Someone who tried to reenter the weight room, ice rink or concert hall and play with his former peers, after a layoff, was going to get badly hurt or badly embarrassed. Someone like Ralph Jackson, though, didn't play games or instruments. He'd "played" warfare, the ultimate contact sport, at the highest level. If he now tried to reenter, cold turkey, after all those years, he wasn't going to be embarrassed or get a muscle pull. He was going to get killed.

Because of his involvement with Hami, Ralph, like it or not, was perilously close to re-entering the fray. Hank wanted him nervous, self-aware. That was part of the reason he pushed him, betting on Jackson's experience to keep him from over-reacting, even now, even stressed like he just was. Sergeant Ralph Jackson retired, had to be reminded of what it was like. He didn't have the same skills, reflexes or emotional callouses he once had. He'd forgotten the power of that first splash of adrenaline and how it affected your thinking and reflexes. Ralph remembered, no doubt, but only dimly, how to adjust for those effects. But, weapons no longer felt like familiar old friends in his hands. Fear was no longer a frequent, if unwanted companion. To be safe, Ralph was going to have to stay out of the way or be very careful and take the time to work himself back into shape. Unfortunately for Ralph Jackson, spare time was in short supply in Baghdad in 2004. Then, there was that temper. It was bad enough that Ralph was likely to get killed if he persisted, but he'd likely get Judge Isha Hami killed as well.

Hank hoped he had just made that less likely.

CHAPTER 19

———◆———

AYAD AL-JABERI WAITED UNTIL THE last man left the shop before speaking.

"Why should we even allow those Kurdish dogs to leave the city alive?"

"Stop for one moment and think this through," Mahmoud Bahr al-Uloum said, exasperated.

Because of his position in the group, Sameer al-Hakim replied with more care.

"The Kurds are right. It was my idea to appoint Isha Hami as Judge and you are the one who wisely reserved the right to revisit the decision."

"I am not saying Hami doesn't need to be removed," said Ayad. "One of the defense lawyers is a friend and he says she will never dismiss this case. He also says she is very skillful, in a female fashion. She must go. But who are these Kurdish savages to come here, amongst civilized people, and threaten us. We should kill those two insolent dogs and then remove Hami. Her removal will give the Kurds what they want, the death of their messengers will remind them that their insolence will not go unpunished."

Mahmoud was on the verge of exploding when Sameer held up his hand like a policeman stopping a car at an intersection. Mahmoud managed to choke back his reply. Sameer spoke in measured tones to Ayad.

"The Kurds are dogs, yes, but we still need them. They did indeed cross an unforgivable line when they presumed to threaten us in our home. However, consider the manner in which they did so. If you or I or Mahmoud had warned the other in such a fashion, we would have considered . . ."

"They are not Arabs, they are Kurds!"

". . . this to have been a measured and respectful warning," concluded Sameer.

"They do not see their delegation as the insult it was. I agree this presumption must be punished, but it need not be punished now. The Kurds are still useful in fighting the Baathists. Until the Baathists are destroyed, I suggest it is wise to ignore this. The Kurds do not know their place, but that is ignorance, not outright defiance. The Kurds don't think they did anything wrong. Let them go on thinking that. Our people know nothing of this. We'll tell the Kurds to keep this matter confidential, then we can avenge their slight at a time of our own choosing."

Ayad Al-Jaberi had listened absently, and then with more intensity, as Sameer al-Hakim spoke. When Sameer finished, Ayad sipped a glass of water, buying time. Mahmoud Bahr al-Uloum's anger at Ayad evaporated while he listened to Sameer and watched Ayad's response.

Sameer al-Hakim is becoming a very dangerous man, Mahmoud thought to himself. Meanwhile, Ayed looked up at the ceiling, lost in thought, so Sameer risked a quick glance at Mahmoud to gauge his reaction. Mahmoud gave Sameer a quick smile and nod of approval while thinking, How can I have Sameer al-Hakim blamed for Hami's removal without implicating myself and without endangering the chances of having her removed?

Ayad looked at Mahmoud and then Sameer. Glancing back at Mahmoud, he said, "I assume you agree with this argument."

"It is persuasive."

"I agree. Like our decision regarding Hami's appointment, I reserve the right to revisit this decision at the proper time. In my father's day these Kurds were waiters, shepherds, shoeshine boys, and other serving men. It is an insult we must even eat with them -- they're little better than pagans."

Sameer bowed his head humbly while thinking, Of course, my opinion does not matter, you pompous asses. As for you, Ayad al-Jaberi, you should live so long as to take revenge on the Kurds. Your son is a weakling and your days are numbered.

"How do we remove Hami, then," asked Ayad, "since we are all agreed upon the necessity?"

"Since Hami was my recommendation, I feel it's my responsibility to correct the situation. Let me ask first, are we agreed that she cannot be removed from her position by using political power?"

Ayad and Mahmoud both spoke at the same time. "No, she cannot be removed politically." The men glanced at each other and then Ayad gestured to Mahmoud to continue.

"You chose too well, Sameer. The Americans would not even consider removing her from office, absent the kind of ironclad proof of corruption even we couldn't manufacture on short notice. The Europeans in particular have been impressed by Hami's appointment. This has eased the pressure on the Americans. Her removal would create a firestorm, not only within the American government but also within the news media, Europe and the United Nations. Finally, don't underestimate her popularity among the people. Her husband was quite a man—at times in my life, I even considered him a friend. Her father, on the other hand, was an enemy, but a very formidable one. This is a woman who has earned respect in her own right and is strengthened even more by family loyalties."

"In that case, she must die," said Sameer al-Hakim.

Ayad al-Jaberi and Mahmoud Bahr al-Uloum both smiled ruefully.

"Of course she must die," said Ayad. "How that is to be accomplished. That is the question."

"It will be difficult, but it can be done. Remember, the Ministry of Justice Building is in South Baghdad. This is my area, these are my people. The U.S. and Iraqi security police are not friends . . . please allow me to address these concerns in my own way."

"The Ministry itself and not her home or vehicle? How do you plan to accomplish this," asked Mahmoud?

"My friend, is it not enough that I will take sole responsibility for this matter? Shouldn't I be allowed to decide this myself? But to answer your question, I don't know yet. I must consult with a few colleagues, consider various plans, contact others who may be of help. All of this will be compartmentalized, so no one knows what anyone else does, except me."

Ayad unexpectedly spoke on behalf of Sameer.

"Come, Mahmoud," said Ayad, "one need not approve of all Sameer al-Hakim does to acknowledge that he's been an honorable and useful colleague in post Saddam Iraq. His advice has been sound and even when it has not, he has been willing to make things right. I say if Sameer can fix this situation, then who are we to ask for his means and methods in advance."

Looking at Sameer he said, "If you take responsibility for the outcome, then I care not how you achieve your result."

Mahmoud Al-Uloum decided at that moment that Sameer al-Hakim would die and die soon. The expression on his face, however, was merely thoughtful.

"Well said, my friend," said Mahmoud. "Responsibility for this matter, Sameer, rests with you. The freedom to choose your own means rightly rests with you. I can only speak for myself when I say you have my complete trust and confidence."

"Thank you both for your confidence. I think it's now best that I take my leave and begin to consider how to justify your trust in this matter."

Mahmoud Bahr al-Uloum and Ayad al-Jaberi both nodded.

"I must leave as well," said Ayad.

The three men rose from their chairs and walked to the front of the restaurant. As they approached, Mahmoud's son unlocked the door and held it open. The three men kissed each other's cheeks, nodded and went off in separate directions. Before Sameer and his entourage reached the end of the block, a black Toyota Corolla sedan pulled beside them.

I will be glad when the political climate in Baghdad permits me to own a Mercedes, Sameer thought, sliding into the backseat. He flipped open a cell phone, hit the speed dial and listened to the number beep out in his ear.

"Yes," answered his chief lieutenant, Ashraf Hamdoun.

Even on cell phones, Sameer al-Hakim was cautious with how much actual information he conveyed. Under the Baathists, he made great use of cell phones to communicate with his men, but the Americans and their fancy technology worried him. So, instead of actually communicating information over the cell phone, he used it to transmit words with prearranged meanings to his employees and confederates.

"I've just left dinner and thought we should get together for coffee, but good coffee for a change."

"Of course, Sameer. How about our favorite shop?"

"Fine."

Sameer hit the "end" button, cutting the connection. In their personal code, Sameer al-Hakim's use of "good" coffee meant a serious meeting and that Hamdoun should bring heavy security with him. Hamdoun's use of "our favorite shop" specified a certain warehouse near the river docks owned and operated by Sameer al-Hakim as the location for their meeting.

As his car was sped toward the docks, Sameer was forming a plan. If Isha Hami was assassinated, the three men with the most interest in her District would naturally be suspect. The three men most interested in Hami's District, of course, were Sameer, Mahmoud Bahr al-Uloum and Ayad al-Jaberi. They'd be subjected to a great deal of scrutiny. Business would suffer.

The best way to eliminate Hami was to do it in way where she didn't seem to be the target. Specifically targeting Hami would be dangerous and Sameer knew that his men might be identified and then traced back to him should they be used against the Judge. After Hami's death, the Americans and Hami's family would be furious and willing to pay to discover who ordered the assassination. The answer, then, was to use men who could never be linked to Sameer. The attack should make Hami appear to be an accidental or at least an incidental casualty.

A terrorist attack, Sameer decided, was just about perfect.

On one hand, the Americans thought him a legitimate collaborator with the occupation force and the new Iraqi government. Knowledgeable Iraqis, on the other hand, knew him to be a professional criminal. Neither of his occupations, collaborator or criminal, would make him a plausible ally of the Baathists. Sameer smiled.

Second, if the Baathists launched the terrorist attack against a government building, of course their targets would be government officials. The more collaborators they could kill, and the higher the position they held, the better. But even if only Hami was killed in the attack, which he thought would require an assault, it would not direct suspicion toward him or his Shia allies. Baathists trying to disrupt the new Iraq would, of course, want to kill Judges.

It just so happened one of his new enterprises was providing safe houses and occasional transportation for the Baathist cells. The men who originally approached him had been both desperate and knowledgeable. They were desperate because the Americans were truly ransacking the entire country. Baathist resistance was shattered, but providing Baathists with services for a fee offered Sameer a lucrative sideline. When the Baathists went underground, they took with them enormous sums of money, denominated in both U.S. dollars and Euros. In fact, at the time, Sameer had tried to steal some of it.

Once the Baathists were defeated militarily, they turn to Sameer al-Hakim since they were well acquainted with him and his capabilities. In Saddam's Iraq he'd always made himself useful, or scarce, depending upon the political climate. Although his criminal enterprises were well known, he was usually able to provide enough service to the government to keep himself safe. During these "calm" periods, his operations went on unmolested. But when he was not needed, when the fickle Baathist powers or Saddam's psychotic sons decided that "corruption" needed to be eliminated, Sameer tried to disappear until common sense reasserted itself. Nevertheless, he was often in danger because he had an insatiable desire for money.

Sameer made an effort to assist the re-emergence of "common sense" by paying money or delivering incriminating photographs or tape recordings of high Baathist officials into the right hands. One way or the other, carrot or stick, Sameer managed to ride Saddam Hussein's tiger for a long time. He managed this feat because he was almost fearless and immensely greedy. The Baathists decided to gamble that Sameer al-Hakim hadn't outgrown his avarice.

So when the Baathists arrived in the middle of the night, Sameer greeted them. Now called insurgents by the Western media, Saddam's thugs were armed not only with A.K. 47's and demolitions, but also with U.S. dollars. Sameer's bodyguards outnumbered the Baathists that night, but the crime lord's resolve to exact vengeance melted when he saw all the greenbacks the Baathists offered. Nadim Allawis, a bitter enemy, sat a nylon bag on Sameer's kitchen table and zipped it open to reveal Two Hundred Fifty Thousand U.S. Dollars.

"There's more where this comes from," said Allawis. "When the Americans grow weary and leave, Saddam and our tribes will not forget those who helped us . . . or those who opposed us."

The implied threat angered Sameer, but it also stuck in his throat.

In parts of his mind he suppressed or tried to ignore, he still feared the Baathists would return to power and exact vengeance. Plus, there was all that money. Two Hundred Fifty Thousand Dollars now and another Two Hundred Fifty Thousand Dollars in two weeks, all for the use of a few warehouses, a few empty houses and a few vehicles, most of which would be returned. He agreed.

It was time to take advantage of his business arrangement with the Baathists. Like a chess master, Sameer thought five or six moves ahead of his present situation. In his still forming plan, he mentally listed his contacts in the new Iraqi police department or military. They'd need a diversion, something to ensure the removal of the American military presence from the Ministry of Justice. He gazed off in the distance, formulating an approach that would convince the Baathists it was their idea. Finally, he wondered how much money he could squeeze out of the Baathists for the right to kill the Judge, for the right to do his bidding. Sameer smiled. Time was short and failure would literally cost him his life. He was balanced on top of a fence. On one side lay death, on the other the elimination of one enemy by another enemy, who would pay Sameer for the privilege of doing his dirty work. The slightest miscalculation would send Sameer plunging to his death. He had perhaps an hour to completely plot his strategy before meeting with the Baathists. He should have been terrified. Instead, his face was pasted with a huge grin. He felt more alive than he had in months.

CHAPTER 20

HANK JENKINS DIDN'T HURRY, BUT he was through the lobby and out the door before Ralph had time to think. He bounded down the stairs and jumped into the Land Cruiser. Just as he was pulling into traffic, his cell phone went off.

"Yes."

"Hank, this is Dave back at the office."

Dave was Dave Barnes, Hank's second in command. He was a young Ivy League guy, but pretty good despite all that.

"What's up?"

"I think you'd better come back to the office sir."

"Can it wait?"

"It can wait about as long as it will take for you to drive back here. I think you'll want to see this."

"I'm on my way."

Forty-five minutes later Hank was in his office holding two separate intercept transcripts. One came from a hard wire landline outside of Mosul. The owner of the phone was a cleaning lady at a large mosque. She wasn't particularly faithful to Islam but held the job as a creature of the Baathists for years. Before the war the Baathists kept their eyes on the mosques and this lady was part of their network. The United States watched and listened to her because she periodically generated useful intelligence. The second intercept came from a cell phone call between two terrorists of different factions. One faction was Baathist, the other a so-called foreign fighter faction. Both conversations indicated that Al Queda leader al-Zarqawi was meeting with two high-level Baathist operatives in a small village, just across the Iranian border. Hank read on and suddenly froze. The three men, one caller crowed, will arrange the end of "the arrogant harlot."

"What's wrong Hank?"

"Did you task the NRO," Hank asked, referring to the super-secret National Reconnaissance Office.

"Yeah, as soon as I read both the transcripts. I also scrambled your operations team."

Hank lifted an eyebrow and smiled a half smile at Barnes.

"Look," Barnes said, "I figured if I did all of this in your name, without your approval, I was in deep. I also figured if I waited until you got back without doing anything I was in deep. I'd just as soon end up in deep crap for killing the guy than letting him go."

Hank laughed along with Barnes.

"Good job, son. How long until the ops team gets here?"

"Probably half an hour."

"Go requisition a couple of choppers, four golf carts with spare batteries and four Iranian uniforms . . . make them border guards. How long until we get the NRO stuff," asked Hank, referring to the satellite photos.

"Before the ops team gets here, maybe fifteen, twenty minutes."

"As soon as you get the photos, bring them in. Until then, I'm going to change and read over these transcripts again. When the boys arrive get them suited up, but tell them I haven't made up my mind yet."

Barnes left, closing the door behind him.

Hank re-read the intercept transcripts and grew increasingly agitated. Maybe it was because he'd just come from his confrontation with Ralph Jackson, but the phrase, "the arrogant harlot" bothered him. Yeah, it could mean America, but she was usually "the great Satan," right? These transcripts were from two separate intercepts at two separate locations. They transcribed two separate conversations each involving two separate insurgent factions. Both confirmed the same conversations and referred to and confirmed the location of the same meeting. When sources from two separate locations and four organizations corroborated the same information, it was a pretty good lead.

Additionally, the lead made sense. Rumors about a meeting between a high-level Al Queda leader and a senior Baathist had been flying around for days. That's what the failed ambush in Gundar was all about. Hank considered the location. A village just inside the Iranian border was a likely place for such a meeting. Although not as bad as Pakistan, the North Western Iranian border was a wild place under only nominal Iranian control. The meeting location and all the rumors, combined with the types of intercepts reflecting two independent sources gave the intelligence reliability.

Hank grabbed a bottle of water from a short office fridge and returned to his desk. The village was also a good place to set up an ambush for Hank and his team. The bad guys knew the Americans were hunting them and that they'd tried to bug every communications device from Turkey to Kuwait. Maybe the terrorists decided it was time to do a little hunting of their own. Hank wanted the satellite photographs. He'd check out the village, then make a final decision.

We should, he thought, be able to see something on the ground that gives it away. If, for example, in addition to everything else the photos showed a large number of parked vehicles, he'd be inclined to take a chance on the intelligence.

After sucking down the last of the water, he dropped the bottle into a can and walked to a green metal locker tucked away in the corner of his office. The locker looked like any gym locker found in the average YMCA. It wasn't. When you were close enough to actually touch it you realized how heavy it was. The metal used to construct this "locker" was twice the normal strength and thickness. It featured a simple, non-electronic keypad lock into which Hank punched a combination. The spring and interior bolt clicked free. There were three assault rifles and two submachine guns leaning in the corners of the locker. A clothes bar was bolted inside and loaded down with an assortment of uniforms. One chest-high shelf was stacked with box upon box of 9 mm ammunition, another held various sorts of web gear, hats and footwear and on the highest shelf were two 9 mm pistols in leather holsters.

Hank slid the hangers apart and found what he wanted, the uniform of an Iranian Intelligence Officer with the rank of Lieutenant Colonel. He took the uniform, matching footwear, web gear, and insignia to his desk and then returned. The two pistols were of Iraqi and Iranian origin so he naturally picked the Iranian one. He looked longingly at the Iranian origin assault rifle and paused, conflicted. On the one hand, he really wanted the full automatic fire capacity of the assault rifle at his disposal. On the other hand, intelligence officers didn't carry such weapons. It's something that would be noticed, and if Hank had one motto in life, it was don't be noticed. He stayed proficient with every weapon in the locker, so he took some comfort with his familiarity with the Iranian pistol. He was still vacillating about the rifle when a knock sounded on his door.

"Barnes, Sir. The NRO photos are here and the team's suiting up."

"Come in"

Barnes slipped in the door, closing it behind him and put the photos on Hank's desk.

"I know you looked at them, so what do they say?"

"They say go."

"Tell the boys. Get the choppers and carts to the airport and get us a van."

Barnes left and Hank impulsively grabbed the assault rifle, three magazines, and boxes of ammunition. Taking everything over to his desk, he emptied out the ammunition boxes and began loading the magazines while looking at the NRO photos. Dave was right. The village was located right where intelligence said it would be and the sand surrounding it was etched and crisscrossed with deep tire tracks. At least four sets of tracks from two different directions led to and disappeared into the village mosque. He flipped through the photos, stopping at the ones that showed village children cavorting along the tire tracks, chasing each other with palm fronds. Besides having good clean fun, the kids were obliterating any evidence of the tire tracks through and outside of the village and taking only minutes to do it.

The mission was a 'go,' Hank decided. The palm fronds trick was just a little too cute to be part of an ambush set up. When you're setting someone up, you don't want to make it too easy, but you can't make it too hard either. It was dumb luck the satellites were positioned to catch the kids wiping out the tire tracks. This was no setup, it was a real, high-level meeting. He felt that familiar surge of adrenaline and realized he had a chance to wipe out two brutal murders in one raid.

He jotted a quick note on his desk blotter, "next report mention kids using palm fronds on tire tracks." It was a great technique. Unless your satellite or aerial recon was timed exactly right, all you'd see was sand, or kids playing in the sand. Even if you caught them in the act, unless you had reason to think something was going on in the village or town, you'd just think it was kids playing. Beyond the village, the wind quickly took over for the kids and erased any trace of the vehicles' arrival.

"Boy, did I just get lucky." Hank smiled.

His mind made up, he finished loading the pistol and rifle magazines, adjusted his Iranian uniform, and found a couple likely hiding places on it for hand grenades. After checking himself in the mirror he slammed the locker door shut, put on his hat, slung his rifle and swept the photographs into a manila file. By now Barnes would have cleared the hallways of personnel. No one would or could see him dressed in an Iranian uniform. He left his office for the secure motor pool where his ops team, four CIA contract employees, awaited him. These were the men who would ride into Iran with him on the electric golf carts. Hank turned into a stairway and pounded down three flights of concrete stairs into the basement. Someone buzzed him through a steel fire door and into a brightly lit garage. An Army Corporal looked him in the face, his finger on the trigger guard of his M16. Hank eyed him back and nodded. The Corporal waited until the door re-latched, then relaxed and turned back to the monitor.

His team was already dressed in Iranian uniforms and milling around a large wooden table loaded with equipment. They looked up long enough to nod at him, then returned to their own preparations. High definition sat photos of the village were scattered across one of the tables. The photos were close-ups, intended for mission planning purposes. They provided the team, in effect, with a detailed map of the village. The center of attention was the mosque, its location, and structural detail. That's where the enemy was and that's where they'd be going. Soon. While each man suited up, they kept their eyes on and tried to memorize the details of every photo on the table. Knowing the entire village layout could mean the difference between life and death.

CHAPTER 21

SAMEER AL-HAKIM'S COROLLA ROLLED TO a stop in front of a generic looking, prefabricated metal warehouse close to the Tigris River in South Baghdad. His driver and bodyguard got out and swept the area with practiced care.

"Looks clear, Sameer," said the driver.

Sameer got out and bounded up the cast iron stairway toward a steel man door. Before he reached it, a second vehicle carrying the rest of his men rolled to a stop. They got out and filed up the steps behind Sameer and his driver.

The men breezed into a large, cavern-like room with vaulted ceilings and crossed over a concrete slab floor to the far end of the building. Other well-armed members of the Sameer organization were waiting and cleared a path up to the staircase landing, nodding respectfully. The entourage swept up the steps and through the landing into a small office overlooking the warehouse floor.

Sameer's Chief Lieutenant, Ashraf Hamdoun, jumped up with the others when his boss arrived. Sameer moved behind the desk and sat down. Hamdoun chose a seat across from him and waited.

"We're presented with a great opportunity and something of a threat," Sameer began. "We have the opportunity to significantly strengthen our position within the Shia community. However, to do so we must deal with the Baathists. How many men did you bring Ashraf?"

"Eighteen, heavily armed, plus the four of us here."

"I have five from the meeting, along with my driver and bodyguard. That should be enough."

"Enough for what?"

"For a meeting with the Baathists. We're going there, now."

Hamdoun raised an eyebrow. "Perhaps we should call first?"

Sameer smiled. "Yes, we'll call, but not until we're on our way. I don't want them to be surprised, but I don't want them prepared either."

"Should we discuss their security," asked Ahmed Khalilzad, another top aide.

Khalilzad and Sameer spent fifteen minutes reviewing the Baathists security dispositions around their makeshift headquarters. Then they decided how to deploy their men. The goal was not only to ensure their own security, but also to intimidate the Baathists before they had time to consider resisting. After a few final minutes ironing out transportation and the final disposition of the men, Sameer stood up, satisfied.

"Shock and Awe," he joked. "Let's go then, I'll call them from the road."

When they reached the warehouse floor, Sameer's three lieutenants, Ahmed Khalilzad, Qassim Zahra, and Abdul Jalal peeled off to brief their men. Sameer and Hamdoun, followed by Sameer's driver and bodyguard all left the warehouse and jumped into the Corolla. The driver waited until Zahra left the warehouse and everyone loaded. Then he pulled out, leading four vehicles full of men and weapons.

The convoy left the warehouse area and merged onto a highway known as River Road. Its only military checkpoint had been entrusted to the Iraqi police. Sameer, of course, made sure that the only policemen assigned to the roadblock were the ones on his payroll. While he dialed Major Nadim Allawis, his underboss, Abdul Jalal, called the police checkpoint. Timing was important and they didn't want to be delayed.

"Yes?" said Allawis.

"It is me," said Sameer. "I'm coming to visit and I'm bringing my entire family, so don't be surprised. Tell your sons to be on their best behavior. I know sometimes our families rub each other the wrong way, but why should this prevent us from meeting or interfere with our friendship?"

"Of course not," said Allawis, struggling to keep the fury out of his voice. "But I don't think today is a good day. I can do much more justice to the honor you pay me if I could be prepared with food, drink, and entertainment. Another day would be much better."

"I'm afraid my schedule won't permit that, my friend, and we really must see each other before I'm unavailable . . . because of business."

"This is just impossible. My humble home isn't prepared for such an honor."

"You're too modest. Even now we can see your home from the highway."

As Sameer spoke, his first vehicle approached the checkpoint. An Iraqi police lieutenant was standing alongside the road, flanked by three other Iraqi policeman carrying assault weapons. A second group of police watched from a nearby machine gun mounted jeep. The lead vehicle slowed and Abdul Jalal rolled down his window and leaned out. The lieutenant stared, recognized Jalal's face and then wind-milled his hand and arm around and over his head, clearing the vehicle through the checkpoint. The convoy sped past the barricade with little delay.

"You're already on your way?" asked Allawis.

"Yes. We're turning onto your street. I'll send some of my boys to help yours with their chores."

Both Sameer and Allawis understood some of Sameer's men would be joining the Baathist sentries posted around the warehouse.

"See you soon," Sameer said, snapping his cell phone closed and cutting the connection.

He allowed himself a smile as he imagined the Baathist cell, still half asleep or half dressed, scrambling for their weapons. Only someone who'd been with him all the times he'd wake in the middle of the night, secretly terrified the Baathists would catch him, could truly savor the moment. As his caravan approached the Baathists' safe house two vehicles split off, sped around and disgorged men near the sentries. Sameer and his main body of men pulled up directly in front of the warehouse and jumped out, wasting no time getting to the warehouse door.

As expected, the door was locked so the first of his men removed a short barreled shotgun brought along for one purpose, door busting. The shotgun was loaded with double 0.0. buckshot, meaning buckshot about the size of marbles. Instead of one shell being full of 100 small pellets, the shell in the shotgun had perhaps eight large projectiles in them.

Boom, click–click, boom.

The man chosen for the job was experienced and the metal fire door was no match for properly placed buckshot. The deadbolt mechanism ripped back from the door itself, allowing a second, larger man to smash his shoulder against it, thrusting it open with the squeal of twisted metal. Sameer's men streamed through the door and scattered throughout the makeshift barracks, shouting in Arabic as they went.

"Don't shoot, don't shoot, we came to talk."

Men clad in only their underwear scrambled for firing positions or dove behind cover as Jalal himself burst through the door.

"Hold fire, hold fire," shouted Major Allawis, as he strode into the middle of the room. "You asses . . . you fools. Forget that this is an insult, it's stupid, dangerous."

Allawis didn't stop until his face was only inches from Jalal's.

"Where is Sameer, where is that...?"

"I speak to you respectfully. Shouldn't you do the same," asked Sameer as he entered the building?

His men waited for the situation to stabilize, then waved him forward. Additional Sameer soldiers with automatic weapons poured through the doorway behind their leader, scattering and taking up defensive positions. Allawis was given no time to protest and only seconds to decide whether to open fire or to await events. The Baathist hesitated and then it was too late. Sameer's men were inside the warehouse, hiding behind boxes of machinery and other shipping cargo. Jalal backed off, allowing Sameer to approach Allawis.

"Why don't we stop this silliness? We need to talk," said Sameer. Allawis was fuming.

"Why should I talk to you after you insult me . . . ?"

"We don't have time for this. When you came to my house last year, did I bring up all the times you and your men chased me from place to place, threatening my life?"

Payback, Major Allawis, or at least, a down payment on an outstanding debt. Recognizing his position, Allawis answered slowly.

"No. If you wish to talk, let's talk."

"Show me where. Just you, me, Ashraf and one of your men."

"Very well. Follow me."

Allawis led them to a small storage room and snapped a switch. A naked bulb hanging from the ceiling illuminated the room in a harsh glare. Ashraf closed the door while Sameer and Allawis each sat on one of the wooden crates filling the room. Their aides stood on opposite sides the door, watching each other warily.

"I will waste no time," Sameer said. "You and your men must leave my building."

The Baathist at the doorway glanced toward Sameer before catching himself and turning back toward Ashraf. Allawis leaned back on his crate, seemingly unconcerned.

"You have a quarter million of our dollars. We have an agreement."

"I know," said Sameer. "I have your money in my car. You're entitled to a refund."

Now Allawis leaned forward. Sameer al-Hakim did not return money, especially U.S. dollars and everyone knew it. Sameer knew what he was thinking. Either this was a trap and a desperate gun battle was about to start, or Sameer was worried to an extent Allawis had never before seen. Rather than snapping, Allawis spoke in a measured, thoughtful manner.

"Of course, this is your building and if you are willing to return our money, we will leave. But will this solve your problem in a way that makes up for your loss of all that money and your alliance with us?"

Before Sameer could speak, Allawis continued.

"There is some reason a businessman like you is willing to part with a relationship as profitable as ours. It must be some sort of serious problem, perhaps even a threat. We have had our differences in the past, but now it seems to me most of your problems, and most threats to you, would also be a problem of mine and a threat to me. Might it not make sense to discuss this with me? If I have nothing useful to contribute, you can still terminate our agreement, return the money and we will leave. But if it is a mutual problem or threat and it is within my power, I am willing to assist you. We can then continue our relationship, to our mutual profit."

Sameer waited in silence, allowing the tension to build.

"There is, of course, a business complication. I do not see how you can help with this, although it is a threat to you as well."

"I know that although they meet with you, neither Ayad al-Jaberi or Mahmoud Bahr al-Uloum are friends."

"Ahh, this is true, but my biggest problem is with the government. Ayad has been making noise about my sympathies to the former Bath Regime and letting all who will listen know I aid and abet what they call 'terrorism.' Some people find these allegations of great interest."

"Who's the collaborationist prosecutor, I'll ..." began the Baathist. Sameer cut him off.

"If the prosecutor is unable to continue, the government will merely appoint another prosecutor. The problem is that two of the three Judges with jurisdiction in South Baghdad are hostile. One Judge is the creature of Ayad al-Jaberi. The other Judge is–"

" I know the other Judge. Hami. I would have thought this woman had learned her lesson. She remains foolish."

"I've heard rumors of the punishment Saddam imposed upon her."

"These are not rumors, they're true. We should have killed her."

"Indeed, it's a shame you did not. One Judge, perhaps, I could deal with, two is impossible. If anything would happen to Hami, then her family, as well as Ayad and Mahmoud, would all instantly suspect me. They would not wait for proof. So, I cannot avoid prosecution without disassociating my activities from your's. Now you know why I am prepared to walk away from Two Hundred Fifty Thousand Dollars. If you have any agents in place or officials who can be influenced, this, I would be interested in."

Sameer was confident Allawis political influence didn't reach that high, but he didn't want the idea of an assault and assassination of Hami and Kalid, Ayad's Judge, to come from him. A terrorist assault as camouflage for a political assassination. Nadim Allawis had to believe the idea was his own, not Sameer's. Allawis had not survived, and thrived, in the regime of Saddam Hussein without a large measure of cunning. If the Baathist had the slightest suspicion Sameer was manipulating him, the entire plan would fail. Allawis had to work this out on his own. Sameer forced his agitation and desire to close the deal down deep, into his stomach.

After what seemed like hours, but in reality was seconds, Allawis spoke.

"Whatever influence we have in this area, we cannot at this time use."

"This is what I thought. I understand."

Sameer channeled his anxiety over his plan into an apparent desire to terminate the interview and get Allawis out of his life. Even as he spoke, he could tell he was successful in transferring his anxiety over one outcome onto the other outcome.

"Wait, Sameer al-Hakim," said Allawis respectfully. "Often times when one is involved in a tactical situation, he doesn't see the board as clearly as one outside of it. I would suggest a different solution to your problem. This is a solution that is within my power and will benefit not only you, but also me."

Sameer allowed himself to sink back onto his crate with a sigh.

"What solution, Major?"

"Your problem is you're threatened by an investigation you can't sidetrack because of two uncooperative Judges. My mission is to disrupt the puppet government of America and discourage Iraqis from collaborating with it. I suggest an attack on the Ministry of Justice building. We will attack when both Judges are there and ensure both are killed."

"This is impossible. How will you get past the American and Iraqi security?"

"For this, I will need your assistance. The Americans are likely to move additional forces north, leaving South Baghdad mostly in the hands of the collaborators. I know you have influence with the South Baghdad police. Prior to our attack, we will create a diversion. If you can convince the leaders of the security detail to respond to the diversion, we'll attack and the Judges will die."

For a full minute, Sameer said nothing. He stared at a spot over Allawis's left shoulder, pursed his lips and stayed silent. Finally, he looked back at Allawis.

"Such a response from the Baghdad Police to anything less than a monumental diversion will prove very expensive to arrange."

"Second," Sameer continued, "although Saddam weakened Hami's family, as well as her husband's family, they still pose a threat. They may not be as powerful as they once were, but they still have power, friends, and respect. If anything happens to Hami, I will be blamed for the attack. I do not relish a confrontation with her families, weakened or not." Lightening his tone, Sameer said, "I do not relish confrontation with anyone. I am a businessman."

"I can't fully understand or address your concerns about retribution from Hami's family. I can, however, provide the money you'll need for the Baghdad police. I think someone as resourceful as you are can come up with a way to deflect suspicion away from you and onto someone else. Why not us? We will claim responsibility for the attack and no one will believe you and I would work together."

"Ayad al-Jaberi would. His Judge is every bit as much a problem as Hami," Sameer lied. "Without his Judge eliminated, for me, it is no better than a 50-50 chance that the investigation will end. Wait," he said as if the thought just occurred to him. "Wait, wait."

Allawis said nothing.

"Prior to your attack, I will abduct a member of Ayad's family. If your men will meet with mine, take him along and leave him, shot of course, at the scene, by the Baghdad Police, will this not look like the work of Ayad al-Jaberi? This is possible, but dangerous Allawis."

Both Allawis and Sameer wrestled with their thoughts. Finally, Allawis spoke.

"I can arrange for Ayad's man to be shot by a police weapon and left dead in the Ministry of Justice. Ayad's Judge, then, must not be harmed, only Hami. This is of no matter to you, Ayad's Judge will be neutered if his patron is blamed for the attack. Finally, you must decide what is in your best interest. Under my plan, you keep this money," he said, gesturing out the door toward Sameer's car. "You make a significant payment to your man in the police, further increasing your leverage over him and his gratitude toward you. Both of us maintain our current relationship. This not only provides you with money and our government with access to your resourcefulness, it also helps us ensure the future. Know this, Sameer," Allawis said, "in the end, we will return to power. I do not say this lightly. I do not say this because we are better than the Shias or the Kurds. I do not say this because we're better than the Americans. I say this because we, like you, are Sunni . . . and we have no choice. If we do not prevail, we die. You, however, now have a choice. I say respectfully, choose."

"I will discuss this with my advisers and consider it. By tomorrow, at 9:00 a.m. I will give you my answer. If my answer is yes, I will tell you the price for the diversion. In the meantime, I will keep the money and you will stay in your barracks. Is this acceptable?"

Major Allawis nodded and both men stood.

"Until tomorrow then," Sameer said.

He left through the door Ashraf had already opened for him. Ashraf followed behind Sameer followed by Allawis and his man. All four men, by gesture and facial expression, assured the men waiting in the warehouse bay all was well. When they reached the center of the warehouse, Sameer stopped and faced Allawis.

"A very interesting conversation, Major. I will consider all that you've said and call you tomorrow with my thoughts."

"I await your call."

When he walked away, Sameer's footsteps echoed off the walls of the cavern like structure. One by one, his men took turns emerging from behind scattered boxes, crates and machinery, and walking backward or sideways, toward the door. The final two men backed out the door and down to a waiting car. The doors slammed shut and they pulled out. Ashraf flipped open his cell and called the men with the Baathist sentries.

"Time to go home."

Sameer's caravan was already out of the Baathist compound and heading back the way it came. Ashraf looked at Sameer with unmasked admiration, but lost in thought, Sameer didn't even notice. The underboss looked like he wanted to ask his leader what he had been thinking and how he was able to turn the conversation the way he wanted. But he knew now was not the time and kept his mouth shut, with difficulty.

This is why Sameer al-Hakim leads us, he probably thought.

CHAPTER 22

———◆———

SOMETHING MADE ISHA STOP AT the patio door. The sun was just dropping behind the dunes. Naba was on Ralph Jackson's knee, whispering to him in English and looking to one side. Isha eased a little further into the doorway. The object of interest was Naba's new dog, lying on his side on the patio floor. They'd named the dog Tabooli, Arabic for a certain kind of split wheat grain salad popular in the Middle East. Choosing the name "Tabooli" was a collaborative effort between Isha and Naba. Ralph wanted to name the dog "Decadent," but Isha felt she had to draw the line somewhere. Tabooli lay sleeping, eyes closed, his little legs moving back and forth, as though he were running. Occasionally, his tail flopped up and down in a slow wag.

Ralph and Naba were giggling like two teenagers.

"SHHH," Ralph said. "If we're too loud, we will wake him up."

"Ralph, is he really dreaming?"

"Yes. Don't you think so?"

"I do. What do you think he is dreaming about, Ralph? I hope he only has good dreams. Sometimes, I have dreams I wish I didn't have. I dream of my mother and my father. This makes me sad. Sometimes I dream of when people were mean to Grandmother and I. It was long ago, but I remember, even though I was only a little girl back then. When I wake from these dreams, I'm afraid. I don't want Tabooli to be afraid. Ralph, do you ever dream and wake up afraid?"

Isha held her breath and tried not to move. Naba had turned from the dog and was looking up into Ralph's face with that solemn expression of hers. Ralph didn't seem the least bit uncomfortable. He looked back and thought for a moment.

"Naba, sometimes I dream and wake up afraid. Everyone I've ever met sometimes dreams and wakes up afraid, but not everyone is the same after they know it was just a dream. Some people wake up from their dream and are afraid. Then they remember it was only a dream. What they were afraid of didn't really happen. That makes them happy because it makes them remember how much good is in their life. For you, when you dream and then wake up, you might think of your grandmother. Or you might remember that no one is mean to you anymore. But not everyone does that. Other people wake up from their dream and they're afraid it will come true. They worry so much about what has never happened, and probably never will happen, that they miss all the good things in life. I try to be afraid only when I'm having a bad dream."

"Tabooli, though," he continued, "is not having bad dreams. Watch. Remember earlier when you and I rolled the ball back and forth?"

Naba smiled and nodded up and down.

"I think that's what he's dreaming about, when we were rolling the ball and Tabooli was chasing it."

"Yes. We let him get it sometimes. You said it had to be fun for him too."

"That's right. And what happened?"

"He ran and ran until he got the ball. Then he stood in between us, with the ball in his mouth, wagging his tail so hard that . . . Oh, Ralph! He's dreaming he's playing ball with us. That's his good dream!"

Ralph smiled at Naba.

"That's what I think, too."

Isha chose that moment to walk out.

"What I think he's dreaming is about running onto the patio, pooping on it and then running away from me. His tail is wagging because he's watching me clean it up!"

"Oh, grandmother!"

Everyone laughed.

———◆———

Later in the evening Isha and Ralph put Naba to bed. They returned to the patio and Isha explained how the desert affected their weather. Ralph was relaxed, letting his gaze drift aimlessly, when he noticed a red brick in the middle of the otherwise sand colored bricks on the outside of the house wall. After a moment of study in the fading light, Ralph could see it was covered with calligraphy.

One more, Ralph thought.

He wasn't very religious, so he didn't think it the least bit sacrilegious to play a game with himself, "Find the Bible verses." Ralph thought of it as a kind of Christian, "Where's Waldo." So far, he found nineteen verses on plates, plaques, bricks, tiles, and embroidery throughout Isha's house. Then, as his eye drifted again he saw her satellite dish jutting off the back roof and smiled, remembering Isha saying, "the best of the old and the best of the new."

The two friends were sitting on the Hamis' patio, part of a traditional courtyard, enclosed with sun dried mud-brick walls in the back of Isha's home. The remnants of dinner were off to the side. The late evening was warm, but a fine breeze kept them both comfortable. Ralph was nursing his last beer while Isha sipped her tea. Tabooli lay at Isha's feet. Ever since Ralph arranged for the dog to receive vaccinations and gave him a flea bath, Isha had begun to warm up to him. Absently, she rubbed the back of Tabooli's neck with her bare foot.

"Don't let Naba see you doing that."

"Ralph, I'm so delighted by how good you are with her. I often think to myself what a fine father you would make. Something haunts you, my friend, but it doesn't seem to have darkened you. Whatever it is, perhaps it's time to let it go."

"You don't understand what I've seen and done Isha." Ralph rolled the beer bottle between his hands and gazed into the desert. In his mind's eye he saw visions of kids, of Republican Guard machine gunners, and stacks of Shia bodies. Suddenly he just wanted to get it all out, to explain it to someone whose opinion really mattered to him. It hadn't taken long before he heard the rumors about what happened to Isha before the invasion. He'd seen Saddam's handiwork, first hand, so he believed them. Here was someone who could understand just how much that final battle cost him.

"I've been to your country before Judge, during the First Gulf War. In fact, I was here before anyone else, training and encouraging your people to rise up against Saddam. I was also here when the first President Bush said 'pull the plug' and we withdrew our support from the Shias. I was in As Salman when the Republican Guard arrived."

Now that he started, he found the words spilled out of him and it felt like air rushing out of a balloon. He told Isha everything he'd experienced and everything he'd learned after the fact. Everything.

Ralph's eyes refocused on Isha, waiting for her condemnation. Instead, she reached out and squeezed his hand. He let out a long breath.

"I formed untrained, poorly armed peasants into a defensive line to oppose that attack. I ordered their children into an old abandoned bunker where they would be "safe." I watched a tank lob a shell into the bunker where I put them and then watched the Iraqi armor chew up their parents. When the tank round exploded, it didn't just explode. It detonated a stockpile of mustard gas shells and covered the children with gas and plasma. I watched them run out of the bunker screaming, their skin literally falling off of their bones. I watched their mothers, whose last sights on this earth were their burning children and their dying husbands.

Anyway, my teammates tackled me and drug me into a helicopter that took us to Kuwait. Forty minutes later I was in an air-conditioned bar. 'Nothing we could have done,' we told each other. I've been in your country before Judge."

They were both quiet for a long time. Finally, Isha spoke.

"You hold yourself responsible for this? Could it be that Saddam, the Republican Guard, President Bush, and even those peasants bear some responsibility for what happened?"

Watching her cross her legs, barefoot in a cotton sundress, Ralph shook his head.

"If you have discussed this with anyone of the least wit before me," Isha said, "you have heard these truths before, yet choose to reject them and punish yourself. I do not know why. I only know that I, personally, would trust you with my life."

"Don't say that, please."

Of course he'd heard and even thought this before, but it always rang cold. Coming from Isha Hami, it sounded different. Now, somehow, something frozen deep down inside of him seemed to loosen.

"Ralph, none of us are strong enough to stand on our own or to bear our own sins. That's why Jesus died for us. Your soul is crying out to Him and you just don't know it."

"Isha, I'm not ready to start going to church, okay?"

Every now and then she invited him to worship with her and he always declined. It wasn't that he had anything against Christians, most of the best people he knew were Christians. Whenever he'd run into an anti-Christian bigot, on the other hand, he was always taken aback by their hypocrisy. If they were "tolerant" as they claimed, then they'd accept both homosexual and Christian viewpoints, for example. Instead, they choose sides and called those that disagreed with them the bigots. Ralph suspected "tolerance" was really just a smoke screen for people who wanted to hate Christians. He couldn't explain it, he liked Christians and disliked their opponents, but it just wasn't for him. Isha looked at him like she could read his mind.

"Sometimes we think something might be good for other people, but not us. Then we find out we didn't know what we were missing." She smiled at him, leaned over and rubbed Tabooli's belly. "Of course, I'm talking about dogs."

Ralph smiled back.

———◆———

Meanwhile in South Baghdad, Sameer, Ashraf, Zabra, and Jalal sat in the warehouse office. They had been rehashing the Allawis meeting for about ten minutes. Everyone agreed to the extent they could weaken Ayad al-Jaberi, their business ventures would prosper. Ayad was a devout Muslim and refused to permit the type of criminal activity Sameer and his colleagues found most lucrative. Should something happen to Ayad, his son, Abdula would take over. Abdula wasn't the same strong leader his father was. Nevertheless, like many fathers, Ayad couldn't see this, so he'd taken precautions to ensure that Abdula would succeed him. As far as Sameer and his associates were concerned, they would do all they could to assist the son in his ascension to power. The weakness of Abdula would aid them in penetrating the South Baghdad neighborhoods where Ayad now held sway as family, clan and tribe leader. It was a prosperous area and held great profit potential.

If the attack on Hami and the Ministry succeeded, Sameer stood to gain. Both sides of Hami's family would see the hand of Ayad al-Jaberi behind her assassination. These proud and powerful men would attack Ayad without regard to the consequences. In the chaos, Sameer predicted to himself, he would either assassinate Ayad or arrange for his arrest. Either way, Abdula became the leader of al-Jaberi's tribe. The strength of Ayad's tribe and confederated families and clans would eventually prove too much for Hami's weakened family. However, by the time Ayad's group prevailed, Ayad al-Jaberi himself would be dead, one way or the other. His family neighborhood would be infiltrated by Sameer's business ventures. Finally, as a result of Ayad's family's weakness from the blood feud and from Sameer's businesses, Ayad's tribal power would begin to wane. This weakness would help Sameer al-Hakim in another way. He had recently decided that he would like to start a political career.

"Very well, then," said Sameer. "Khalilzad, contact our Police Lieutenant and arrange for his support during the attack on the Ministry. Don't tell him about the attack. Imply we have an operation, criminal in nature, and prefer that his attention be directed elsewhere. Find something in the immediate area, a large enough prize to be plausible, but not so well guarded as to cause difficulty. If I have to choose, I'd prefer the Lieutenant be a little suspicious because the job is small, rather than any of our men be caught, killed or wounded because we picked to big a job. The purpose of this robbery is strictly cover for our diversion. 'What a coincidence,' we'll say to the Lieutenant. Give him Ten Thousand Dollars. Half in Dinar bills and half in U.S. Dollars. If he becomes difficult, we'll consider cutting him in for a percentage of the robbery. Is all this clear?"

"This is clear and I will arrange it," replied Khalilzad.

"Zahra, we need surveillance on active members of Ayad al-Jaberi's inner circle. Let's keep at least three of them under constant observation from now on. Get two teams of men ready to abduct Ayad's men. Look into some special equipment. There's something called a 'taser' which I see used on television all the time. Buy two, no, buy three. Once we've selected the targets, we'll plan two abductions, 20 minutes apart. If the first one fails, we initiate the second. If the first one succeeds that's it, we call off the second. The fewer loose ends the better. We'll call Allawis tomorrow and accept his offer. I've decided the diversion will cost

One Hundred Thousand Dollars. It's high, but not too high. Anyone have objections? Does anyone have questions? Then we're through. Jalal, arrange for transportation to my home."

At 9:00 a.m. the next morning, Khalilzad called Nadim Allawis's cell phone. On the third ring, Allawis answered.

"Yes."

"This is Ali, your landlord's nephew."

"Yes Ali, I thought you would call."

"My uncle needs food for one hundred. Please remember all of his guests have American tastes."

Since they never spoke in amounts of less than a thousand dollars, Allawis would know Sameer wanted One Hundred Thousand Dollars to bride the police. By telling him the guests had American tastes, Khalilzad was advising him that this amount would have to be paid in U.S. dollars.

Khalilzad was somewhat surprised that Allawis agreed immediately.

"Yes, I can find the food."

"Very well. My uncle will call you soon."

"I can only guarantee the food for the next couple days."

Anxious to get off the cell phone, which could be traced, Khalilzad said, "Of course," and hung up.

———◆———

Nadim Allawis closed his phone and thought, Only One Hundred Thousand Dollars? Pondering the amount led the Major to conclude Sameer was worried. Allawis had been prepared to pay at least Two Hundred Fifty Thousand Dollars, especially since he'd already paid that, twice, for the warehouse barracks. If Sameer was willing to accept such a sum for his bribe and commission, it was serious. The attack would have to succeed. Morale was low in some of the Baath cells, so an assault on the Justice Ministry, if successful, would demonstrate the continuing strength of the Baath party. It would encourage the Sunnis and disrupt the collaborators. But most importantly, Sameer was a resource of more current value to the Baath Regime than money.

While Saddam and his generals watched the United States prepare for war, they made their own preparations. One of them was to cachet hundreds of millions of U.S. oil dollars in secret, but accessible locations. Each cell leader was told where some of the cash hordes were hidden. Together, Baath cell leaders controlled enormous sums of money. Essentially, there were a lot more U.S. dollars available to the Baathist cells than there were men like Sameer Al-Hakim. Major Allawis called for his assistant. He was already formulating the attack plan.

CHAPTER 23

———

THE FOUR MEN GEARING UP around the table were contract employees from the Central Intelligence Agency's Special Activities Division. They currently comprised Hank's operational team, but would soon rotate back to the States, having served out their contracts. Some of his guys were only with him for a month, some were with him for four or five months, but none were full-time CIA employees.

The Central Intelligence Agency maintained lists of current and ex-military members who were available for covert paramilitary operations of short duration. These "contract operators" had security clearances and supplied skills required by the Agency on an "as needed" basis. Their background checks were kept up to date to ensure they remained reliable and available on short notice. These pre-cleared operators comprised what was known as the "C" list. In exchange for dangerous service, they were paid anywhere from Ten to Thirty Thousand Dollars a month, tax free, depending upon the operation and the individual's skills. In addition to the pay, health care was guaranteed and a government owned life insurance company insured their families would receive a generous death benefit in the event they were killed "in the line of duty."

Typically they were men who could disappear from their regular lives for short periods of time without being missed. Some of them were active military and used their accumulated vacation time to pick up some extra cash or work a mission they really believed in. Others, after being discharged from the military, were attending college and needed extra money. Their college spring and summer breaks provided them with perfect opportunities to take "vacations" without raising suspicion. Other operatives had prior military service and worked as Realtors, pharmaceutical salesmen, or in other occupations which let them control their schedules.

Throughout his career Hank learned some of these men risked their lives for strange, mundane or even noble reasons. Usually though, they worked for college educations for their kids, to pay off a mortgage or business debt, or to pad their retirement accounts. In every case, they believed in the mission. Contract operators were always briefed about the general nature of the mission in advance. If they were uncomfortable with the contract offered, they could walk away. The Agency learned operators were motivated by a complex combination of greed and patriotism. If patriotism weren't a prime motivation, they could have made more money working on the black market as mercenaries. They were all good, but these men were some of the best Hank had worked with. He was glad they'd be the ones going with him into Iran. Following the CIA's proven philosophy, he briefed them.

"We've received reliable intelligence that a meeting between Major Nadim Allawis and Abu Musab Al-Zarqawi will take place tonight. That's right, Zarqawi. The location of the meeting is a village outside of Avroman, just inside the Iranian border. If we violate Iranian airspace, they'll send out a patrol to see what's up, so we'll go in from the Iraqi side. Here's how we'll work it. We've already initiated air activity along the Iraqi side of the insertion point."

"That radio," Hank said, pointing, "is set to monitor air traffic along the border, so pay attention to it. At staggered intervals over the next three hours we'll buzz the Iranian border with fixed and rotary wing aircraft at various altitudes. Once we've provoked an Iranian response, we'll continue the flights, tracking North to Camp Cobra Air Base, outside Mosul. When the Iranians get bored and stand down, we'll suit up and air insert by MH-47Ds. We off-load with four electric golf carts with spare batteries and drive em across the border. Once we're about a mile from the target we'll stash three of the carts and take the fourth one into the village."

They were going in with a small team on short notice so Hank wanted the men to know Fred Littell would provide their only mission support. Littell was a sniper. In this operation he was not only a sniper, he was also their artillery and air support, all rolled into one.

"How about a brief on the sentries and support, Fred."

The team was relying upon Littell to compensate for the enemy's numeric advantage, so he gave them an in-depth explanation of his tactical plan and its background. For this mission, he'd selected a .50 cal. Barrett M82A1 BMG Rifle.

"I first ran across the M82 when my platoon was engaging a Republican Guard Unit during Operation Desert Storm."

He explained his Company had attacked a resupply convoy that managed to escape into a nearby cave system. At first, the Marines called in an air strike, but as the aircraft approached, the Iraqis fired off two-hand held anti-aircraft missiles of some kind. Whatever kind they were, the second missile almost knocked down an American "Warthog" jet flying close air support. In that mountainous area, with enemy anti-aircraft missiles and limited room for a plane to maneuver, the air strikes were called off.

No infantryman wanted to lose close support aircraft but they didn't want to get chewed up trying to assault the cave system either. In a flash of brilliance, Littell's Company Commander called in a U.S. Army Explosive Ordnance Disposal (EOD) unit for advice. One of the EOD guys checked out the cave system from a distance of almost a mile. Smiling, he put down the binoculars.

"Watch this."

Out came the M82 Rifle, then used to blow up unexploded ordnance. Basically, the Army guys used M82 to blow up un-exploded bombs by shooting them, preferably while the bomb maker was still standing alongside it. Fred had never seen one before and was fascinated. The EOD guy spread the bi-pods and put one round, treated with phosphorous, down range. It hit one truck that was visible just inside the cave mouth. The truck was carrying demolitions and exploded. Moments later the whole cave system went up with primary, and then secondary, explosions.

Fred Littell was in love.

The M82 was a semi-automatic sniper rifle with a ten-round magazine, which meant he could keep pulling the trigger ten times without stopping. The men already knew a .50 caliber bullet was for all intents and purposes a small cannon shell. It could penetrate light vehicles and enemy emplacements in unfortified buildings. For night vision, Littell had the Morovision 760 Gen 3 Night Vision Riflescope, with 6X magnification. Waterproof and nitrogen purged, the 760 was guaranteed by the manufacturer to stay sighted in.

"Otherwise, they give your next of kin your money back." Fred smiled.

The 760 featured an adjustable red on green Mil Dot reticle for precise shot placement, a top mounted objective focus, exposed micro-click windage elevation target turrets and a built-in Weaver style mount. Using the M82's self-leveling bipod legs, Littell figured he could take out the sentries before the first gunshot boom even reached the compound. With the illegal sound suppressor for the barrel, it was unlikely anyone inside the buildings in the village would even hear the boom from 3/4 of a mile out.

Everyone looked satisfied, so Hank wrapped it up.

"Fred gets out of the cart three-quarters of a mile outside the village and sets up. Once we locate the sentries, Fred takes them out and we drive into the village in the carts. With Littell and his night scope as our long distance support, we roll right up to the mosque. Once inside, we capture anyone we can. The big fish, of course, are Allawis and Al-Zarqawi. That's his photo, there, and Allawis's over there. Memorize them. If we capture them, good. Gentlemen, the United States does not sanction assassination. It does sanction this mission and you are specifically authorized to fire in self-defense and in furtherance of the mission. Any questions?"

For the next six hours, the men lounged in the motor pool, killing time with restless small talk. They reviewed the satellite photographs like a nervous tick, glancing at them even while talking about their kids, baseball or what idiots some of the journalists were. Hank stayed in the garage but sat apart from the team. He didn't want the men to see how tired he was or how jittery he was soon to be. He'd been awake all night for the ambush in Baghdad on Sunday. Early Monday morning he got the call from Henderson about the Hami subpoenas. Then he confronted Ralph Jackson inside his apartment building and then got the call from Barnes. Hank stole a glance at his watch. It was now zero ten hours early Tuesday morning. He hadn't slept since Saturday, but it seemed like a week ago.

Who cares, he thought, I'll sleep tomorrow.

To compensate for the lack of sleep, Hank swallowed what the Army euphemistically called a "stay awake" tab. It was really a highly engineered amphetamine capsule. He knew his men would notice the telltale signs indicating he had taken the tab, so he kept himself busy and away from them. Everyone on the team had been in a similar situation, where you hadn't slept but had to function. They knew how the tabs affected a man. It was like drinking gallons of coffee all day along. Worse, despite all the supposed improvements, the tabs affected your judgment. Even someone like Hank, who'd learned to mentally adjust for the side effects, tended to become overly aggressive and jumpy.

No one would blame him if they knew he took the tab, but they would watch him. Hank didn't want anyone second-guessing his decisions once they crossed the border. They couldn't afford it. So he sat apart from everyone else and tried to look bored. He passed the time absently rifling through the satellite photos and listening to the radio traffic from their aircraft along the Iraq / Iranian border. It took effort, but he forced himself to act calm despite the butterflies and fidgetiness that was part anticipating the stress of the mission and part, no doubt, feeling the effects of the drug. Eventually an unmanned drone with an infrared camera detected movement. The Iranians mobilized what appeared to be a mechanized infantry platoon and sent it to the general area of the insertion point. The mission light just turned yellow. Hank waited to receive word the Iranians had withdrawn and the light was green.

Five hours later, they were still waiting. Hank was getting nervous. The drone could only stay airborne for another hour, plus he'd taken that stay awake tab. If, for whatever reason, the Iranians didn't withdraw before the drone returned ran out of gas, he might have to scrap the whole operation.

He didn't want to miss the opportunity. Al-Zarqawi was responsible for some of the worse carnage of the war. Then there was Allawis. "War criminal" was too kind of a word for Nadim Allawis after the atrocities he'd carried out against dissident groups within his own country. Both men were murderers of the worst kind. If Hank couldn't capture them, he'd kill them -- in self-defense. The radio squawked and a drone operator from a joint CIA Army observation facility spoke.

"Baghdad, I'm picking up movement. It looks like your boys are leaving. I can stay on station for another twenty-five, thirty minutes, tops. After that, I've got to land this bird."

"Roger that," Hank replied. "If there's any change, let me know. Stay on station until the end of your fuel parameters."

"Willco."

"Showtime, boys. The Iranians are going home."

———————

Nadim Allawis stood apart from the rest of the men, admiring the calligraphy on the mosque walls and ceiling. Even in such a small, poor village, the effort and skill that went into its mosque attested to the power of Islam. While his men teamed up with al-Zarqawi's to load the trucks, he reviewed his plan. He'd formed the outline of it right after his meeting with Sameer al-Hakim, The easiest way to kill Hami, of course, would be to attack her vehicle or home, but unfortunately, neither was an option. If Hami were specifically targeted, the world would search for suspects. However, if she were merely a target of opportunity in a large assault upon the collaborationist government, there would be no suspects beyond the "terrorists." The impression Allawis wanted to convey was the insurgents launched a suicide attack targeting high Justice Ministry officials and Hami just happened to be the one they got. Disguising Hami's assassination meant an attack on the Ministry itself.

This was no easy task. First, the Americans and their collaborators maintained a security cordon around the Ministry. In addition, the Iraqi Justice Ministry maintained a security force of 40 men inside the building. At any given time, five men patrolled the building. Thirty-five men, however, were stationed inside the Security Office in the Ministry itself. These men were heavily armed and highly motivated. No one publicized the fact, but the Justice Ministry only recruited Shias who lost family members under the Bath Regime for these positions. There was no corrupting them.

However, Allawis did have two men working undercover in the Ministry's Commissary Department. One of them was in charge of supplies for the kitchen. It was a stroke of luck that the kitchen's pantries were located in the rear of the building, not only just one floor below but directly underneath the security force barracks and armory. Allawis inside men placed a large order for cleaning supplies and foodstuffs. Other Baathist operatives were standing by, waiting to hijack the shipment, open the cartons and re-pack them with explosives. They'd use a simple kitchen timer hooked up to a battery and a blasting cap for detonation. At a prearranged time the supply foreman would set the timer and leave the building. The massive explosion would eliminate the entire ministry security force, leaving only, if they were lucky, isolated policemen and the five patrolling security officers.

They'd enter through the same lightly guarded service entrance used to check in the supplies. The explosion would be large enough to not only take out the entire security complex one floor above, but it would also blow out sideways. The police detachment at the service entrance would be killed, wounded or so stunned by the blast that by the time they recovered, the foreign fighter assault team Allawis recruited would already be through the doors. The Baathist Major was inserting four of his best men into the fighters force. Once inside, they'd split off from the main force, locate and kill Isha Hami. While the rest of the ridiculous but deadly foreign fighters roamed around killing until they were killed, his men would switch into "new" Iraqi police uniforms and escape out the rear.

Unfortunately, the "dry goods" shipment would have to pass through security. It would be x-rayed, some of the packages randomly opened and the non-food items subjected to dog searches. The random searches might be overcome by packaging and the efforts of his kitchen men could distract the screeners. The dogs and x-rays were a problem. The dogs were specially trained to detect explosives and the x-rays detected metal fragments embedded in manufactured explosives. Two pounds of explosives might sneak through. Since Allawis was using 2000 pounds, his plan required some way to get the explosives past those security checks.

———◆———

Hank's team was moving. They'd conducted a mental inventory of their weapons and gear while loading all of it into a beat-up van with darkened windows. The men threw in their gear, climbed in behind it and slammed the van's doors closed.

"Airport," Hank told the driver. "Tell them we're on the way."

The driver punched at an automatic door opener, grabbed a radio handset and notified the airport the assault team was on its way. It would take a few minutes for the ground crew to get the golf carts up the rear ramps of the helicopters and Hank didn't want to wait. He'd tasked two MH-47Ds for the mission. The MH-47D Adverse Weather Cockpit Chinook is a twin-engine, heavy assault helicopter, specifically modified for long range flights. It was equipped with weather avoidance/search radar; a Personnel Locator System and Infrared night vision for rescues; and two M-134 machine-guns and one M-60D machine-gun, among other goodies. The pilots were from the 160th Special Operations Aviation Regiment. They didn't need to be told to get their pre-flight checks done. By the time Hank's team got there, the rotors should be spinning on both birds, ready to go.

Traffic was light, so the van was at the airport in under fifteen minutes. They entered through a gate under the exclusive control of the American military and pulled right up to the helicopters. The carts were loaded and their helicopters' rotors already roaring. The team spilled out of the van and into the rotor wash. They split into two groups, two and three. While the swirling wind flapped at their clothes and gear, they climbed up the rear ramps. The men secured their gear and squeezed into the space left between the golf carts and skin of the aircraft.

"Team one, team two," Hank radioed.

"Team two, go."

"Equipment status?"

"Secured."

Hank signaled the crew chief and five minutes later they were airborne, heading toward the northern border, skimming along at what would have been treetop level had there been any trees. The plan called for the helicopters to race toward the insertion point, flare, drop the ramps and allow Hank's team to drive the golf carts off the helicopters' back ramps simultaneously. Both aircraft would then pull up and take off the instant the carts cleared the ramp, reducing the "time on target" to a minimum. The idea was to convince a radar operator, or anyone close enough to hear the helicopters, to question whether or not the birds had even stopped.

The team would head toward the village in silent, sand resistant, specially modified electric golf carts. Beyond twenty yards
the carts were virtually soundless, so the odds of the team arriving
undetected were high. After Fred eliminated the sentries on the
western side of the village, Hank hoped to roll right into it before
they were observed. Using the Iranian uniforms, they'd move
through the village and breach the mosque. Once inside they'd
drop the guards, tase or sedate Al-Zarqawi and Allawis, put them
in the carts and roll out. As soon as they crossed the border, they'd
call the choppers and fly into Camp Cobra.

No muss, no fuss.

Of course, there was a lot that could go wrong. Hank's biggest concern was they wouldn't be able to locate all the sentries.
Granted, security at the village would be light. Large security con-
tingents drew the attention of US satellites, warbirds and drones,
the last thing Al-Zarqawi and Allawis wanted. They'd travel light.
Though the Americans would be outnumbered, the opposing
force should be relatively small. Every one of Hank's team members had state-of-the-art night vision goggles which would further
even things out. Still, if they couldn't spot the sentries, they would
face hard choices. That was Hank's biggest concern. If they found
the sentries, no problem. Fred Littell, retired Marine Corps sniper
and current Wyoming big game hunting guide, would take them
down. No doubt. But, if they missed a sentry, more likely than not
Hank and his team would roll up into a hail of gunfire. They'd
never even get a chance to show off their authentic Iranian uniforms. Hank let it go, zoned out, and got ready.

Fifteen minutes out, Hank moved to the rear of the helicopter.
It was almost twenty feet wide, big enough to accommodate the
width of the cart with at least four feet on either side to spare.
They were long enough that two carts, bumper to bumper, still
left enough room at the front and back for the flight crew to operate. An angry red light designed to help preserve his men's night
vision illuminated the interior of the helicopter. The "night light"
always left Hank with the impression that everything was covered
with blood. The symbolism, and irony, wasn't lost on him. Vibrating along with the chopper, Hank looked at his watch, shook his
head and was about to order everybody into their golf carts when
his earpiece crackled.

———

Allawis' search led him here, to this mosque, waiting while his men loaded two tons of Semtex plastic explosive onto the waiting trucks. As easy to slip through airport security as nylons, Semtex had been the terrorists' top choice of explosive since its creation in 1968. The original Czechoslovakian Semtex felt like Play Dough, had no smell, and was undetectable by dogs and airport security devices. Over the past decades, terrorists use Semtex in several deadly attacks, including the 1988 explosion of Pan Am Flight 103 over Lockerbie, Scotland, and the 1998 bombing of the US Embassy in Nairobi, Kenya. And no one had found a reliable way to combat it.

In the 1988 Lockerbie explosion, just 12 ounces of the substance, molded inside a Toshiba cassette recorder, blasted Pan Am flight 103 out of the sky, killing 270 people. The secret, according to its creator, was in the styrene-butadiene rubber binder, which "had a very positive effect on the consistency." The "effect" was so "positive" that the Czechs, under pressure because of Lockerbie added metal components and a distinct odor to the explosive to make Semtex easier to detect. Because of this change, Semtex was referred to among professionals as either Semtex or "Sweet Semtex," or the "sweet stuff." The sweet stuff was the Semtex made before the Czechs added metal chips or the odor to the manufacturing process.

Before Lockerbie, the Czechs had exported 900 tons of "sweet" Semtex to Colonel Moammar Qaddafi's Libya and another 1,000 tons to other unstable states, such as Syria, North Korea, Iraq, and Iran. Some experts put worldwide stockpiles of pre-Lockerbie Semtex at 40,000 tons. Semtex has an indefinite shelf life and is far stronger than traditional explosives such as TNT. Therefore, there was a real demand for sweet Semtex on the open market, because it was the kind of explosive you could get past dogs and screeners. Anyone who had the old version began to hoard it like gold. All Semtex was suitable for military and industrial applications, so the new stuff was kept in inventory and used routinely. The sweet stuff was kept in cool vaults for special occasions.

Which is why Nadim Allawis brought in Al-Zarqawi. For his

plan to work, the explosives had to get past the Ministry Security. To do that, he needed access to some of the "sweet stuff" and the only one he knew who had access to sweet Semtex on such short notice was Al-Zarqawi. So he contacted Al-Zarqawi's network and negotiated a purchase. The negotiations were done via messenger, not cell phone or other vulnerable communications systems since cell phones, used, or even left on for any length of time, were the same as painting a set of crosshairs on your chest. The Americans zeroed in on you. Sometimes, Allawis wondered how they were ever going to win.

We don't have to, he thought, catching himself, the American's will beat themselves like they always do.

He and Al-Zarqawi finally met face to face, completed the transaction and had been comparing notes for the last hour. It was unlikely they would ever speak to each other again because it was simply too dangerous for them to meet. Now that the meeting was over, Allawis was distracted and anxious to leave. He was careful to turn on his satellite phone at designated intervals in case of an emergency. The Baathist Major was confident in their precautions and trade-craft, but survival was dependent upon discipline. The warning call network was his creation. Nevertheless, he was surprised when his phone rang. The Major answered, intending to listen for no more than two seconds.

"Yes."

"Water," a voice said in Arabic. The phone went dead. Allawis snapped his off.

"STOP. That's all, quit loading, secure what you've got and let's move," he shouted. "We leave in five minutes."

The men looked up from their work and froze.

"Now! Move! Anyone not on the truck gets left behind."

He was already walking toward the trucks himself and the men responded, scurrying around, securing loads and slamming shut tailgates. Al-Zarqawi came out of a back room, stone-faced, but before he could speak, Allawis did.

"I have men in positions that know things. We are going to be attacked, very soon. Load the assault team with my men and evacuate the rest of your men."

Al-Zarqawi wasted no time on words. He returned to his men, issuing his own orders as he went. Meanwhile, Allawis wistfully

JOSEPH MAX LEWIS

glanced at the explosives still on the mosque floor. He probably had three-quarters of the load. It would have to do. The rest had to be left with the foreigners. He suspected two tons was enough, but Allawis believed in overkill. It was part of his discipline. There was no choice. The Americans were coming.

"Water" was a code word indicating someone reliable had learned of an imminent attack. It told Allawis, "Run!" The only code word more urgent instructed the insurgents to stay in place, destroy all confidential materials and prepare to fight because it was too late to run away. "Water" meant they had perhaps minutes, no more than half an hour before the village was attacked. His men knew the importance of speed. Already, less than two minutes after receiving the call, engines roared to life and the first truck pulled out.

———◆———

The lead chopper pilot spoke into Hank's earpiece with an update.

"Sir, I've got Baghdad Ops on the line."

"Patch it."

Hank heard a click in his ear as the pilot patched the exterior radio traffic through the helicopter's interior intercom system.

"Jenkins."

"It's Barnes, Sir," the voice metallically said. Hank had a bad feeling.

"What?"

"Twenty minutes ago the Fourth Infantry Division released a drone they'd tasked to chase some suspicious looking vehicles in Northern Iraq. Turned out to be two beat up flatbed trucks loaded with sheep. I was monitoring the traffic, saw it was in our area of operations so I countermanded the return order and grabbed it off of 4th ID. We flew it in a standoff observation pattern, two miles away from Avroman at 15,000 feet. Sir, our targets are on the move."

"Where are they at now? Feed the coordinates to my pilot."

"Mr. Jenkins, that's not all."

Hank wanted to take off his headset and smash it against the floor of the aircraft, over and over, until nothing but pieces were left. Al-Zarqawi and Allawis were responsible for tens of thousands of lost or ruined lives. Even if he hadn't been able to capture them, killing them would have been an incredible victory in the war on terror. No way. He wasn't giving up on it.

"Dave, just tell me what you saw and how long ago. Then tell me what you see now."

"Five minutes ago I got the bird on station. I ordered the drone to paint the village with its infrared beam and to watch the paint with its binoculars."

Barnes was using slang. He'd ordered the drone pilot to turn on a high-powered infrared beam carried under the drone. The drone, or small, unmanned airplane, emitted a powerful beam, undetectable to the naked eye, which lit the village. An internal camera mounted beside the IR beam was equipped with a magnifying lens and the technology to view infrared light and enable the operator to see what was happening in the village.

"The place was like a hive. Figures running out of the surrounding buildings and into the mosque – the one we targeted. Minutes later, four vehicles appeared from out of nowhere, from inside the mosque. All four headed into the interior of Iran, two went Northeast, two headed due East. As soon as I was sure of the direction of travel, I called your bird."

"Five minutes? No problem, we'll get the northeast group out in the open desert. We'll drop the team ahead of their line of travel and we'll use the choppers' mini-guns for support. OK, follow the flatbeds and feed me speed and direction."

"Sir, the Iranians launched attack helicopters. Allawis or Al-Zarqawi must have tipped them off. We've got to get the drones down or we might lose them."

"Satellites?"

"Nothing we can move fast enough. Sir, those attack helicopters won't just take down the drones, they can take you down, too," Barnes said, telling Hank what he already knew.

"All right Dave. We're aborting." Hank tried to keep the frustration out of his voice.

"Sorry, Sir."

"Not your fault. This was the real deal, we were off by minutes. Jenkins out." Hank leaned back against the nylon mess and banged his head against the helicopter's skin. Half an hour, he thought, and I would have had them.

"Sixty seconds to insertion, Sir," came the pilot's voice over the intercom.

"Abort the mission," Hank said. "Return to Baghdad immediately."

"Say again."

"Repeat, abort mission, return to Baghdad immeadiately."

He switched his microphone from internal cockpit communications to a direct link to the team in the second chopper.

"Gentlemen, the mission is scratched. The targets took off, we missed them."

The guys in his helicopter looked at him to make sure they'd heard right. Hank looked at them and drew his forefinger across his throat. He took off his headset, threw it on the seat beside him and closed his eyes. The other two men backed off. Hank wasn't ready to talk about it. He'd let them know what happened back in Baghdad.

All the men in the helicopters, but particularly the assault team, began to experience a slight sense of euphoria. Even Hank, frustrated beyond measure, wasn't immune from the sensation. For the past six hours they'd been preparing themselves to face a situation where they might die. Now everything was called off. No danger. They reacted accordingly, unconsciously, with an involuntarily sense of mild euphoria. Hank knew he'd missed an important opportunity, an opportunity to save the lives of people he would probably never meet. Still, he couldn't help feeling good.

———◆———

Nadim Allawis scrambled off of the makeshift loading dock and into the cab of the second truck. Five minutes later the Baathist convoy was a half-mile away, in route to a rendezvous point where the explosives would be transferred to more innocent looking vehicles. Those would be the trucks used to smuggle the explosives into Baghdad. As his truck crested a hill and the lights of the village disappeared from view, Allawis thought about just how close he'd been to death or capture. It shook him. The Americans were on to them, somehow. Surely they couldn't know he planned an attack on the Justice Ministry, because only he and Al-Zarqawi knew that. Even Sameer didn't know in any detail what Allawis planned. That left Al-Zarqawi. Could he trust him? What about

Sameer?

Yes, Allawis concluded, but he couldn't trust those who Al-Zarqawi and Sameer trusted. It was just a matter of time until crucial information made its way to the Americans.

We can't wait. We'll have to attack tomorrow, he thought. He decided he'd also launch another operation he'd been working on for some time. The plan was complete, the men and materials in place. All he had to do was pull the trigger. That would be his diversion for the Ministry attack. He didn't need Sameer or anyone else involved. It was the best way, really.

CHAPTER 24

———◆———

IN AN APARTMENT IN THE Dora section of Baghdad, a troubled man sat at an old wooden table in a straight-backed wooden chair, wrestling with demons of his own creation. His table sat in a nondescript room with original white plaster walls, now the color of mocha from decades of accumulated cigarette smoke and grime. Off to his left a small kitchenette was visible, as was a red plastic trash receptacle that overflowed with half empty cans, food scraps, and a tottering, empty whiskey bottle. The heat in the room swirled around the flopping blades of an ancient ceiling fan. Otherwise, the room was deathly quiet.

The man stood and stretched before collapsing back into the chair. He was about 5' 10" and obviously fit, but battered looking. His eyes were a startling combination of red, white and blue, the result of bursting blood vessels, an extended drinking binge and inability to sleep. He wore a pair of khaki shorts and a sweat stained Tee shirt, neither of which had been changed in a week. The front of the shirt was covered with particles of something, most likely vomit. He stank.

"Pills or pistol," Ralph Jackson muttered to himself.

Leaning back, he looked over the table top for other potential accomplices, but his search was hampered by alcohol-induced tunnel vision. Close at hand sat a bottle of Valium and a .38 caliber pistol. The pistol, for some reason, seemed to keep finding its way into his hand before he knew it was there. With effort he managed to shift his gaze further out toward the other items scattered on his tabletop.

To his left were the books. THE UCMJ, or Uniform Code of Military Justice, the Provisional Authority's "Rules and Regulations Governing Conduct in Iraq" and the pre-war, "Republic of Iraq, Civil and Criminal Code," in four volumes, translated into English, all sat silent.

The only response audible over the ever-present chant of "she's dead, you killed her, she's dead, you killed her," originated, he thought, from a half empty bottle of Jack Daniels. Blame it on no sleep and a blood alcohol count well in excess of .20 if you wish, but Mr. Daniels told him, in so many words, he'd be glad to help no matter which instrumentality he chose.

Instrumentality.

That was Jack, putting on airs because he wasn't strong enough to do the job himself. Ralph had been letting him try for over six days without visible effect.

Okay, except for seeking suicide advice from inanimate objects.

Further out were his pictures, his nephews and nieces, a picture of him with his midget soccer team and one of him and his little brother from when he was in Big Brothers. Ralph managed to focus on the last two framed pictures, one of Isha and one of Isha and Naba together. He half smiled, wearily.

Finally, he shifted his gaze to the edge of the table. There, on his right, stood the final occupant of his cluttered table, an almost empty bottle of Jack Daniels. Six Daniels cousins sat empty in Ralph's kitchen trash.

Mr. Daniels, you've already had your chance, but maybe I'll let you help.He picked up the pistol and pulled back the hammer. Turning the weapon backward, he stared down the barrel of the revolver with his thumb on the trigger. Hollow point bullets on either side of the barrel stared back at him with a dull gleam.

It would be quick, he thought, granted, but messy.

The sensation of holding the weapon flashed him back six days earlier. He watched his hand grip the same pistol as he ran full speed toward the Iraqi Ministry of Justice and Isha's chambers. Seconds earlier, he'd had been shaken by a huge explosion from inside the Ministry. Racing closer, he heard gunfire inside.

Not Isha, Ralph thought, as he ran up the stairs toward her chambers. He had no doubt that she was one of the targets of the assault.

At least Naba stayed at home today, he thought at the time. Often Naba went to work with her grandmother.

He should have known some kind of attack was likely, even imminent. Hank had warned him. The Amani case was a powder keg that brought together all the explosive materials in Iraq. It was Shias against Sunnis, Baathists against new Iraqis, the law against chaos. Even the American military involvement was an issue.

Or as Isha put it, "This was all witnessed by an American patrol from the same unit which suffered the casualties from the IED. There is some question as to how aggressively they intervened. The Army is conducting a parallel investigation."

"Well," he thought, coming back to the present, "pretty soon there'll be plenty of parallel investigations going on."

"She's dead, you've killed her, she's dead, you've killed her," rang out in his head.

Ralph grimaced, switched his grip on the pistol, and turned the barrel away from his face.

"How the hell did the pistol get up there," he wondered.

Ralph didn't remember picking up the pistol, but it's what happened in some of his dreams. He pulled the trigger while his thumb was on the hammer, allowing it to slowly descend upon the firing pin. He'd decide for himself.

"Pills or pistol," the voices ask.

Ralph wondered about the deadline and checked his watch.

There's still plenty of time and I haven't finished the whiskey yet, he thought.

———◆———

On the other side of Baghdad, behind the so-called Green Line, Hank Jenkins moved carefully. The chair, like his desk and the rest of his furnishings, was Governmental Spartan, constructed of sturdy steel and painted a gunmetal gray. The walls were glazed cream rectangular bricks, separated by the gray mortar and the ceiling cheap acoustic tile. Windowless, the room was nevertheless large enough to accommodate large metal lockers, extra metal side chairs, stacks of files and envelopes and an unfinished, concrete slab floor. From the office, you would never have guessed the importance of the man at the desk, which was just the way he liked things.

Under the circumstances, he would have accepted a more comfortable chair. He'd already re-opened the shoulder wound earlier that morning. His head throbbed and the deep bullet graze along the outside of his thigh, along with everything else, made it hard to get comfortable. A soft chair would have helped. Nothing could help soothe his sense of frustration and loss. He picked up the newspaper, reread its account of the attack and shook his head.

"Baghdad Burning."

He was disappointed, yeah, but he didn't feel responsible. The Jackson kid did feel responsible though, for at least two of the deaths. Ralph Jackson and Hank Jenkins had been antagonists for months, but all that was resolved when they rescued Judge Hami. Hank was on his way to the Ministry but still a block away when he heard and felt the explosion. Approaching from the Tigris River side, he left his Jeep and rushed toward the building, armed with only a handgun. He was greeted by the kind of destruction that can only be caused a wrecking ball or a couple of tons of explosives. Part of the first floor was missing. A large section of the second floor had collapsed onto the ground floor, scattering bodies and debris everywhere.

This is Allawis, I know it is, Hank thought.

He picked his way through the rubble, squinting against the dust. The service entrance was partially collapsed and its security detail wiped out. Stepping over the bodies, it suddenly struck him that the now missing second floor had been where the Ministry Security contingent was located. The Ministry staff, including the Judges, were defenseless.

On the other side of the building, Ralph was coming to the same conclusion. Both had the same idea.

Get Hami.

Although they were only carrying pistols, each man engaged the heavily armed terrorists in running gun battles. Hank escaped with two minor gunshot wounds after dropping at least four terrorists. Ralph killed two terrorists and together, he and Hank managed to get Hami out of the building alive. The cost, however, had been high. Physically, Ralph was unscathed, but mentally and emotionally? Hank was worried.

"Come on kid, you know better than that," he'd said, afterward.

"Bull, I don't know better, Hank," Ralph said. "I'm the one that pressed for lunch. I'm the one who couldn't make it on time. If I'd been here, like I said I would, we would've been at the restaurant.

I would never have entered that building and things would be different. You know my track record. Once might just be bad luck. Isha almost had me believing that. But twice?"

Hank argued with him, but he could tell he wasn't getting anywhere. Ralph's eyes focused just past Hanks' head while he was talking. When the older man paused for breath, Ralph patted him on his uninjured shoulder.

"Sorry about being an ass," Ralph said. "I was wrong about you."

With that, Ralph walked off.

"I'll call you in a couple days," Hank yelled.

Because of a complication with one of his wounds, Hank was hospitalized for six days and had just been released that morning. During the interim he hadn't spoken to Ralph, but did arrange for Baghdad police check on him a couple times to gather, "more information." Evidently, Ralph was drinking. Hank didn't blame him.

I might as well get caught up, he thought.

His desk was stacked with copies of international versions of the Herald Journal, transcripts of cell phone conversations and the mail intercepts of suspects. Listlessly, he sorted through the various piles. One of the piles was of mail that was intercepted by the PA, or Provisional Authority after it was sent by, or before it was received by, certain targeted individuals. After the suspect deposited the mail with Fed Ex, UPS or Iraq's budding postal service, it was diverted to Hank Jenkins. When it arrived it was X-rayed and scanned in the basement. Then the envelopes and packages were brought to Hanks' office and stacked.

He found it in the mail intercept stacks. A bright colored Federal Express envelope with his name as the addressee.

What 'target' would mail me a letter?

Hank's personal mail, for obvious reasons, didn't come to his real office, it went to a Post Box drop point. He jerked the envelope out from the pile.

What's going on?

Once he got it clear of the stack he spotted Ralph Jackson's name and address as the sender. Now he was really curious. Ralph had been under surveillance ever since the Western media leaks regarding the Amani murder case. Wounded and hospitalized, Hank never thought to or had the opportunity to cancel the order, so it continued in place. Anything Ralph mailed to anyone still ended up on Hank's desk. It was ironic a letter to Hank was intercepted and diverted to . . . Hank . . . a day sooner than in the normal course of delivery. He hissed under his breath, struggling to get the folder between his two knees, flap pointed up. The date on the intercept stamp indicated it was picked up earlier that very morning. With one arm in a sling, he used his knees, one good hand and the tip of his ballpoint pen to half cut, half rip open the envelope flap. He stuck the pen into the arm sling, grabbed the envelope by the bottom and shook it until a stack of papers clipped to a letter fell out.

Nervous, Hank picked up the packet and read the note.

Ralph!

Hank flipped through his Rolodex and found Ralph's profile card. No landline, just a cell, probably turned off. Still. He punched the numbers into his landline.

"I'm sorry, that number is currently unavailable."

Unless he acted fast a good man was going to die. He tossed the suicide note on his desk and called his secretary.

"Get me to the switchboard. Now!"

In a moment Hank was connected.

"Get me the lobby of the Quays Apartment Building in Dora." After a short delay, the operator came back on.

"Sir, the lines in that part of town are out, have been ever since the attacks. Supposedly, the 15th Signal Battalion and the Iraqis will have them operating by tomorrow."

"Get me Iraqi police dispatch."

Ralph's apartment was in an area of Baghdad the Americans turned over to the new Iraqi Security Forces. Except for isolated advisors, there were no US military personnel in that part of town.

The peculiar sound of a foreign telephone service buzzed in Hank's ear.

"Baghdad Police, Precinct 14," someone said in Arabic.

"Speak English. This is the Provisional Authority and my Arabic is limited."

"Very well, Sir," the dispatcher responded in passable English. "How can I help you?"

"Get me your watch commander immediately."

Seconds later a second voice, speaking better English, came on the line.

"This is Police Captain Zalmay Kamil, how may I help you?"

"I've got a real emergency here Captain," Hank said. "I've just opened a mail intercept and must contact an American in the Quays Apartment Building in Dora. 'Now' would be too late. All the phone lines are out and it is no exaggeration to say it is a matter of life-and-death. Do you have any police units in the area?"

Silence.

"Captain?"

"I'm here Mr. Jenkins. You must be looking for Ralph Jackson if it's that apartment building." Hank was taken aback. Ralph was hardly a well-known personality in Iraq, but he didn't have time to decide what this meant.

"I am."

"I have an officer en route to Jackson's apartment right now."

"Why? No, never mind, patch me through to the vehicle."

"I cannot patch you through to the vehicle, Mr. Jenkins. That particular police unit was damaged by a terrorist attack yesterday and its radio does not operate. The unit was ..."

The Captain paused.

"Well, you have heard, I am sure, about Judge Isha Hami and her granddaughter, Naba?"

"Of course," Hank snapped.

What Kamil said next left Hank flabbergasted. His mouth moved, but no words came out.

"Mr. Jenkins?"

"I'm here. Please call any vehicle or unit in the area and send them with sirens to Jackson's apartment. Tell Ralph just what you told me. Every word. This is on Provisional Authority orders. I've got to go. Captain Kamil, thank you."

Hank hung up on Kamil and called his own dispatcher.

"Get the best vehicle and driver you have. I want them ready and waiting for me in Bay One in five minutes."

The deadline was set at twelve o'clock. Ralph's apartment was a forty-five minute drive from Hank's building. It was 11:12 a.m.

"And a radio," he added as an afterthought. He hung up the phone, shoved Ralph's papers back into the envelope and took it with him as he hobbled toward the staircase.

In many ways, Hank thought, Ralph and Isha were casualties of the First Gulf War. They'd been walking wounded for a long time. If the first war hadn't been able to kill Ralph Jackson, Hank was damned before he was going to let the second one do it.

CHAPTER 25

———◆———

RALPH WAS STILL IN HIS wooden chair, at his wooden table, woodenly replaying that last day in his mind. He barely noticed his splitting headache or the pistol in his hand.

"It's not on Tariq Street, it's on Baba Street and you've never been there before."

Isha and Ralph were on the phone, bantering.

"Just because you grew up here doesn't mean you know every good restaurant in Baghdad. Some reporter from the Washington Times recommended it and it's still undiscovered."

"But today I agreed to meet Judge Bashir and Judge Aziz at the Kesef if I could."

"Come on Isha, that's not an appointment, ditch em. Go with me."

"But Ralph . . ."

"Come on Judge, come on."

"All right," she said laughing, "I'll see them tomorrow, but you and I have a hearing tomorrow at 1:45."

"Of course, of course. I'll be there at 11:30 sharp. That gives us plenty of time to eat and get back."

"Unless you run into some interesting situation or person, of course you will be on time."

"I promise, Judge."

Still laughing, Isha said, "Don't make promises you can't keep, Ralph. But ever trusting, I will be ready at 11:30 and probably still be waiting at 12:15."

She hung up and Ralph smiled, certain she'd be delighted. The "Yellow Submarine" was a theme restaurant opened by an Iraqi who returned to Baghdad after years in Detroit. Like Isha, this expatriate had an obsession with the Beatles and everything related to the Beatles. He only played Beatles music over the sound system, a large plastic yellow submarine hung from the ceiling, and posters, pictures, and all sorts of Beatles memorabilia, brought by the owner from Detroit to Baghdad, covered the walls.

Humming, Ralph jumped in and out of the shower and got ready for lunch. This time, he swore he'd be on time. He was late. Ralph met a young man, perhaps fourteen, working a pedal sewing machine on the street about two blocks from the Ministry. The kid was delighted to brag about how he could repair worn and discarded U.S. military boots and resell them. Before he finished an enormous explosion shook the ground. The blast emanated from the direction of the Justice Ministry.

No, Ralph thought, not from the direction of the Ministry, from the Ministry.

He didn't need to look at his watch, he knew he was late. He and Isha should have been sitting at the Yellow Submarine, waiting for an early lunch. Ralph broke into a run. The closer he got closer to the Ministry, to stronger the smell of blown Semtex and concrete dust. Flames reflected through and off of the window panes. He reached the building's front door at an all-out sprint, hurdling large pieces of concrete that had been blasted loose and were now strewn across his path. Shots rang out, but maddened, he dashed past the Iraqi security barricade, zig-zagging as he neared the shattered doorway at the main entrance.

No U.S. military presence at all, he thought.

Bullets rained down from the top of the building, kicking up asphalt chips from the street surface as he passed. Three suicidal Iraqi Policemen leaped up and followed him, screaming something in Arabic. Ralph stopped inside long enough to catch his breath while the three policemen poured in through the doorway. The men knelt with their weapons, forming a perimeter.

Ralph didn't give them a chance to say anything. He ran past them and up the stairs leading to the second floor Judges' chambers. Thick white dust and smoke limited his vision, but he could see well enough to avoid the bodies strewn along the staircase. Several of the bodies had obvious bullet wounds in the back or head, so it was clear the terrorists sent in an assault force after detonating the explosives. Ralph shot a man raising an AK-47 assault rifle just before he reached the top of the staircase.

Gunfire erupted from somewhere further down the long hall-way. He moved in a crouch to his left. A figure appeared out of the smoke and sent a stab of flame toward him. Ralph felt something whistle over his right shoulder and fired back without breaking stride. The man dropped and he flashed passed his body, through an open door and into the chambers of Judge Hami. Her secre-tary lay on the uncarpeted floor near her desk in a pool of blood. Alongside her was an equally dead terrorist. Ralph panicked and bolted toward Hami's door. His feet slipped from under him as he hit the slick pool near the woman's head. He landed on his stomach and slid, head first, through the open inner door into the Judge's chambers. She lay about ten feet away, gasping. Little red bubbles percolated from between her lips.

———◆———

While Ralph sat alone, Hank moved. By the time he made it down the three flights of stairs his vehicle was waiting. It was a brand-new Ford Explorer with Paul Hill, a graduate of the State Department's evasive driving course sitting behind the wheel. Hank heard the guy could turn a wheel. Maybe there was a chance after all. Hill had the window down and was staring at him.

"You don't do this very often. Tell me."

"If we don't make it to Quays Apartments in Dora in thirty minutes we're going to lose a good man," Hank said.

He rounded the front of the vehicle and climbed in. Hill was moving before he got the door closed.

"You know where we're going, right," Hank said.

"Yeah. It's going to be tight."

While Hill concentrated on getting out of the garage and into traffic, Hank took a second look at Ralph's papers. The note and the Last Will and Testament were clipped together with a large, black metal binder clip. He pushed down on the clip with his good hand and got the letter. It was written in a shaky hand and barely legible.

"Hank, I don't expect you to understand this, but I'm going to die. I'll tell you this much. For the last twelve years, I don't think I've slept for more than two or three hours at a time. I wake up with the same dream, with the same kids, screaming the same screams. You wear down. I came back to Iraq, hoping the dreams would go away, and for a while they did. But now I've killed more of the innocent. The dreams are back, worse than ever. I can smell the flesh burning. By the time you get this, I'll be dead. I haven't decided how I'm going to do it yet, but I know when. Twelve o'clock, when I should have been with Isha and Naba at the Ministry."

Hank found Ralph's number on his cell and re-dialed it. Still "unavailable" and likely to stay that way.

He held up the envelope to get a look at the courier postmark. The time stamp was from earlier that morning. Ralph hadn't wanted him to get the stuff until after he was dead. Hank Jenkins definitely believed God moved in mysterious ways. If he hadn't been hospitalized he knew he would have canceled the mail intercept. Without the intercept, he wouldn't have gotten the suicide note until after Ralph was dead. He took a moment to offer up a quick prayer for Ralph, then opened his eyes.

"Let's move," Hank said.

"Where am I supposed to go, Mr. Jenkins?"

They had rounded a bend only to find themselves at the end of blocks of bumper to bumper traffic. Hill slowed, then stopped behind the last car in line. A long chain of old cars, military Jeeps, Hummers, and other vehicles stretched ahead. The intersection itself was still ten blocks away. Sitting up high as he was, Hank could see the traffic pattern. Only someone who's been in the Middle East could appreciate what it looked like. At least thirty five cars were jammed into the intersection, pointing in all four directions. Some vehicles were stopped perpendicular to another's side door, while others were at the bumper or grill of the vehicle ahead or behind them. Everybody used their horn and curses rang out in a half a dozen languages. You would think nothing short of tow trucks, bulldozers and demolitions could ever clear the intersection. Incredibly, as Hank well knew, eventually, somehow, some way, the Arabs would maneuver, honk and curse until every vehicle moved and the intersection was clear. No one could ever explain how it happened, but it did. Unfortunately, this mysterious process took time and time was the one commodity Hank Jenkins was short on.

"I thought you were a certified evasive driver. You're supposed to be one of the best drivers in the world. I got a good man who'll die because you either don't have the guts or the skill to get me where I need to go."

"No need to be nasty. All you had to do was say 'get me there.'"

Immediately, Hill jerked the wheel to his right and smashed into the back of the truck in front of him. He reached down, put the vehicle in four-wheel-drive and pushed the pickup truck ahead about two feet, ignoring the shouts from the driver. Then he shifted into reverse and slammed into the front of the vehicle behind him, keeping his foot on the gas until that vehicle was pushed about a foot back. This gave him enough room to pull out of traffic and swing onto what passed for a Baghdad sidewalk. Since his horn was useless, he rolled down his window and yelled.

"Get out of away, get out of the way."

His Arabic was horrible. Meanwhile he accelerated and shot down the sidewalk. Bags of produce flew in the air as men and women scurried out of his way. Some dove into doorways but with traffic at a standstill and Hill hurtling down the sidewalk, smashing through small carts and vegetable stands, the middle-of-the-road was the refuge of choice.

He gripped the steering wheel in both hands, twisting it back and forth as he drove, somehow managing to miss pedestrians, kiosks and stray livestock as the SUV lumbered along. Hank found himself wondering how long he could keep it up. Often, they'd have two wheels on the sidewalk and two wheels on the berm of the road. Without warning Hill veered to the left or the right, grazing walls on the passenger side, then sideswiping vehicles still stuck in traffic with the driver's side door. Seconds seemed to drag on for hours, even for Hank, who was no coward. Hill's eyelids opened as far as possible, making him appear bug-eyed. Hank hadn't seen him blink for minutes.

"Get the map, get the map," Hill said. Before Hank could ask "what map," Hill whipped them to the left, sideswiped an old panel truck, and then bounced back onto the sidewalk."Where, what map," Hank shouted to be heard above the din of collisions, horns and screaming pedestrians.

"In the glove box, the glove box."

Hank punched at the button on the glove box but it stuck. It was still resisting his efforts when he was thrown off balance by another one of Hill's quick swerves.

Ralph, Hank thought, you're going to owe me for this.

The glove box relented, popped open and released an avalanche of debris: napkins, small spiral notebooks, and an empty Coke can among other items. Hank couldn't find any maps, so he bent over, head between his knees and pawed through the pile on the floor. About the time he got his hands on the map, Hill jammed on the brakes, bouncing Hank's head off of the glove box.

"Crap."

Hill accelerated again, throwing them both into their seats. Somewhere in the process, Hank lost his grip on the map.

"Are you doing this on purpose?"

Hank looked over and the man didn't seem to be joking. He was still driving bug-eyed. His eyes were red and tears puddled in the corners, then ran down his cheeks. Hank dove back in for the map. This time he grabbed it and sat up before Hill braked. They'd already covered five blocks in seconds and Hank knew this was one of the finest displays of driving he'd ever seen.

"Don't just sit there, open the map and find Ra Shid Street in central Baghdad."

Hank unfolded the map, searching for the right section of Baghdad.

"We need to make a turn toward the river real soon, Mr. Jenkins. If we miss the turn, it'll cost us twenty minutes."

Hank could image Ralph picking up that revolver of his and putting it to his temple. He flipped through the map but couldn't locate their position. Meanwhile, they were bouncing down the sidewalk at high speed.

"Ra Shid, Ra Shid," he mumbled under his breath.

In his mind's eye, he saw Jackson pull the hammer back on the .38. Hank could actually see the cylinder turn.

"Got it. What are you looking for, what side street?"

"Ishan Avenue. We just passed Hussein Alley."

Hank ran his forefinger across the map, down the black line that was Ra Shid Street. He was looking on the river side of the street at the names of the small side alleys. He found Hussein Alley and ran his finger along its path, fighting against the sway of the vehicle.

Glancing up, he gasped.

"Turn here, turn here," he shouted. There was no way they were going to make the turn.

Hill responded instantly by twisting the wheel violently toward the right. The front end of the SUV lurched to the right, but the rear slid around, squealing tire and rocking. Just when it seemed they'd tip over, Hill twisted the wheel first left, then right. The Explorer straightened and shot down the narrow alleyway, accelerating with a deep-throated rumble.

"Now where," Hank asked.

"As soon as we get to the end of this alley, we should be staring right at the Tigris River. Take a look at the map and make sure I'm right. There's an improved dirt road that parallels the river. If we can follow that for about three kilometers, Hussein Avenue makes a bend and follows the river and alley. I think the Explorer can climb that embankment - all the way up to the highway. Then we'll pop right back onto the road."

While Hill was talking, Hank ran his finger down the map. If Hill was right, they would have completed an end around the traffic jam and hopped back onto the highway. When he looked up Hill seemed a little more relaxed. Nevertheless, the Explorer was really moving. They were already two-thirds of the way down the alleyway, rushing toward the river.

"According to this map, you're right," Hank said. "At the end of the alley make a left and follow the river for what looks like two miles. Then we come to . . . What is this?"

Hank pointed at a black line with diagonal lines across it.

Hill leaned to see the map.

"Where . . . oh, OK. That's just a gas line, the maps are weird here. Don't worry about it."

When they looked up, they were already at the end of the alley, headed directly for the river. Hill twisted the wheel to the left and hit the brakes. The Explorer's tail end slid toward the river bank in a shower of dirt. Its right rear wheel actually straddled the precipice between the river bank and the road. The Explorer twisted toward the river and the wheels spun dirt, searching for traction. If they rolled off the bank, even if they didn't get injured in the fall, they could forget about getting to Ralph in time.

"Come on baby, come on," Hank said.

Just when it seemed gravity would win the battle, the mighty

Explorer popped back over the rim of the embankment. It was already shooting down the road when Hill looked over at Hank with a big smile. Holding the wheel with his left hand, he patted the center of the dashboard with his open right palm saying, "good girl."

Hank opened his mouth to reply, but a Bedouin with a flock of sheep appeared seemingly out of nowhere and stood in the middle of the dirt road. The look on his face must have registered with Hill, because the driver looked ahead, saw the Bedouin and twisted the wheel, all at the same time. The small flock heading to the water were immediate casualties.

They managed to avoid the shepherd only by plunging into the midst of the sheep. The lambs cried with the eerie voices of human children. Hill shuddered at the sound, but he didn't let up on the gas. In the meantime, the first three sheep wedged underneath the Explorer and were drug along as it moved forward. These dead and dying sheep formed an organic cow catcher which directed the path of their compatriots up toward the grill and over the hood. The next sheep in line were diverted by the other animals upward, against, up and over the grill, rolling onto the Explorer's hood, hooves banging against the metal. The fourth sheep came rolling, head first, toward the passenger's side of the windshield. The cute sheep snoot with the black wet nose flew like an arrowhead directly toward Hank's face. The creature bleated pathetically. Hank Jenkins, survivor of enemy interrogation, multiple gun battles, at least six manhunts, and parenting four teenagers, shrunk back in his seat. He threw an arm up in front of his face. The sheep collided with the safety glass and created a spider web crack before bouncing off.

As quickly as it started, it ended. They bounced over two or three more sheep and cleared the flock. The Explorer roared and barreled down the dirt road, accelerating. Hill began to laugh. He kept his eyes on the road and spoke in the slightly pretentious, ponderous tone used by some American TV news anchormen.

"The terrorists have developed a new weapon of mass destruction which strikes fear into the heart of even the most hardened American operative. The suicide sheep."

He looked at Hank. Hank snorted and let it go.

Both men were laughing until Hank's attention was drawn out

his side window by distant buzzing. The river bank sloped down steeply to the water's edge, the slope chalky white with the white cobbled stones or powder white limestone gravel Saddam's government used to lend stability to the river bank. Near the river the white gave way to lush green vegetation that sprouted thickly along the water's edge. At this time of day, the blue water of the Tigris complemented the clear blue Iraqi sky. The river was dotted with brightly colored wooden boats, their white canvas stretched over the deck as shelter from a brutal sun. The buzzing came from the boats' powerful outboard motors which sent them skipping here and there across the water's surface. False alarm.

Hill drove as fast along the Tigris River as he dared, headed toward the point where Hussein Avenue bent close. Drawing near, they could hear sirens in the distance.

"I think that's Baghdad Police sending units to Ralph's apartment."

CHAPTER 26

R ALPH WAS LOST, RELIVING THE day of the attack, reaching out his hand, crawling toward her.

"Ralph," Isha managed. She actually smiled.

Thinking about the missing U.S. security, he hissed, "Jenkins is
a dead man."

Isha shook her head "no," turned her eyes toward the dead terrorist and then back. A Caucasian civilian with a pistol lay crumpled
alongside one of her bookcases. His chest was crisscrossed with
bright red buttons marking the bullet holes. No doubt he was one
of Hank Jenkins' American operatives.

That explains the dead terrorist, Ralph thought. When he
kneeled over Isha, she tried to speak.

"Quiet," he said, "save your strength."

Ralph pulled the tablecloth off of a side table, sending a clock
and candy dish crashing to the floor. Wadding up the fabric, he
used it to apply pressure to Isha's chest, directly over top of her
single bullet wound. The bubbling on her lips and the location of
the wound meant she was shot in the lung. Without help her time
was short.

Ralph centered his pistol on the chest of an Iraqi policeman
without thinking.

"No," the policeman said, spreading his arms and going pale. It
was one of the men who followed him into the building. Ralph
lowered the pistol.

"Must move Judge," the cop said. "Still Baathists here."

"We can't move the Judge without killing her."

"Leave Judge here, kill her anyway."

The man looked frightened but in control of himself. Ralph

considered.

"She'll bleed to death if we move her."

"If we don't move her now we're all going to bleed to death, rather quickly I think," a third voice said.

It was Hank Jenkins. One of his pant legs was wet with blood.

"I came up front from the service entrance in the rear," he said. "Most of the security staff and Court personnel are already dead."

"Understood," Ralph said. "So we hole up here and wait for the U.S. to respond-"

"Baghdad Burning."

"What?"

"It's a U.S. Army voice code, known to only company commanders and up. It means the enemy's launched multiple, coordinated, city wide attacks. You can hear units calling it out over the dead cops' radios. Whoever did this pulled out all the stops."

"Must move Judge now," the Iraqi said.

Ralph looked at Isha and hesitated. He couldn't carry her and keep pressure on her wound at the same time. She might bleed out.

"Forget about help," Hank said, "we're it. There are at least three terrorist assault teams working their way to this end of the building. As soon as they're sure the rest of the Ministry's clear, they'll push to the front. I killed two outriders just down the hall and it won't take long for the rest to get here. They know what they're doing, Mr. Jackson."

Hank looked over the policeman's shoulder at Isha. Blood continued to ooze out of her chest, soaking her blouse, the tablecloth, and Ralph's hands. His face turned grim.

"Pick her up, Ralph."

"Right."

Ralph holstered his pistol and as gently as he could, lifted her off the floor. You could hear the air wheezing out. Characteristic of a lung shot, he thought. That's when it first popped into his head, "she's dead, you've killed her, she's dead, you've killed her," like a drum beat, nothing dramatic, just relentless.

Lord, he thought, she's lost a lot of blood.

The three men gathered at the door long enough to organize themselves. Ralph carried Isha, Jenkins and the Iraqi carried pistols.

"Okay," Hank said. "On three, one, two, three!"

They ran out into the hallway. Small arms fire erupted to their left. Hank and the Iraqi fired back. Ralph took Isha in the other direction. The men followed after him, firing as they ran. Ralph almost skidded to a stop when a terrorist appeared out of nowhere, right in front of him. Before the man could even bring up his weapon, a bullet whistled past Ralph's ear and found its target. A bright red hole appeared in the terrorist's forehead. He tottered and fell.

"Run! Run," Hank yelled.

Ralph ran toward the main staircase and gunfire broke out behind him again. The Iraqi policemen went down and Hank, suddenly stumbling, fired off a few rounds and then limped after him. Ralph wanted to help Hank, but he had to get Isha out of the Ministry and into a hospital. He kept running. He made it to the main staircase and then pounded down the steps. Bullets scraped off the walls and passed over his head. He sprinted past the last two policemen at the base of the staircase and looked over his shoulder. The police were firing behind and to either side of Hank as he made his way down.

He could feel Isha's blood soaking through his shirt. The front and sleeves were sticking against his flesh. Without waiting for anyone he ran out the door, into the street and toward the Jersey barrier barricade. The pallor in Isha's face told him that without a blood transfusion, she'd soon die. He weaved through and behind the barrier, then toward a line of police vehicles.

He laid her behind a Humvee. She was still bleeding but the flow had really slowed. Her skin had taken on a pale, pasty color. Ralph heard footfalls and turned in time to see Hank half limp, half trot to him. The spy sat on the pavement and leaned against the vehicle, taking in great gulps of air.

"The cops didn't make it," he said, gasping. Hank was bleeding from his left shoulder and right thigh.

"If we don't do something, Isha's not going to make it either," Ralph said. "I know you're hit, but can you hold this until I get to a radio?"

Ralph gestured to the tablecloth he was still holding on Isha's chest. Hank nodded, heaved himself to his knees and placed his hands beside Ralph's on the makeshift bandage.

"Better hurry. I'm a little light headed."

Ralph jumped up and ran to another Iraqi Humvee, one with a radio aerial. Incredibly, bullets whizzed over his head. When he turned, some of the terrorists were already trying to get out through the front doorway. A small group of Iraqi Police officers fired at the Ministry's doors and windows, driving them back inside.

Ralph ducked into the Humvee, stretched out on the floor and grabbed the radio handset.

"Baghdad dispatch, Baghdad dispatch, this is Iraqi Police Unit . . .," Ralph looked at the radio chassis and located the vehicle unit number stenciled on the side.

"This is Police Unit 14 B. The Justice Ministry is under sustained terrorist attack. The building is occupied by terrorists. No more than ten officers on the scene. Wounded Judge, critical condition, need immediate ambulance or medivac."

Ralph's voice was calm and professional. The other voices flooding the radio, in both English and Arabic were not. He ignored them and repeated his message over and over, receiving no response.

Hank was right. Baghdad Burning was repeated, over and over, in English and Arabic.

Finally the frustration got to him, made him more strident in tone and attitude. Eventually, an Iraqi police dispatcher speaking passable English came on the air.

"Unit 14 B, be advised, attacks on multiple targets throughout Baghdad still in progress. Access to Ministry blocked. Attack on President of Governing Council. Reinforcements and medivac impossible at this time. Baghdad Burning."

Ralph squeezed the microphone key, screaming at the dispatcher first in English, then with a few pornographic Arabic phrases he'd picked up over the years. The fit subsided. Right in front of him, by his face on the floor lay a US Army M-5 medical bag. Ralph grabbed the bag, wiggled out of the Humvee and sprinted back to Isha.

Hank had passed out and was laying alongside her with one hand still over the makeshift compression bandage. Shushing Isha, Ralph ripped open the M-5 bag and removed the I.V. line and plasma bag. He didn't bother swabbing her arm, he just found a vein, inserted a needle, and got the flow started.

She watched him the whole time without trying to speak. He slumped against the tire, watching the plasma and looking at Isha.

The rest of the day, he didn't even remember. Everything was a blur. Sometime during the day help finally arrived, but only after it was too late. In the end, his friend raised her hand and Ralph fell silent. Leaning over her side, he bent down close. She smiled at him and raised her hand, her fingers touching his cheek. He managed to get his arms around her. Even in the heat, she was so cold.

"I wish I'd met you earlier, before all of this," she said.

"So do I," he choked out. "Hold on, hold on."

"Ralph, please, promise me you'll try Church."

"Isha–"

"For me. Please."

"I promise."

"There's one more thing . . . I need to ask you to . . ."

Her voice faded with every word until, with a small shiver, and then a gasp, she died in his arms.

The U.S. paratroopers who finally arrived treated Hank and gave him whole blood. Ralph remembered talking to him when they were loading him onto the ambulance, but he couldn't remember what they said. Somehow, he made it home and got his whiskey.

———◆———

Ralph Jackson woke up with a piercing headache and a feeling he might be drowning. He'd passed out at the table, holding the revolver in his right hand. He knew he'd been grinding the barrel into his head, but had no idea how the pistol got in his hand, let alone against his temple. Ralph put the pistol down and placed both hands on the edge of the table. He tried to catch his breath. It was another dream, worse than the others, and he'd been trying so hard not to fall asleep. When he awoke, the putrid odor of burning flesh lingered in his nostrils. Isha came out of the As Salman bunker with her skin falling off.

"Why Ralph, why?" Naba stood to one side, watching her grandmother suffer.

Ralph discovered he was holding the pistol again. He watched and didn't really want to, or did he, but his arm seemed filled with helium because it floated toward his head with no effort on his part.

"Why, why did you kill my grandmother? I hate you. I never want to see you again."

Behind Isha, a line of melting children filed out of the bunker, their screams like fingernails on a chalkboard. They marched past him and he remembered their names and faces.

"You . . . did this!"

Ralph used his left hand to pull down the errant right one. He sat the pistol on the table and contemplated his quivering right hand.

"Tricky s.o.b."

Ralph would've never imagined himself capable of suicide. Suicide was giving up and giving up was for . . . All his life the one thing Ralph Jackson believed in was never giving up.

It's hard to explain, how it wears you down, he thought. At first it was a little weird and sad, but after days, weeks, when you can't turn it off, every chant is a screech, like fingernails on a blackboard, but a bit louder, a bit more intolerable each time.

He decided to start with the tranquilizers. Just a few at a time at first and see how it went. It was 11:30 a.m. and he had to be dead by noon. That was important, only fair. It was restitution.

If they don't work fast enough or I just feel sleepy, I'll pick up the gun and use it, he thought.

She's dead you've killed her, she's dead you've killed her.

Ralph picked up a blue ceramic ashtray sitting on top of his old black and white TV and returned to the table. He threw the ashtray on the table top, grabbed the prescription bottle and re-read the dosage instructions. He wasn't a particularly big man and decided ten should do it, especially after all the whiskey. He snapped off the white cap, spilled a bunch of tablets, more than enough, onto the ashtray, then snapped the lid on. He took a long pull on the whiskey and swallowed three pills. The rest went into the blue ashtray.

A car door slammed, surprising him out of an unexpected stupor. Once again, he was holding the revolver. Ralph walked over to an open window just in time to see the back of an olive green pant leg entering his building. A marked police jeep was sitting below his window. He checked his watch. 11:45 a.m. Close enough.

That settles it, he thought. I'll let fate decide.

Sweeping up all the remaining tranquilizers from the ashtray, he put the pistol away and swallowed the pills with the willing assistance of three or four ounces of Mr. Daniels. If the cops wanted to take him to the Ministry, he'd excuse himself to get a fresh shirt, grab the pistol and blow his brains out. If they only wanted to check on him or schedule an appointment for later, okay. That would only take a couple minutes. He'd talk to them, then sit in his easy chair and die watching black and white reruns of Baywatch.

———◆———

A few blocks away, Hank Jenkins glanced at Ralph's note.

Hill looked at him.

"What's going on Mr. Jenkins?"

"This guy sent me a letter and his Will. The letter said he was going to kill himself today, at noon."

"It's 11:45 now."

"Right."

"Why?"

"He was a friend and colleague of Judge Isha Hami. He's had enough training and experience to think he should've been able to protect her. He wasn't. None of us were. I was in the hospital and missed the funeral, but at the funeral, the Priests and some sixth cousins of Hami wouldn't let the guy see the granddaughter, Naba. Dave Barnes said the girl was staring at the ground the whole time. He didn't even think she knew he was there. The relatives and Priests told him Naba hated him for killing her grandmother. They told Naba our guy went home to America without even saying goodbye. It's more complicated than that, but that's the gist of it. I don't want anyone else to ever know this, okay?"

"Yeah. He must be a good man."

"He is."

Hill nodded.

"Then let's get him."

Hank returned to the note.

"I also named you Executor of my Will. You probably wish I still thought you were an ass. Except for a few family items, I left everything to Naba Hami. She's almost like a daughter to me. Please tell my brothers why I left everything to her instead of my nieces and nephews. Naba is now all alone in a country that has little compassion for the innocent or the vulnerable. Money might make be the difference between her surviving or not. You might make all the difference, Hank. I would've done more, but you know what happened at the funeral."

If I could just tell him, Hank thought.

"One last thing," Ralph wrote. "You were right. Just because I dropped out doesn't mean everyone else can. Don't. Ralph."

"Hank, look up."

In the distance red lights flickered at the top of a fast approaching thirty-five foot embankment. Baghdad Police were blocked from Dora by a traffic accident. The roadway itself loomed a quarter mile ahead. Hill evaluated his approach. The embankment was sloped at a forty-five-degree angle, so he began edging the driver's side wheels toward the hillside. He eased back on the gas, approached the incline and began climbing. Once all four wheels were off the road he accelerated. The Explorer tilted at a frightening angle. As it picked up speed, Hill eased the wheel to his left, climbing the bank. His initial approach angle had been gentle, but now, as the vehicle picked up speed, he straightened out, increasing his angle of attack. He didn't want to try to drive straight up, but he didn't want to roll it either.

Hill looked just like he had when he was driving on the sidewalks. His knuckles tightened on the wheel, he opened his eyelids unnaturally wide and he leaned forward. By the time Hank felt the Explorer begin to tip, Hill had already corrected for it. By the time he felt the rear wheels spin, Hill was decreasing the angle of attack. Then the Ford crested the embankment, popped out through a gap in the guardrail and left the accident far behind.

"Good job," Hank said, casually. "We're on the hardball so let's make tracks."

Hill swung the Explorer off the berm and on to the highway, accelerating. They didn't need maps to get to Ralph's apartment. Hank knew the way. They were far ahead of the Iraqi Police and already nearing the turnoff.

"Two streets down, make a right."

"Hold on," Hill warned, swinging the Explorer into a sharp, right-hand turn.

"Third building on the left-hand side," Hank said, pointing across Hill's body. We're too late, I've lost another one, he thought to himself. His watch said 12:00 Noon, but that didn't mean

Ralph wasn't dead. Hank steadied himself for the gunshot about to ring out. Hill cut across traffic, parking the SUV diagonally in front of the entrance. Hank threw his door open and ran toward the apartment, yelling as loud as he could, trying to impart the only information that he knew would make Ralph change his mind . . . and save his life.

———◆———

Ralph Jackson had always been a man who felt the weight of the world lifted from his shoulders once he'd made a difficult decision. Now, with a clear path in front of him, he responded to the door buzzer with a bounce in his step. Kind of. Still, one way or another, the chanting and nightmares would end. He pulled open the door and gaped, glancing from an Iraqi police officer, who was telling him something that wasn't registering, back to his companion, back and forth.

He understood the broken English, but the meaning just didn't sink in. The policeman handed him a packet of papers which he managed to grasp, but couldn't get his eyes to focus on. Eventually he managed to read the entire first page, and then pushed the papers back into the cop's hand. He ran to the bathroom, bent over the toilet and stuck his finger so far down his throat he could feel it in his stomach. Up came about a gallon and a half of Jack Daniels, part of a falafel, and 15 or 20 little white pills.

I must have miscounted, Ralph thought. He rocked back on his heels and leaned against the wall, sniffling and gasping. The Iraqi cop was shouting from the door.

"Just a moment," Ralph shouted back.

He flushed the contents of his stomach down the toilet, grabbed a washcloth and invited his visitors to take seats inside. He told them he'd been ill and needed to clean up. When Ralph reentered the living room he was wearing a fresh shirt and pants and gave his best smile to the cop's beautiful companion. Little Naba didn't have the gray hair her grandmother so proudly displayed, or the age spots she tried so hard to hide. She certainly didn't yet have the Judge's height. In fact, she looked like a smaller version of Isha from the first picture on his table. That one was taken when Isha was his age, 34, at her 1973 "Inns of the Court" graduation in London. He looked down at Naba, 31 years later. She gazed back up at him, tentatively smiling the Judge's smile, looking at him with the Judge's eyes, and clutching the doll he'd given her.

Ralph took the documents from the policeman, flipped over the cover sheet and looked at a multi-page Last Will and Testament, written in Arabic. Then he re-read the cover sheet, a hand-written note in English.

"Ralph, I have given all that I own to my granddaughter, Naba. I have given all that I value to my friend, you. I've appointed you Naba's legal guardian. She and I have no one else, but even if we did, I could think of no finer choice. You have deep wounds that never healed because you failed to save many. Perhaps you can finally find peace by saving just one. Love, Isha."

Ralph felt a tug and looked down to find Naba taking his hand and looking up at him, so brave. He realized the voices had stopped. Somewhere, deep inside, spring finally returned and the thaw began.

ABOUT THE AUTHOR

———➤———

JOSEPH MAX LEWIS SERVED AS A member of an Operational Detachment in the U.S. Army's Seventh Special Forces Group, the storied Green Berets. During his service Lewis received antiterrorist training and his detachment was tasked to "Special Projects." Afterward, he served as an instructor at the Special Forces Qualification Course. Lewis attended the Pennsylvania State University, where he was elected to Phi Beta Kappa, the University of Tel Aviv in Israel, and the University of Pittsburgh, receiving degrees in International Politics and Law while being certified in Middle East Studies.

After living and studying abroad, first in the Middle East and then Southeast Asia, Lewis returned home to practice law. He's a columnist in the New Bethlehem Leader-Vindicator and currently lives, writes, and practices law in and around Pittsburgh, Pennsylvania.

Find Joseph at *www.josephmaxlewis.com*

43808939R00158

Made in the USA
Middletown, DE
02 May 2019